BOOKS BY THOMAS WILLIAMS

# THE
# FOLLOWED MAN
## Thomas Williams

Richard Marek Publishers, New York

First printing

Library of Congress Cataloging in Publication Data

Williams, Thomas, 1926–
  The followed man.

  I.  Title.
PZ4.W7275Fo  [ PS3573.I456]    813'.5'4    78-16629

SBN: 399-90025-x
Printed in the United States of America

*For Liz*

"Okay. Say, you doing anything tonight? You want to come for supper?"

"No, thanks, Martin, but thanks, anyway. I'm going to read that book you sent and go to bed early."

"Okay," Martin said. "Take it easy, now. See you tomorrow."

Luke put down the phone and lay back on the bed. He felt like a ghost. He was the one who always returned, bringing alone with him the memories of those who would never return. He still belonged to another world. Still, after six months, he could not manage to think of himself as a single unit. After having a wife and children for nineteen years he did not have a wife and children, because they were dead.

The thought was like a choke, his mind suddenly blocked and spasmic. In strobic flashes he saw the fair faces, in sunlight, of his son and daughter, framed sometimes by darkness and sometimes by a gray absence of vision. His wife's turns, angles, hollows of body moved toward him only to fade, only the pale face left as he tried to determine what her expression meant. These visions came from his own mind and memory, yet they were so powerful and uncontrollable they seemed to bear messages from outside. It had been six months and he could not look at any of their photographs. The magnitude of his response to their deaths seemed strange to him; it was nothing he could have foreseen. There were husbands and fathers who were far more deeply involved with their families than he had ever been, though he had been responsible enough. It had hardly bothered him, while they were alive and seemed permanent, that he was always a little detached, a little cool. Perhaps he hadn't been. He didn't think they'd thought him cool.

He hadn't flown with them to his wife's mother's funeral because, he'd said, he had to work. But he had chosen not to go and the two-engine prop-jet had crashed into a low, wooded hill and he was alone in places so deep he'd never even considered them before. He didn't want to name his children or his wife, to think of the strange solidity of their names, common names: John Wilson Carr, Grace Lois Carr, Helen Sarah (Benton) Carr.

He had buried his family in Ohio, in the Benton family plot. He

10

and Helen had never thought of having a plot; it wasn't the kind of thing they'd ever considered—a place to put their dead.

Then, after he had returned to Wellesley and the empty house, his uncle, Shem Carr, died alone in New Hampshire at the age of eighty-three, a death more mete, more timely, one that could be pondered without a sudden loss of breath.

When Martin Troup had called last week he had been half-asleep in his clothes on the living room couch. That voice from the functioning world had made him look around and even begin to smell the funk around him. Without Helen's care the house had seemed to wilt and rot. And then Martin spoke of death, more death, and how we are so busily and aggressively formulating and building traps for ourselves. This time twenty people in a second or two. It was death that had paralyzed him and so, recognizing his desperation, he had agreed to go where death was, to the abomination itself, and see if he could face it again.

He got up and took from his briefcase the book, *Ferroconcrete Construction*. The coefficients of the thermal expansion of steel and concrete are nearly the same, therefore the tensile strength of one and the non-compressibility of the other combine with tremendous strength. After the concrete sets, that is—a continuing process depending upon many factors, such as heat, moisture content, air content, quality of mix, etc. One summer while he was in college, Luke had worked for a shady contractor and when the owner of the house whose foundation they were pouring came by, the word was whispered, "If he asks, tell him it's five to one." The mixture of gravel and sand to cement was more like ten to one. But maybe it was not that kind of greed that had caused the skyscraper's floor to collapse and kill. Haste, error, who knew? It was not his job to find out why it had happened, but to report its effects and perhaps to comment upon what Martin Troup had once called New York City's "edifice complex." Everywhere the old was being violently torn down and the new and shoddy as violently thrown up. Those sterile, inefficient glass and metal verticalities.

He put *Ferroconcrete Construction* down and went to his briefcase, where he found two letters. The first was postmarked Leah,

11

New Hampshire, March 3—three months ago. It was written in pencil on lined tablet paper.

> Dear Luke, well the snow was just to heavy last month and now I live in the kitchen but a bunch of God damned busybodies want to burn this place and send me to the county farm. It does not leak much except in the pantry but what God damned business is it of theres. If you would come and tell them I think they would haul off. I am not leaving here standing up and that is God's own God damned truth.
>
> Sincerely yours<br>Your Uncle<br>Shem G. Carr

And Shem hadn't left there alive. While Luke was in mourning, or whatever his inactive state might have been called, Shem had died in the kitchen of the old farmhouse, evidently the only room left that kept out most of the snow-melt and rain. Phyllis Bateman, the town clerk, had called to tell him the news. She had his address because he had paid the taxes on the old place for years. Shem had a World War I pension and some social security because of the time during the Second World War when he had worked in the woolen mill. It was enough to keep him, but he wasn't good at paying taxes, or for anything that wasn't directly tangible, so Luke had taken care of that—a matter of four hundred dollars a year on the hundred and sixty acres. The barns and sheds had all fallen in, the fields had grown up in poplar, birch, cherry, maple, ash and softwoods. And now the rocky hill farm was his. He hadn't seen the place in years, hadn't gone to Shem's funeral, which was conducted by the Veterans of Foreign Wars. He had sent them a check to help pay for it.

To say "My uncle," just as it had once been to say, "My mother," or "My father," had been a hedge against death. Those older people were, after all, in the first line. Each time he'd mentioned Shem, while Shem was alive, he'd thought of this, as if he were using the old man in a slightly dishonorable way.

He remembered when the tops of Shem's rubber boots, as he went authoritatively about the work of the farm, were as high as

Luke's waist. Looking up at the man working, as Shem always was then, seemed to make him more distant and forbidding, unlike his own more urban father, whom he saw only after work, at home. Shem had seemed more important than his father, his essentially good-humored jokes funny yet dangerous, coming as they did from up there where the grizzled beard was, high above the manure or soil or oily wood his great boots trod.

But when Shem's wife died, and then his only son, Samuel—a strange, silent boy who never went anywhere, never married—and he passed into his seventies, all he did was cut and split wood for his stove. The animals were all gone; his last dog, a beagle named Gretchen who lived fourteen years, also dead. He had a 1941 half-ton Chevy pickup that never quite seemed to die, although it was certainly rusted out and asthmatic. But then he hadn't bothered to register it for years, just put the white-on-green plates on in even years, the green-on-white in odd. The local police knew this, but finally it got to be so much of a joke in town the State Police heard of it. By then he didn't see too well anyway, and with the truck settling in a shed that soon settled over it, neighbors brought him supplies every few weeks. Spam and beans, canned corn and peas, a loaf of Wonder Bread, potatoes, coffee and tobacco. He'd used to drink hard cider he made himself, but in the last ten years his stomach couldn't take that anymore. And he never changed his pants, stank, wasn't polite to anyone who came by, whether it was to help him or not. He wouldn't look at the television set someone gave him, or listen to the radio, or read anything. what did he do all the years of days in the collapsing house? He wouldn't leave it; upon that rock of intention he lived out his time, until his eighty-third year, when he stopped.

When he finished this assignment Luke would go up to New Hampshire and look at Shem's grave, buy him a stone, and see what was left of the farmhouse and the fields he remembered as if they were two places—the working hill farm of his childhood and the jungle of growth and rot he'd last seen several years ago. Six years ago, to be exact, when he'd been in New Hampshire to do an article about a commune of young people trying to subsistence farm a long-abandoned mountain place as unpromising as

13

sponsibilities, heavy with unavoidable love. In the middle still, fragmented like a blown cloud, he began to fall, not a cloud but pieces of a man.

It was unbelievable to him and must be wrong, or if true it all must be undone.

Into the irrational again, said a voice that must have been one of his own cooler voices. It was important, the voice claimed, that he hold on, right now. And also not to fall into the bottle, because drinking while unhappy was the certain way of the lost.

All he seemed to remember of his past were the times he had wanted to be free. The first was when he and Helen had been married about three months. Helen was out shopping and he was sitting alone in the little apartment they'd had on Beacon Hill. Suddenly, out of no context at all came a cool chill down his back and the firm knowledge that he couldn't just take his passport and go alone to Paris. He was twenty-six, Helen twenty-three. She was working for a publisher of religious and philosophical books and tracts, not making very much. He was a subeditor on the house organ of AFEMCO, a ubiquitous corporation whose acronym he translated as the Anti-Free Enterprise Monopoly Cartel Organization, famous for price fixing, restraint of trade and fierce celebration of the American Free Enterprise System.

Okay, think of that sort of thing instead, he thought, breaking it off in the wound. Johnny was the first born. In his arms he held the hard little body, sturdy and muscular even as a baby, always wanting to climb. Three years later came Gracie, whose green eyes always looked steadily at him, seeming to ask questions long before she had words.

But there were times he'd wanted to be free of them all. How he had misunderstood! How could the theoretical be so wrong? It was the three wishes of a fairy tale, and the first thoughtless wish had been granted. But where were the other two wishes, the ones that might undo the first illicit one? In the bottle? No, he'd found no wishes lurking there. Now it was a question of living, or not living. Wasn't the world forever new, fascinating, beautiful? It all seemed such an abstract idea, the world.

Yes, but he was not really sympathetic to the idea that life was not worthwhile. He was breathing, wasn't he? He had some money. Some might even consider him well-off, with money in the bank, a house in Wellesley, Massachusetts, with no more than ten thousand left in the mortgage, a car one year old and another three years old, the house full of all the furniture and appliances and gadgets and toys of the middle class. Then there had been the envelope with the flight insurance policies, addressed to him in Helen's hand. Hello from the Other Kingdom, in haste, with love.

How far had the airplane fallen; how many minutes or seconds had they known, or half-known, that something was awfully wrong? Johnny pushes his feet against the footrest under the seat ahead of him, his square hands tight on his armrests, his body straight, his stomach doing the windmill of knowledge. Gracie senses it all, and asks, asks; no one can answer. Helen reaches for Gracie's hand, always to reassure, but Gracie sees that her mother's neck is pale, blue-veined. Helen's woman-center is cold with the anxiety that is exactly intolerable. For herself, for them. Here it comes.

Why did human animals get so entangled in love for each other, if at the same time they insisted upon all this height and speed and the insane momentum of their uncontrollable playthings?

Maybe he couldn't face this assignment. He would call Martin Troup and tell him he was sorry, he couldn't. But that decision looked like the entrance to a long, sloping corridor stinking of booze and self-hatred.

He must put an end to the memory of his wish for freedom. It was not so uncommon, after all, and perhaps his guilt was a form of self-indulgence. Now he would go out of this quiet, old-fashioned room, down the long carpeted corridors to the old elevators, then out into the high lobby, a man of indeterminate age and condition dressed in a medium-expensive gray suit of lightweight material, sturdy shoes, conservative tie—a man not to be remembered very clearly by anyone whose attention he might fleetingly engage. He would eat, come back and read some more about ferroconcrete, see the television news and then go to bed and shut his eyes.

He'd thought of walking a few blocks to a Japanese-Korean res-

17

with several older women, none of whom he knew by name. There was something gleaming and unfresh and urgent about the little face and sharp blue eyes. All around his feet were the leather boxes and straps of his profession.

"He's the best there is," Martin said. "I wanted the best writer and the best photographer for this job, and now I've got 'em both. Oh, hey, you met Annie before, right?"

A thin dark girl with the mild, hardly unattractive wounds of an ancient acne, and the deep, luminous eyes that seem to go with that disease, had appeared in the doorway.

"Yes, we've met," she said. "When you did the piece on Attica, Mr. Carr."

"A long time ago," Luke said.

"Hey, Luke," Martin said. "You want to do another piece on Attica?"

"You didn't like what I said about Oswald last time," Luke said. Martin had wanted to cast Russell Oswald, the Commissioner of the Department of Correction, as a sort of hero, a man in the middle, but after Luke had spent a day in Albany with the man, his own reaction had been more complicated than that. In fact his study of prisons, prisoners and their keepers had led him to believe the situation hadn't the slightest hope of amelioration from any quarter.

Martin laughed and hit Luke on the shoulder with his fist, hard—something they had once instinctively done to each other. Now Martin dropped his arm and looked embarrassed, not knowing what to say, as though he'd been importunate at a funeral. Luke tried to smile it away, but Martin was too embarrassed for that.

Annie said, "I've got some more addresses for you, Mr. Carr," and handed him some Xeroxed sheets.

"How come you call him 'Mr. Carr?' " Martin asked her. "He ain't more than fifteen years older'n you, Annie."

"Because he's so sad and distant," she said.

"And old?" Luke said.

"Oh!" she said, turning dark, a rather beautiful flawed rose. "I forgot. I forgot about your tragedy, Mr. Carr."

22

"Is there something I should know?" Robin Flash said.

Luke explained as quickly and plainly as he could.

"Wow. Heavy," Robin Flash said.

They were silent for a long moment until Luke said, "Anything else I ought to know, Martin?"

"Well . . ." Martin said, not looking Luke exactly in the eyes. "You handle it the way you want. Only one thing. You're going to find a lot of . . . defensiveness in some quarters. Depends on what you think you want to look for. I mean about the cause of it all. They haven't found out exactly why the floor gave way, at least as far as we can find out. Or at least they're not telling it straight."

"I don't want to be a detective anyway," Luke said. A nerve had begun to jump somewhere alongside his sternum, and a breath came short. "I know how these things can happen. A mistake here, a bad coincidence there. . . ."

"Yeah, right!" Martin said, apparently very much relieved. "You and Robin handle it the way you want. And, Luke . . . I mean, if it gets to you, all the death . . . Maybe it's too soon after. You know. Well, no matter. . . ."

"Do I look that bad?" Luke said.

"I know you're a pro, Luke. You're the best. That's why you always get so goddam involved. Anyway, you know what I mean."

"Okay, Martin." Luke turned to Robin Flash, trying to assume a bravado he certainly didn't feel. It was dread he felt, and he could place it anatomically. It was in his diaphragm, slightly to the left of center, and it seemed to have a color—a mottled gray—and a shape somewhat like a certain clinker of slag he had once removed from a coal-burning furnace. "Robin, shall we go and diagnose the sickness of this town?"

He must have dreamed last night, because fragments of dream queried him now, passing close, not letting him quite grasp them. He was on a snowy road, driving a bug-eyed Sprite, of all cars. He'd never owned one. No, he wasn't driving, someone else was. He was in an editorial meeting, and a girl—a woman—was crying. She had a wide face and long, horizontal dark eyes—a tigerish look—and she was crying out of sorrow. What was her tragedy? He meant to get up and ask her what the matter was, but he asked

23

its traffic, its builders and destroyers. Robin looked up at him curiously. "It's a living, right?" he said.

Luke felt himself smiling and recognized that constriction of the face. It was one of the possible reactions to incipient combat, mortal danger. But certainly the hard hats were not going to kill either one of them. It was, however, as unpleasant a prospect—he heard in his head the words, "as unpleasant a prospect" and smiled harder, wanting to laugh because he was terrified. He was more terrified than he had ever been at the prospect of actual death by shell fragments or machine gun fire, and maybe it was because he was home—this was his country and he had lived in this city and these were his people. They were not strangers at all, any of them, even the manipulators and moneymen who were causing all of this. He thought quickly of suggesting to Robin that they go to a nearby bar and have a drink and think it over. No. He had to go here first and see what the initial, somewhat official, reaction would be. Then he could take the names and addresses supplied by Annie and see what had happened to those people who were survivors and relatives. And all the time he was writing the article in his head. The silently screaming black man would be in it, yes; and the taxi driver, the ancient seductress in wig and miniskirt, the mad sledgehammerer and the blind man.

"Let's go," he said to Robin, just as a young ironworker passed them and went up the steps. He was an Indian, from his looks, and just a boy, his brown face round and plump, wearing horn-rimmed glasses that gave him a scholarly look even in his hard hat. Luke followed him up the steps, Robin coming along behind. The young Indian opened the door and went in. Luke hesitated a moment, then knocked on the doorframe and went in himself. The young Indian, an older man who was probably a supervisor, and a younger man, all in hard hats, turned to look at Luke and Robin.

In his nervousness Luke was hardly aware of his words, but he said who they were and asked if they could talk to the men and take some pictures.

The younger man, who wore chino pants and a Marine shirt with a lance corporal chevron on one of the sleeves, suddenly said,

"*Gentleman!* You want to take a picture of my ass?"—turned, bent over and presented his gaunt, muscular rear end to them, a strange form of violence Luke would think about. *Gentleman* had, he supposed, a risqué reputation from years back when it was a rather naughty magazine with its airbrushed, long-legged but never nude cartoon girls. But the young man's reaction had to be some kind of hysteria. Luke didn't have time to sort out this inter-pretation, however, because the supervisor's attitude was more explicit. His large red face, stubbled with gray bristles, grew red-der in places, white in certain wrinkled areas.

"I got a *buildnabuild!*" he yelled.

"Well, we know that," Luke said.

"I ain't authorized to let *nobody* on this job, you understand that?"

"Sure."

"Fuckin' ghouls, anyway," he said, turning away, dismissing them. He handed some papers to the young Indian. "Joe Hayes your new pusher. Report to him." Then, over his shoulder in a milder tone he said, "I can't talk to nobody, neither. I can't keep you off the sidewalk and I can't keep you from taking pictures or talking to the men on their lunch breaks. But don't come on the job and bother me or nobody. We got a *buildnabuild*. You got that straight?"

"Sure," Luke said. "Thank you."

The supervisor looked at Robin, his nose and upper lip wrin-kling. "Shuh!" he said in disgust.

So they left the trailer-office, its impressions printed in Luke's mind. Relief to be leaving, of course, but there were the piles of red hard hats in one corner, a desk with sheaves of architectural drawings soiled all around their edges, a dark corner with hot plate, a strange domestic corner with lamp and chair. This was the real world, not what he and Robin would seem to them—hobgob-lins from *Gentleman*.

But *Gentleman* meant something powerful and fascinating to the men. At eleven-thirty when the lunch breaks began, Luke and Robin stood on the sidewalk, Robin taking all the pictures he wanted, Luke trying to talk to too many of the men at once. The

31

word had flown all over the job, vertically and horizontally, that they were there. Soon Robin, with a wink, a shrug and a crypto bump and grind, left crosstown for his assignation with the giant-ess, and Luke was left trying to get names, titles and the state-ments of the men written down in his spiral notebook.

They came on, at first, with a kind of arrogance that almost amounted to shoving. Later he did feel that he had been shoved up against the brick wall behind him, or that his tie had been grasped in a fist as some of them spoke. But they hadn't actually touched him. What did he want? they wanted to know. A shop steward wanted to know what the hell a girly magazine wanted to know about the construction the hell *for*, anyway. A connector, down forty stories by vertical column, ladders and elevator, want-ed to make sure Luke knew that it was a goddam dangerous job, but somebody had to do it. Why couldn't they get insurance that didn't cost more than the goddam payments on a car? You took your chance and the pay was good and when you fell or a cable whipped your fucking arm off or a column or a header or the fucking hooks squashed your head it was good-bye and good luck, baby. It was a complicated business and there were a thousand and three ways to kill a man on the steel or down below.

"Never mind him," another man said. "He thinks he's Tarzan of the fucking Apes." This was said with a certain amount of em-barrassment because the first connector had come on so strongly about the dangers of the profession. "I been connecting since he was a punk, and I still got all my ex*tree*mities."

They laughed, but the information had been given, and none of them were about to deny it. Out of the declarations, jokes, in-sults and demandingly precise terminology Luke began, at least, to sense how little he knew and how much he would have to ask before he could ask what he wanted to ask. They all knew he was here because of the one horrendous accident, and they were skep-tical, growing a little narrow-eyed when he said that he was less in-terested in it than in its aftermath, and in their work itself.

"Yeah," one dark, small man said. "Them things always hap-pen. Guy's just as dead if it happens one at a time, right?"

Though Luke hadn't said much, and hadn't had to, he saw that

32

they were beginning to know him. He had always had that strange talent, that they began to know him. The dark, wrinkled-faced man was Mike Rizzo, an oiler, which meant that he maintained a crane; an engineer ran it and Mike Rizzo kept it oiled and greased and running. "Luke," he said when the others had begun to return to their work, "I'll tell you something. I used to work on the steel. I fell twenty-five feet once, landed in a sand pile, didn't hurt a bit. Let me tell you. I was thirty years old, now I'm fifty-two, and I can't climb up a seven and a half foot stepladder without getting the shakes. You follow me?"

Mike was a small, wiry man, his dark face creased and whorled as a walnut. He looked fierce, but he was a talker, slightly patronized by the others, who were exasperated by him though fond of him.

"Luke," Mike said, "nobody knows exactly what happened— you follow me? Maybe there ain't nobody to blame. A little mistake here, a little legal cutting of a corner there, maybe the steel a little out of plumb here, maybe a guy pours a little too much in the hopper there, maybe a rodman's got a sore arm or a hangover here—you follow me? Maybe the architect pushed the wrong button on his calculator—hit the divide instead of the multiplier— you follow me? Too much sand, not enough air in the concrete? Scuttlebutt, Luke; even scuttlebutt don't know the answer. Anyway, Luke, I wouldn't shit you, now. You know that? You follow me, Luke?"

"Sure, Mike," Luke said. "Sure. It's a dangerous occupation."

"A dangerous occupation. You hit the nail on the head, Luke." Mike nodded seriously, tipped his hard hat and smoothed back his sparse gray hair.

"Hey, Rizzo! Hey, *Rizzo!*" someone was shouting from across the street. "Hey, Rizzo, you going to bullshit all day? Jesus Christ!"

"My engineer," Mike said, pointing to the square mass of the crane on its base of crossed timbers. It looked substantial enough until Luke followed the boom up, up, far beyond what all of his calculations about leverage, all of his experiences in childhood and after had told him was the very edge of possibility. But the boom still rose into the yellow haze, beyond logic and sanity.

33

He followed Mike over to the crane and its engineer, Jimmo McLeod, who, in spite of his angry yelling, seemed now a mild, friendly man of thirty-five or so who shook Luke's hand with pleasure.

"It's too high," Luke said, pointing up at the boom.

"That's nothing," Mike said. "You could put a jib on it and add another sixty-five feet."

"I can't believe how high it is now," Luke said. "How can you expect me to believe that?"

Jimmo McLeod laughed, pleased. "It rocks a bit sometimes," he said.

Beneath the outriggers that were extended from the base of the crane, old square timbers were stacked to take the strain off the huge truck tires beneath. Then he saw what he might have expected to see anywhere else but here on a creosoted timber. A dragonfly had alighted, its four shimmering wings faintly vibrating in their stillness, the irridescent green body absolutely still. This desert of fumes and asphalt and metal seemed no place at all for such delicate wild fragility.

"I miss old Mickey, though, I'll tell you that," Mike said.

"Oh! Yeah," Jimmo said. Luke looked up to see Jimmo's plain pale face squeeze together, startled and sorrowful.

After a moment Luke said, "Mickey?" carefully.

"Mickey Rutherford," Mike said. "Engineer."

"Derrick operator," Jimmo said.

"Everything fell on him," Mike said.

34

# 3.

Luke walked back across Manhattan the way he and Robin Flash had come by taxi that morning. Jimmo and Mike had gone back to work and Luke had stayed to see the crane hoist a steel beam or header almost out of sight in the soiled sky. Then he crossed Broadway again, still continually startled almost to the point of fatigue by the strange people who seemed to move with a jerky intensity that reminded him of people at a racetrack. "This is where the money is," he remembered the young businessman saying that morning in the Biltmore. But it seemed more than money; they all moved toward some drama, tragic or triumphant, their eyes shining with excitement or hatred or avarice. Except for the boy nodder, who had still been on his bench in the filtered sunlight. The gray-faced old woman had left, as had the young black who had soundlessly harangued the city.

He remembered the name, Rutherford, in the first list of next-of-kin Annie had sent him, and a first name. Margo? Marjorie? He would go back to his room and look at those lists. He would look at them carefully, but to call any of those people seemed right now out of the question. It would be too brutal to demand anything from them.

35

He walked the long blocks between the avenues. The midday air was at once sultry and full of nerves, weary in its heat yet clanging with sudden hard sounds, the only movement in it the harsh gusts of exhaust and traffic. A fat man in a soiled brown suit, his face and mustache the color of iron, let slam a metal trapdoor in the sidewalk. A truck's air horn, meant to be heard at highway speeds, shrieked beside him among the stalled trucks and cars. He thought of all the hot grease in those axles and transmissions, the trapped pistons in the cylinders, moved by fire; explosion was the final desperate action of the imprisoned gas.

He was not hungry. He went into a bar and bought a pack of cigarettes, wondering, as he lit one, that the cigarette seemed not an addition to the poisons of the air but a kind of deadly antidote. The bar was dark, narrow, full of the yeasty bread smell of old beer, sour but nostalgic. It was a cell, this place that seemed to have no name and was as narrow and deep as a railroad car. He took a stool at the wooden bar and ordered a draft beer, his eyes opening to the dim light where people sat quietly in near-darkness. Once he had felt a pleasant but undefined promise in places like this, not of people but of the powerful magic in all the potions dispensed by bartenders much like this one, a dim man with a flash of white apron, competent in his movements to spigot, sink, register, wiping cloth.

The beer, too, seemed an antidote; its bitter aftertaste made him remember the first time he had tasted beer, though it didn't taste the way it had then. Most of the power had gone. He finished the beer and cigarette and left, having a chill just as he re-entered the heat and noise of the street.

In his room he again stood at the windows and looked down across the relatively quiet canyon, across to the massive dome of Grand Central. How grand it thought man was. But all was transitory now, having more to do with the abstractions of bookkeeping than with any human use. It all seemed insane, like the hive of manic wasps and the queen dead.

Marjorie Rutherford was left without a warm husband, without money.

He looked back at the old hotel room, its faded but not quite

36

shoddy wallpaper—expensive and from another time. For six months he hadn't slept with a woman beside him, that matching other half. Now fading in a grave, motionless, drying into blue-gray, the sordid color of death. No, don't go there to the coffin. Coffins, all of his were in coffins. Caskets, vaults, the fallow grave-yard earth. How surprised he'd been when he first wished that he were the one dead, and they were still in the air and sunlight.

If he found it impossible within the next hour or two to call and talk to the survivors, he would call Martin and quit this project.

Marjorie Rutherford, Michael G. Rutherford's widow, lived on Mosholu Parkway, in the Bronx. There was the telephone, here was the number. He reached for the telephone, called room serv-ice and ordered a turkey club sandwich, toasted, and two bottles of Heineken beer. That done, he lit a cigarette and went to the windows, where he could see all those windows across the way, a wall of windows like his own. They all seemed dark, black, the rooms behind them unoccupied.

The phone rang, startling him. Thinking that it was room serv-ice calling back, he picked it up and said hello.

"Luke?" It was Robin Flash.

"Yeah, Robin," he said. "How're you doing?"

"Right now I'm lathered all over with honey, man. But what's new? You get a line on anything?"

"I'm trying to get up enough nerve to call a widow, and I'm not sure I can get up enough nerve, but I'll let you know if I do. Tell me where you'll be."

"Okay. But do you mind if I come over there and take a show-er? My old lady's got a nose for love's sweet effluent, man."

"Sure, Robin. Be my guest."

"Thanks. I'll see you in a while."

A waiter brought him his club sandwich and the two cold green bottles of beer, including two glasses. Into one glass he put a half inch of bourbon; in the other he poured light beer. A grown man, of course, should not have to do this.

Marjorie Rutherford's telephone number, its seven unmemora-ble digits, was there before him. Out of the unimaginable number of unknown people in the city, the mind-boggling millions and

37

millions, that number focused down upon the one person, just the one. If he called that number and she were home in her apartment she would answer, he would hear her voice, and through that one voice her loss would attach itself forever to him.

The bourbon nearly gagged him; the cool beer made him dizzy for a moment. Anxiety's static charges, small but as unmistakable as pinched nerves, for a moment stopped his breath. Another cigarette appeared, lighted, in his lips. Why, exactly, was he so much afraid of Marjorie Rutherford? Somehow he had chosen her, and that choice could not be amended. One practical reason was that he would find out more about her husband from Mike Rizzo and Jimmo McLeod, who he would see again tomorrow at noon.

The hotel switchboard dialed her number, which rang once, twice, far away across seething Manhattan, across the hazy terra incognita of the Bronx.

"Hello?" said a breathless woman from over there.

"Mrs. Rutherford?" His voice trembled.

"Yuh."

"My name is Luke Carr, and I'm doing a magazine article on the tragic accident that took your husband's life. I wonder if I might talk to you sometime."

God, what horrible words to hear coming from his own mouth.

"Magazine article?" She seemed surprised, not suspicious but confused. Her voice was low, breathy, with a city accent: *magizine aatikle*, he spelled in his head.

"Yes, for *Gentleman* magazine. It's a follow-up story on the accident. If you'd like to check on it, you can call the editorial offices of *Gentleman* and ask them about me."

"Lewkah?"

"Luke, Carr—C–a–r–r. Two names. "

"Okay, but you better let me call you back. I got two kids in the tub."

"All right. I'm at the Biltmore, Room 1040. The hotel's number is Murray Hill 7-7000. But you might want to check with *Gentleman*. The editor is Martin Troup. You could ask for him."

"Just a second while I write that number down. Them kids are splashing all over the place. I can hear . . . Marcia! Mickey! You

38

stop that splashing!" Her shouting was dimmer, her hand no doubt partly over the mouthpiece. He expected to have to give her the information again, but after a moment she said, "Okay, I'll call you back in a little while."

"Thank you," he said.

"Good-bye now."

He put the phone down. Now that the first part of it was over he felt great relief, as though he had done something admirable. But the relief could hardly last; if Marjorie Rutherford did call back it would mean that she would see him and then he would have to talk to her. Where? In her home, of course, so that he could run his judging eyes over her possessions and come to all sorts of easy sociological conclusions. He could do that so well. He had done it so many times before and probably much of it was true, but a chill waited for him here. Now it would be a widow, young enough to have two kids splashing in the bathtub. What had she ever done to deserve the cool regard of the readership of *Gentleman*?

A knock on the door. It was Robin Flash, straps and boxes, glinting clothes, disheveled blond hair. To Luke's nose, love's sweet effluent seemed a bit sour as Robin passed beneath it. Sour but nostalgic, if nostalgia did not mean the recreation of desire but only its recollection. He did remember the desire to pump himself into a woman's sweet receptive bulk, there where she was broadest and deepest. Whether or not he would ever feel that way again did not seem terribly important, and that was only sad.

Robin half-strutted into the room, talking and seeming athletic in his wiry, moist way. He wiped his brow with the back of his hand. "Cool in here! Better. Jesus, it was hot in that goddam Toronado. Sweating brown and white meat all over the upholstery— I'll bet we looked like a turkey roll." He put down his equipment and from a leather box took a cellophane package containing a new pair of jockey shorts. "It's funny, you know. She took a dislike to me—that was obvious—and when we went at it, she's glaring at me all the time. Some way, that made it even sexier, even if she could have squashed me like a lead soldier if she wanted to put a scissors on me. But you know that glare I mean? Those brown eyes bugging out? I mean, you know that devil-god mothering

39

mammy-glare? And she wouldn't say a word. Not one goddam word!"

While he spoke he pulled off his clothes, his hairy, muscular body almost the miniature of a grown man's. "I mean, I know she does it for money, and Ruiz would cut her ass if she didn't do what he said, but still . . ." He stood next to the bathroom door, in his shorts, shaking his head in wonder. "But, still, here we were, man, as close as you can get without coming out on the other side. I mean, she's a woman and I'm a man, and all the glands and membranes and ducts are working like crazy out of their minds except she *hates* me. Figure that one out sometime. I mean, don't use my name, but write that all out sometime."

"I'll put it in my article," Luke said.

"Well, maybe you better not," Robin said, laughing. Then he turned pensive again. "I mean, I know fucking is not love, but the two are not fucking *incompatible*, right?"

"I wouldn't think so," Luke said.

"But do you really know? I mean everybody says so, but do you really know? I mean out of your *own* goddam experience, Luke, can you truly-bluely say, so help you God, that you *know?*"

"I'm beginning to forget the question."

"No, you're not."

"Okay. While you take take your shower I'll think about it. Meanwhile, can I order you anything? I'm waiting on a phone call."

"Yeah. Order me a hot pastrami on light rye, yellow mustard, and a Coke."

When Robin came out of the shower, Marjorie Rutherford still hadn't called. Room service came with the hot pastrami Robin said was medium cold, the Coke, and another bottle of Heineken.

"I never drink alcohol," Robin said. "Who needs it? Not that I've got anything against it, but I'd rather fuck."

"Are the two incompatible?" Luke said.

"Alcohol dulls the senses, right?"

"I suppose so."

"Then who needs it?"

"Those who need their senses dulled," Luke said.

"Profound, man. *Profound!* And is that kind of the answer to the first question?"

"Robin," Luke said, feeling affection for this little satyr, "I'm sure we'd be able to answer any question if the question were properly posed; but I feel that we haven't really posed the question you want answered."

"Pro-fucking-*found*, man," Robin said admiringly, and took another bite of his pastrami.

Then the phone rang. "Mr. Cah?"

"Yes," he said. "Mrs. Rutherford?"

"Yes," she said, and he felt that she wouldn't ordinarily have said "yes"—that she was imitating something high-class she thought she had detected in his voice.

They arranged to meet at her "home" the next afternoon at three. There seemed to be some hesitation, or even embarrassment on her part, and then she said that her friend would be there, too, if he didn't mind. He assured her that it was all right if she wanted to have a friend present, that he just wanted to ask some questions and if she didn't want to answer any of the questions that was fine; he didn't want to invade her privacy.

Robin was chewing and grinning at him from across the room.

Luke's assurances seemed to cheer her up, and she said, "Good-bye now," with a light, pleased, anticipatory lilt.

"You didn't tell her about your friend with the cameras," Robin said.

"I thought I ought to go first and then, if she begins to trust me, suggest the need for the pictures." But he knew she would have agreed, probably, to the pictures. He hadn't wanted to add that to his demands, that was all.

"Yeah, maybe you're right," Robin said. "But they really go for the photos, man. I mean unless they're really gross freaks, and happen to know it, they really cream off having their picture in the papers."

"Well, I wonder what she does look like," Luke said.

"She's a vision of loveliness," Robin said. "What kind d'you like, anyway, Luke?"

"What kind do I like?" For a moment he didn't know what Ro-

41

bin was asking. The kind of person to interview? Then he said, "My God, what an idea."

"You mean you never thought of it?"

"You mean trying to put the make on this poor widow?"

"Why not? What is she, some kind of a Martian or something? Some kind of an *it?* Maybe she's a good-looking chick, man, horny as a snake. You mean you wouldn't even consider it?"

"Now you sound moral about the whole thing," Luke said, then suddenly gave out a horrified little laugh that he felt to be demeaning and inadequate.

"I mean, don't you ever think about it?" Robin asked, with what seemed to be sincere curiosity.

"Look," Luke said, "I'm thinking about her situation. She's got at least two little kids that splash too much in the bathtub, and probably token insurance from his union and maybe no other kind, unless he was in the service and that wouldn't amount to much. It's a matter of survival I'm thinking about, and sorrow and grief and no resources. Maybe I'm wrong, but how can I . . ."

"Maybe because of your family and all that?" Robin said hesitantly. "I can understand . . ."

"Maybe that's part of it. Or maybe it's that I think this whole city is a cancerous growth of some kind."

"Hey, man! Wow! I mean, that's pretty heavy, huh? This city? It's where we all *are*. It's what's going on."

Yes, it was what was going on everywhere, and that was not to be thought about, but he couldn't not think. That sense should be dulled. Now he wanted Robin gone. He could not dislike the shining little man, though Robin's energies seemed to him half-mad.

Robin did leave soon, both of them having agreed to meet tomorrow noon at the building site. Then he was alone again in this old, expensive room, a place where, perhaps because of the imperative of the two rigidly geometrical beds, he could not think of sitting down to work. Not at that desk-bureau with its thick glass top, not in that stuffed chair. The shape of the room, its amber, used shadows, the height and breadth of the windows, the high moist cell of its bathroom, its closet of hangers like disembodied shoulders—all was wrong for sitting down with his pencil and

42

notes and that last twisting of the mind that might turn chaos into thought.

He had a quick desire for whiskey that jerked his shoulders toward the bottle as though cords had snapped—a weakness, almost like falling, before he caught his balance again. He said out loud, "If I could think of what to do, where to be, I would not need that drug." The voice remained alive in the room, directed by some other self toward his listening self, which now lost all pride or independence at all. As he poured some whiskey in a glass the other voice said shame, death: there are places in this world which, without your self-pitying despair, are beautiful beyond imagination, the very models of our conception of heaven.

And then he did see a world, strangely a place of deep winter, with himself in it. In moonlight, a small field half-grown-up in gray birch and poplar, surrounded by dark woods. The moon was cold, distant, almost at the full, its miracle a pale silence in which the cold, glittering across the snow, seemed to have frozen the air itself. It was a world of crystal, deathly blue-silver, brittle, motionless. A step would cause the snow to scream, if a step could be taken in this interstellar cold. But at one edge of the field a small window gave a dim yellow light. There was a cabin there, nearly submerged in the deep snow; that one small yellow eye, and a white ray of smoke that rose straight as a column, proved that something here was alive.

Now he became embodied in this wilderness. He was on cross-country skis, the light wooden wands bearing him easily, as if he were nearly weightless. He was cold, feet and fingers and face, but not chilled. He wore a light pack on his back, and his arms as they held his long bamboo poles were weary yet strong. He glided easily toward the small windowlight, the snow squeaking cleanly along his narrow skis. What would he find in that buried cabin? What would it be like? As he approached he seemed to know the cabin with a maker's knowledge, and at the same time it was new to him.

The snow had pillowed up over the cabin from the west, drifted in a whorl over the low gable, and he saw as he approached its roofed porch and log columns that it was the classic, neolithic log cabin which lent, it was said, its spatial harmonies to the Parthe-

43

non. Sidestepping, he skied down the several feet of a snowdrift into the blue shadows of the porch where split hardwood—maple, ash and beech—had been stacked so evenly, each two-foot stick fitted so carefully, the piled warmth seemed a work of architecture itself.

He removed his skis in the dim light from the small window beside the heavy wooden door, cleaned their bindings of snow and leaned them against the firewood. Inside he knew he would find warmth in that yellow light, but now he stood before the door, his light cross-country boots in a skein of drifted powder. He raised his hand to knock on the door, then knew that he shouldn't knock because it was not necessary. It was his right to enter the warm interior with its peeled log walls, sturdy furniture of the same lustrous wood gleaming in lamplight and a dark-enameled woodstove alive with heat. In fact he must enter, because he had skied too far through the frozen wilderness. He knew in his body the exact reserves of vigor and warmth that were left, and to try to return the long miles would be to risk death.

There the vision stopped and the sighs and distant clashings of the city pushed into his tenth floor room. The interior of that cabin would have to be perfect, because it would have to be the room in which he could be alone, content to be alone, serene in his oneness. In it would be a sturdy desk and a chair, placed and lighted so that the four walls, the beams and purlins, the frosted windows, the stove, the bed, the kitchen, all of the harmonious and practical interior would enable him to write the truth that had either escaped him or that he had avoided all his life. When the stove cooled into embers he would rake the ashes, add the heavy wood and return, warmed and grateful, to his work. Outside, only the clean and implacable cold would search the joinings and closures of his shelter.

# 4.

Jimmo McLeod opened his lunchbox and without looking into it brought out a sandwich wrapped in a Baggie, the soft bread compressed like pale flesh. "You don't *live* here," he said, his sandwich hand indicating the streets, the whole city. "You exist. This is where the money is." He sat on one of the timbers that supported his crane. Mike Rizzo sat below him on an upturned galvanized bucket. Luke wondered if the bucket rested on soil or some sort of pavement covered by a compressed layer of fallout resembling dirt. Where was soil here? Once this same Broadway was a dirt road among working farms, lowing cattle, moist sweet hay; before that had been the purity of wilderness. This morning he had looked down a long cross street to the Hudson River and for a moment had a sense of the lay of the land, as if Murray Hill were a hill again, and he felt nostalgia for an island he had never seen, though he had lived here as a child.

"Hey, Luke," Mike said. "You a vet?"

"Three years in the army," Luke said.

"Any combat?"

"In Korea."

"What branch you in?"

"Infantry. Twenty-fourth Division."

"I was in the Eighty-second Airborne. One combat jump and three battle stars."

"In Europe, then," Luke said.

"The Bulge. Bastogne. I got shell fragments in the ass, this son of a bitch cook beat me to my own foxhole."

"I remember that war. I was just a kid," Jimmo said. "Mickey Rutherford got wounded in Vietnam."

"You know his wife Marjorie?" Luke asked hesitantly. "I'm going to talk to her this afternoon."

"What about?" Jimmo said, frowning, his jaws no longer chewing. Mike looked at him sternly, too.

"About the accident. How she's making it. Background stuff—you know."

Both of them seemed reassured by the professional-sounding words, and nodded.

"Sure, I know Marjorie," Jimmo said. "Mickey and me were in the same lodge—Elks. Mickey was a great family man, you know. He was always heading for home. I drunk many a beer at his house. Marjorie's one handsome-looking woman, she was crazy about old Mick, too. And their two kids, well, for the both of them those kids hung the moon." He shook his head and the sides of his mouth turned down. "Without a father, I don't know. Christ if it ain't hard enough as it is."

"Yeah," Mike said, "hard enough as it is. Hard enough as it is."

"You said it," Jimmo said.

"I don't know what's going on," Mike said. "I'm a Catholic and I don't even know what's going on with the Church, not to mention the kids. You follow me? You Jewish, Luke?"

"No," Luke said.

"I just wondered, you being a writer. What I mean is, they just sit around like zombies. Even out on the street, just standing around like zombies. You follow me? We used to play stickball, ringalevio, swim in the East River, you follow me? Only maybe they're smarter than we were, I read that somewhere lately. Maybe they get that from the television, but none of the kids do anything anymore. I get that impression, I don't know. I got a daughter eighteen, she don't want to do nothing. She don't want to go on to college, she don't want to get married, what the hell does she want? And now they say we're going to have married priests, homosexual priests, morphodite priests, woman priests. What's a man supposed to believe? You follow me, Luke?"

"Yeah, I do, Mike." He had wanted to think that what Mike said was funny, and Mike wanted him to think that it was, in part at least, funny, but the lined, dark, walnut-grained face was in real consternation and doubt. It was as if Mike were asking him, perhaps because he was a writer, because of the power or magic attached to that title, for a real answer. For a moment he felt his eyebrows knot, his skin turn hot, and he bade himself not to express the sudden unattached sorrow he felt.

"Lot of guys out of work these days," Jimmo said. "It ain't even as steady as it used to be—if you could call that steady."

Mike said, "I mean I was drafted and proud to go put my life on the line for my country, but now it's okay, just tell the country to shove it up the ass and it's okay. You follow me?"

Because of the din of the traffic and the constant engine noises, various clangs and booms, they were all half shouting. In this general mood of consternation they talked until the lunch break was over. Other workers had been watching the three of them, somewhat surreptitiously, and as Luke turned to leave, one of them, the young man in the Marine lance corporal's shirt who had yesterday presented his rear end when he had heard the name *Gentleman*, came striding toward him as if propelled. It was as if his earlier hesitation were a gun that finally projected him toward Luke, striding on stiff legs, swaggering. Luke watched him come, recognizing it all, knowing that he had no need to flinch away from the red face and its pressures.

"Minds!" the worker shouted. "We got minds, but we also got hands!" He held out his hands. "Hands that do the work! You understand that? We got the hands that do the work! We built this country! We're the ones that build the country, you understand that?"

Before Luke could answer, the man snorted triumphantly and turned away. "Huh! Huh!" he said, nodding his head violently as he strode away.

47

And Luke, since he didn't want to appear to hang around, walked away too, thinking of what he had or hadn't learned so far. No one knew for certain what had caused the accident; most likely it was a chain of large and small errors, incompetencies scattered over several trades and men of different unions, different employers, including the engineer-architects. There was the John Hancock building in Boston, for instance, all glass except that the glass panels blew out to shatter like fragmentation bombs hundreds of feet below in the streets. There were dams that burst, bridges that took off in a gale like broken birds. Mickey Rutherford's command post at his derrick's bells, lights and control levers was inside the building, below the floors that had collapsed. They didn't get his body out for several hours. His head was in his hat, and his hat was in his lap. He was thirty-one. If something could happen, it would happen. People would be rent apart, crushed, dismembered, burned, suffocated, dropped through space to their deaths.

But unless it was quick it must hurt terribly when it happened; there was such a thing as agony. He walked up Broadway thinking that he must be very alert, though he was filled with a strange lassitude that was, again, like sorrow. What in hell did all these people *want?* For a moment he would disregard the blacks who would like very much the eight dollars an hour Mickey Rutherford had earned; not many blacks in the International Union of Operating Engineers. But that was another question. He would take the subway past Harlem, that dangerous continent, on his way to the Bronx.

He walked north, toward Central Park. He still had a slight scar on his calf he'd got skating in Central Park when he was twelve and cut himself with the blade of his own skate. They all wore knickers, then; he remembered the cut through the stocking, even the pattern and color of the stocking, which was like the designs on old linoleum. The cut wasn't deep, needed no stitches, but unlike other superficial cuts this one had left a scar that never went away.

On a newsstand he saw the headlines of the *Daily News*: CRAZED VET KILLS WIFE, CHILD, SELF.

In Korea he carried a BAR until he made corporal, and then he carried a carbine, which was considerably lighter and had no sharp corners to dig into his back. Once, on detached service with the First Cavalry, he'd carried a .45 automatic for a few weeks. He was thinking about weapons because of the knife-wielding punks who would decide to mug him on the subway, of course. Amazing to think of *being* a force again, instead of being forced. The .45 would do nicely, with its enormous 230 grain bullet: a cartridge designed specifically to stop gooks and other dark-skinned types in their wild-eyed, teeth-bared, slavering charges. A lot of gooks had been laid down in Korea. Bloody ragged holes. That was a bullet war, particularly intimate on those terrible hills because you shot at men you could see. Not with the .45 much, though. With Garands and BARs and the cal. .30 M1914A4 machine gun.

How strange it was to think back to those days when he was in his teens, to at least think in such a prosaic way about what was a symptom of the disease that frightened him now. Those deaths were thought aberrant because they occurred in war, which was then considered a temporary phenomenon. There was only one man he was certain that he and he alone had killed, but his bullets must have entered many other bodies through the bulky cotton quilting of those winter uniforms.

He didn't know how long it would take him to get to Mosholu Parkway, but he had nothing else to do, so he might as well go up and look at the Bronx until three. He found the right subway out of an ancient memory.

Mosholu Parkway did have some soiled grass in its boulevard lanes, and some plane and linden trees that seemed in suspended animation. He found Marjorie Rutherford's building, a brown brick structure in a row of similar three-story buildings that were shabby, as if they had been smeared too often by dirty hands, but without the detritus of poverty. He was half an hour early, so he looked around the neighborhood and found a café with clean windows and dim furnishings from the thirties, sat at the counter and ordered a cup of coffee from a heavy, pink-uniformed waitress who served him without actually looking at him.

Robin was supposed to have met him at the construction site, but hadn't shown up. Perhaps he was locked in the death grip of those great terrestrial thighs, in the pleasure-agony of opisthotonos, his head mashed into the rich carpeting of a driveshaft hump. A plausible vision that matched, because of whatever humor it contained, his own near hysteria. The coffee cup rattled against its saucer as he put it down. The cigarette was as dry as the wind in an alley.

After twenty minutes he left the café and walked back to Marjorie Rutherford's building. Be not, he thought, conscious of your feet in your shoes. Be not conscious of each foot in its own shoe, nor of each toe cramped in its own fashion too intimately next to its fellows in the dark of cloth and leather. Be not conscious of parts.

Above the row of mailbox doors in the entryway was an old Elks sticker from the Vietnam war, varnished by age: OUR FLAG—LOVE IT OR LEAVE. Old Glory undulant, faded as an antique painting. Below the mailboxes the word SHIT had been incompletely erased, and three identical spray can graffiti signatures in black were undecipherable but done with flair.

In one corner of the foyer was a grimy abandoned teddy bear, split along its seams, its granulated yellow stuffing coming out. Luke would never see a stuffed toy without having to remember how, long ago, his Uncle Shem had a bluetick hound that had been ripped open by one of the wild boars that escaped from Corbin's Park after the 1938 hurricane, and how all down along the hound's ribcage and flank was the stitched scar that hair had never grown back to cover. "Ayuh," Shem said, "that's where they put the stuffin' in old Sport." And Luke, who was eight, for a moment thought yes; but the dog was alive and running around in its pen, so how could he be a stuffed dog? Just for a few seconds it had seemed possible and the world had opened up so that the fantasy of Pooh and Piglet and Tigger was real. The possibility faded slowly, leaving a sort of welt, a heavy place in his mind, like a vivid dream that took a while to shake off. As now, again, he shook off the memory and pushed the black button below the Rutherfords' mailbox.

In a moment her voice asked, "Who is it?" and he thought *ha-wizzut?* while he answered.

"I'll be right down," she said. "The buzzer don't work."

He waited for the widow to come down the stairs to the solid, brown-painted door he faced. He heard nothing from the other side until the door opened, then had the sense of looking up at her; though she was about his height, her blond hair was built up straight above her forehead in a kind of shako, or busby, of shining gold, circled by a black velvet ribbon. Her eyes, surrounded by mascara, seemed too round and small and dark for her large pale face and whitened lips.

"Come on in," she said, motioning him past. "I got to make sure the door locks when it shuts."

She wore fawn colored slacks and a white blouse; her forearms were rose and white, glinting with golden fuzz. As he followed her up the stairs he thought of the word "strapping," and watched the power of her buttocks and long legs as they filled and moved beneath the thin cloth. Largeness was not invulnerability, he knew. This was a large and basically cheerful woman whose man was dead. God knew what she might do when they spoke of him, but now she said what a nice day it was, not too hot for June. Her apartment was on the second floor, her friend, a not so cheerful smaller woman, standing in the open door.

"My friend, Mrs. Ryan," Marjorie Rutherford said of the smaller woman, who merely nodded, turned and went ahead of them into the apartment.

The hallway had been yellow-brown, an undecorated, indifferently soiled public place, impersonal as a chute, but once inside the apartment the drabness ended in a bright plane of color, a hot red wall that met a brighter yellow one.

He wondered if his expectations were about to be confounded; maybe Marjorie and Mickey Rutherford were odd, at least in their taste in interior decoration. But then he saw that the colors were only a touch of the Scandinavian, or whatever that fashion for broad primary surfaces was. The sofa was a plaid print, covered as permanently in transparent plastic as were the ruffled white lamp-

51

shades. On the bathroom door a varnished maple board bore the carved words, MICK IN THOUGHT, and there on the dining alcove wall was the coated copper sunburst clock, and an ornate plastic plaque with the motto, ILLIGITIMI NON CARBORUNDUM.

Two small children sat on the orange shag rug looking at the large color television, which was tuned at this hour to an audience participation show full of screamed numbers and shrieks of gladness.

Mrs. Ryan saw her role to be the protector, fierce though silent. She sat carefully in the chair that matched the sofa. Marjorie Rutherford had the children stand to be introduced: Mickey and Marcia, Mickey dark and jumpy and shy, Marcia blond and looking at him. They were seven and five.

"Well," Marjorie said, "sit down, Mr. Carr. Can I get you anything? A gin and tonic?"

"That would be nice," he said, thinking how a gin and tonic would be a high-class drink to offer on a June afternoon on Mosholu Parkway, noting his snobbish eye as it documented, documented; though only in her thirties, Mrs. Ryan wore harlequin glasses. She was pale, sallow in fact—a friend of the large woman who had just gone to the kitchenette to make him a gin and tonic. She sat with her nylons touching at ankle and knee. What history, he wondered, of mergings and accommodations with Mr. Ryan, with her children, if any? Any joy? Do not judge so, he told himself, though she seemed cold and defensive.

"You're Mrs. Rutherford's friend," he said, letting her treat it as a question, or not.

"Five years," she said, nodding once for each word.

"A terrible accident," he said, signifying by a conspiratorial glance that neither Marjorie, who was tinkling ice in the kitchenette, nor the television-bound children were listening.

Mrs. Ryan shook her head, sad all at once. "Yes. Terrible. Terrible, and the children no father. What will happen? What will happen to them, the poor dears?"

He could only shake his head. Whatever he was here for, it was not to help, and this woman, with her sternness gone, was no longer definable.

52

Marjorie brought him his gin and tonic. He was sitting on the plastic-covered sofa, and the coffee table, full of potted plants, was over against the wall next to the television set, so he held the wet glass in his hand, sipped the cool liquid and felt the lemon slice touch his lip. Marjorie took a straight chair from the dining alcove, placed it at a distance from him that seemed precise to the inch, then carefully sat on it, her knees together, her hands in her lap. She looked at him brightly. Over her shoulder was the room's one window, heavily armored with metal latticework secured by a padlock. From the top of the television set, gold-framed Kodacolor photographs of two smiling children looked down upon their subjects, who did not smile but gazed with grave faces at the now muted excitements of the picture tube.

She was telling him about how much it cost to garage the car, the Ford station wagon in which they had taken trips to the country; the garage rent was forty dollars a month and now it was going to be raised to sixty. They couldn't leave it outside because it would be vandalized, or stolen, as it had been once. She was afraid to take the subway into Manhattan. Mickey had taught her how to drive. She didn't want to sell the car but was afraid she'd have to now. All this told cheerfully, brightly. These were mere facts, were they not? She didn't mean to give the impression of complaint, or at least not more than the usual, ordinary, ongoing complaints about the city.

Marcia scuttled over on her knees and turned the volume up, a sea-crash of undifferentiated breathings and cries, transcended by the man's joking, patronizing voice: *Yes, my dear Mrs. Mustig! And now . . . and now! Yes! Yes! Here it is . . . .*

"Honey, Honey!" Marjorie called across the noise. "We can't hear! Turn it down!"

Marcia, on her knees in front of the haze of color and sound, paid no attention to her mother. Mickey looked at his mother once, quickly, then at Marcia with an amusement he tried to conceal; evidently he considered his little sister a character. Marjorie got up, big and graceful, and turned the volume down. Marcia waited until her mother was seated again before she turned the volume back up.

53

"If you don't turn it down we'll have to turn it off!" Marjorie called to her.

There was more of this, Luke feeling the detachment of the observer, the nervousness of one who feels embarrassment in others, until Marcia was crying and pouting. Finally Mrs. Ryan said, "I'll take them out, Marge. Here, let me get them ready." She had decided to trust him, as they always trusted him unless they were slightly insane. "Mickey, go get your clothes changed. We'll go to the playground." She took Marcia's hand and led her into a bedroom, Marcia's face red and wet, her lower lip still swollen into a pout.

He took a swig of his gin and tonic and Marjorie said, "Here, let me freshen your drink. Maybe I'll have one, too. It's hard for kids just sitting around, but what can you do?"

He shook his head. She took his half-full glass away and he heard the prying fracture of ice in an ice tray, the thud of the refrigerator, its hiccup before it hummed—domestic noises he hadn't heard for several months unless they were ones he had made himself.

At first there had been the friends who came to see how he was taking it, husbands and wives bringing food. And the few neighbors he knew in that dormitory suburb stopped by with not much to say at first except the half-mute words of consolation and the touching of hands. Later some came to offer advice, his dissolution apparent but not too obvious because he did the dishes and picked things up, more or less. But evidently there were ways beyond his ken in which Helen had kept the house fresh and new; after a while an aura, or patina, of staleness and neglect had sifted through the house like a fog.

Marjorie brought back two gin and tonics. This time she sat in the deeper chair, her long legs crossed, and offered him a cigarette, which he accepted. She got up to get him an ashtray, a heavy metal square with a thin, Giacometti-like figure standing on one edge of it, arms raised in a supplicating pose.

"What's this?" he asked, surprised; even though it decorated an ashtray, the figure was unlike any other object he'd seen in the apartment.

54

"It used to have a saying on it," she said, hastening to explain that it was incomplete as it was. " 'Lord, why hast Thou forsaken me?' "

Yes, for a moment, in that strangely precise way in which the eye assesses value, it had been wrong for this place. Now he looked more closely at the supplicating figure and saw that it hadn't the rough unsentimentality of Giacometti; each limb and feature, though skeletal enough, merely implored.

When Mrs. Ryan and the children, who now wore their playground dungarees, had left, Marjorie asked why he wanted to talk to her, really.

"So I can write about your experience, I guess," he said. "What it's been like for you."

"But why me in particular?" she asked, blushing a little around the edges of her makeup, which now seemed a mask he wished she hadn't wanted to wear, though that mask was part of what he must observe. To her, he supposed, it wasn't a mask at all, but simple reality; one wore makeup in certain situations just as one wore clothes, and clothes were not necessarily a mask.

"Because Jimmo McLeod and Mike Rizzo talked to me about your husband, and your name and address were on a list I got from *Gentleman*."

"Sheila—Mrs. Ryan—made me call and check on you," she said.

"And I passed?"

"They said you were a well-known writer. Then Sheila—Mrs. Ryan—looked up *Gentleman* in the book and it was the same number you gave me, so we figured you were you." She laughed, then stopped suddenly, as though her easy laugh had been wrong. "But what could you write about me?"

"I want to find out who you are, what it was like before and after. I know my questions might make you unhappy and if you don't want to answer them, please don't. I don't want to add to your tragedy, even in little ways."

"Is that what reporters say?"

"It's what I say, anyway," he said.

"I thought just now you were going to cry," she said. "Now, if *I* do, my mascara will get all gooey and my false eyelashes might fall

55

off. You know, tears look funny on pancake makeup. They sort of roll down like they were on oil or something." She laughed again, her eyes, which he now saw were light green, looking out of their heavily darkened rims at him.

"Why do you wear it?" he asked, a question he hadn't intended.

She thought, frowning at him, though not in anger. She blinked, and he wondered if her lids felt sticky. Closed, her eyes were ragged black slits in fleshcolored paste.

"If I'm going to have to cry I'll take it all off," she said. "I don't know why I didn't think I'd have to cry. You're going to ask about Mickey and where we went when we went on trips to the country. We went to Pennsylvania sometimes, sometimes Vermont, or Atlantic City. Sometimes on Sunday we just drove around in the suburbs looking at houses. You know, with a yard, a garage and grass. Neither of us ever lived in a house, but I always wanted to try it. Just think! Your own house? Do you live in a house?"

"Yes," he said.

"Is it nice? Trees and grass and all?"

"Yes, it's nice. You'd like it."

"I'd like to see it sometime. Where is it?"

"In Wellesley, Massachusetts."

"But you know, with all those doors and windows on every side, don't you feel funny? Like, somebody could look in, or break in. Like, here, we got the door with the police lock, and bars on the windows. I mean if somebody tries to get in at least I know what door." She stopped and shook her head, the high golden crown of her hair seeming too massive to rotate that quickly. "But you want to ask questions, right?"

"Well, you're answering them before I even ask," he said.

"You mean you want to know things like we wanted to live somewhere else? Anyway, who wouldn't?"

He asked her about her life before she was married, and she told him that she came from the Bronx, grew up in the Bronx, graduated from high school and worked as a receptionist-secretary in a private clinic. She met Mickey Rutherford because she sometimes dated his younger brother, who was in high school when she was. Mickey never went to regular high school, but he

got an equivalency certificate in the army, where he was a techni-
cian—a mechanic. In Vietnam he was wounded in the back when
a rocket landed thirty feet away from him. Then when he got out
of the army his uncle, who was a shop steward, got him into the
IUOE. He was only on permit a year before he got his card.

Mickey loved his kids. He was a home-loving man. "I still can't
believe sometimes he's not coming home. Sometimes I have to
shake myself, around five or six, because without knowing it I
been expecting to hear his key in the lock. And then I got to know
he's not ever going to come busting in and grab me and the kids
ever again."

She put her fingers to her eyes, then looked at them. "I better
go wash my face," she said. "Look, I don't want to weep all over
the place. I'm not a crybaby. . . . " She got up, trying to suppress
a high whinny of grief, and went into the bathroom past the sign,
MICK IN THOUGHT.

As the water ran in the bathroom he considered flight from her,
but that would be betrayal. She wouldn't know why he had left.
She would wonder, and feel bad on that account as well. He liked
her, and felt that she was good. He was aware of his mental note-
taking: ILLIGITIMI NON CARBORUNDUM on that plaque from a gift
house or souvenir shop supposedly meant, Don't let the bastards
wear you down. A conversation piece. He thought about the social
implications of that, of everything; but the woman behind the
bathroom door was real, a system of life exquisitely tuned to feel
pain.

All his life he'd had the feeling that he thought about things
other people didn't think about—not because of their lack of
imagination or intelligence, but because they acted upon some
ethical or moral code that he had somehow missed, as though he'd
been out of school the term it had been introduced into everyone
else's consciousness. And so now he thought of her naked
haunches, and how they would be vast and warm as sand dunes,
sea grasses blowing between. This vision was not sexual, it was just
there, tawny and immense.

After a few minutes she came out of the bathroom, her hair tied
back and with a different face made of honest shiny skin incor-

57

porating pores, the inner shadings of her own blood, green eyes rimmed by the faint rosiness caused by tears, and a small white scar at her left temple.

"This is what I really look like," she said, blushing.

"You look more real," he said.

"More's the pity."

The telephone rang, and she got up quickly to answer it. "It's for you," she said, surprised as one always is in that circumstance.

As she handed him the receiver their fingers touched, then it was Robin's voice at his ear. "Hey, Luke? I'm sorry I didn't make it today, but I got hung up." Luke thought of dogs in the rut. "But is it okay if I come over and get the pictures? Have you asked her about it?"

"No, not yet. Let me ask." He turned to her and said, "It's the photographer. He'd like to take pictures of the apartment and you and the kids. Would you mind that?"

"Like this?" she said, putting her hands on her washed and shining face. "My God!" Then she said, "You didn't tell me about any pictures."

"I was going to ask you. Anyway, it can be some other time." He wanted to say that it could be never, if she didn't want them to take pictures, and in leaving out this option he felt the twinge of coercion.

"Oh," she said. "Well . . . "

"I don't want to intrude," he said. But he didn't want her to say no to the photographs, either. Even now there was the sense of getting this assignment over with. But then what would he do? She nodded, and he told Robin to come.

"All right," she said. "Let's sit down." They sat down and lit cigarettes. "Mickey didn't smoke. He used to get disgusted with me. 'Why smoke that garbage?' he always said."

"A good question," he said. "I always used to think—maybe I still do—that if I could live a certain kind of life, with everything just right, I'd never even think of smoking."

"When you're sound asleep, maybe," she said. "We're fellow addicts, you know?"

He considered telling her that they had more in common than

that, but he was afraid of that connection, and also of a loss of control. It seemed a meanness in him that he could not share it with her, and in not confessing his own loss he felt cruel and small. He had never trusted secrets; in many ways they seemed more powerfully evil than lies.

She found him easy to talk to. She said this. She told him about Mickey, when they first dated and he'd taken her to his social club, The Nocturnes, and later when they'd had an engagement sort of party there, with the club—it was a dingy sort of basement, really—all festooned in crepe paper. Her maiden name was Burns and she wasn't Catholic, but Mickey was and now Mickey Jr. and Marcia were Catholic, which was all right but it made her feel funny sometimes. Was he a Catholic?

"No," he said.

"Carr. Is that German? Jewish?"

"English, or Scottish, I think. Maybe it was once spelled K–e–r–r—you know, like Deborah Kerr."

"Oh, the actress! Yeah, sure. I always used to pronounce it Curr. I saw her on the Late Late Show with Burt Lancaster and Montgomery Clift. I been watching the Late Late Show a lot lately."

When he asked her about her finances she spoke as openly; the money seemed like a lot, but she knew it wouldn't last long unless she went to work. She'd been putting that off, because of Mickey Jr. and Marcia, but she'd have to go looking soon.

He found that she was afraid of blacks, though without the intensity or even shrillness that usually came with that fear; she had no programs for a solution to that problem. She knew Mickey felt stronger on the subject, but he also said many blacks couldn't get jobs, so maybe they had to steal. She'd heard him say that. And he admired black athletes. He was crazy about Muhammad Ali, though he always called him Cassius Clay. He couldn't admire that man enough; whatever he said just broke Mickey up.

She showed him pictures of Mickey, her hands trembling and her voice tremulous at first. In one picture the family sat at a picnic table among long-needled pines, a blue lake behind them. Mickey's curly fair hair was thick, and his wide red face grinned more intensely than anyone else's. "This old lady came along and Mickey got her to take the picture," Marjorie said. "She really loved doing it but he had to teach her how to hold it and look through the viewfinder and push the button. That's at Lake George, last summer."

She knelt beside him, her red fingernail pointing out the blue lake, the far shore. Her round arm, reddish and fuzzed, gave off heat, and again he saw her monumentally naked, tawny dunes and grasses shimmering, baking under the force of sunlike energy.

She got up and slipped the pictures back into a maroon album that had the words, *Our Family* stamped in gold on the leatherette cover. "I got to stick them all in there sometime. I never got around to last summer's."

She was nervous, smoothing her undone hair back, taking a step toward the kitchen, running her hand over the edge of the dining table and looking at her fingers for dust. "It's strange you being here," she said, blushing at what that might mean.

"I understand," he said.

"But everything's strange. What are you going to write about me?"

"The way you are, I hope, and how you're taking it, and how you look. I'll let you read it first."

"How I *look!* God, I look awful."

"Not to me."

"You don't like makeup, huh?"

"Why paint skin? It's already got its own color."

"You're a wierdo, you know that?" She laughed, then looked at him seriously and shook her head. "I feel like I ought to call you by your first name, now. Luke, right? You call me Marge, okay?"

"Okay, Marge."

"That's better," she said, and sat down again, this time with a little carelessness, as if the upholstered chair were sturdier than it had been before. "Luke? You go around talking to people all the time that had something bad happen to them? Is that what you do all the time? I mean, news is bad news, right? And you're after the news. What I mean is, how can you stand it? I mean really."

"News isn't always bad," he said. "Just most of the time."

"It bothered you a lot to come here, right?"

"Yes."

"You don't have to show me first. You know—what you write about me."

"I will, though, if I write anything."

"You mean you don't have to write the article?"

"Not if I don't feel like it."

"But it's how you make a living, right?"

"Partly, anyway."

"You're awful sad, you know that?" she said, frowning, worried for him. "Let me get us another gin and tonic. Got to cheer you up, Luke."

She made them another gin and tonic, and told him, their ice tinkling and their fingers on the cold moist glasses, about her father and mother. Her father was the super in an apartment building with forty units—forty families in it and somebody got mugged in the elevator last week. It was getting worse and they ought to have a security guard in the lobby. Her mother had a heart condition. Her brother was in the navy and her little sister was getting married next month to an optometrist. Marjorie seemed happy to talk, to look at him and smile and sip her gin and tonic.

"You're married, Luke, right? And you got a family up there in Wellesley, Massachusetts. I can tell."

"How can you tell?" he said. Of course she had to ask that question sooner or later and force him into a choice of answers, each option having a precise moral value—yes, or the truth. "No, I didn't mean to ask you how you could tell. I had a family but in January my wife and two children were killed in an accident."

For a moment her face was still, and then she said, "Your whole family? My God!"

"Yes," he said.

"Oh, my God! Your wife and children?" She kept looking straight at him, tears running from her green eyes. Blood infused the rims of her eyes beneath the glitter of the tears.

"I shouldn't have told you," he said. "I didn't mean to bring

61

anything like that here, and I'm sorry. I don't know why I told you. I'm sorry."

"I've still got Mickey and Marcia, but you got nobody. Lord Jesus God, you think you got troubles and you're the only one and then you find out other people got troubles worse than you."

His throat was tight, not painful but in a stasis caused by a familiar apprehension. All at once she had taken on the power of certain ordinary people he had encountered every once in a while all his life, people who had, for no reason he could find of vanity or gain, demonstrated that intensity of sympathy for someone else. He had always felt smaller than those people, alien to them, and no matter what successes had come to him in life he had always been haunted by the possible existence of another race that was in some way more generous and real than his own.

"But how could you stand it?" she asked. She pushed her large hands down her thighs toward him, smoothing the fawn material of her slacks.

"I'm here to find out how you can stand your loss," he said.

"I didn't think I could, but I'm not the first woman they came and told her her husband was dead."

"No, that's true," he said.

She looked at her small silver wristwatch. "Sheila ought to be back with Mickey and Marcia." Within a few seconds the buzzer rang and soon they were back, all of the doors' locks undone, including the police lock's iron buttress, the angle of which suggested immediate and violent siege. The children, still in a wild, playground mood, caromed off each other and the furniture.

Soon the buzzer rang again, and it was Robin. Luke went down to his car with him to hold the building's door open while Robin carried his floodlights and other paraphernalia up to the apartment.

Then there were serious discussions, Robin extremely expert in these matters, of a barrette for Marjorie's long hair, of a touch of powder, a suspicion of eye shadow, of the children's clothes and the qualities of direct and reflected light. Marjorie was patient and cooperative while Robin, it seemed to Luke, assumed Mad Hatter-like dictatorial powers, moving or having moved for each shot

62

nearly every movable object in the apartment. After their initial fascination, the children were not so patient. When not forced into place they wandered here and there, touching the equipment in spite of Mrs. Ryan's horror at their doing that.

After more than an hour of this the children began to get hungry and querulous, so he and Robin put the apartment back the way it had been, each piece of funiture covering its shadow pattern against non-faded carpet or wall. When all of Robin's equipment was boxed, telescoped and strapped again, they were ready to say good-bye.

Marjorie was still flushed and excited by all of it. As they were ready to leave, her hand moved toward Luke's nervously, as if to touch his hand or shake his hand. Her gesture had been strange, at least according to his social instincts about her, so his hand was a second late. When their hesitations were over and their hands did meet, her large hand warm within his, it had become an event, and they smiled about it.

"If I have any more questions, can I call you?" he said.

"Sure," she said. "Call me anytime, Luke."

# 5.

That evening as he was about to go out to eat he got a call from Ham Jones, a Wellesley real estate man he'd known for a couple of years as an occasional tennis partner and less occasional poker player. On Luke's way to New York they'd met at the Eastern shuttle in Logan airport and had an early, airplane-nervousness drink together. Ham had just come in from La Guardia, so his drink was in celebration of survival. Luke had mentioned that eventually he would want to sell his house, but had been no more specific than that. But now Ham told him that he had a buyer who would pay a little more than twice what the house had cost to build ten years ago.

"This is firm, Luke. These people have A-1 credit and they're nuts about your house just from looking in the windows. What do you say? Are you ready to sell? I think they'll buy the furniture and lawn stuff and just about anything else. Buddy, they are hot to trot! The guy's in electronics on Route 128, pretty good outfit, I've checked it out. Are you there? I didn't mean to push you or anything, but the minute I saw these folks I knew exactly what they'd want, and what they want is your house. What do you say?"

He could see Ham Jones in his plaid pants and maroon jacket with the Rockwell calculator making a slight bulge in the inside breast pocket along with the worn mortgage tables. Not that Ham was worn—he was a twenty-year air force officer who had retired on pension at forty and was so invigorated by his new career he seemed in his twenties.

"Can I think about it?" Luke said. He felt the sudden vacuum of not having his house, his home place that was full of all those years.

"Well, they've just been transferred from L.A. and they're in a hurry to settle in. I don't know. Do you really want to sell it, Luke?"

"Can I call you tomorrow night? Right now I don't know what I want to do. I know I'm not going to live there but I've got to sort things out for a while yet."

"Twenty-four hours? Will a day do it?"

"It might," Luke said. Already he was going up the front walk, at the step in the middle where the Japanese yews formed a sort of gateway. The landscaping would be difficult to return to because Helen had done all of it, and now the weeds had grown up through the sedum and thyme, through the low mugho pine and ground juniper borders. There would be no moss roses this year because they were annuals and she hadn't been there to plant them. Everywhere the weeds knew how to prove that absence.

He promised to call at the same time tomorrow night, and again Ham said he hoped he hadn't pushed him into something he didn't want to do.

Then he was alone with this conception, one he had often fooled with in the past when it was just fooling: which of his possessions did he actually need? The question came from a desire for efficiency, not, he thought, from any ascetic urge.

Also, how did the glass of bourbon and water materialize in his fist? Were the two questions related?? There were those who would settle for the bottle and a warm place to drink.

Now he was still on the front walk of his house in Wellesley, approaching the front door. He didn't want to be there, because this time he would be in the possession of the idea of farewell. Beside the front door was a plant, a soft round silvery mound called *ar-timesia,* or something near that; he had never seen it spelled. Once when they were driving back from New Hampshire Helen wanted to stop at a nursery they happened to be passing. They turned in and went past Lombardy poplars and arborvitae to greenhouses and moist acres where they met the old man who owned the place. At his feet were peat boxes from which the silvery plant, which Helen had never seen before, almost glittered in the late after-noon light. They bought one of the boxes and the old man looked up at them and said, hefting the box, "The trouble with a nursery is you don't just sell your plants, you sell your soil."

Now he was at the dark, heavy door itself, the silver-mound glowing in the periphery of vision. Strange to be about to enter his own front door; a formal occasion. The door was unlocked, and swung inward on its three brass hinges with a groan.

"Sell the house. You can't handle it," he said out loud, and took a drink. How much of loss, or any strange, new or dramatic situa-tion, was an excuse for reward? A voice seemed to answer him, but he could neither identify the voice nor understand its words. He did believe that the voice came from his own mind, some-where from within that labyrinth of inefficiencies. A statement or question needed an answer, even a ghost answer.

Now, at least, he was back in a hotel room in New York City, with this article to write, some theme or other to pursue—perhaps that the queen was dead or dying or demented and the workers—good troupers, most of them—went on building, building. Seen from a distance they were mad, and took on the hateful attributes of whatever forces exploited them, but when you got them alone they could be, some of them at least, sensitive, kind, transcending it all, which made it worse. Now, if he were the proper monster he could write it easily, brilliantly, because the truth would never constrain syntax, which would then be free, unalloyed, and could make all sorts entertaining discoveries. That those discoveries might be wrong, unfair, destructive, pure vanity, wouldn't matter, because Artifice was all, was it not? He should explain to Martin Troup that this whole idea of sending writers around interview-ing people was wrong, even criminal, because the results were

66

credible lies and people would *never* learn not to believe the lies, especially the liars who wrote the lies.

This was depression, fear and booze talking in his head. He would go out, now, and eat.

On the way down in the big elevator he lost any desire to eat and it seemed worse than that because, alone in the plushy old elevator, descending to where the people were, it was all desire, desire for anything in the world, that he seemed to have lost. And so again he went to the dark steak and chop place off the lobby and ordered a steak, a salad and a beer. He felt full and dull, his taste dull. He put A-1 sauce on his meat, something he never did, and the meat tasted like something out of a can. The salad was too sweet, the beer bulk liquid sloshing in his stomach.

In the elevator again, this time accompanied by a young black woman in some sort of hotel uniform who carried a small vacuum cleaner and a clipboard, the whole column of the elevator shaft began to lean to the left. He held on to the handrail as the elevator, its cables and pulleys unaware of the lean, rose at an increasing angle to the surface of the earth. The hotel was falling over and he was helpless, emptied of breath by vertigo. The young black woman, her straightened hair glossy, her plum-colored lips in profile more protrusive than her nose, stood at that angle with no support and of course he knew that the imbalance of the world was in his head. He would hold on, hoping that her floor was first, or that he would find level again before he had to get off on the tenth floor. Vision, or his inner ear, or some lower, more primary system of control had gone astray and the muscles of his legs were not getting the proper messages. It seemed he supported his whole weight with his right arm. The low call of nausea had begun, a silent warble deep in his throat.

The young woman got off at the eighth floor, not having looked at him, and he waited for the elevator to close its doors, hesitate, and then, with worn mechanical suddenness, rise.

His eyes insisted that they knew what was vertical, but before he reached his room his shoulder hit the corridor wall several times. After the business of the key and lock he got into the room and nearly missed the bed he chose to fall upon, holding himself upon

67

its canted surface with a desperate swing of his arm. The damask texture of the bedspread against his cheek was the only normal, almost reassuring, signal from outside his head.

The room tilted slowly to the left until it was nearly on its side and then, with no apparent return or change, was vertical and as remorselessly tilting to the left again. Nausea came precisely at the impossible return, then subsided as the tilt progressed, only to begin again, each time a little stronger, as the room, with no sound or stress, was vertical and again beginning its tilt. He crawled to the bathroom and knelt upon the stained hexagonal tiles, put his face over the ancient toilet and emptied himself of chunks and bitter brown liquids. How long? he wondered. How long? Not to be nauseated; that would be a great gift. To be neither anxious nor nauseated—what a wonderful gift that would be.

When he thought he was empty he crawled back to the bed on his soiled knees, his hands still shaped by the cold saline rim of the toilet.

In the night he awoke, only the distant rhythms of the city, crashes and horns so muted they had lost all insistence, calling from beyond the brown canyons of the Biltmore. The amber room was stable and the nausea was gone. At first he lay still, his mind free of all the events of the past, and enjoyed the smoothness and neutrality of balance. What was level was level without thought, even though he was in a small cubicle on the tenth floor of a huge and doubtful structure built on an island that was itself unstable, lying as it did near a long fault in the system of continents. All could dissolve into rubbish at any moment. Then the recent past was back with all of its black and white, no amelioration, no making the best of it. No, he was at least free. There must be some value in that.

In the morning he called Martin Troup and said he was going home. He would need to do some research on the article, which would deal with construction, Manhattan, the bodies crushed, wounded and bereft, and he would have it done in a week. Martin said two weeks would be okay and wished him well. Then he called Robin Flash and told him. Robin had been to his developer already that morning and it seemed the kids had fooled with his strobe and half the pictures taken in Marjorie's apartment were underexposed, so he'd have to go back and do them over.

"Will you be down here again, Luke?" Robin asked.

"Sometime, anyway," Luke said. "I'm going to sell my house but I'll be there for a few days. I'll let you and Martin know where I'll be."

"Marjorie's going to be disappointed not to see you again, man."

"Oh, come on, Robin."

Robin laughed, and his voice was still precarious with mirth when they hung up.

Luke called Ham Jones at his office in Wellesley and told him to go ahead with the sale; he'd take the noon shuttle and be back this afternoon. With all this done he felt a sense of accomplishment. He would finish the article because he'd said he would. That was now settled, and although he had no way in mind to get into it, he'd always been able to write five thousand words. He'd just do it and get it over with. It would be about nightmare but it wouldn't be nightmare to do because he would sit down and do it, if he had to, out of the cold skill of his profession. In it would be the black man on Broadway screaming silently, the din, the fouled air, the stupid inefficiency and impermanence, and in the foreground in a different light the clear faces of the people. Maybe—if he saw clarity there when he came to look more closely, when memory increased and made its surprising juxtapositions and comparisons. He would see, but he would have to do the work that made him see, letting the words lie as little as possible. The weight of that task hovered over him as he prepared to leave the old hotel.

At eleven-fifteen he sat at a small bar in La Guardia near the entrance to the shuttle, holding a bourbon and water in his hand. He looked across the bar to the dim, rusty-colored mirror behind the bottles, where he saw a man leaning over a bourbon and water, looking back at him. Was that man drinking because he needed the drug to reduce anxiety, or was he using the anxiety as an excuse for drinking? He wished it weren't necessary to keep asking that question. He must change his life.

Finally he did go through it all—the electronic arch, the tunnel, the entrance into the long machine, the wait, the rumbly taxiing, the demeaning thrust and whine of the takeoff. There were no incidents other than the ghost ones that could have happened at any stage, that he monitored as if his nerves were split into the monitoring systems of the airplane. In an anxious limbo, he wondered how boredom and fear could be so mixed. Then the descent, and the landing upon the precious, stable earth. Ugly or not, cemented and asphalted to the horizons or not, it was terra firma and he would take it.

On the way to Wellesley in his three-year-old station wagon, in the statistically greater danger of traffic, his own systems calmed somewhat, and later in the afternoon he stood in the shaded driveway beside his house, in the lush vibrations of summer.

The house was more or less like the others in the neighborhood, and was what Helen had wanted—modern, mostly at the back where the window-walls looked out upon lawn and hedge, but in front shingled and dark stained, with a low, eaved, bungalowish look among the plantings.

A female hummingbird worked in the bee balm, shimmering, hovering, its black needle of a beak quickly probing the red flowers. A cicada's scratchy metallic call rose over the humming of the little bird. If he listened, birds were calling everywhere. A phoebe swooped from the garage, where every year they built a nest on the raised garage door and every year someone shut the door and spilled the nest into a small liquid disaster on the cement, yolks and whites and the muddy grass nest unhinged. It was just one of those small collisions, mildly sad. The air was moist and warm, the leaves at their most tumid thickness.

And amongst all this rich shade and sunlight was the house, unused, empty of all visible life except for the spiders in the high corners and their small prey. He went out to the mailbox and brought back an armful of paper, let himself by key into the kitchen and let the mail fall onto the counter. A few actual letters and bills could be winnowed from the junk, and these he took into the living room to look at, sitting on the deep leather couch, the mail on the red coffee table in the light of a wall of windows.

70

There was a letter from Phyllis Batemen, the Cascom town clerk.

RFD#3. Cascom, N.H. 03898

Dear Luke,
We have in our shed a big wooden chest that belonged to your Uncle Shem. It weighs about 150-200 lbs. and is locked with an old padlock so we don't know what is inside. We can keep it as it is not in the way at all but we thought you ought to know we have it.

Sincerely,
Phyllis Bateman

He had to be interested in what was in that chest—probably tools, or old ledgers, he supposed. But he did remember a big chest of rough hardwood that took up much space beside Shem's woodburning range. He'd thought it a woodbox. Perhaps it was full of stove wood, and Shem had decided to padlock it for some old, old man's reason. Wood was heat, and in the long New Hampshire winter heat could be as valuable as any thing. Shem might even have dreamed that someone came in the night and stole his precious fuel, sneaking in when he went to the outhouse or during the erratic sleep of his old age. He had always been a man who believed what he alone had reasoned out.

He read the letter again, hearing in it disapproval, just the slightest, taking-everything-into-consideration disapproval, of his absence from Shem's funeral, including, maybe, his long absence from Cascom. He had known Phyllis Bateman for many years, beginning when he was three or four and she was in her teens, long before she married George Bateman. Her maiden name was Follansbee. She was pretty then, with black hair, though she was always squarish and plump. He hadn't seen her for six years, and now she must be getting to be an old woman. Years ago there had been a tragedy in her family—the suicide of one of her sons—but he couldn't remember the son's name.

He would have to go to New Hampshire and buy Shem a stone, a ritual he did not anticipate with pleasure,

71

A telephone bill, overdue. He must pay for messages that had all been unhappy.

Then a stamped envelope with no return address, his name and address typed in an elite face that was more immediately recognizable than he expected it to be. He opened the envelope, thinking that maybe it wasn't the semiliterate Avenger striking again, also thinking that he really didn't need this, God damn it, but if this were a second message maybe this wacko was for real after all. Again the postmark was Grand Central Annex.

Luke Carr:
    How is God offended that your filth entered her Sacred Body!
    The Day will come, I have promised Him!

All right, he thought. If it were tapering off from murder toward theological niceties maybe the whole thing would eventually go away. But what woman did this person have in mind? Helen? Another woman? He didn't want to think about old lusts and passions. And of all the women he could think of, none had been any less an accomplice than he. But that case probably wasn't arguable in the court of the Avenger's mind. A joke—maybe this was all a joke, he tried to think, done by somebody who didn't know what had happened. But he couldn't make that believable. Of course it was possible that he might even know the Avenger; one could know someone for a long time without learning what bells gonged in the silence of the head. He had once been clearly betrayed by a friend, which had been a shock deeper than any historical or literary example had prepared him for.

Suddenly he realized that he was exhausted, that he hadn't slept much last night and the only thing he had taken into his system, and kept there, was the bourbon at the airport. The rest of the mail looked like bills, so he left it for later. When he got up his body was weak. "Dangerously weak," he said aloud in the peopleless room. "Dangerously weak—did you hear that? Do you hear me?" Who? He half staggered out to the car and brought in his suitcase and briefcase, then fell on the couch. His head seemed lighter as he lay back, but that symptom, which said not to lie back, was not warning enough against the weakness. He was like a fluid, lighter than water. He thought, at the last, that he should lock the kitchen door.

He was awake, aware of the loss of time, that bereavement of life that always saddened and depressed him when he slept in daylight and awoke to find the day ending. The southern window-wall, meant to catch the low winter sun but eaved against the high summer sun, revealed the hay of the neglected lawn in a twilight that seemed ancient.

He had been helpless in his sleep—sick, unconscious and visible; he should at least have locked the kitchen door. The inside of his mouth was sticky. He wondered if the letter had made him this apprehensive, or if he would ordinarily have been aware of an unlocked door in Wellesley on a summer afternoon, a car in the garage and one in the driveway, no mail in the mailbox. The unkempt lawn might tempt a burglar, but that was all. He'd meant to get a neighborhood high school boy to mow it, but had kept forgetting. Ah, these responsible little domestic impulses. He used to like to mow the lawn, making and remaking that finished emerald smoothness in which his family's house was set.

The phone in the kitchen began to ring. When he got up he started to faint, but bent over and let the dizziness slide away.

It was Ham Jones. "Luke? Glad to have you back, buddy! Your mind still made up?"

"I guess so," Luke said.

"Okay! Can I bring these people over tomorrow morning, say around ten?"

"Sure. Okay."

"Okay! See you then! No problems! Good-bye!"

So. What that meant was that he would go through with it. It didn't seem his proper sort of duty to have to go through the rooms and pick out what would be saved, what given to the Salvation Army, what thrown out. Helen was good at that sort of thing. What would he do with things like the trophy Johnny won swimming at Camp Ontowah? The cheap, brave, silver-colored statuette stood on Johnny's chest of drawers between a Sopwith Pup and a Fokker D-VII. The clothes would go to the Salvation Army.

What about the books? There must be a thousand books in the house—cookbooks, gardening books, kids' books, novels, reference books, history books, the *Encyclopaedia Britannica*, dictionaries, scrapbooks, notebooks, photograph albums, ledgers, bankbooks, checkbooks, paperback books, little magazines, non-books, fashionable books, unread books, unreadable books. And things, gadgets—TV sets, radios, hi-fi, calculators, skis, sleds, skates, hair driers, mixers, toys, bicycles, sprayers, shoes, paints, boots, brushes, medicines, hammers, wrenches, screwdrivers, snowblower, mowers, clippers, bulbs, watches, saws, clocks, musical instruments, vacuum cleaner, plumber's helpers, brooms, mops, pots and pans and broilers, silver and condiments and cutlery and nutcrackers; God, he had hardly begun. Where did all those things come from? How could there be room here for all of those things? The energy and expense that had gone into their acquisition was stunning; and now what a shock it was to be left alone, as if with your sins at the final reckoning, with all this dreck that once must have seemed absolutely necessary when the living ones were here.

Before those people came tomorrow to look at the house he must clean out the children's rooms of their clothes and toys, books and trophies. And Helen's closet and bureau, their bathroom's douches, toothbrushes, shampoos, creams and menstrual supplies. He must remove all of the evidence. Those poor people, knowing what had happened—if they saw the rooms as they were right now it would hurt them. It would break their hearts.

He had to eat something first or he would fall down. He was not thinking very well. He would have the movers come and pack and store everything—everything down to the last worn toothbrush and book of paper matches with two matches left in it, the relics of his family put away in the dark until he could face the choices.

He couldn't be here when those people came tomorrow. He didn't have to be here. Let Ham Jones earn his commission; he would leave a note on each door, and be gone when they arrived. He would travel light. Ah. He would go to New Hampshire. He must be practical now. Let us flee the past with all its accidents and betrayals.

74

He stood in front of the refrigerator, wondering why the word betrayal had come back. He wondered why he was standing in front of the refrigerator. Because there might be something inside it, and he had to eat something today.

The door opened, its magnets reluctant. Something was rotten in there—the cold sour stench of refrigerated meat gone bad. It was a pound of hamburger he'd bought and never opened. He tore the bloody plastic from the body of it and pushed the meat into the disposal, where it roared stickily into the nether regions. The milk was sour, so it went down as well, with a wash of cold water as a chaser. The disposal, unburdened, hummed contentedly before he turned it off, hearing, as it wound down and stopped, the last few clicks of its teeth.

In the freezer compartment he found a package of green beans and some pork chops, but the idea of cooking those things was beyond consideration. He went to the canned goods cupboard and found a small can of pork and beans, opened it on the electric can opener, took a spoon and wolfed the beans down cold. There. The electric can opener still held the can cover, so he took it away, plucking it free and into the trash, the little disc sailing down among its own, gold-silvery, with a clink.

It was getting dark, now, the kitchen's white countertops and bright metal fading. He took his suitcase from the hall and went upstairs to their bedroom, dreamlike in the growing darkness. He put down his suitcase and went out into the hallway, then to Gracie's room, its Raggedy Ann rug smiling up at his lowered eyes as in a dream. On her dresser was a small cloisonné box, a gift from Helen. He opened it and found there, just still visible, seven folded dollar bills and forty-three cents in tarnished coins. Gracie was a saver of her allowance. Money was not ever personal; yes, he did think that, and put that saved, time-cured money in his pocket. Her dolls, drawings, her bed made neatly for going on a trip, her small possessions flickering across his vision, he left her room and went down the hall to Johnny's. There was the trophy between the two jaunty model airplanes, and on the wall the poster of "The First American," a red Indian, noble and long in the cranium. The trophy's glued-on plaque was engraved, *John Carr, 1st Place,*

75

*Across the Lake Swim, Camp Ontowah, 1976.* He left Johnny's room, closed the door, and went back to their room, where the big bed faded slowly in the dusk.

He slid open the door of Helen's closet and put his hands in among her hanging clothes, the skirts and blouses giving way with liquid acquiescence, slippery and cool. A vague, clean yet powerful scent was still there. He took his hands away from the garments so light on their hangers, and shut the door.

# 6.

He woke up, naked on their bed, to the clamor of partly remembered dreams and an erection that was so dead and distant,
so purely physiological, that the thick organ might have been connected to him by a leather strap.

There was always the small distance of the return from dream
to the facts of his life now, and he slid along that ice until he was
completely aware of where he was. The digital clock in the radio
said 7:50. He would get up and do the mechanical things, dress in
dungarees, work shirt and leather boots for his evasive trip to
New Hampshire. Evasive was a strange word to come to mind; he
had no one to whom he owed his presence. It was like the word
betrayal that had come into his head last night as he stood in front
of the refrigerator. Never mind. He would leave notes on the
doors for Ham Jones, the keys on the counter. He would call Ham
tonight.

He looked into his study before he left. Dust covered his typewriter's dustcover. Manuscript pages seemed to be turning faintly
yellow at their edges. The idea of sitting down to write was so alien
to him it gave him a twinge of actual nausea. It was as though the

man who once worked in this room had been doing something so frivolous and inaccurate as to be dishonorable. Dishonorable— another of those abstractions that seemed to follow him, baggage from a previous life. No words seemed to apply to his present situation. He didn't seem to *be* in a situation, to have a situation; he was a man without a situation.

He was not even hungry. His body moved through the tasks he had set for it this morning without pain or stress.

He took the Plymouth station wagon, which had been, more or less, his car. Helen had chosen the newer car, the Hornet, because she had been impressed by its guarantee. It had sat there in the garage for six months without being used; probably its battery was dead, its tires low, its oil stratified and gummy. He would sell it when the time came—or maybe turn it and the Plymouth in on something else. A small flash of nostalgic interest there, because he had once been quite interested in cars, even in their mechanics and engineering.

He stopped before Route 128 for gas, then went on. He still wasn't hungry. A cigarette, in the draft of the open window, burned in his lips like a small forge. He snuffed it out, thinking as always that it would be the last one he would ever light and inhale and crush out. On Interstate 93 he passed into New Hampshire, no perceptible difference in the landscape or in the commercial drabness of the buildings. Occasionally an old white farmhouse would appear, high and many-windowed, framed by dead or dying elms, television antennae another skein above dark brick chimneys.

By noon he was above Concord, where he left the interstate and entered Saxon County on a two lane road that climbed hills and circled mountains. This part of the journey had hardly changed since he was a boy, before the interstate, when they had to go through the centers of towns and cities. The land here had changed only in that the fields were smaller and fewer, the trees coming in over wall and brook to cover them as the old farms died and the farmhouses either rotted or had the sterile, over-painted look of summer places. There were a few working farms left, but not many now. His father once told him that he could remember

78

when there were four places up the mountain beyond Shem's, but now those cellar holes and barn foundations were all shaded by deep woods, the day lilies, roses, lilacs, and even the apple trees, though they would try in the end to stretch up into the sun, all dead of the green shade.

There was no restaurant or even a store left in Cascom, so he went past the green square, the wooden church, the former Grange Hall that was now the Town Hall, then five miles further into the larger town of Leah, where he stopped downtown at the Welkum Diner. One must put food into the body, which was, after all, a machine. He would let all those involuntary processes continue.

The old diner was the same, the short order cook another in a long line of cadaverous bottle-hiders. When he was ten he would rather have eaten the Welkum Diner's hamburgers and hot greasy French fries, with an Orange Crush, than any other food in the world. It had always been a treat when his father took him here. And even now, whenever he passed a diner that looked old enough, its exhaust fan's greasy dustlets a swath down a side of it, he still thought of food that was so different from home, so good, so bad for you that he remembered with pleasure that old complicity between him and his father.

One change was that the Welkum Diner now had a liquor license, which seemed the wrong sort of bad influence altogether. He had coffee with his hamburger and fries, feeling in himself at least a relic of that lost appetite. He and his father always sat at the counter, never in one of the narrow booths, so they could watch the great chromed boilers, gauges and spigots of the coffee machine, and the bubbling glass dome full of a purple drink he had never seen anyone order.

He entered the food into his body, paid for it and went across the street to his car. It was one of those June days that are so bright and still they seem improbable, out of time, as if they could only occur during vacation. A few thick white fair weather clouds moved like trains across the blue, coming from Vermont and traveling straight east, their speed so silent, the air here so still, there seemed a disconnection between that element and this, as if he

79

were watching a vast silent movie. His car was sultry, baking, but then as he drove back over the hills to Cascom it caused its own wind and clamor.

George and Phyllis Bateman lived in a small white clapboard house on the Cascom town square, with a large garden behind it extending to a pine woods that someone had planted in even rows at least forty years before. He drove into their gravel driveway and parked behind their pickup truck. George was in the garden so he went around back and walked down its edge. George, wearing the dark green chino work pants and shirt that were the rural working man's uniform, was bent with the intensity of a woodchuck over the row of carrots he was thinning. With that same alert attention he suddenly turned his head and saw Luke, picked out one of the pencil-sized carrots, and while still looking at Luke drew it through his fingers to wipe the dirt from it and ate it. Luke didn't know if he was recognized. The gray-stubbled chin chomped the thin carrot until only the fringy green top was left.

George was in his late sixties, a short, square-faced, husky man. He had been a stonemason, among other things, for most of his life. From beneath gray eyebrows the faded gray eyes calmly examined him, then George nodded once and said slowly, "I thought you looked kind of natural."

"You recognize me, then?" Luke said.

"Well, it's been a while. You're Shem Carr's brother's boy, Luke." George wrung off the tops of his culled carrots, picked up the colander and carefully stepped over the rows of carrots, chard and beans. He wiped his right hand on his thigh and they shook hands. "Been a while," he said, smiling, though Luke thought he heard some disapproval in George's words. Then George's face went stern. "About your family, now, Luke. When we heard, it was like the world come to a stop." He looked away, embarrassed, scowling so hard he might have been threatening someone. "The goddam things that happen," he said. "Ayuh, and you never get used to 'em. Come on in the house. Phyllis was wondering if you'd come and see us one of these days. She'll be glad you did."

Luke thought of the suicide of one of their sons, so long ago. He remembered, too, that at one time George had a reputation as

80

a violent and disputatious man. One story was that once he'd thrown all of the furniture in his house out onto the front lawn.

George went on ahead, then stopped and turned at the kitchen door, his voice lowered. "She's got the arthritis pretty bad now, you know. You'll notice she don't get around the way she used to." He scraped and stamped the garden dirt from his boots before he opened the screened door, then went in first himself, because he was the one burdened, to put his colander in the sink.

Luke followed him into the dark, cool kitchen, the small double-hung windows filled with potted plants. At first it smelled like a greenhouse, but then came an old farmhouse's grave-whiff of cellar, and of ferment—vinegar, cider, and then the faint odor of creosote from the somnolent cast iron woodstove, its fires out for the summer. In winter the black range, whose name, cast into its oven door, was FORTRESS UNION, would be the warm center of the kitchen, but now it had lost its power and was in the shadows, with potted plants on its warming shelves. A small white-enameled gas stove beside the sink cooked the summer meals.

After George had washed the garden dirt from his hands they went through the small dining room with its oilcloth-covered table and crowded glass-fronted cabinets full of dishes, over the big floor register and into the front room. Phyllis sat with her back to them at a maple rolltop desk, her thick back as upright as if she were playing a piano. When she turned on her swivel chair she was startled, took off her hornrimmed glasses and peered at Luke.

"Well, well, it's Luke Carr," she said. "You think I wouldn't know you after all these years, when I used to take care of you and change your diapers?"

"I'll bet I was too old for that," Luke said.

"No, you weren't. When you was three and four you used to have accidents. Maybe it wasn't diapers, but it was six of one and half a dozen of the other."

She looked at him excitedly and fondly. Her face was puffy, soft white, her hair in a loose bun and half gray. He always remembered her absolutely black hair, so black and lusterless it seemed all one piece. He remembered one time when he must have been five or six, and she twenty or twenty-one, when he was staying overnight one summer at her parents' farm on the River Road, and she'd let him climb into her bed and stay. Her belly and smooth white sides were snowfields, heaven and sin to slide himself against. That fresh cool skin he could touch, nothing else, but at that time it was all he could imagine of pleasure. Now that same girl was sixty years old, but as she smiled and nodded and moved her swollen hands, the flesh of her forearms swinging loosely on the bones, he saw her as she had changed, becoming the old woman but still being that unmarried young girl, Phyllis Follansbee, bored with her life, who would every once in a while go into a sad, staring mood and give a great romantic sigh.

She was a reader, though she hadn't been able to go to college— that wasn't a possibility her family would have considered then. Six years ago, when he had been here last, she and George were having a garage sale and among the items were three hundred paperback books at a nickel each. Before her marriage she had read all of the books, every one, in the little brown granite Carnegie Free Library across from the church. She had told him six years ago how she waited for the Bookmobile before Nixon vetoed Federal funds for such things. And in this room books were everywhere, though there weren't any bookcases in the house, as far as he could see. Books were piled along the wall beside the sofa, piled on top of the rolltop desk. Her books, from libraries or her own, fiction and non-fiction on any subject at all, were mostly piled on their sides, rarely on end, though here and there two piles formed bookends for a few upright ones.

"So you come to see us," Phyllis said. "It's been a long time, and all the terrible things that happened. You know you're always welcome here with us. We can put you up in the spare bedroom if you're staying over. Will you have supper with us?"

"I'd like to have supper with you, but I've got to go back tonight. I'm selling my house."

"You mean you can, or you can't?" Phyllis said.

"I mean I can, but I can't stay the night."

"Well, why didn't you say so right out? George, get some deer chops out of the freezer. We'll have the little carrots . . . any size to 'em? And dandelion greens, bread-and-butter pickles, heat up the rest of the scalloped potatoes. . . ."

"Now, Mother," George said, "don't you get all heated up. You just order what you want and I'll take care of it."

"Luke hasn't had a good meal in months, I can tell. He's been eating restaurant junk. Look at his eyes, George."

George shrugged and glanced apologetically at Luke's eyes.

Luke said, "Before supper I'd like to go to Leah and pick out a stone for Shem's grave. I was there around noon and forgot all about it. Anyway, is there anything I can get you while I'm over there?"

George frowned and looked embarrassed. "Well, now, Luke, you know . . ." he said, then paused for a while to think. "The Buzzell-Nadeau Post and the VFW, we kind of got together and bought Shem a stone a couple months ago. Concord granite, kind of plain, but a handsome piece of stone, if I do say so. Weighed over five hundred pounds, two by three by eight inches, what's sticking out of the ground. I tend to think you'd approve of it."

Luke didn't know how to cope with George's embarrassment. George evidently felt that he'd been responsible for butting in on a family affair.

"George, I'm grateful to all of you," he said. "You've got to let me pay for it, though. All right?"

George seemed relieved. "You're not offended we went ahead on it, now?"

"No, I'm not. I'm grateful, and that's all. I just want to pay for it."

"Well, nobody's going to have no objections to that." George thought for a moment. "Maybe we was a little hasty. We should of known you was going to take care of it. But Shem was the oldest living vet in town, you know. He had quite a record in the first war, I don't know how much your family told you, in the Argonne and all. Now, that wasn't my war, nor yours, but the boys take it pretty serious. Shem Carr was a cantankerous old cuss, but he was pretty well respected, just the same."

That was a lot of words for George, and he seemed to be thinking over what he'd just said and trying to figure out if he'd said the right thing.

Phyllis changed the subject. "So you're selling your house in Massachusetts."

"Yeah," Luke said, nodding.

"Where you going to live, then? You going to the city?"

"I don't know yet."

"You going to sell the farm? Land prices are out of sight, as they say. Pretty near ridiculous, to tell the honest truth."

"No, not until the taxes get too bad, anyway."

Phyllis turned to George. "You going to get those deer chops out of the freezer? Give 'em some time to thaw if we're going to pan fry 'em. I'll take care of the carrots and. . . . "

"You'll take care of nothing," George said. There was an edge of anger in his voice that seemed excessive for what he'd just said, but it was probably his continuing embarrassment about having butted into someone else's business.

"You got your country clothes on," Phyllis said, changing the subject again. "You intend to look at the farm, or you just wear your boots when you come to New Hampshire?"

"I wasn't slumming, if that's what you mean."

Phyllis laughed and then grimaced; her neck hurt when she raised her chin. "George, go get them chops out of the freezer," she said in a voice that meant there had been enough discussion of that subject. George went.

"Now, Luke," she said. "You want to go see the stone that caused all this nervousness. Shem's in the old high cemetery, you know. You can stop on the way to the farm, if that's where you're going. We'll eat kind of late, say seven-thirty, after the TV news, so you got time enough to look around. I don't know why I kept you standing up all this time when there's a perfectly good sofa right there beneath the books. And if you change your mind about staying over, why that's fine. Now get along. We'll see you at supper." She waved him away with a bent hand that was painfully shiny at the finger joints.

He took the Cascom Mountain road, the rounded mountain itself appearing time and again, always a little startling, as if it had a tendency to move to different points of the compass. Its top, at about three thousand feet, was bare granite, though not above the timberline at this latitude; a forest fire in the 1880's had burned its humus into dust which had blown and washed away. The trees,

84

hardwood changing to stunted spruce and small white birch, had been slowly climbing back since then.

The narrow asphalt road turned and climbed, crossed beneath a power line, passed the houses of several old, grown-over farms, summer places now. Just before the high cemetery, the road turned to gravel, and his own dust moved over him as he stopped. The cemetery was small, about an acre in all, and he found Shem's stone with no trouble. Even though he had been here as a child, and would always remember the odd thoughts he'd had then at seeing this place of the dead, he was surprised to find so many Carrs here, the earliest death 1834, the latest Shem's. There were more of the Biblical names, those ancient Hebrew syllables—Hepzibah, Ezekiel, Japhet, Amos, Ezra, Rachel. And Shem Gorham Carr, 1894–1977. Shem's son, Samuel Gorham Carr, 1921–1949, had a small stone near his father and his mother, Carrie Watson Carr, 1900–1960. Samuel was the strange son who had never married, hardly ever spoke. Luke had never heard how Samuel died.

The sun seemed hotter over the graves. Shem's gray granite stone was more modern than most; the earliest were black slate. Small American flags, the size of dollar bills, faded in cast iron holders at the graves of the veterans. The bodies, half-imagined, seemed to suck the sun down into the lush, uncut grass. Once elms that spread in the air like great fountains had shaded this place, but now their stumps were moldering at the stone walls, losing definition.

He went back across the grass and through the opening in the stone wall to his dusty car. The road rose as it followed the Cascom River, rapids visible here and there through the dense leaves. The brook that flowed through Shem's farm, Zach Brook, was one of its tributaries. There was a Carr Brook, too, but it was named after another branch of the family, and emptied into another small, rocky river in the next valley, though they all fed Cascom Lake in the main valley below.

The road left the Cascom River, climbing more. On steep stretches his tires bounced on the washboard, gravel ticking on the car's gas tank and fender wells. Here the trees sometimes covered the road, and the air grew cooler. At one point the road was actual ledge. The only houses he saw were two small hunting camps with slab siding and rusty stovepipes, side by side in a small opening.

A half-mile farther and he came to the side road, grassed in the middle, that descended through deep spruce toward the farm. Under the trees, if he looked closely enough, he could see large stones, vaguely rectangular in pattern, that had been the foundation of one of the fourteen schoolhouses that Cascom had once supported. Shem's father had attended that school. Now the only school in Cascom was the one-room grammar school down in the village.

The wire from the power pole at the road disappeared overhead in branches that should have been brushed out long ago. At the small frog pond beside the road he bottomed in a deep puddle; a culvert was needed here, and a few loads of gravel. Then he wondered why the maintenance of this road seemed that immediate a responsibility.

The road emerged from the dark spruce, as if that cool, primitive shade had been a tunnel, an entranceway into a lighter world, because he was out of the twilight into saplings and steeplejack, with patches of juniper and even tasseling hay. There should be the cellar hole, where the driveway was still clearly open among poplar and gray birch sprouts. Ghost images from childhood flickered upon the green. The garden had been there, the barn there, with its slough of manure flowing down the barnyard slope, then the connecting sheds leading from the barn to the white clapboard farmhouse. It was hardest to visualize the lush pastures that once spread far back over the hummocky slopes behind the house and barn to what had been the edge of the sugarbush. The old maples were still there, higher and darker than the saplings that had grown up to them, but all that open distance had gone.

A light breeze came from the west, from the mountain that seemed improbably close here, as if this must be the only real view of it. Weather had always come over the mountain. He remembered those summer storms that built and rolled up from the west, the ominous turbulence over the mountain, then the gray rain approaching, ridge by ridge as each shuttered out and then

86

the almost horizontal sheets flashing across the barn and house. Thunder echoed from the mountain so that each crack or rumble was double or quadruple. Blue arcs would climb, as if on invisible stairs, from the transformer on the pole across the road.

He walked up the drive to the cellar hole. One squared corner of the kitchen still rose from it at an angle, like the bow of a sinking ship, the rest submerged and going down. The wood of the corner trim was still flecked here and there with eggshells of paint, but the gray wood was damp and limp, all the life gone out of it. He pulled a rusty nail from the soggy wood with his fingers, and it came out as easily as if from clay. Wood lasted forever unless water got to it. At what point in Shem's life had he stopped making, because of infirmity or not caring, the small repairs that would have kept his house alive?

One of the connecting sheds rested upon Shem's '41 Chevy pickup truck, a dark caul over the sinking machine. The truck's rusted wheel rims had pressed through the tires and into the earth. A two-gallon motor oil can, among many cans and sheets of steel or iron worn thin by rust, seemed kept alive by its contents. *Amalie.* Odd bottles had turned lead-colored and untransparent in the rain and dust. None of the rafters of the sheds or the hewn sills and beams of the collapsed barn were salvageable, though their former symmetry and strength could be remembered. He had jumped from the barn's thick beams and cross members, when they were square and sound, into sweet dusty hay. Somewhere in the brush and saplings would be a hayrake, stoneboat, cutterbar, harrow, manure spreader, maybe even the old John Deere somewhere with a poplar as thick as his leg growing up between its axles. Once they had all been greased and oiled, silver in their moving places, but now the keepers and protectors of this place were all dead, a civilization gone and its relics and monuments going down under humus, becoming humus. He felt like an archaeologist who had come upon his own bones.

The breeze died for a moment and the leaves of the poplar, or aspen, green coins unstable in the wind, gradually stopped their quaking and rustling. A breath that continued was the distant rushing of the brook, a few hundred yards down the slope to the west. The road by the house had once continued down that slope to a log and plank bridge over the brook and then two miles or more up the mountain to the cellar holes of other farms abandoned long before his memory. He found the road, now canopied by branches, grown up in basswood, or witch hobble, as Shem had called it, and a grass that seemed aquatic in its wide-bladed greenness, whose name he had never been told. As he pushed his way down toward the brook, thinking of the lush and nameless grass he realized how much he had learned in those summers, how Shem had always taken great pains to teach him the names of things—plants, tools, parts, animals, machines—and he seemed never to have forgotten the big man's instructions, though Shem had always half-frightened him. He remembered one time in the barn when Shem and his quiet son, Samuel, were milking and he was sitting on the barn sill watching. "Look there," Shem had said. "See the snake." He thought Shem was trying to scare him, but Shem pointed over the stanchion to a joist and there, along the crack between the joist and the barn floor above was a black, brown and tan patterned snake about a yard long.

"Milk snake," Shem said. "Only he don't drink milk, he eats the goddam mice, is why he hangs around the barn." Two scrawny barn cats were sitting next to Shem hoping for a squirt, and Shem gave them a couple of squirts that plastered their faces. They both contentedly stroked their whiskers with their paws and licked off the warm milk. "King snake's the right name for him. A lot of shit-for-brains farmers'd kill him on sight."

The hill farmers were not like those on the rich river bottoms because they were closer to the wilderness, and also to starvation. They were loggers, hunters and gatherers, always looking for sustenance wherever they could find it. Frosts came late and early in these upper valleys. Apples, potatoes, corn and timber, Shem had told him, were their mainstays, and "They et a lot of johnnycake." They knew wild food, and blueberries, strawberries, raspberries and blackberries, in the order of their seasons. As for game, there were no hours or seasons, and they counted out their shells and cartridges one by one.

On the way to the brook the road had been gullied in places to

88

the ledge. All the old waterbars that Shem repaired each year had been washed away in the spring runoffs, so instead of being shunted off to the side the rivulets had taken the road itself for their channel and washed it down to base rock.

The rush of the still invisible brook grew louder as he descended. A deerfly found him and circled his head slowly, with a kind of bullying insistence. He stood still, waited for it to land and then crushed it against his scalp. Blackflies, here in the damper shade, had found him too, but they were not thick enough or ferocious enough on this dry day to bother him.

He came on the brook sooner than he had expected to. The log and plank bridge was gone entirely. The boulders and stone slabs of its abutments, which had been built up eight feet from the bed of the brook over a hundred years ago, were still there in spite of the white torrent the brook became in spring, when the snow melted from the mountain. Then whole trees would come shooting past like pile drivers, and you could hear and feel the rumble of boulders hurtling along below.

Now the brook sighed in its small rapids, was so calm and clear in its pools he could see the smallest pebbles on the bottom. A small brook trout felt his shadow and sped across what seemed nothing but air, to hide in a crevice. Only a slightly more golden tone in that element told him the water was deep.

The far side of the brook, now grown up in alders and beyond the alders in gray birch and poplar, had once been a smooth field called the lower pasture. Downstream, around a bend bordered by an outcropping of ledge, was the chute and pool that had been called the swimming hole, though the pool was only a few feet deep and twenty in diameter. He left the road and found a way through the trees along the steep bank. The pool was bordered on one side by ledge and on the other by several loose but immovable boulders, one as big as a room. The floor of the pool was a smoothed dip in the bedrock that in flood would scour itself clean of stones and sand, leaves, waterlogged branches and the remains of all the living things that inhabited the brook. This early in the summer the scoured stone was still bright, and the water coming down the stone chute that used to be his slide entered the pool with a quiet rush and disappeared except for the large bubbles that rose, wobbling and silver, back up to the air.

He considered taking off his clothes and sliding into that clean cold water that was as pure and enlivening as any he had ever known, but it was cool here in this dim, mossy-banked place. It would be good to cut out the trees on the southwestern side and let in the afternoon sunlight. The tall hemlocks on the eastern bank could stay; their shade and acidic needles kept the bank on this side smooth and clear of brush. That thought, and thoughts of a bridge for the old abutments, culverts and gravel for the road, the clearing of brush so that at this time of day the sun would slant across long vistas of the green hay he remembered, gentle and hazy in the summer light, began to work in him a change he couldn't define, to infect him with a purpose that was not to be seriously considered.

He took off his boots and socks, his feet on the hemlock needles feeling tender and unnatural. The hemlock needles, and a root that emerged and then submerged again, were cool and harsh to his naked soles. He took off the rest of his clothes and stretched his air-touched nakedness vertically, like the narrow bodies of the trees.

When he stepped down to the stones, they felt harsh yet familiar to his feet. The water seemed cold only at its surface, though almost unbearable there. His legs, below the nearly invisible surface, seemed to belong to a water organism unconnected to the chilled body above. He started to shiver violently, then gave it all up and made a shallow dive up toward the head of the pool. He was warm, numb, cold as refrigerated meat, slow-jointed. He opened his eyes underwater and seemed to be swimming in a great golden salver. The invisible turbulence from the chute was, in its motion, like arms and hands. A silver bubble touched his thigh and belly as it rose. The energy of the moving water, its gentle yet powerful kneadings of his flesh, seemed a form of life in connection with him, each shove and pull an opinion made kinetic, like an embrace.

He climbed out of the water feeling taut and compacted, hard as rubber, his scrotum like cold boiled eggs, his penis narrow as a bent dowel. He wiped the water from his body with his hands, then put on his clothes that were now soft and unsubstantial. His boots felt light and good on his feet. He was thankful that he'd had the nerve—only it wasn't exactly nerve, but more a surplus of heat and force, something like the almost forgotten joy children had in the motions and changes with which they tested their bodies.

This pool, these woods and disappearing fields, this small arc-fragment of the earth's surface would, after probate, be his in name. Shem had died intestate but as far as he knew there would be no other claimants to this land.

He crossed the brook on stones below the pool, wanting to see what was left of the lower pasture. There had once been a black-smith shop by the bridge. The stone walls, some of them five feet across, had been piled by men, oxen and stoneboat. Before that had been stump fences, stumps piled on their sides and inter-locked. The walls had sunken and been tumbled in places by frost. Birch and poplar, pincherry and steeplejack had come in across the fields, but there were patches of meadow left; it could be cleared again. He walked across between the saplings, feeling the once-openness of the place, then remembered his daydream, partly night-dream, of the field and cabin in cold February moon-light, the cross-country skis, the one yellow windowlight of the shelter waiting for his return. In winter the mountain would be ice-white, and he would hear the sigh of the iced-over brook.

On the other side of a thick wall to the southwest was a dense grove of spruce in which it was night. To enter its deep dusk one would need a flashlight, if the lower branches would let anyone into its mysteries. A red squirrel, invisible, screamed alarm and outrage at his presence, or at the presence of some other car-nivore. In a patch of grass, three yard-long, kidney-shaped depressions in the green were the recent beds of white-tailed deer, and there were the raisin-like turds one of them had left as it departed.

An alien, not an alien, he had company in this wilderness. If he looked he would find the signs of a thousand animals. At his feet were wild strawberries, so he went to the ground and searched them out, their tang and sweetness, pale red washing his fingers. Grasshoppers were down here, and leafhoppers, and there was a lucky glimpse of a departing green snake. In the underthatch ran old white-footed mouse passages from the past winter, when the snow had roofed them over. A broad tailed hawk's plaintive whistle made him look up from the warm grass to where it patrolled this salient, turning on an invisible plane. A mosquito sucked the blood of his wrist, proving that at least in some measure he was accepted by this world and its forces.

On the way back up the tunnel of a road to his car he heard one more evidence of life. A partridge drummed, the sound hard to locate, an air-thudding that gathered momentum until it stopped, leaving an uncertain memory of its direction or even of its having occurred. But it was there, the large grouse somewhere in the woods fanning its powerful wings.

# 7.

When George brought the small deer chops, a whole platter of them, to the table, he was smiling in a mysterious, hard to repress sort of way. Then he couldn't resist and said, "You know where I shot this doe?" Knowing of course that Luke couldn't guess, he went on. "In Shem's lower pasture, is where. 'Bout seven o'clock, first day of the season, dry and noisy. I was about to light my pipe when I heard this tickety-tick-tick-tick and out steps this pretty little doe, free as you please. Now, that don't happen too often in a man's lifetime! I drew a bead on her neck, she wasn't more than two rods from me, I was using the old thirty-forty Krag with the iron sights, and bang she goes down like a sack of meal. Tagged her, cleaned her, drug her across the brook and up the hill to the truck and I was back home by nine. She only weighed eighty pounds but I'll settle for tender meat anytime."

"I saw three beds down there today," Luke said.

"Ayuh, they come in there, all right. Popple, old apple trees, sprouts. There's a buck in there with a track as big as a heifer I'd like to see sometime. You wait till there's snow on the ground, you see them tracks you wonder if it ain't a breechy cow got loose from somewheres."

93

The deer chops were tender, rosy on the inside, leaving a smooth, tallowy aftertaste that the acidic dandelion greens cut. George had poured them each a half tumbler of hard cider that was clear as water and slightly effervescent. He said, "You want to go easy on that if you're still intent on drivin' back to Massachusetts tonight—which you don't have to, you know."

"We'll be happy to put you up, Luke, as we already told you," Phyllis said.

"As for me," George said, "I admit to some common curiosity as to what's inside that chest we got out in the shed. My program for the evening is we haul it in here in the light, Luke and me, pry off that padlock and look inside. Now, we got plenty of cider, which goes good with curiosity but bad with drivin'." George stopped, and frowned at himself. "None of my goddam business, of course. What in the bejesus got into me?"

"Now, George," Phyllis said.

George's face had turned red and dark, rigid and unforgiving. Luke hastened to say that he'd like to do just that. He'd call his real estate man, find out what was going on, and stay and drink up all the cider in the house. "I'm curious, too," he said.

George still looked suspicious, but he did relent enough to take a drink of his cider and offer Luke another deer chop and some more scalloped potatoes. "I ain't a bad cook, if I do say so myself," he said. "Though I can't hold a candle to mother, here, when her arthritis ain't acting up."

"It comes and it goes," Phyllis said. "Sometimes the aspirin and a little cider or wine can handle the pain pretty good, sometimes I just got to sit and let George do everything for me. He put in the downstairs bathroom there off the kitchen, plumbing and all, where the pantry used to be, so I don't have to climb the stairs."

"Hell, I done plenty of plumbin' in my life," George said, looking more cheerful.

After supper George decanted more cider, then he and Luke cleared the table and went out to wrestle in the rough wooden chest. "Bigger than a footlocker by far," George said. In spite of his age at the time, which was thirty-six, George had gone into the army in World War II and served in North Africa, Sicily and France in the Engineers.

94

George had a dolly which he'd used to carry bricks and cement blocks, so they roped the chest on that and finally, with much straining and planning about steps, doors and sills, rugs and angles, got the chest into the dining room next to the table.

"I reckon you got some slivers out of that session," George said. Luke looked at his soft white hands and found that it was true—the chest was made of unplaned oak, though carefully joined. He would have to borrow a needle to dig out the slivers. George's hands, of course, were tough as gloves, a matter of pride.

"Now, how we going to get that padlock off there? I looked the chest over, hoping there'd be a key nailed on the underside somewheres, but no luck," George said.

The padlock looked rugged, one of the kind made out of layers of steel held together with steel pins.

"We could pry off the hasp, I suppose," Luke said.

"You don't want to ruin the chest," George said. "Let me get a hacksaw and see if it'll cut the lock. We cut it where the U-bolt goes into the body and it might want to swing loose."

The hacksaw just barely would cut the lock bar. They took turns at it and finally cut it through, though the saw blade was ruined. "Hot!" George said as he turned the lock open. Luke undid the hasp and opened the chest, which had leather straps, cracked though still working, to keep the cover from falling back against the hinges. Phyllis moved her chair closer so she could see. On top was a wooden tray a few inches deep, and in the tray was the gleam of many shades of metals, shapes of silver and blue-black that at first meant only heaviness and value, a treasure of tools—brass, steel and smooth hardwood shaped for a man's hand.

"It's his tools," George said. "It's his tools, all right. Shem Carr always took good care of his tools." George hesitated to reach into the tray, though it was obvious he wanted to put his hands on the smooth handles and heft them all. There were chisels, a set of them in widths from a quarter-inch to two inches, in quarters, each made of one piece of steel with ash inlays for handles, so they could be used by hand only or malleted at the butt, wooden and brass mallets and persuaders, screwdrivers, box wrenches, adjustable wrenches, an auger set with bits; burnishers, a small pry-bar.

Luke recognized some of them, seeing the old-fashioned one-piece screwdrivers, for instance, in Shem's big hand. There was a small square with its spirit level, the bubble in its yellow oil still free to find the center of the earth. Luke picked the tools out, one by one, and handed them to George, who hefted them, named them, then replaced them with the reverent attention given to objects on an altar. There were pliers with various jaws, a bolt-cutter, cold chisels, a ballpeen hammer and a balanced carpenter's hammer for common nails. No rust was anywhere, just a film of light oil on the metal that was browned with age, or citizen's blued, or of the silver revealed in the steel by a finishing whetstone. There were stones, too—aluminum oxide, fine and coarse, Iwashita, India, Arkansas soft and hard, each in its wooden box. A short-bladed but long-handled bench knife suggested the power of a muscular hand, given leverage.

Luke said, "Shem told me once when I was about ten that it was better to walk fifty yards to get the right tool, then walk all the way back, even if you had to climb two fences on the way, than to mash up what you were trying to fix. I remember that as if it were yesterday."

"Amen," George said. He was examining a small, fine-toothed cabinetmaker's saw that had its own canvas sheath. There were also a set of spade drills, a spokeshave, calipers and Allen wrenches, thread pitch gauges, a set of three wooden planes, clamps, tin snips, a miter saw and coping saw, a drawshave and more wrenches, including an eighteen-inch pipe wrench.

When they had looked at all the things in the tray they lifted it off to find another tray of the same size, but this one was compartmented and lined with green velour, and it held guns and their accessories—ammunition, cleaning equipment and gunsmith's tools. First was a single-barreled, single shot Harrington and Richardson twelve-gauge shotgun. Luke remembered it; he had been allowed to shoot it once, and remembered the kick. He took the forearm off the barrel, put barrel and action together, snapped on the forearm and held the assembled gun in his hands. It seemed much smaller now, which wasn't strange.

"Barrel's sawed off a few inches," George said. "Makes it cylinder bore instead of full choke. Handier. I recall when you could buy one of them brand new for under twenty dollars." Next was a Marlin lever action .22 rifle with the old square bolt and an adjustable tang sight.

What they found after that made George sigh. In matching fleece-lined cases were what looked at first like matched .45 automatic pistols. Luke put them down side by side. One was marked U.S. and was the M1911 Al army issue Browning, but the other, though the same size and weight, was chambered and barreled for the .22 long rifle cartridge. It was made by Colt and had, on closer inspection, a slightly lighter, smoother job of blueing.

"Look at that!" George said. "I bet that one cost an arm and a leg. The other one, Shem probably got in the first war and then sometime he got the other one made up so's he could shoot the smaller shells. Damn." He picked up the .22 and looked it over. "Don't see how a .22 long rifle cartridge would have the power to blow that action back. Maybe it's a single shot, or you got to pull the slide back by hand each time." He took out the clip. "Clip's made for the .22 all right. Wait, now. Hold on here a minute. Seems the slide's lighter, made of an alloy. 'Course, the barrel's got to be heavier 'cause it's got so small a hole in it." He picked up the regulation .45. "Near the same weight overall, almost the same balance. That's pretty slick. Now, that ain't no barrel insert, that's a whole barrel just made for that gun." He looked at the .45 again. "That ain't the regulation sight, neither. It's your wide Patridge. He must of had that done, too."

There was the one holster, marked U.S. on the full flap, that fit both guns, and an issue webbed belt.

"I carried a .45 for a while in Korea," Luke said.

"Not much different from that one, I imagine. I carried one in Africa and Europe, and then about twenty years ago I got one, surplus, through the NRA for fifteen bucks. I can't afford to shoot it much, not at a quarter a goddam round, or thereabouts. My son Bill brought me a case of shells, once, he liberated from the army, but we went to the dump and wasted most of 'em on rats. I got maybe fifty rounds left in case they come and try to take my guns away from me."

97

"That's why George has all his guns," Phyllis said, "so they can't come and take them away."

"This ain't goddam Massachusetts," George said. "Not yet, anyways. We always had our guns and we're always going to have our guns, and no holier-than-thou goddam liberals going to say we can't, 'less they want their goddam legs blowed off." George's voice had turned ominous. "Goddam busybodies. What am I supposed to do, some crook comes to the house, call Lester Wilson? He's chief of the whole police force, which consists of himself, and he drives one of them souped up supercars, which makes a noise like a wood chipper and half the time has a dead battery anyways. Not to mention Lester couldn't hit the broad side of a barn and I never seen him yet he didn't have most of a six-pack under his belt. He's about thirty years old. No, sir, I got my .45 up by the bed and loaded, and by the Jesus, mother, you can say what you like!"

"It's all right, George. It's just that I'd hate to see you shoot somebody."

George calmed down and shook his head in mock frustration. "Well, I never meant to go on about it, but by God, Luke, it does fry my ass."

They looked over the ammunition, and George recommended that he throw out the old .22s and if he shot the .45s he'd better clean the pistol well because it looked to him they might be so old they'd have the old, corrosive mercuric primers. "They'll shoot all right, probably, but you want to clean her right away."

Under that tray was the body of the chest, and here they found, among other things, a block and tackle with old, slivery hemp rope on it, an adz, a broadax with no handle, a double-bitted ax, a set of iron wedges, a splitting maul, a sledge, two steel squares, hand auger bits and handle, extra ax handles, a Hudson Bay ax, a glass jar of blasting powder and eight feet or more of fuse, a tin box full of fishing equipment including rod eyelets and tips, hooks, swivels and an ancient Hardy trout reel, a can of Dupont FFF black powder, several cans of number nine percussion caps, a sewing awl and waxed thread, a roll of thick tanned leather and a ball of oily rawhide, a sight level and other bottles and cans of nails, screws, washers and bolts.

"Damn," George said. "I'd say you were pretty well equipped, Luke, I don't exactly know what for."

Phyllis said, "What are you going to do with your life, now, Luke? I know you always sort of gravitated toward the city, with your writing and all."

"I've got to finish the assignment I told you about, but then I don't know." He looked from one to the other, and found them curious, sympathetic, a little avid somehow—at least Phyllis was. She had something in mind for him. George evidently knew about it and, though curious, he disapproved of it, or at least washed his hands of it. He poured them more cider and sighed at the devious schemes of women.

"I mean, are you going to spend some time here in Cascom after you get your assignment done?" Phyllis said.

"I wonder what Shem was doing with that triple F powder and them number nine caps," George said. "He must of had a muzzle loader at one time."

"Weren't you going to call about your house?" Phyllis said.

It was ten o'clock. George pulled out his pocket watch and looked at the time too.

"I guess I'd better call. I'll charge it to my own number," Luke said. He went into the front room and sat at Phyllis's desk to phone. George came in and turned on the television, the volume hardly audible; he must have had a program he wanted to see at ten, and that accounted for his looking at his watch. While Luke waited for someone to answer at Ham's house he glanced at the television, a large old black and white console, and saw that the program was a documentary on the battles of World War II. That was George's war and in a sense his youth, as it had been Luke's youth, too, having dominated so much of his thoughts in grammar school and high school.

Ham's wife, Jane, answered and seemed joyful to be talking to him, although they had once had an argument over politics during which she'd accused him of patronizing her. She'd been very cool toward him for at least a year afterward. Now she asked when he could come for dinner, and why didn't he stop in and see them anytime? She was a tall California girl who had that brassy physical symmetry that made him think such people had bigger, straighter and brighter, though fewer, teeth than other people, or perhaps one less finger on each hand, like animated cartoon characters. Maybe he had patronized her. Maybe he hadn't signaled strongly enough that he found her attractive, if that was what she wanted. God knew. He promised to come see them. Then Ham came to the phone.

"Luke, if you want to go through with it, it's pretty much in the bag. Hell, we can set a closing date anytime."

"All right, Ham."

"You mean it, now? You're one hundred percent sure?"

Luke thought of Shem's farm, all its land and trees silent in the darkness of the summer night, the brook flowing in the dark. He felt himself there, alone with a clean terror of the dark.

"I'll see you tomorrow sometime, okay?"

"Come for dinner. Jane wants you to."

"All right. That's nice of you people."

"Just a minute—Jane wants to talk to you. See you tomorrow."

"Luke?" Jane said in her American voice that seemed totally clean of any regional inflections. "What would you like for dinner? How about a cookout? Drinks at five or so and barbecued spareribs or something when we're properly mellow? Would you rather have steak? Lobster? You name it."

He'd have to name one thing or she'd think him too indifferent. "Spareribs and your famous tossed salad," he said, feeling a touch of dishonor.

"Super! We'll see you at five or so. Bye bye, Luke."

From the television came the muted, portentous voice of Richard Burton. George's rough, compressed face seemed in black and white too as the ancient explosions of the British barrage before El Alamein rumbled from the set.

George looked up. "North Africa. Monty. Rommel. You remember?"

"Yes, I do," Luke said.

"When we come in we got our asses whipped at Kasserine Pass, but they said—some Kraut general said it—was the Americans always fouled up at first, but once blooded nobody learned faster. That's what this Kraut general said, anyways."

100

Phyllis came slowly into the room and George fixed her chair for her. She read a book while they watched the last days of the Afrika Korps. They watched in silence, and when it was over, the last columns of dusty prisoners trudging along in their visored caps, George sighed and clapped his palms down on his knees. "Well, we won that one," he said. "You always know how it's going to come out."

They wrestled the wooden chest onto the dolly, then out of the house and back to the shed. "You can leave her here as long as you like. It ain't in the way," George said. He sat down on the chest and filled his pipe. Luke found himself reaching for a cigarette for the first time that evening. He hadn't thought of having one, even though he just now remembered from six years ago that George didn't smoke in the house.

Suddenly George got up and said, "Now, what in the hell got into me? I got another box of Shem's belongings in the house I plain forgot! I'm losing my wits in my old age!" He put his unlit pipe back in his pocket, and Luke put his unlit cigarette back in the package. "I'll get it for you. Go ahead and smoke your cigarette. I'll bring it out here."

George brought back a shoe box, which they opened under the shed's cobwebby light bulb. "We found these on him, or near him," he said.

Inside the box was a large old-fashioned wallet with many compartments, the light tan leather disintegrating with age, rather than use. In it were some of the papers and documents of Shem's life—his discharge papers, Social Security card, Luke's address, old newspaper clippings, odd stubs, letters and his driver's license for the year 1960, among other things; Luke would look at them more carefully later. There was a worn black briar pipe and a package of Beechnut tobacco, and a large jackknife with staghorn slab handles smoothed by use down to the ivory, its largest blade honed narrow. Luke could hear Shem telling him that the blades were called clip, sheepfoot and spay, and that the knife "walked and talked," which had to do with how healthy a click the blades made when opened or shut. Back when Shem showed it to him his fingernails were not large enough or strong enough to dig into

101

the blade nicks and open it. But now they were, and it still walked and talked. Also in the box were five one-dollar bills and forty cents in change, a silver necklace set with dark blue stones, a thick brass fountain pen and a split ring with several keys on it.

"There's salvageable stuff in that kitchen you might want to poke around for," George said, knocking out his pipe at the shed door. "It was pretty near flat when we found him. Hell of a blizzard the night before, no telling how long before the plow'd get up there, so I borrowed my neighbor's snowmobile, and Jim Pillsbury—he's the game warden now—he took his and we went up to check. That's when we found him."

Their silence was the comment upon that fact.

Luke finally said, "I'd like to leave all this stuff here for a few weeks, if you don't mind. Except for the knife, I guess." He put the knife in his pocket, then found room in the chest for the shoe box.

"You might as well take the money," George said. "Ain't no sentimental value to it." Luke put the dollar bills next to those that had belonged to Gracie.

When they went back in the house they found that Phyllis had gone upstairs to make up a bed for Luke, which exasperated George, who went up after her. "God damn it, mother!" Luke heard him say. "It hurts you to lick a goddam postage stamp, and now . . . " A door shut. Luke looked at the book Phyllis had been reading. It was a novel, *Time Out of Mind,* by Rachel Field, published a generation ago. He wondered if Rachel Field were still alive, and what she might have thought if she knew that her scenes and people lived again in another mind.

Phyllis stayed upstairs, said good night from the landing, told him about towels and asked what he wanted for breakfast. George muttered that he'd take care of all that, and came back downstairs.

"I don't know why she won't sit still for a goddam minute," he said. "She's in pain every time she moves."

"But it comes and goes, she said?"

"Mostly it comes," George said. "But let me tell you, she's a fine woman, Luke. Well. I'm going to have myself a little nightcap and go out on the steps and smoke my pipe, if you'd care to join me, and then hit the sack."

The nightcap was blended whiskey poured over an ice cube in a juice glass. Their glasses tinkled as they sat on the front steps, sipped the whiskey and looked across the green square. One streetlight, the only one in town, grew out of its circle of green and softly brought the white church and the white town hall out of a darkness roofed by trees. Fireflies made their dotted lines of greenish yellow as they flew slowly over the grass, a light Luke knew was cold, not given for him or his purposes. He wanted to say to George, "Look, from all I know you're a fine man, too." But that would be a doubtful and demeaning simplification and would not do. He did say, "I want to thank you for all you've done, George."

"Weren't nothing," George said.

"I mean it, though."

"You paid his taxes for him and sent him money. It was little enough for me to look in on him once in a while and do some grocery shopping for him." George puffed on his pipe a few times. "Anyway, I owed Shem. Maybe you don't know, but I lived with him and Carrie four years, starting when I was thirteen and my mother went to the lunatic asylum. Samuel was just a baby then. I done chores and let me tell you I worked my tailbone off. But they took me in, and no kin of theirs. My father run off to Manchester, to the mills. He couldn't handle me."

"No, I didn't know that."

"Shem taught me a lot," George said. "He sure wouldn't take no sass, neither. Ouch!"

"He used to scare me a little when I was a kid," Luke said.

"Nobody screwed around with Shem Carr. He put them blue eyes on you and your gizzard froze up solid!" George chuckled and then finished his whiskey, rattled his ice cube and took the last drop. "Anyways, I owed him," he said.

Luke finished his own whiskey, wishing he had more of it, wishing that he didn't want any more of it. He field-stripped his cigarette and put the filter in his breast pocket. George was watching him, which startled him a little. Out of the corner of his eye, in the light from the window, he saw George nod.

"Well," George said, yawning the words, "I guess I'm going to hit the sack. What time you want to get up in the morning?"

103

"Whenever you do."

"You got the room to the left, head of the stairs. She had it all made up, God bless her."

They said good night. Luke used the downstairs bathroom, then found his room, the overhead light left on for him. His bed was old, swaybacked, made of iron. He had slept on such beds before, at the farm, at Phyllis's—maybe this very bed.

In the middle of the night he woke up in the deep woods, in absolute darkness, where he'd made his bed in a gulley overhung with branches. Water was coming, which would flood him out unless he climbed out of the gulley through the thick brush. The sides were steep, and he gathered up his sheets, blanket and pillow and tried to climb out, reaching up for purchase with his right hand, which grasped a string and pulled it. The overhead light came on and he was standing in the middle of the swaybacked old bed in Phyllis Bateman's house in Cascom, with all the bedclothes clutched to him. The unnerving recognition of the dream came first, but then it was all pleasant. He had to go to the bathroom, yes, and perhaps that was the water part of it, but it seemed such a beautiful adventure, one to be remembered and treasured. He put the sheets back on the bed, went to the bathroom down the hall, and came back to the bed that was now so safe and old that he melted down into it.

# 8.

In the morning Phyllis was so painfully stiff George had to help her into the bathroom and Luke and George had to help her down the stairs to the breakfast table in the kitchen. She wore an old blue bathrobe, frayed at its cuffs and seams, and men's leather slippers with elastic at the sides.

"I don't like to be helped," she said. "I never liked to be helped and I never will and that's a great disadvantage in your old age."

"Hell, you're only sixty," George said. "You ain't even at retirement age yet."

George made coffee and toast and fried eggs on the bottled gas stove, while Luke set the table under Phyllis's supervision.

After they had eaten they had more coffee, and as they sat there Phyllis had that secretive, yet slightly avid look that meant she was having plans for Luke. Even when he was a little boy he knew she wasn't good at secrets.

"When you sell your house are you going to come back to Cascom sometimes?" she asked.

"I'll come back and visit," he said.

"There's some awful interesting new people in town you ought to meet."

105

"You going to look after the land at all?" George said, changing the subject. "There's some timber. Yellow birch, white birch, maple—veneer logs in there worth a lot of money. Hemlock, pine—not so many—spruce, beech, ash. You got seventy acres of woods ain't been logged in thirty years. You should ought to do some thinning."

"I was thinking when I was there yesterday I'd like to clear the old pastures."

"Ayuh," George said, nodding. "It's a damn shame to let it all close in like that. Ain't good for much but red squirrels and porcupines once the brush grows up in trees."

"Maybe I will sometime," Luke said.

George looked at him skeptically, his gray eyes just visible, like little glints of washed metal in the complicated folds of his old eyelids. "Naw, you won't," he said.

Luke felt heat in his cheeks, as if he'd been accused, correctly, of lying. He wanted to deny it. He thought of the dream last night of the black woods. There had been other dreams last night, too; they reached for his mind as if with hands, but he could not quite remember them.

The farm had been a place where he was before he was a husband and father. Cascom was like that too, the weight of his earlier past seeming heavier here.

"Did you swim in the brook when you were a kid?" he asked George.

"I'd go down to fetch the cows in the lower pasture on a hot day, you can bet I was out of my overalls quick as a wink and down the chute. That was the coldest water! I swear it was almost too cold to drink!"

"I took a short dip there yesterday. I thought I was paralyzed for a minute."

"I got a great affection for that place up there," George said. "I hate to see it go back, but I guess that's what's happening to all the old farms. Sometimes you wonder how any of 'em ever made half a living, but what I seem to recall is plenty of good company and good food. Weren't much cash money, but in them days a man could pretty near fix anything that broke, doctor his animals,

106

build what he wanted and shoot the varmints." He shook his head once, a jerk of his bristly chin to the right and back. "Now it does feel a long time ago."

Phyllis said, "When you come back, maybe I'll be up and around and we can have some people in for supper."

"That would be nice," Luke said with something like dread—a minor form of dread.

Before he left he made George call around and find out how much Shem's stone had cost altogether, then made a check out to George for it. Phyllis made him promise again to come back soon, and George said he was always welcome. Suddenly without thinking much about it, because if he had he would have seen how complicated it was, he told George he wanted to give him the .22 caliber pistol on the .45 frame.

George was startled and not exactly pleased. "That's a matched pair!" he said.

"It'll match your .45 as well as Shem's," Luke said. "I'll keep the .45 and the holster, but I want you to have the .22 and whatever tools go with it."

"Naw!" George said.

"Yes," Luke said. "We'll go shoot rats with it at the dump when I come back. It's yours, George, I mean it."

"Well, God damn it, I'll think about it!"

"All right!"

George wouldn't quite smile. Luke knew how the pistol fascinated him, but he also knew that the gift of such an elaborate and expensive object would seem beyond the pale to George, an act of irresponsibility, and somehow suspect. But George wanted to play with the pistol, and shoot it, and now he would have permission in his own mind to do that much, anyway.

That afternoon Luke turned into the shaded driveway of his house in Wellesley and stopped behind the Hornet, which protruded slightly from the garage because of bicycles and other gear. The other half of the garage was full of lawn furniture and other summer things he hadn't taken out.

He didn't want to open the car door. The magnitude of the

107

tasks before him was too great. He wondered, even began to calculate, the expense of shame and general self-hatred and disgust it would cost him to just stop functioning in any responsible way. Let everything go, let everything rot. He didn't want to sell anything, store anything, have anything, except maybe a drink.

The engine creaked, cooling. His hands on the steering wheel looked craggy and old. You could always tell the true age by the hands, someone once told him, but who cared. He looked at his hands and discovered the slivers from the old wooden chest, deep and turning the skin around them red. They looked like a flight of little arrows embedded in his flesh. He needed a tool, and there was Shem's jackknife in his pocket, so he took it out and opened the longest, or clip, blade, which had a sharp point. *John Fredericton Knives, Stamford, Conn.* was etched in tiny letters on the handle. It was a fine knife, a fine thing, perfect in its detailing, fit for a man to carry all his life and leave to his descendants. Without bothering to sterilize the tip he sternly and efficiently dug out each sliver. The pain seemed to come from far away, diminished by travel. He licked the salty blood from the blade, wiped it well on his dungarees, clicked (walked or talked) it back into the handle and slid the knife into his right front pants pocket, where it had made a shape for itself and seemed to belong.

In the house he would find antiseptic and a couple of adhesive bandages. The surgery seemed to bring him back into the world, so he got out of the car and out of habit went to the mailbox, brought the mail into the kitchen and let it fall onto the counter. There was no letter from the Avenger. Two windowed envelopes looked like bills and the rest were ads and solicitations, tabloids full of exclamations and coupons. Helen used to clip the coupons out and use them while shopping; he couldn't imagine ever doing that.

In the bathroom he found himself brushing his teeth. A grainy feeling discovered by his tongue had resulted in this action directly, involuntarily—part of the sympathetic nervous system, no doubt. Also, he would shave, and did. He had a few hours before he was supposed to be at the Joneses, so he collected trunks and boxes from the various storage places and began to pack those possessions he would put into storage.

How many souvenirs of his family, if any, did a man need? There must be some system here. He must make choices based upon some reading of intensity. What did he want to remember? What would he use each object for? Would he in his old age sit in a room in softly nostalgic light and muse fondly upon the mementoes of his lost son and daughter? His old age wasn't that far away and he foresaw no such room or mood. His wife, whose companionable body and soul he knew, mole and freckle, wound and phobia, irrationality and loyalty—what *souvenirs* would he keep of her?

There must be four categories: 1. Those things he would keep with him. 2. Those things he would store for possible later use. 3. Those things that might be useful to such an organization as the Salvation Army. 4. Those things that would go to the dump. *Use* seemed the principle here.

He would keep: photographs and letters. Naturally; no thought involved there. He did not want to look at them but there were albums and drawers full of loose photographs and envelopes of negatives. There were albums of his babyhood and youth, albums of Helen's babyhood and youth, albums belonging to Johnny and Gracie, albums that he'd forgotten about. He stopped in the upstairs hallway and put down a cardboard box full of albums and loose photographs. He could not do it this way. If he went into each room and removed one category of objects from each, he would never finish. He must do this in terms of space, cubic feet, not categories. He had never been good at any category except miscellaneous; categories overlapped and slid together like a shuffled deck of cards.

What he needed was a female relative, one with a warm yet unsentimental mind like Helen's, one of the kind who used to wash the family corpses, wind them in sheets and lay them out for ceremony and burial while the men, heavy with muscle and bone, kept out of the way.

He left the box in the hall, went down to the kitchen and got a

109

beer out of the refrigerator. He went into the living room and found that he could not bear to look through the window wall at the unmown lawn, so he went on into his study and examined with a cool sort of interest the dusty possessions and objects of someone who seemed to have gone away.

The phone rang. At first he felt that it must be for someone else, that no one was officially in this house. Then it insisted, so he went out to answer it.

"Hello?" he said, hearing that strange neutral tone of voice and at the same time noticing on the telephone table the June issue of *Gentleman,* its cover a photograph of a girl, in chromed lug-studded leather G-string and bra, carrying a bullwhip.

"Luke?" It was Robin Flash. "How you making it, man?"

"Pretty good, Robin."

"Hey, man, we got complications. I tried to get you last night. . . ." Robin paused.

"Like what?" Luke said.

"Marjorie's had a change of heart, you might say. I mean, she's getting really prissy about the whole thing—you know, like maybe even lawyers and the whole bit."

"Well, what happened, Robin?"

"Ooo, I hear in my little juvenile delinquent soul that you have a theory already. My mother used to say 'Robin' just like that. Did anyone ever tell you that us New Yorkers tend to *hear* you New England types like that?"

"Okay, what did you do when you went back to get your pictures?"

"Aw, Luke, damn it all. I meant no harm, man!"

"Tell me, Robin, was your strobe really off the first time?"

"Oh-oh! 'Tell me, Robin . . .' Okay, it really *was* off, Luke, I swear on my fucking Hasselblad, it was! This just happened, man!"

"You put the make on her . . ."

"Well, that's a quaint way of putting it. Listen, when I got there she'd been hitting the gin pretty hard. That chaperone of hers— Mrs. McDoughface or whatever her name is—wasn't there, okay? So we took the pictures, put the kids to bed and sort of sat around

110

while she had a couple more. Actually, we were talking about you. She wanted to know all about you and maybe I made up some stuff I didn't know, like you got the Purple Heart in Korea and like that. Hope you don't mind. Anyway, I can see she's getting so goddam horny, along with the booze, she can't see straight. That Mickey Rutherford must have been a pretty regular stud. . . ."

Luke was startled by the strength of his disapproval, and a sense of betrayal, of virtue debased; yet at the same moment he heard his own voice grimly and crudely cutting into the whole delicate, scandalous mess, saying, "Did you nail her, or not?"

"Luke, were you in love with her or something?"

"Or something," he said. "I didn't think she was the type."

"Well, man, I'm sorry. But listen, it turns out that Mickey Rutherford was a kind of short, blondish guy like me, and she likes kind of short, blondish guys, so it turns out, man, that in a way it wasn't like this little fucking insect crawled into her pants when she wasn't looking, you know! I mean, this slimy little Jew with the monster libido, you know!"

They were silent over the distance, Robin the one waiting, his life noises coming across the circuits, a sort of basal hum of concern and unfinished connection.

"What do you think I am, some kind of *animal?*" Robin finally shouted into the phone.

"Well, yes. Some kind of animal. That doesn't mean I'm judging you."

"Well, *shit!* Of course you're judging me! You're a writer, for one thing—who knows what's going on in your goddam head? And then your whole family got wiped out, right? So you're some kind of a prophet or a saint or a fucking oracle or something! You better not forget it!"

"Hey, Robin."

Again there were no words for a while, only the gray noises and the knowledge of their connection. Luke thought he could hear Robin's pulse over the distance, or someone's—maybe his own.

"Hey, Luke, I'm sorry," Robin said.

"Okay."

"Anyway, I guess when she thought about it the next morning

111

she got tear-assed and called *Gentleman* and threatened everybody with the law and libel and all that. She's got you mixed up in it too. She called me, and thank God I answered the phone, I was about to go out, and said if I told you she'd tell my wife, and all kinds of hysterical shit. I mean, Luke, listen—she got laid and she liked it, all seventeen goddam different ways she liked it, and I can't understand it, man. Anyway, if you ever see her again don't tell her I told you. Amy found out about one other time and it took six months before she could see straight. She's old-fashioned in these matters and I don't think my nervous system could take another session like that. I mean she jabbed me with a table fork I've still got the scar on my left pectoral and from then on I never knew what the fuck she'd pick up and bash the shit out of me with. She'd look perfectly sane one minute and the next she'd be fucking ape."

"Have you talked to Martin Troup?"

"Yeah, he called me, but there's something funny going on at *Gentleman,* anyway. Maybe they're folding, I don't know. You hear rumors. Anyway, Martin seemed sort of preoccupied. He didn't sound too interested in it one way or the other."

"I wonder," Luke said.

"Everybody goes into a sort of coma in New York in the summer. Maybe that's it," Robin said.

"I wonder," Luke said again. He was sorry for Marjorie and touched that she didn't want him to know. It was truly not like her to get drunk and let herself be taken to bed by a stranger, but then she'd never been a widow with all that new strange singleness like a great vacuum ahead of her, that tired adventure. At the same time he recognized that he would take any excuse not to write the article, for which he hadn't done enough interviewing and research. If *Gentleman* folded he wouldn't have to write it. Even in an attempt at truth, words were misleading approximations, and mostly they were in the service of liars. There were too many ways to make a sentence. The very idea of a paragraph made him apprehensive.

It was the farm, now wilderness, that had begun to press upon him and his dreams; it was shameful to let the old house rot into

112

its cellar hole. He should clean up that grave with his own hands.

"What do you think, Luke?" Robin said.

"Maybe it's not too late for Martin to get another writer."

"He probably won't bother with it," Robin said. "Oh, well, I could have used the money, but at least I made a couple hundred and expenses. Easy come, easy go and all that jazz."

"No hard feelings if I quit?"

"Shit, no. Anyway, it was me that kind of screwed you up. I just never thought she'd take it this way."

"Let me think about it for a day or two. I can't make up my mind to quit. I don't know what I want to do."

With that they said good-bye and Luke was left alone in his house feeling that he'd almost come to a momentous decision—as if he'd either had a near disaster or a near triumph, and he didn't know which.

He put the empty beer bottle in the trash and opened another, thinking of Marjorie in her bright apartment, down the squalid hallway, behind the buttress of the police lock and the other locks, in shame and consternation, putting out too many cigarettes in her fake Giacometti ashtray. The kids would be watching television and she would be large, moving, self-violated, her eyelids raw. He would like to comfort her and the idea terrified him.

But it was time to take a shower and get ready to go to the Joneses'. He had promised to do that.

It was a calm, hot afternoon, the sun seeming too high for five o'clock, the air grayish with humidity if he looked toward any distance. Trees down a block lost their names and were just trees, of a flat green grayed by the heavy air. Since the Joneses favored light clothes, but clothes with a certain formality about them, and he didn't happen to own anything with their California flair, he got out an old seersucker suit and wore it without a tie. He had never quite understood these matters but Helen had, and there was probably something wrong about his costume that he regretted for her sake, though he was now free of the always surprising precision of her knowledge. No, it didn't matter now because it had only mattered for her sake.

113

The Joneses' house had been built about the same time as his own, a few years before Ham had retired from the air force and moved here. It was long and low, with one higher gable over the large living room, obviously a very expensive house and lot, and Luke had wondered how Ham could afford it until he remembered the pension that underlay all of Ham's activities. Twenty-some years, ending as a colonel, would give him a financial base anyone might envy. He'd often wondered what the other real estate people in town thought of competition that was so subsidized, but had never asked.

He drove up the long driveway between rows of arborvitae and parked beside Ham's station wagon.

A sign tacked to a stick, cut out to represent a pointing hand, directed him through the breezeway. On the wrist and palm of the hand was the word, *Drinks.* Jane liked signs, which she made out of colored matting paper. There were always signs of this sort stuck here and there when the Joneses had people in. On the other side of the breezeway another sign in the shape of a hand directed him to the left. On this one was the word, *Pool.*

And there was the pool, the aboveground kind where you walked up a few redwood steps to a deck that surrounded a great blue plastic bag full of water. Jane, in all her tanned and nearly flawless length, lay on her back holding a sheet of aluminum foil so that the reflected light of the afternoon sun might tan her under her chin. She was forty, and except for a few leathery but good humored wrinkles on her sun-cured face, and the silvery, untannable stretch marks that descended toward, but never reached, her yellow bikini, she might have been the bride of a second lieutenant decorating the officers' club pool at Hickam Field or some other subtropical base. He'd often thought it must be some trick of mangoes, or breadfruit, that had kept her bones so straight and her flesh so firm, but more likely it was Coca-Cola and cheeseburgers.

When she saw him she rolled over toward him, handling her legs with a smoothness that seemed to have come from long and necessary practice, there was so much distance between their articulations.

114

"Luke's here!" she called to Ham, though she looked at him. She motioned him up to her, pulled his head through the deck railing and kissed him on the lips, hers tasting of gin and suntan lotion. Then she said, "God, it's hot," and rolled neatly over into the pool, her submergence slowly bulging the blue water into a wave that became a series of crossing and returning waves. Her head appeared, her blond hair streaming over her shoulders, water beading on her oiled skin. "Ham will get you a pair of shorts," she said. "Go get yourself a drink and get out of that ridiculous suit. Oh, oh! Did that hurt your feelings?"

"No," he said. "Just remember that here in the East we're a little stodgy."

"God, how true!" she said. "No one over thirty is supposed to take off her girdle."

"That wouldn't apply to you in any case, Jane. I was thinking when I came around the corner that you looked about twenty-nine at the most."

"Twenty-nine, huh?" she said, carefully considering. He had a suspicion that it was the wrong number; he wasn't very good at that sort of thing.

He found Ham in the kitchen stirring a large pitcher of martinis with a glass rod. "Here you are, sport!" Ham said. "This utensil, or whatever you call it, is your very own. Grab the glass of your choice and the garbage of your choice and let's proceed to get agreeably smashed." He wore a pair of red shorts that bisected his wet, hairy body so tightly they gave the impression of a tourniquet. "But first get out of those clothes. There's some shorts and a towel in the bathroom there." He frowned as he looked at Luke. "You do want martinis, straight up—or don't I remember right?"

"Yes, but how many of them are *in* there?"

"Enough for a starter. Green olives, right? You like green goddam olives! I'll get em!"

Ham went to the refrigerator and Luke found the shorts, which were too big for him, but would do. He and Ham carried pitchers and glasses to the pool and Luke dove into the tepid, slightly chlorinated water. Yesterday he swam in the waters of Zach Brook.

He didn't open his eyes under this water, but turned around,

115

came to the surface and pulled himself up beside his pitcher of martinis, which was beside Jane. Ham sat on the other side of her with his pitcher of what looked like Manhattans. Jane's drink was gin and tonic. They sat on the edge of the round pool with their legs in the water, the sultry heat pressing against them. The first sip of Luke's martini seemed about as cold as Zach Brook, though with a different power. He felt the alcohol immediately as a loosening of a guard he hadn't been aware of before he felt it slipping away. The Joneses had been acquaintances who were more eager to be friends than he and Helen had been. He couldn't, and Helen hadn't, put words to what it was about the Joneses that made them wince slightly, but now he supposed it was a matter of a very fine difference in humor, or an aggressiveness that was suggestive but not quite real. Ham flirted with Helen (or did he?) and Jane was always touching Luke, winking, saying cryptic things that could have implied that they were lovers, or at least knew more about each other than they did. At these times Ham would seem to back off from Jane's and Luke's intimacy and be strictly neutral, or else he would speak only to Helen, and on another subject.

The Joneses had one child, a daughter who was eighteen and had her mother's physical presence. She had her own life; though she lived at home she was seen only in passing.

As Luke let more of the gin, with its cold clarity but slight film of oil, slide over his tongue and into his system, he felt the need to speak, and these people, who had been so solicitous and kind after the accident, would do. He couldn't remember why, long ago, he would have been careful. He didn't know what he might have had to be careful about.

There was the Avenger, of course; he had told no one about the Avenger, and he still didn't want to tell anyone about that.

"You're drinking awful slow," Ham said. "You thinking about that article you're writing?"

"No. I may never do it, in fact."

"Hell, you don't have to," Ham said.

"It's sort of a habit to do what I've said I'd do, I guess."

Jane said she always knew he was a Puritan. "You've got a bad case of the Work Ethic, that's what you've got. So uptight!"

116

"Am I?"

"Yes, *always!* You never let go for a minute! Always thinking about what you're going to say or do. It's your New England up-bringing, I suppose." Jane said this and lay back with her arms over her head and her knees apart, as if to prove how un-uptight she was. He found himself looking at the smooth swell where her bikini crossed her thigh, and looked away.

"Oh, yes," she said. "Up *tight.*"

"Well, I am getting tight," he said.

"But not up!" Ham said, and laughed.

Jane ignored his laughter and told him it was time to light the charcoal. The spareribs were in the oven but they would finish them over the charcoal with the barbecue sauce, in about forty-five minutes. "Are you hungry, Luke? Will you be hungry by then?" she said, touching his leg. Her fingernails were long and polished, silvery and slightly curved, like woodcarving chisels. They raked slowly through the light hairs above his knee as she retrieved her hand.

Ham had gone to light the briquettes in the outdoor grill, and they watched him for a moment as he showered the charcoal with a can of lighter fluid. His crewcut black hair stood up in clumps. Though he was tall and not fat, rolls of flesh at his kidneys came out over the waistband of his red shorts, giving his torso a soft white, indeterminate look at its base. Black hair grew symmetrical-ly on the two rolls as though genetically planned for them.

"If you sell your house, where are you going to live?" Jane asked.

"I don't know. I suppose in motels or hotels for a while."

"We could put you up for as long as you want, you know. We've got rooms to spare."

The alcohol made this offer seem less dangerous, though its complications were still apparent to him. If sober he would have thanked her for the offer quickly, thinking of regrets, but now he let the silence continue for a little too long. She moved her sun-glasses up on her forehead and looked at him, meaning that he should see her eyes looking at him.

"I don't think that would be exactly wise," he said nervously.

117

She patted his thigh and smiled; that was evidently the compliment she wanted. But he hadn't meant it as flattery or any sort of game. He had never played such games, and the words for what would have been unwise were near the surface of his mind, direct and powerful; they were magic and shouldn't be used, or implied, or joked about if the possibility of the action they described was real. He drank the rest of the gin in his glass, crunched and swallowed the Spanish olive and poured himself another drink. If he kept drinking he might say the words and that would cause trouble—or maybe not. Maybe the Joneses were swingers who hadn't quite been literal about it because of his and Helen's "puritanism." Maybe that was what had kept him and Helen a little edgy about the Joneses. Jesus Christ, he thought, who knew? He went about his life considering certain things powerful and dangerous (Helen had been powerful and dangerous, loving him and watching him, treating their union with extreme attention, knowing all implications).

There didn't seem to be much danger though, here in this sunny yard, by this artificial water. Otherwise they wouldn't be drinking their senses dull. They were all friends here. He and Jane had made up their little political argument long ago, except that it hadn't been quite political, no. But who cared. He at least had nothing to lose, so he drank.

Later, after more warm water splashing and swimming, Ham was cooking the spareribs, turning them with giant tweezers and painting them with red sauce. Jane and Luke sat at the rim of the pool.

Jane said, "Do you ever touch women? I mean do you ever sort of spontaneously reach out your hand and touch them?"

"I'm afraid I'm getting on toward the dirty old man category," he said. "When I was young and pretty I did."

"Old! Huh!"

"Maybe I'm afraid if I touch them I won't be able to let go and I'll have to take them down and tear off their clothes and fuck 'em and eat 'em and in general act pretty unsocial."

"You're only partly kidding," she said, giving him a long, deep, how-interesting look. Evidently she thought him tame enough,

118

and in the circumstances, at least, she was probably right. His thinking was vague, a little circular, or perhaps spiral, because he couldn't quite come back to where he began.

"No," he said, listening to himself with an interest that was at best fragmentary, "no, I guess I'm not totally kidding." Now, that sounded, in retrospect, pretty logical and intelligent. But what had he been going to say next? "Jane, Jane," he said, "I'm pretty well drunk and confused. I had something I was going to say that would have made you feel just right, but I'm absolutely fucked if I can remember what it was."

He immediately forgot what he'd just said, and was surprised at her anger.

"Why do you think you're so *superior?*" she said in a low voice. "You were going to tell me something that would make me feel good? Well, *fuck you!*" She slid into the pool and swam the twenty yards or so to the other side, where she turned without looking at him and floated on her back.

He lay back and tried to remember what exactly had happened, but couldn't. Ham came over, climbed the steps to the deck and announced that the spareribs were done. If Jane would get the rolls and salad, they could eat. Then he recognized the antagonism and said, "Oh oh, another goddam argument? Nixon's long gone, so what's it about this time?"

Jane swam back and without a word climbed out, irritated that one of her buttocks had slid clear of the bikini, which she violently corrected and went toward the kitchen. There had been a red pimple on that white buttock, Luke observed cruelly to himself, a fairly angry sort with a good deal of—what was the word? *Mass* to it. It must have been kind of painful to sit on.

Ham shook his head tolerantly and went to set the outside trestle table, where they ate, Jane still imperiously silent. Luke was a little unstable physically, though he had an appetite and ate a lot. They had white wine in large stemmed glasses which he drank, he thought, not quite at the swilling level.

At one point he kept hearing little popcorn-popping sounds, little angry ticks and cracks he first thought were in his own head, but they came from an electric insect executioner on a pedestal, palely bluish on the inside, that fried moths and bugs at an alarming rate. "Damn," he said. "Look at that mother eat its way through the cosmos!" Darkness was coming on, though it was still humid and hot. "Jane," he said, moving his head to the side to catch her averted eyes, "I love your spareribs! Did we have an argument? I can't for the life of me remember any argument. Listen! According to the Bible, Eve was a sparerib, though I don't exactly know what I'm saying. . . ."

In the morning sometime he woke up in a strange room. It was not his room at the Biltmore. It was not the bedroom at home. When it became clear that it was a room in the Joneses' house an absolute avalanche of doubtful, possibly shameful memories fell upon him and crushed him down into the springs and stuffing. "Oh, God!" he said out loud. It seemed there were more and more things he'd said and done that wouldn't be good at all in retrospect. Was it true that he'd shit into the aspidistra? No, and it was no use being flippant at this hour, whatever hour it was. It was true that Ham, good old good-natured Ham Jones, had gotten very angry when Jane had insisted on skinny-dipping in the pool at midnight. That was her word for it, and drunk as Luke was he could tell that she was trying to punish both of them, but why did he have to enter into a domestic squabble? Who did he think he was, anyway, some kind of superior idiot who could arbitrate twenty years of grievances?

Yet he was fascinated and not quite embarrassed enough when Jane stripped off her yellow bikini, revealing a white one beneath that was untanned skin, except, of course, for her light brown triangle of pubic hair. She had undressed in the living room, and it struck him that a bikini, small as it was, actually did cover an awful lot, because without it she assumed power. Her sarcasm, none of which he could remember, was directed mostly against him, and that also angered Ham because one shouldn't treat a guest that way. Her breasts had blue veins in them, and seemed vulnerable, milk white but authoritative in their heaviness and their eye-like wide brown nipples that moved as she yelled.

He supposed it was not entirely his fault, actually, that he found himself wrestling with both husband and wife, ostensibly trying to keep them from hurting each other. He was lucky he wasn't killed.

Oh, *God,* that rolling around on the shag carpet, wall to wall. He moved and the sheets stung the raw scratches on his ribs. There were bruises, too, one from the corner of the marble-topped coffee table. Once he grabbed Ham by one of his hairy kidney rolls, a texture like fresh bread. But Ham had finally snuck a quick slap across his shoulder that caught Jane on the side of her face and then there were no more cries of "bitch!" "cocksucker!" "bastard!" and the like, but tears and moans and sobs from both Jane and Ham. It was then Luke Carr, priest, psychiatrist, medicine man, counselor, tearful himself, evidently conducted some kind of therapy session complete with weeping confession, abject apology, birth trauma, self-flagellation, kissing, feeling and hugging. . . . The portentous sentiments contained in Reverend Doctor Carr's sermons and admonitions burned shamefully at the edges of the alcohol shadow that lay ominously across his memory.

It was also his idea that they should, after all, do what Jane wanted and go skinny-dipping in the tepid pool in the light of a hazy moon. Chlorine therapy, or something. And it was there that Gail, their daughter, returning from somewhere, found them all palely floating.

"What in hell happened to the living room?" she asked.

"We had a little argument, dear," Jane said, submerging all but her head.

"Jesus! Well, good night!" Gail said.

Other moments would emerge later, he supposed. He held his head in both hands, as if it were a vase. Physical and mental pain too often occurred together. Wounds (non-fatal ones) were all right in sports, work, or war but he couldn't stand the ones he had now.

It was eight o'clock. He tried to think that his pain and embarrassment might indicate that he was getting used to the deaths. He did care about his life now, whether he knew it or not, and he

121

must get away from all these people. Maybe he could leave a note and sneak out before the Joneses woke up to their own pain. He would go and hide, change his name, disappear.

His toes nearly disappeared in the thick carpet. This was a guest room, with the ever-new and moribund look of guest rooms. All naps were unworn, all the little pictures were straight, there were no cobwebs, no worn trails, no dents, no scratches. The connecting bathroom gleamed with onyx tile and chrome; the toilet seat was covered in thick mauve pile, the purple towels were two fuzzy inches thick on their silver rods and rings, the shower curtain was frosted glass. Though he liked warmth and hot water as much as anyone, bathrooms had always offended him a little because they seemed to imply a worshipful horror of piss and shit that he couldn't quite manage to understand, even in himself. The power of shit— God knew he'd had his hands in it often enough. People, people. He always made a hurtful fool of himself.

He took a shower, his scratches raw, and put on his clothes. Shem's knife was a hard, utilitarian lump in the pocket of the light pants. He hoped the Joneses were not up, but to leave without seeing them would cause its own complications, and unless he went out a window he would have to pass the kitchen. They, too, must be mortified by all that had happened last night.

As he came to the kitchen Ham called, "He's up! He's up!" and came out and grabbed him above the elbows. Ham was dapper in white tennis shorts, sneakers and tennis sweater. "We heard the shower going so we knew you were a survivor! Didn't we tie one on for sure? Come and have some coffee, Sport!" And pulled him into the kitchen. Jane was still in a robe, one cheek darker than the other, but aside from that she looked pretty fresh.

"What a blast!" she said, her fingers at her temples. "Gail sure thought us old crocks were out of our gourds!"

"Us old crocks *were* out of our gourds," Ham said. "But that's our goddam privilege, right?"

They gave Luke coffee, and tomato juice with secret ingredients in it that he identified as Worcestershire sauce and probably vodka.

"Too bad about the quarreling," Ham said brightly, a little

122

bleary in the eyes if one looked too closely. "But so it goes, huh? Nothing serious. We're all friends here, right?"

"All friends," Luke said.

"Jesus," Ham said. "Didn't we tie one on?"

"Sozzeled, absolutely," Luke said.

"Mashed, squashed, pie-eyed," Ham said.

"All bent out of shape," Jane said.

"Yeah, you better believe it!" Ham said.

# 9.

In the next few days, out of some sort of penance, Luke believed, he went through things, chose and discarded, packed and transported, and finally all of those possessions he had saved for some vague future use took up a space in Joe the Mover's warehouse about the size of a small room. He sold hundreds of ephemeral books to a secondhand book jobber, selling them because he couldn't just throw them away. He borrowed a battery charger from the local service station, got the Hornet running and sold it at a loss to the dealer Helen had bought it from. He gave clothes, toys and other things to the Salvation Army and to neighbors. The number, the sheer bulk, the complexity, the horrendous initial expense, of the machines, utensils, implements, equipment, furniture, vestments, supplies *contained* in his house amazed him; if all the houses on his street, in the town and across the vast country were so crammed with goods, what had happened to necessity and use in his civilization? And yet the discarding was hard—with each choice a surprisingly deep dismemberment occurred: wouldn't he ever have a use for an electric food processor called a Cuisinart? He could not see his life ahead of him, and so he didn't know, but instinct told him to discard, sell, divest himself of possessions.

Now that daydream of years ago came back as reality, a wish that had been cursed as it was made. What did a man need? His eyes and ears, his good arms and legs. Some clothes. A good knife. A horse (his beat-up station wagon). But when you got into horses the world began to get complicated again, with saddle and bridle, blanket and cinch and other tools and tack.

Until he had some idea of where he was going, how could he put anything into his car except his toothbrush, which was worn out and should be replaced anyway?

He stood alone in the kitchen, the house bare of those things that had been personal, except for a couple of suitcases of clothes that were seasonal and a few cardboard boxes full of working papers, a few books, one dictionary, pens and pencils and notebooks, a few things that were unclassifiable as to need, such as a clipboard, an ashtray Gracie had made for him in second grade before she stopped condoning his smoking, a stapler—a birthday present from Johnny—and his typewriter. From one of the cardboard boxes he took an address book and looked through it. It was an old one, not kept up to date very well, many of the addresses surely obsolete. At one time it had seemed to him that he had many friends, maybe too many, before they had scattered to far places. What had happened to Dick Knight, who had, at least as of ten years ago, been teaching at a college in northern California? Or Dick Mulner, who when last heard from was running for Congress from Marin County, whatever district that was in? Or, to keep on with Dicks, Dickie Greenblatt, who took over his father's woolen mill in New Hampshire? Other couples—John and Rose, Jerry and Vera, John and Lois, Weldon and Dot, George and Fumiko, Nathan and Angela. How attractive all the young wives were, and Helen was: there was a season when all the women wore simple dresses called chemises, which showed how young and slender and graceful they were. He was in love with all of them, as if all their variousness of height and color were somehow invested in Helen's own vividness at night when he made love to her. They were all pregnant or not, nursing or not, and the whole race

125

seemed beautiful then. Wives were named Fern, and Fran and Pat. In those days he and Helen, or any of their friends, could have packed all of their belongings into a small U-Haul trailer and been gone. Which happened, though none of them thought of loss then. They seemed to have no secrets from each other, none at all, though there was much tact between men and men, women and women, men and women. Small strangenesses and quirks that surely would later become irritating or even ugly were then, within the tense purity of youthful flesh, merely interesting oddities of character. Many were now divorced. Some were dead, some insane, whether ambulatory or not. Or had been when last heard of. But they had all been so valuable in their equality and potential. Then, as he had moved from place to place, from more or less regular jobs to his present independence from one place of work, most of those old friends had faded into their own lives, in near or distant places. Most of them were as unsure of his present state and address as he was of theirs, he knew. Some still sent Christmas cards or an occasional note, but in their communications was the feeling of how long ago it had all been, how the years had gone, how amazing it was that time had flown so quickly and left them older, established in other worlds.

Then came a crisis of loss, in which his vision shattered. The sunlight on the counters turned prismatic, and the windows cracked silently without falling from their frames. The house was full of empty closets and drawers, which changed its basic echo, even that of his own pulse. The bodies of his family were not here and he would never hear their voices.

On Wednesday he went to the closing at the savings bank. Ham was there, and Luke's lawyer for this occasion, an older man named Lewis who was partly deaf, and Glennis and Clifford Ruppert, both in their late thirties, and their lawyer, and an officer of the bank. Ham's commission was surprisingly large, but evidently the standard one. Insurance, taxes, water and so on would be prorated, Luke paying through the second week of June and then no more. He would receive $244.53 every month for twenty years, a sum and a time which once would have seemed large and long.

Afterwards Ham reminded him to terminate the electricity and telephone, and to get his deposit back. They walked out onto the street with Clifford Ruppert, a soft, balding man with protuberant brown eyes. His wife, whose name Luke had already forgotten, had to do some shopping nearby, so Ruppert suggested that they have a drink on it. They went into the chilled darkness of a bar and sat in a leather or Naugahyde booth in the slowly lightening gloom.

'So everything's about concluded," Ham said. "A pretty good deal for all, I'd say."

"I'll go along with that," Ruppert said. A waitress came and Ruppert supervised the ordering of drinks. He had been looking at Luke with an intensity that implied a question he wanted to ask but didn't yet know how. When his Scotch came and he'd taken a couple of good swallows, he said, "So you've got everything stored or sold and what you need is all packed in your car, right?"

"Right," Luke said.

"So you can just slide behind the wheel, turn the key and go wherever you want!" He shook his head, curious and eager, his big eyes gleaming with envy.

"I've got a little unfinished business here and there," Luke said.

"Your article. Right," Ham said.

"Yeah, there's always something," Ruppert said. "Sometimes if I think about all the things I've got to do I get depressed. I mean from the IRS to getting the oil changed and a lube job to a haircut to insurance to filling out forms or getting somebody to fix something or honor a warranty or if it isn't one thing it's another." But he was still looking at Luke with envy, and it was those main responsibilities of wife and family that he considered being free of. The sheen in those soft brown eyes was moist and libidinous, a quality that could not be hidden for a moment. Ah, the easy and willing young women of a generation he had missed out on by a few years! Maybe Luke was being unfair to this husband, but Ruppert was of the age to hear that music, those distant, slippery, liquid notes, and young enough not to divine the truth about granted wishes.

By four in the afternoon he was back again at the house he no longer owned. Ham had asked him to come for dinner, but he'd

127

lied and said he had to leave town this afternoon. On the way back he'd stopped at the Post Office and told them to hold his mail in General Delivery until he had an address, but there was today's mail in his mailbox. He immediately recognized the elite typeface on a stamped envelope. This time the postmark was Wellesley, MA. He looked up and down the street, across lawns, then all around once more as he closed the kitchen door. Wellesley was too close; the exercise was suddenly more than literary. In the house he found a place by the hall telephone where he couldn't be observed through any window as he opened the envelope.

Dearest Lukie-Dukie,
   You prickie-wickie I have got you in my sites and I am going to pull the trigger-wigger.
                                                              Mr. Death

His revulsion was somewhat postponed until he read the note again. The mind revealed here was frightening and boring at the same time, talentless and needful, banal and self-satisfied, and it came to him with an absolute clarity he hoped was not permanent that the only thing to do with a being that bored and frightened at the same time was to kill it.

This was the third note; the reality of the Avenger increased. Presumably the police were there to cope with this sort of thing, but he had dealt with the police on other matters and he didn't want to get involved with them now. If he must be alone he would be alone, free, singular, responsible to no one. Either this blob was seriously going to try to kill him or was just being creative. He had no idea who it might be and therefore neither would the police, who would have to wait until further developments, such as an actual attempt on his life. Well, he would wait for that alone, without the cop-civilian dialogue he could, if he wished, write out beforehand in his mind.

Then an interesting, almost thrilling little instinctive thing happened to his right hand. It went to a holster that was not at his waist—was, in fact, in a wooden chest in New Hampshire. His index finger had familiarly curled to undo the clasp of the holster

128

flap, the hand moving without thought through the complications of the leather to the firm butt of the pistol. If it had been there the pistol would now be in his hand, the hammer cocked, the grip safety properly depressed so that the heavy yet precise instrument would be ready to fire at his will, a lethal vector of force extending from his hand. In Korea he had found that he was a good shot, single-or double-handed; he'd had the patience to take the short time necessary to care more for the alignment of his sights than the clarity of his target, which would soon have a large hole in it anyway and could be examined at leisure.

The Avenger, or Blob, unless these notes were improbably deceptive, called gunsights, "sites," which seemed to cancel out his familiarity, and thus his skill, with at least one order of lethal machines. But that might be a false conclusion. He knew nothing about the Avenger except the most important and technically useless thing of all—that in these notes he revealed what Luke perhaps hated most in his fellow man. It was not the semiliteracy, but the supreme confidence of tone. Yes, exactly *tone,* always the nasty little progenitor of hurt—literary, conversational, carnal, mortal—every little backstabber's game and justification.

He would leave here. The house and garage had been stripped of all that the Rupperts hadn't wanted to buy. There was something he should do. The telephone. The Rupperts would take care of the electricity. He called the telephone company and in his official voice arranged all that. No, he didn't want another telephone at another address, not yet; he would let them know.

He took one last quick look through the house and was surprised to find that he hadn't looked into the kitchen liquor cabinet. Among opened bottles of bourbon, blended whiskey, gin and vermouth, and also various unsavory liqueurs that had been there forever, was a fifth of good Scotch, unopened. He threw out the liqueurs, put all the whiskey, gin and vermouth in one of the cardboard boxes in the rear of the station wagon, and left the Scotch on the counter as a present.

He was leaving. At the last moment, having some room in the car he hadn't expected to have, he took the dented old toolbox and its contents from the garage. He seemed to be supplying himself for a trip, but a trip to where? All he had to do, as Clifford Ruppert had said, was slide himself behind the wheel, turn the key and go anywhere he wanted to go.

One more quick look through the house, and the telephone caught him.

"Mr. Luke Carrr?" said a man's voice, a sneezy, high, phlegmy man's voice with a rising inflection in the slurred last syllable of his name.

"Yes," Luke said.

"This is Mr. Smarmalurgis from the Prumalator Company?"

"Yes?"

"There's the matter of the bifold invoices indicating a leased debit balance of one hundred thirteen dollars and fifty-nine cents overdue now seven and one-half months?"

"What was the name of your company again?"

"The Permolator Company, Mr. Carr? A division of Weston, Watts, Porgis Corporation? At two percent interest per month the immediate sum, if remitted on or before six, fifteen, amounts to one hundred twenty-six dollars and ninety cents?"

"What, exactly, is a permolator, Mr. Smarmalurgis?"

"Hormel N. Sturgis, Mr. Carr. A perfulator monitors your water system as to ionization and turbidity?"

"A perfulator? I don't think I have a perfulator."

"A permulator, Mr. Carr. If you will look you will find a white enameled tank one foot in diameter by four diameters appended to your main?"

In the silence following this apparently reasonable statement, knowing that he never thought very well over the telephone, Luke tried to choose from among several clamoring attitudes the one he would take toward this fellow. If he'd heard correctly, and it was certainly possible he hadn't, the man—or maybe the voice was that of a throaty woman—was not being consistent in its pronunciations. For a moment caution won. "Why don't you send me a bill, Mr. Sturgis?"

"This was a non-billing lease, Mr. Carr, meaning three points less per annum? I have the lease before me, signed by one Mrs. L. Carr, dated five, one, seventy-six?"

130

"Well, Mr. Sturgis, append the three annum points and send me a bill, okay?" Now he was on the edge of saying something outrageous, but caution was still there. What was this device, some kind of water softener that Helen had had installed? He was tired and bored, bored with the telephone that connected him to all the vacuousness of the world out there, and this strange hermaphroditic voice.

"Very well, Mr. Carr. In that case the due amount will be increased three dollars and eighty-one cents, making the total one hundred thirty dollars and seventy-one cents?"

"Yes, fine," he said.

"As you instruct us, Mr. Carr."

"Right. Good-bye."

He would have paid one hundred and whatever dollars and cents not to have had that call, but now it was too late. Evidently the telephone company hadn't immediately disconnected his phone, which reminded him that he hadn't called Robin to say whether or not he'd go on with the *Gentleman* piece. He just couldn't make up his mind. Maybe cancelling the phone had been a decision not to do the piece, but then he'd put his typewriter and notes and other material in the car, so he was still hanging there, not wanting to do it, unable to give up, hating the words he would have to write down and type and rewrite and proofread—that whole process he'd once found rewarding.

A permolator? Permulator? Prufolator? A white enameled tank? He went down to the basement and traced the water pipe from the meter. The only white enameled tank was the electric water heater, called a Hot Roc, made by Ford Steel Products Corp., Tarrytown, N.Y. He traced the lines to the washing machine and up to kitchen and bathrooms and there was no prufolator or permolator or simply any room for such a thing in any closet or wall. There was no tank one foot in diameter and four feet long in this house.

Still, he was willing to believe that he had been the one to misunderstand, that his mind, always precarious on the telephone, had jumped to all sorts of visual conclusions about some white enameled tank. Maybe the tank was somewhere else, in some other building somewhere. Maybe it was installed inside or underneath the water heater. But he knew better, and when the telephone rang right beside him he jumped, thinking that the strange damp voice of Mr. or Ms. Sturgis must be the one waiting for him to answer.

"Hello? Luke Carr?" It was not that voice, but a familiar one, a woman's, harshened by the circuits. It was Marjorie Rutherford, and his hands shook with embarrassment.

He said, "Yes?" a lie because he knew.

"Luke." She was quiet for a few seconds. "Luke, this is Marjorie Rutherford, in New York. You know."

"How are you, Marge?"

"Terrible."

"What's the matter?"

"I know Robin told you."

Now he was silent, trying to make up his mind. He was silent a little too long.

"He did tell you. I knew it! Men always tell everything about women!" She was crying, and angry too.

"Hey, Marge," he said. "I understand. Jesus, of course I do. Come on, it's all right." His soothing voice.

"I don't think it's all right!" She cried the words, and he couldn't help trying to visualize some sort of phonetic spelling: *Aien non thing utz alraieeent!* But at the same time the words, which he felt tear her throat, twisted his own throat.

"So I don't want you to write about me!"

"Do you think I'd write that?"

"I don't know! I read the *Gentleman* for this month and they said terrible things about everybody. *Horrible* things about real live people!"

*Gentleman* still lay on the telephone table in front of him, the studded leather whip-woman leering. "I guess I don't blame you," he said. He could see how her capitulation to Robin could be used, all right. The breakdown of everything, including the poured floors of skyscrapers, the mad wasps regurgitating and building for no procreative reason because the center itself rotted, and so on. Mike Rizzo's priests were "morphodites" and Jimmo McLeod's

132

life was nothing but existence, self-admitted. And below, in the garbage-strewn streets, among the rats, were the blacks, the blacks, waiting for the lights to go out. They'd love that at *Gentleman;* this was the age of interesting literary simplifications, and apocalypse was nothing if not fashionable.

"I bet you both thought it was a big joke, didn't you!"

"No. Robin wouldn't have told me if you hadn't called *Gentleman,* I'm sure."

"'Cause you'd be ashamed of me!"

"I was surprised, maybe, but I think I understand."

*"Understand!"* she cried, and went on crying. He held the black telephone, from which a woman sobbed, against his head.

Soon she stopped sobbing and breathed a few deep, moist breaths. "I'm sorry," she said. "None of it's your fault. I just wish you never called me in the first place."

"It looks as if I won't write the article anyway," he said.

"I wanted to have our pictures in *Gentleman,* I don't know why. It would make us sort of out of the ordinary," Marjorie said.

He didn't know how much longer he could stand here, not knowing what to say or wanting to say anything. He felt that he didn't understand people at all and should have nothing to do with them. He never knew what they wanted or what they were going to do or say next. He could hear the television in the room in the Bronx, where Mickey and Marcia were no doubt watching some late afternoon soap opera; all that feigned emotion, those widened eyes and dramatic statements—he wondered if they understood any of it. Maybe they just watched the people move and talk and weep, not knowing why or even following the simplest words. Enough, maybe, that they looked like real people and something seemed to happen each moment.

He was now planning his escape.

"I'd like to see you again, Luke," she said. "I liked talking to you."

"Me, too," he said. "Maybe we'll see each other again sometime, Marge." No, no, they never would.

"You never can tell," she said. "Maybe I'll come up there to Massachusetts and visit you sometime."

133

"Sure, why not?"

"Sure. Yeah. Well, it was nice talking to you. I hope everything works out for you."

"You, too."

"Good-bye, Luke," she said, and the connection ended.

Why should he have to feel that he was no help? Well, he wouldn't be of any help. In the issue of *Gentleman* that lay before him was an article about the joys of "bondage," its straps and whips—tongue in cheek, of course, as they liked to say, and God, they liked to say. Also the straight chic poop on "snuff" movies, in which the actress, after having participated in the usual oral, anal, what-have-you exercises, is informed on camera that she is going to die, and actually does go screaming and whimpering to actual death, for the gratification of the viewers. Hey, man, you know, the *real thing.*

If he stayed around this echoing house much longer someone would show up—Ham or the Rupperts—so he left. All he had to do was slide under the wheel, turn the key, and go anywhere he wanted. The loaded car moved through the balmy June air, heavy and steady on its wheels. In a little while he was on Route 128, heading north. There was only one place on earth that was his, where he would not have to rent or be a guest, where no one else had a right to be and wouldn't be.

# 10.

When the interstate crossed the New Hampshire line he first consciously looked in his rearview mirror to see if he were being followed. The official sign at the border said:

LIVE FREE OR DIE
BIENVENUE AU
WELCOME TO
NEW HAMPSHIRE

Now, as if the line were really a frontier, he examined those who might follow him across. If he were not being followed, say, by that blue Oldsmobile Cutlass he now realized had been behind him for some time, then no one knew where he was going. He couldn't remember telling anyone in Wellesley or in New York that he might go to New Hampshire, because he hadn't really known it then himself.

It was seven o'clock; there would be at least two more hours of light, so he would get to the farm at dusk. It was a destination that would at least give him two hours of definition. He was going somewhere.

135

The blue Cutlass with Massachusetts plates was fifty yards behind him, its driver alone in the car. He kept his speed at fifty-nine, which seemed to satisfy the driver of the Cutlass, who might have been a man or a woman, he couldn't tell.

If he were actually being followed he would become angry in a way no threatening letter or strange telephone call would ever cause. He watched the Cutlass carefully as it came with him on curve and rise, keeping its distance as the landscape passed. That the Cutlass had appropriated his exact speed seemed in itself a violation of his freedom, and he began to sense the first aura of a rage that he had felt only a few times in his life. He would not knowingly be followed; his freedom would not be abridged that way.

There was a time when he and Helen had been married only a few months and hadn't yet found out what they were as married people, defined by marriage, that declaration of permanence and emotional license. They hadn't even had much of an argument between them then. But one night they were driving back to their apartment and a pickup truck turned out of a side street directly in front of them, so he had to swerve to miss it and accelerate to pass it, no doubt looking reckless as he did so. The truck, which had some sort of municipal decal on its cab door, followed them, and pulled up beside them as he parked. Helen was frightened by his reaction, and he couldn't blame her. It was the physical following, the presumption of that power, that caused him to pull the man out of the cab of his truck onto his knees on the street and to scream at him; " Are you following me, you son of a bitch? Are you following me?"

"All right, all right," the man said, whatever chiding or lecture he'd had in mind forgotten, and Luke let him get back in his truck and drive away.

Helen was silent and thoughtful for the rest of the evening. The next morning she said, "I never saw you act like that before."

He tried to explain how the man had nearly caused an accident and then followed him to give *him* a lecture, and it was just bloody infuriating, but he was truly sorry he'd acted that way.

She was still pensive, no matter what he said. They moved care-

136

fully with each other, then, through touching to discussion, slowly in their different ways, using for each other what they did know, until the matter grew less important. But in truth he still felt that the crime deserved punishment, and he had never been sorry about what he'd done.

And there behind him was the blue Cutlass, bound to him by that driver's intention. That the Avenger might want to kill him caused caution and a certain amount of nervousness, yes, but it was the following itself that began the anger. He would not change his speed because that might give away his suspicions and put him at a disadvantage. The anger brought with it a coolness of thought on that simple level; it was the son of a bitch who followed him who was in the clearest danger.

But then the blue Cutlass fell back a little and peeled onto an off-ramp, like an airplane turning away. Slowly his anger subsided, leaving him free again. He remembered the anger as an abstraction only, as if its force had occurred in some other person whose emotions were not his at all.

When he left the interstate north of Concord, no one followed him onto the two lane highway. He thought briefly of stopping somewhere to eat, but that might cause him to arrive after dark, so he went on. When he had climbed the mountain road out of Cascom, its last part gravel, and passed through the long tunnel of spruce into the lighter air of the farm, the sun had just gone behind Cascom Mountain, though the sky seemed as bright as midday.

There was the sinking hulk of the house, the collapsed barn and the sheds bent down over whatever metal they had once sheltered, but the sprouting fields and trees were fresh, full of a light that seemed to issue from stem and leaf rather than the blue-white sky. In this weather there would be another three-quarters of an hour of light, so he must make his camp, knowing now exactly where, among all the acres of meadow and woods, he would sleep. He had been coming toward the farm for a long time, even toward the specific place in the lower pasture, across the brook—a level expanse of meadow grass beside a cairn of stones he would make into his fireplace.

137

He went to the rear of the station wagon and pulled out Johnny's nylon pack bag, which contained in its various zippered pockets all of Johnny's Camp Ontowah gear, each piece lovingly cleaned and polished at the end of last summer in anticipation of the next year's canoe trip on the Allagash (where Johnny would have been right now, on June's high water). He looked through the pack, found a small bottle of insect repellent and used it before he did anything else. From the cardboard box of canned goods and staples he'd taken from the kitchen cupboards he chose a can of baked beans, a package of Swedish hardtack, a bottle of instant coffee and a can of red salmon, and put them in Johnny's pack. He thought for a moment before he put the half-full bottle of bourbon in there too, saying out loud, "We shall see."

From the old toolbox he took a hatchet, and that seemed to be enough. Even though he'd be only a quarter of a mile from the car he didn't want to have to come back to it until tomorrow. He changed quickly into dungarees and boots, though not quickly enough to avoid one or two mosquitoes. Johnny's pack would contain everything else he needed. He lengthened its straps, put it on and descended through the overhanging brush of the old road toward the brook and the lower pasture. The valley's coolness came up over him like ghost water as he went down into its darkening green. The sigh of the brook grew louder until he could identify individual rapids along its curve through the small valley.

At the brook he filled the quart polyethylene water bottles from the side pockets of the pack, crossed on stones and then crossed the pasture around juniper and between aspen until he came to the cairn of stones and the still-open grass. Here it was far enough from the brook so that the rush of water would not cover the sounds of wind and the night flutters and calls of animals.

By full dark, the cool air passing and folding over him from the west where the great wooded mountain was a world-heavy presence, he had strung a nylon tarp over saplings to keep out the dew, spread a nylon groundcloth and the thin foam pad beneath Johnny's light summer sleeping bag, and had a small fire of deadwood going in the cairn between two stones that supported an aluminum billy full of water. He sat Indian fashion on the tarp, on

138

the soft sod of the meadow, in a small island of orange light that flickered and pulsed in the light wind. The can of beans, punctured a few times in the top by the clip blade point of Shem's knife, half floated in the water in the billy, warming fast enough while he sipped bourbon and cold brook water from Johnny's mess kit cup and smoked a cigarette. He felt good, now, a mountain himself because he was so alone, so far from any other of his kind in this pre-moon darkness. Miles of woods and nearly a thousand feet of altitude were between him and any other person.

He knew that later, in the damp of night, after sleep's sponging away of force and confidence, he would awake half-blind, his fire out, to a more vulnerable mood, more near nakedness and ancient terror. He would wake in the midst of that fear, he knew, but now the small fire crackled and gave light, and the valley, though wild and dark all around him, seemed at peace with his presence here. A great horned owl in the woods to the south gave his breathy hoots in series, to the rhythm of *hip-hip, hip-hip, hooray,* a sad-sounding but not really mournful cheer from that predatory night world.

The animals, except for those small fliers who wanted only a pinhead's worth of his blood, whose high voltaic whines he could ignore, would know very well that he was here and would not challenge him because they were sane, their business being survival; men were dangerous. But another part of his education told him he was vulnerable in the open, before a fire that not only made him visible but by its small cracklings made him unable to hear sounds within a certain range of decibels. The lessons of bivouac and infiltration (where was his pistol?) did not apply here except in his imagination. No mortar rounds, grenades or snipers' bullets would come from these woods. No Chinese bugles would signal a charge that would turn into tracers and burnt cordite.

But who was the Avenger? First, being carefully logical about it, if the Avenger was that strange sexless voice on the telephone, he was (or she was) cleverer than his notes would indicate, and in fact the word "sites " applying to the sights on a rifle, might have been deliberately misleading. If so, and if the Avenger had somehow followed him, his head might be in those sights right now.

139

This was ridiculous; his sudden, involuntary ducking of his head was ridiculous, a boggle. No one knew he was here, unless someone in Cascom happened to recognize his car. But the whole thing was boggling. If there were an authority to appeal to he would shout in an outraged voice, "What's happening here? I'm a man who's lost his family!"

That was not logical, just reasonable. If he could stop being outraged long enough to think, he might try to figure it out. Recently, on the radio, he'd heard this reasonable story: a man, driving his car out onto the street from his driveway, swerved to avoid a gray squirrel. His door, not properly closed, swung open and his left foot slid out of the car. Another car, also trying to avoid the squirrel, hit his open door, which closed, cleanly severing his left foot above the ankle. On the man's rear bumper was a sticker saying, "I Brake for Animals." No, that wasn't part of the news item, that fatuous, sanctimonious bumper sticker; you can find, or create, meaning in the misfortune of another, so do it in your own case, or in Marjorie Rutherford's case.

The water in the billy boiled with a hiss. It didn't really matter if the beans were warm or not, just so the pot backened on the fire and he was alone. In Johnny's pack he found a two-cell flashlight with weak but functioning batteries, and a GI thumb-style can opener. He also found a folding tin and mica candle lantern and a supply of short steroid candles, so he set the lantern up on its own rock, undid the spoon, fork and knife set, opened the beans and ate them with the spoon.

He was alone here; no needful or hurtful person had followed him. That was why he was here. This dark valley had its own power, this benevolent night being only a small respite in its seasons. The small chill between his shoulders was a reminder of crisp, pure, deadly cold to come.

Beans, hardtack, bourbon and the cold water of Zach Brook—there was a proper meal. The Civil War had been fought on such a diet, among the other wars, shoot-outs, rapes and fiascos that had occupied his ancestors. Add a little beef. Now he was the last of his line, though there were plenty of people named Carr, and he wasn't sure how such things were reckoned. His grandfather

140

was born on this land, and now it was his—though not quite so much at night. There were things he would not think about because he didn't have to think about them here; they didn't exist here. He took off his boots, blew out the candle lantern and got into the thin sleeping bag. The fire was quietly embering now. The cool earth was close beneath him, a bed miles wide.

He awoke knowing from his swept mind and odd fragments of dreams that he had slept for several hours. His coverings seemed frail though he was not cold. The world had two colors, pale silver and blue, and every blade of grass, stone, coverlet and line was as wet as if immersed in water. He had to get out of his dry bed and urinate, a function that could be put off, but not forever and at the price of no more sleep. He could read his watch by the three-quarter moon: two thirty-five.

The wet grass was cold, old stalks from the year before like little spikes against his tender feet. A mosquito got him on the ankle before he finished, a tiny imperative his other foot had to rub, the wet like cool oil against the feverish little itch. Back in the sleeping bag his feet would dry and the chills would leave his back, but as he ducked beneath the suspended tarp a rivulet of moon-cold water ran down his back, as if to remind him that in the wilderness there were hazards he would have to learn again.

Back in the dry warmth of the bag he removed his shirt and pushed it down toward his feet. Anything in the outside air would be soaked by morning. He found his cigarettes and matches down there in one of his boots, lit a cigarette and lay propped on his elbow watching the silver smoke drift out and away. The woods and field were drenched and silent, the brook a whisper from the east where the dark blue woods rose up the hill toward the ruined buildings of the farm. Even though those buildings were fallen and rotted, their people all dead, in that direction was a far civilization where people at least lived at one time. Down here was the beginning of wilderness, where the bear marked their trees and dug up anthills and rotten stumps for grubs. It had been that way even when he was a child and the farm was still a farm. So he felt now like a child who had through a dare made in daylight agreed to sleep out and away from the warmth of light and company, in the night world that was so different from the world in sunlight.

141

Though he knew he was not in any real danger, an ancient, bone-deep, deeper than bone, a marrow of the bone terror was still there, waiting, not to be quite thought away because it was primal, racial, before thought. How flickering and puny was his warmth here below the moon's distant and indifferent light. It was animal loneliness, not a desire for any named person—as if he were not just the last of his line, but the last of his race. He could put on his boots and get out of here, go back across the field and brook and up the dark hill to his car, that familiar room with its engine noise and lights. There was that cowardly choice to make.

He put out his cigarette in the dew and after its last hiss listened to the night. The owl had stopped its hooting or moved over a ridge. The woods dripped with dew. It would begin to turn toward dawn in an hour and a half or so, he thought, though he was out of touch with dawns. He would not go back to his car and to that world. He would tremble if he must, and listen with the fearful intensity of the hunted if he must. In the morning he would rise, wash and eat, then make plans for his permanent shelter here. As he imagined that shelter, it would be of stone and wood, built against this enlivening terror as well as against water, wind and cold. By winter he would be snug, solitary, cousin of the black bear and the yarded deer.

That thought had the power of a resolution. Made in spite of night fear, it seemed as binding as whatever resolution had caused Shem Carr to live out his life alone on this land. Why should he need other people with their wants he could never quite anticipate, like their wanting him to love them, or even their wanting to kill him?

It was the vision of a room, part log cabin, part massive stone, that he saw now, with its warmth and soft yellow light. He might be near that room or even within the yards of space it would surround. In the morning he would look and see, thinking of its orientation and elevations, drainage, footings and joinings. His rough construction skills would return in the service of that shelter. He could see the clean stone and wood surrounding a spare, sinewy man who would age and cure in his labors, hurting no one, surviving no one.

He slept again for a while, this time waking cold, with a cold light growing behind the wooded eastern hill. Chickadees and bluejays began their morning business, and a red squirrel sang in the dark spruce. Soon the granite of the mountain in the west turned a warm rose, the spruce on its slopes a paler green than they would be in full daylight. He watched as the shadowy dimness washed out from the valley and changed its nature; just to be able to see into its interior spaces changed it, and as the darkness passed, his loneliness passed. When the sun itself came above the trees its warmth slowly reversed his chill. Heat then came from outside his covers, toward him rather than from the energy of his own body, so that nature supported his comfort.

When the dew burned off his little pile of dead branches he rekindled the fire and boiled water for coffee, opened the can of red salmon and ate its cold delicate chunks and bones with hardtack and the coffee.

The new sun grew warm and then hot. Soon his clothes, tarps and pack were dry, as was the meadow hay and the trunks and leaves of the saplings. He packed up, leaving only the drowned ashes of his fire to show he'd been here. The pressed grass would rise back within a few days, like the beds of the deer.

If the cabin were here, if he had spent a night alone within its future walls, he would have meadow to the south, deep spruce to the north, and the brook down across the meadow to the east. The dense spruce would protect him from the north and northwest winds, and from the south would come the radiant heat of the low winter sun. The cabin would be the perfect shelter; he must study this. He had read many things about heat and cold and thermal efficiency in the last few years, as had everyone, he supposed, and he had some theories of his own. In his mind the cabin grew, changed, widened. Logs fit upon logs; stone (a bad insulator— think about that) fit into near-eternal mosaics, storing heat and letting it go. There were inflexible laws he must know and use, because he would be solitary in a February blizzard followed by weeks of below zero weather. He'd been in the woods when the sun seemed to have no heat in it at all, just cold light. In those times the deer didn't move because they would lose more energy

143

finding food than they could get from the food. The bear drowsed in their dens, living off their own bodies, and the partridge flew deep into the snow, away from the killing air, and waited. The deer could starve then, and the partridge might be caught by a quick melt and a freeze, imprisoned beneath the crust until they died. That was the dangerous season, life at its most precarious balance, and he yearned for his own readiness then. He would be here, alone in a clean and deadly world, knowing his comfort.

# 11.

His tasks now had no hurtful or pleasurable significance to anyone else; they were his alone—finite, immediate, once done, done. Memories came to him at will, many in Shem's voice: "A softwood log peels in spring. You can run a spud right down the length of it slicker'n goose grease."

He bought a chainsaw, a Homelite with a sixteen-inch bar at Follansbees' in Leah. He'd used one years ago, most recently helping a friend remove a tree blown down on a suburban lawn, but he read the directions carefully. So much power to cut was there in the light machine, its engine not much bigger than his two fists, his hand on the grip and trigger throttle causing it to roar and heave with torque. Its teeth didn't know what they cut.

At first he stayed at the Hi-Way Motel in Leah, ate breakfast at dawn at the Welkum Diner and drove to the farm. In the evenings he drew tentative plans and calculated the number of spruce logs he would need. He would cut at least half again as many as his vague dimensions called for—another message of Shem's from long ago: "If it's wood, get once and a half as much as you think you need. If it's stone, double that and add a third more. If it's

145

shit, don't worry, you'll have plenty." He picked out the straightest spruce, each a foot or more in diameter at the base, cut and limbed with the snarling saw, then peeled them using the chisel end of his car's lug wrench. The sap was thin, hardly sticky, and the bark that looked so rugged on the outside was skin-smooth and slippery beneath. The logs lay white and naked through the spruce groves, smelling fresh and sweet for a day or so until the watery sap dried. His hands blistered, cracked and hardened.

Phyllis and George Bateman would know he was in town, so after a few days he stopped in to see them.

"Been cuttin' wood, have you?" George said. "I see you got wood chips in your bootlaces. Spruce, by the looks of it."

Phyllis nailed him to a date for supper with the interesting new people she'd mentioned before. He could find no way to refuse. Her arthritis was better, so she could get around in the kitchen and do the cooking she wanted to do. "No saying how long it'll last," she said. "I just know you'll like these folks, Luke."

George was interested in the woodcutting, so Luke told him he was building a camp, which was almost not a lie, out of logs.

"Lots of tricks to a log house," George said. "You know how to do it?"

"I'm going to study up on it as soon as I get my logs peeled."

"Cut a half more than you think you'll need," George said. They went to the shed to Shem's wooden chest, and while Luke selected an ax, ax handle, wedges, a peavey head, a tape measure and folding rule, they talked about it. They sat, smoking, until it was supper time and Luke had to stay for supper.

George said he had an old twelve-by-twelve tent Luke could use, if it wasn't rotted out. It hadn't been used in ten years. So they went to the shed loft and found the big bundle of khaki canvas with its ropes wound around it, and five wooden poles.

"If it's rotted, burn it," George said. "Don't give it a thought. But it seems to me I dried it out good before I put it away, so it might do to keep the rain off. No sign of mice in it I can see."

They put the tent and poles in Luke's car, and then, that bundle of canvas suggesting that he would actually set up his camp in the wilderness, Luke went back to Shem's chest and opened it to the shelf containing the guns. He took out the .45 automatic, its holster, a cleaning kit and two boxes of the old ammunition. The .22 version was still there, so he took it in to George, who had gone back to the house.

"This is yours, you know. Did you try it?" he said.

"I tried it, and I been studying up on it. That ain't a Colt conversion unit, you know. Some hotshot gunsmith did that special and it's probably worth a fortune. It works like a charm."

"Well, whatever it's worth, it's yours."

"Don't know as I can accept it."

"I'll take it out in trade. I want you to teach me how to lay up stone."

"That's some camp you're going to build, anyway," George said, which was at least a partial acceptance of the gift.

They'd discussed location, foundations, roofing materials. Luke brought up solar orientation, which George wasn't much interested in. He liked double-hung windows and not very many of them.

After supper they sat at the table having coffee.

"I'll show you how to lay up stone," George said, "but it ain't something you can learn right off, you know. You got to look right into a stone to find its proper face, and some don't even have a face. You can turn 'em over a thousand times and you still won't find a face. Some of 'em have false faces that'll trick you if you don't know stones. As I say, it ain't something you learn right off." His gray skin and gray eyes seemed to have been coated with a fine oil.

Phyllis said, "When you get sick of your own cooking up there, you come for supper anytime. There's always plenty here."

"Thanks, Phyllis," Luke said. "Anyway, I'll remember next Saturday. Don't worry about that." He felt the vague dread again about new people.

That night at the motel he drew plans for a cabin, finding that it kept getting larger. Too many aesthetic ideas of space and design kept getting in his way. He should begin again with the smallest space he needed, the minimum number of cubic feet to heat and care for. But there was that baronial vision of cavernous beams and a tall stone fireplace column, the lone romantic figure by the

147

great fire while in the eaves the wind howled its white fury across the mountains. " . . . A crag of a wind-grieved Apennine . . . " Tennyson? Wordsworth? Beyond the general condescension he had been taught in school, why shouldn't that vision have its appeal?

He folded his sketchy designs and dropped them in the plastic wastebasket. The motel room was smooth, carpeted, polished at the factories that had made its parts. As soon as he had the tent up and a few more things he needed he would leave.

He was well-tired by physical work, with a sense of the shapes of his muscles. His upper arms had grown larger, hard to sleep on. His waist felt slimmer, his hips and thighs indicating to him their unity of nerve, tendon and bone. He took a shower and slid like a muscular eel into the cool sheets.

He would have thought of a woman, then, except for the woman who was dead, who had been the shape and color and presence of the woman he wanted. While Helen was alive he had occasionally lusted after other women, but now he was only curious about the impotence of his imagination. He brought Marjorie Rutherford into the room and had her sit down, there, on the bed beside him, her large healthy body wanting his, her handsome face curious and willing. Then Jane Jones—pretty, ambivalent, fierce; she would reach a long arm down over his belly to test her effect on him.

He had lost that urgency, but if the sense of its loss were lost, where was the loss? Friendliness remained, and care remained, but the center would not gather its force. The object of love could not be the object of lust. All was diffused, spirit, memory, grief-shrouded, gratitude-shrouded, flesh no longer.

In the morning after breakfast he went to the Leah Post Office and made out a card to have his mail forwarded from Wellesley. He knew he had decided not to write the piece for *Gentleman*, but he still felt responsible. No, he didn't know what he'd decided, so he should keep in touch with that world. His hardened hands seemed not made for writing. The Post Office ballpoint pen was fragile in his stained fingers, and his printing was crude.

He drove to Cascom, up the mountain road to the farm and

parked near the sunken house. His temporary camp, for conven-
ience, would be up here while he cleaned up the junk around the
house foundation, sheds and barn. Another day or so and he
would have all his logs cut and peeled. Then would come more
work and planning. He would have to clear the road down to the
brook and make a bridge in order to get his materials to the field.
He would need a machine to snake out the logs, carry sand, stone,
mortar, water, lumber and roofing. There would be nails, hardware, glass, stain, paint, and he was starting with so little. There
was also the foundation excavation—a backhoe would have to
make it down the hill and across the bridge, the unbuilt bridge.
Eventually would come the equipment to make him a well. And
he would want REA electricity for its power to preserve food and
run tools; at least four more poles would be needed past the one
at the farm. He would want auxillary power, too, for the winter
ice storms that would take trees down upon the main line up the
mountain.

There was so much to do, now that he'd begun to think more
about it. Just the traveling to supply and lumber companies would
take a lot of time. But he would do it all, beginning right now.
This was what his time was for, all that his time was for.

He had a great deal of money now and could buy any truck,
tractor or crawler he wanted. Death had profitted him and would
profit him even more, probably, when the final decisions on com-
pensation were made. It was only money, not anything but
money, and he could buy what he wanted with it. Reflex—the
reflex of the dutiful middle class—had made him take care of his
taxes, his books, his debits and credits and interest in April when
the season for that sort of thing had come, but then the large
figures had meant nothing but arithmetic, squared green numbers on a calculator. There was nothing he wanted then that
money could buy.

On the way through the leaved tunnel of the road to the brook
he heard a strange sound from down there, a cry that made him
stop, put down his saw, tools and gas and oil cans. It was high and
fluty, but not like the call of any bird or animal he knew. Without
quite thinking that the sound was human he turned, a chilly place

149

between his shoulders, went back to his car, got the .45 automatic and holster from under the seat, loaded the clip and chamber and put the weapon on his belt. This sudden turn toward caution, or even fear, angered him and made him walk quietly as he returned. He left his equipment and went carefully toward the sound, which came again in undulations that rose and were cut off as though breath ran out at their highest pitch.

Whatever it was seemed to be right at the brook, below the old bridge abutments, probably at the chute and pool. The water would mask his noises as he felt his way down through the hemlocks. The nearest the sound came to any animal cry was the nearly hysterical whining of porcupines as they argued with each other in a den, but this sound was more breathless and sporadic, not a dialogue.

As he slowly descended the hill, keeping trees between himself and the pool, the cry seemed that of a young child who had been hurt, but still he could not believe it human. Then, through the hemlocks' green fronds, he saw a white thing move, a small plane of white. There was a gleam of bright red, too, though this was stationary and separate from the moving white. He pressed slowly through the young hemlocks, the cry growing louder and more convincing, even though he could still hardly believe it; if it had stopped and nothing were there at the pool but an early turning maple branch and a reflection on the water of the gray-clouded sky, he would still be able to believe it had been the call of a bird of some kind—say a hawk's strangely lamenting complaint, and in its complete absence wonder if he had really heard it at all.

He moved closer, the cry so near and real something had to be there, just below him. He had been in the woods enough in his life to know that he might find nothing at all, the crier flown. He pressed himself forward between two small hemlocks whose branches intertwined, the needles soft against his face, until their hazy greenness grew thin, like disappearing fog, and there was the chute and the pool. The whiteness was a naked young woman standing thigh deep at the pool's edge, and the cries came from a black-haired child she now picked up and stood on a rock, a boy about four or five years old. The red he had seen was a packframe and bag on the opposite bank, next to the clothes they had removed. The boy was crying and sputtering; he had water in his nose, and she was trying to soothe him, kissing his chest as he waved his arms and howled, then sneezed and gasped for breath before howling again.

They were no more than ten yards below him. She stood straight as she held the boy steady on the rock, her small slim body shining, whiter in bands around her breasts and below, where she had worn a scant bathing suit in the sun. She was so familiar to him that at first, staring at her breasts and thighs, it didn't seem improper that he observe her nakedness; she had Helen's body when Helen was in her twenties, and Helen's dark blond hair. Her pose was one Helen had often assumed, holding a child out like that at arms' length, her own small body proud, slim and athletic.

He was so shocked by her perfection he was out of breath. He might have been prepared to see a woman and a child, but not these, and not here at his childhood pool. Helen and Johnny had been here with him, and Helen had stood just there one summer afternoon long ago.

She was talking to the child, crooning words to him; her face was not Helen's but seemed lively and sweet, her eyebrows darker than her hair, her lips thin, with a gleam of small teeth. Her waist was Helen's, the lateral rise of muscle below the small of her back Helen's, but one buttock, that approximation of roundness that was so complicated and precise it hurt him, was signed near the cleft with a brown mole the size of a penny.

He had never been jealous of a child with a woman, but now, perhaps because he didn't know her and might never know her, he at least understood the possibility of that feeling in a grown man. She kissed the child's forehead, then his nipples, then his navel, and then, the child responding with a sudden laugh to all these kisses, she knelt lower and kissed his small, cold-rigid penis as he laughed and turned, wanting back into the clear water.

Luke stood like a stone with eyes as they waded and swam in the water that was so clear its surface could be discerned only by optical distortions of their nakedness—an arm foreshortened, her hips wide, then flattened, then a submerged squiggle of flesh col-

151

or. As she surfaced and stood, gooseflesh erected her nipples. She held the boy in the heavy flow from the chute while he yelled with excitement and a little fear. The longer Luke watched the more he seemed to be taking something from the young woman he didn't deserve. His eyes almost cruelly searched out her colors and proportions. She noticed that the boy's lips were getting blue, though he didn't want to leave the water, and she picked him up under her arm and carried him to the bank. As she bent to her pack, Luke's probing eyes saw the down on her coccyx, her penny-sized mole like the mark of one of his fingers, her anus the warm color of tea and her water-pointed brush. They were not given for him to see and thus violate, because she didn't know he was there. But all the time he stared, keeping nothing from his eyes.

Kneeling beside the boy, she wiped him with her shirt, then dressed him, sat him on a stone and put on his stockings and shoes while he pulled her wet hair over her eyes. When he was dressed and impatient she squatted briefly to urinate, then splashed herself with a handful of water from the brook. She put on her wet cotton shirt, her jeans and stubby, professional looking hiking boots. Her red nylon pack and frame looked fairly heavy, with a rolled sleeping bag tied on top, but with good strength she swung it to her shoulders, worked her arms into its straps and settled it on her back. She looked around carefully to see that they hadn't left anything, and then she and the boy went on down the other side of the brook among the alders and were gone.

The water rushed down the stone chute and submerged into itself, the silvery bubbles wobbling to a surface that instantly received them into nothingness—air into air. The tawny pool was clear and empty, as he might have found it in spite of the flute-like cries, its deep turbulence hardly visible. He had seen the two delicate creatures at play here, a scene innocent and ephemeral except for his presence. At least he thought he had seen them, not a memory fleshed out by his mind. There was the mole, and the child's black hair, but imagination had the talent to convince itself by adding surprising and disarming details. Maybe he had imagined, if the mind was the last to know of its own instability, something of what had been lost. A version of his loss.

He went on down to the pool, crossed on the stones below it, and looked for a footprint in water on a stone, or a splash that wouldn't have been caused by the brook itself, but found none. She had dressed the boy here, sat him on that stone to put on his shoes, and squatted to urinate there. That last would be all the evidence of her existence an animal would need, and since he was an animal in some doubt he knelt, put his face down to the musky leaves and received with the most primitive of the senses the sea-briny proof of her.

Later, in the black and green spruce grove, the saw snarled as it ripped the heavy limbs from the spruce, exposing jagged light wood where the teeth raked. More of the pale logs lay drying in the openings they had once filled as thickly branched trees.

He could think while cutting spruce of the scene at the pool, which was clear, cool and separate from the hot blast of his saw, but the scene faded in the repetition of memory. He'd cut and stripped the long slabs of bark from so many logs today he was quite certain he had enough and more, but he would have to count them and do his figuring later. The imperatives of the hard, noisy physical work made that sort of calculation impossible until he could stop, calm down and let his ears clear of the rip of explosions.

He peeled the last three logs he had cut. Flayed, they were too slippery to move with his hands, but he cut an ash sapling and made a handle for the peavey, then lifted and rolled them up on their own piled branches to dry. He went through both of the spruce groves he had worked, counting logs. The cabin, he thought, would be about twenty by thirty feet, with fairly low eaves—although those dimensions were the largest he had considered. The logs, over their useful length, averaged about eight inches in diameter. Lengths varied, but his rough calculations, not taking door and window openings into consideration, indicated that he could build two such cabins with what he had. This seemed wasteful to him, and he promised himself he would be a great deal more precise with bought lumber and sash.

When he had finished counting the logs and measuring them with Shem's folding wooden rule, it was six o'clock and he was hungry, tired and happy—the feeling there in the finished task;

153

now the air and sun would work for him every clear day. This day it would soon rain, if he could read the sky over the mountain as he could as a boy. It was his luck that the rain had held off for so long, and he didn't want to leave the place of his work, where he had changed the woods. These trees would be his house, a miraculous change he would continue. But it would rain, so he gathered up his pistol and the rest of his equipment and lugged it all back up the hill to his car and the big tent, which loomed there like a surprise.

This would be his last night in the motel. In the morning he would buy what he needed to set up camp in the tent. Then he would begin clearing up the collapsed buildings here, salvage what he could, clear the old dug well and put up a base near the tent for the electric meter and have it connected. What he wanted left of the farm buildings was smooth earth, green meadow, where the granite foundation stones, ancient ruins here on the edge of the wilderness, could weather in the manner of Easter Island or Stonehenge. Then Shem's ghost would be free of oilcans, bottles, rusted iron and junk, and memories of the working farm could recede gravely, with dignity.

He would need a truck. Now it became more serious—as if he weren't serious before. A Ford F-100? A Chevy, a Dodge, a Jeep, an International? Stick shift, six-cylinder, four-wheel drive? Half-ton or three-quarter? When, not thinking why, had he studied these things? Though he might not know enough about anything, he knew more than he thought he did. It was as if, in all the projects, assignments, and in the various jobs he'd held in his life, he'd been picking out certain kinds of information and storing it away. Ballistics, for instance, or the names of trees, the qualities of wood, the nature of torque, leverage, tensility and mass. He had been many things—that is, he had done certain jobs for money and thus "been" a carpenter, a welder, a plumber, a sawyer and planer, a painter, a bulldozer operator, a truck driver, a mechanic, a janitor, a rifleman. He would study the tangible and useful, like an auger, a beam, a chainfall or a truck.

In bed in the motel, his bones and muscles said to him as they grew heavy and calm that they had labored and would rest.

154

He slept, then in the beginning of dawn he woke, full of the strange memories of sleep. His thick left arm, swollen taut from wielding the saw, was uncomfortable to sleep upon, and it was that which woke him, as if the strange hard arm belonged to someone else.

He'd had a dream about Helen, though she hadn't seemed to have been in the dream, just him alone in a canoe on a swift river with high smooth banks, the water green and folding in an insane silent run. A quarter of a mile ahead the river turned and descended like a chute, gathering speed, and he didn't know what rocks and rapids, or even waterfalls, were down and around that turn, just that there was no way for him to stop, no way at all, and fear took his breath. It was the silence and speed of the green water that was so ominous. In the dream he thought, as if he were speaking to Helen, How tough the body is, how hard to dismember or crush, yet life goes out of it so easily.

155

# 12.

Follansbees' store was an anachronism in Leah. It had escaped the great fire of 1958 when most of the business section of the town had burned, and stood alone. It was three stories high, clapboarded, white with green trim. A fixed beam with a pulley protruded from the gable in order to lower kegs of nails and other hardware from its attic storerooms. This vertical use of space, along with the store's carrying everything from fresh meat and groceries to plumbing supplies and oakum, was part of the anachronism; in the new shopping malls to the north of town all was horizontal, acres of floors of merchandise under uniform fluorescent light.

After a hundred and twenty years, Follansbees' was still owned and run by the Follansbees, a family that must have had some sort of genetic fix for storekeeping, which included knowing exactly where everything could be found and how it worked. There were Follansbees who knew all the trades and tackle, who knew meat, guns, masonry, glazing, pickling and roofing, baking and fishing, plumbing and sewing, soldering and painting.

From one of these enthusiasts, a young, balding Follansbee

Luke thought he remembered from six years ago as a thin apprentice with much hair, he bought the supplies on his list and also a fifty-round box of new .45 ACP cartridges. The young Follansbee helped him carry everything to his car, which was still full of the things he'd brought from Wellesley, and immediately supervised the rearranging and loading. "There you go," he said when all was properly stowed.

"Thanks," Luke said, and the competent young Follansbee nodded in the manner of his ancestors.

Luke stopped at the Post Office to find that his mail hadn't yet been forwarded, a small reprieve, then drove to Cascom and up the mountain to the farm, passing through the quiet spruce into the light again.

After pulling the small trees and brush from the tent floor he smoothed the dirt and grass down as much as possible and unloaded most of the things from the car. When the tent was reasonably settled he took the box of new ammunition, unloaded the old shells from the pistol's clip and put seven of the bright new ones into it against its spring, slid it up into the pistol handle until it locked, then pulled the slide back and let it go forward again. The pistol was now loaded. He let the hammer down on half-cock and placed the pistol in its holster.

From his briefcase he took a sheet of typing paper and drew a circle on it with a felt marking pen, then filled it in, a black dot about as large as a fifty-cent piece, and tacked the paper to a rotten barn board. He paced off twenty yards and turned, the pistol large in his hand, bigger than he remembered the gun to be, as though his hand, or his indifference to violence, had diminished since his war. The .45 had been called "a hand cannon," or "pocket artillery" often enough, and the myth—or perhaps it was the truth—about it was that its cartridge had been designed specifically to stop suicidally charging Huk tribesmen. The .45 ACP bullet, which was almost twice as heavy as a military rifle bullet, extinguished such passion. The gun itself was originally designed by John Moses Browning, that odd genius responsible for so many weapons. Luke had seen at least four of his inventions firing at the same time—this pistol, the Browning automatic rifle, the .30 cali-

157

ber light machine gun and the .50 caliber machine gun. And there was the 37 millimeter antiaircraft gun, the Browning and Remington semiautomatic shotguns—legions of animals and men had fallen before his barrels, cams, inertia sleeves, extractors and feeders.

The loaded pistol was in his hand, ready to blast the air apart with its contained explosions, the copper-jacketed lead bullets stabilized in flight by a counterclockwise twist. It would blast the silence of this quiet, misty day. The echo would come and come again from the western hill. But did he want to make such a statement to the valley? It was better to creep in, kill silently and be gone.

He must shoot the gun, and no one would hear, or if hearing know what the shot was or where it came from. No one was here to kill or be killed. This was his land and he could do anything he wanted here. He sat down, cocked the hammer and held the pistol in both hands, his elbows around his knees for stability. The black dot swayed, the square sights wavering in and out of alignment in a way he could not remember. He took a deep breath and let it half out, willing the sights steady as he pulled the pad of his right index finger toward him on the trigger. Always the first shot was anticipated with mild apprehension, but then the pistol jumped backward, the explosion not so much loud as a tremendous vacuum of sound, and a smaller black dot appeared a few inches from his bullseye. Now he remembered the kick, which was smooth and pleasant; the pistol had reloaded itself and was ready. Echoes reverberated across the valley until they died, and a bluejay flew screaming from a birch.

He fired six more times, until the valley seemed as used to the sound and its rolling as an orchestral hall. His bullets moved a little closer together, near enough together and to the bull so that he wouldn't bother to adjust the sights. He might never fire the pistol again, but he would have it somewhere nearby in its holster, just the clip loaded. He knew that much, but not exactly why. He hadn't come here to be in Indian territory. The enemy he wanted was the inevitable and beautiful turning of the spheres that turned the seasons, not creatures that had to be shot. There was the Avenger, who was so far purely literary, except perhaps for

158

the telephone call, though he had just about come to believe that some other Carr was involved there.

But there was the pistol, now on his belt in its large protective holster, and it spoke to him of a sort of partnership, indissoluble, as though a contract had come to be written which specified a certain nearness, a distance in reach, a multiple of the length of his arm but only such and such a multiple. Or time—three seconds from awareness of need to the bulky feel of steel and walnut; or two seconds, the feel also the weight of seven cartridges and the mild give and tick as the grip safety released under the pressure of the crotch of his hand.

Something moved exactly behind him, ten feet behind him, and he turned quickly, all of his senses shocked by a presence. It was a dog, its brown eyes now apprehensive at the quick defensive movement, but still and questioning. It was a black and tan beagle, or part beagle, looking straight at him with the ancient question always expressed by the whole body of a hound: Friend, or not?

"Friend," Luke said.

The white tip of the tail moved an inch, back an inch, and stopped. The eyes of this hound were unusually bright and deep.

"Friend or not, it doesn't matter, does it?" Luke said, but he squatted down, keeping his hands on his knees. The dog came forward without cringing or hesitation and smelled his hands, then wagged his tail a few times, calmly, to indicate friendship or the possibility of it. The dog was also interested in smelling the holster of the freshly fired pistol, and may have come to the shots. Luke scratched behind the long, soft ears. On the dog's collar was a tag, pop-riveted to the leather rather than hung from a link.

MY NAME IS
JAKE
I BELONG TO
LESTER WILSON
CASCOM, N.H.

"Hello, Jake," Luke said. At the sound of his name, the dog looked up at Luke's eyes again.

Lester Wilson seemed a familiar name, one Luke had heard

lately. George or Phyllis Bateman must have mentioned it in some context or other, but he couldn't remember.

Jake made a tour of the tent, car, collapsed buildings, left his scent on a corner of the house foundation, then came back to Luke, who was still unloading the car, barked his hound yowl once, as if to say good-bye, and ranged off into the brush to the south.

Jake may have been a roamer, like many beagles, but if Lester Wilson lived down in the village, the dog was at least seven miles from home. Maybe Lester Wilson was fishing a mountain brook and was not too far away. Certainly no hunting season was open. He'd have to ask George or Phyllis who Lester Wilson was.

George had talked about Luke's nearest neighbors in this upper valley. The two hunting camps on the road below belonged to Massachusetts people who came up weekends in deer season, seldom any other time of year. Three miles on, over the shoulder of the mountain, some "hippies," according to George, had built shacks and a cabin and periodically tried to be farmers, going away often to earn money enough to come back for a while and try to farm the inhospitable land again. Beyond the hippies was the extensive land and the old log lodge of the Cascom Mountain Club, a semipublic group of hikers and skiers based in Boston. The young woman and child at the brook, if he had actually seen them—the memory was so vivid yet out of place here it flickered in and out of actuality—might have come from there. But from what he had heard of the CMC people over the years, they maintained their own trails and stayed on them, rarely if ever bushwhacking.

Then he remembered who Lester Wilson was—the young part-time chief of police with the supercar and six-pack George spoke of during his right-to-bear-arms outburst. It seemed strange that he now remembered George's reference to Lester Wilson, as if such skill in remembering an odd name were exemplary in some way, a talent he hadn't known he had. And then he thought, looking over at the submerging kitchen corner of the farmhouse, that he should have come to see Shem once more before Shem died. The old man had always liked him, looked at him a little more

160

fiercely, grinned harder at him than at other people. "He learns pretty good," Shem had once told his father, and when his father told him what Shem had said, he was a little more afraid of Shem.

He thought he knew that Shem hadn't meant to frighten him. Maybe not anyone. He thought he knew it as a child, but was still frightened and fascinated. Whenever one of his own statements or jokes had caused that sort of tension in another, he had been surprised, because he had never meant to cause tension or fear. But it had happened. One never knew one's own power to threaten, and others hid their vulnerability. But Shem was dead and he was alone.

It took him some time to fit a shovel handle, to fit the peavey handle better than he had done it in haste at the spruce grove, and to cut some saplings for braces. Then he began to pry, brace and dig his way through the slanted and collapsed walls into what had been the kitchen.

Here all was damp and must, wood leached of its color and strength, slabs of ancient wallpaper, lath still embraced by grainy plaster, clapboards that had twisted and sprung as the studding buckled. He chopped into the large old two-by-fours. Some still had a little hardness and life in them, and some received his ax with the slow giving of cheese. Part of one wall, freed of its joinings, he pushed outward with a sapling and let it fall with a rotten softness to the grass. Half of the kitchen had been one story high, and the main part of the house, the second story that half-covered it, had collapsed to the north, so he soon began to see a recognizable though canted kitchen floor, with its brown wear-runs in the patterned linoleum. The old wood stove seemed intact, though rusted in its ungreasy places to a sand-textured primer red. The faint odor of the old kitchen was still there in its walls, or it might have been a memory of baking meat, sweet and brown, steam, acid, spice, bread, cider, all now set, cold and faint amid the potatoey, cellary fresh chill of rot.

He came upon the old kitchen table, protected somewhat by its ragged oilcloth, its varnished wooden chairs surprisingly intact, though damp and gray with mildew on their leather seats. There

161

was Shem's cot, mice in the shredded blankets, the pillow open to feathers soggy as fresh mortar. The floor there was doubtful; the rusted metal cot, its sodden mattress and bedclothes brown with stains that had been there long before the house fell in, would slide in the general list toward the cellar hole below.

Pots and pans, silverware, bowls, glasses, kitchen knives and utensils he collected, saving all of them, remembering all of them, even odd forks, a knife worn to a thin ribbon of steel, a spoon etched with a scene from Wichita, Kansas, an aluminum potato masher which squeezed a boiled potato out into white worms, a greasy spatula he remembered clean and shining in a drawer. All the old white plates were gone, and all of the cups, though there were many saucers stacked in a tilted cabinet. In the slate sink were an enameled cup, a blue-enameled pie plate, a cast iron frying pan and a large silver-plated spoon, all gleaned by the teeth of mice. Shem's Morris chair was salvageable, but not its cushions.

He would clear out the rotten wood and pile it to burn, then himself glean from the house whatever he could use. He could see now that it would take him days to find everything that he wanted to find here. Shem's spectacles, his pipes, a tomato can half-full of pipe ashes, the old television set now cracked in its wooden veneer, the tube's face a dead gray—these he would let fall to the cellar hole, but he must touch them first, and catalogue them in his mind. The hand-pump at the sink he would remove and set up at the dug well in the yard, using new plastic pipe. The other plumbing, including the electric pump that Shem hadn't used for years, might not be worth probing for, but he would see. When he was through, this ruin would no longer be a junkyard; it would be smooth as a grave.

He worked all day in the wreck of the house, until the rot and soddenness of what he remembered square and had thought eternal depressed him and made him yearn for the fresh logs and uncreated, unspoiled dimensions of his own cabin, which would grow clean and bright on new land.

It was eight o'clock, the sky still light but a darkness sliding into the shadows, when he stopped, cleaned up the kitchen table and chairs by rubbing off their mold with his hands, and took them to

162

his tent. With the oilcloth removed the table top was dark as mahogany, though made of pine. He set his new stove up on the table and opened a can of beef stew and a can of stewed tomatoes, then had a drink while the stove hissed blue flame.

Someday he was not going to feel the newness and relief of being alone. As the light died he sat in the doorway of the tent and watched the mountain grow black and flat against the sky, then the sky fade little by little as if by the blinks of his eyes, into the night that always came. A bat flew, fluttering silently and swiftly through its angular courses, then still flew when it could not be seen. The evening star fell toward the mountain and a cold haze grew in the southeast as the moon rose. The night was cold, for June, though it was usually several degrees colder up here than down in the town. All the people were down there, now, with the farms gone from the hills and the trees coming in. There was a place on the farm, a granite knob—or really Kinsman monzonite, he'd discovered in some research project or other—from which the lake and distant lights could be seen, miles down and away to the southeast. Driving to town didn't seem that far, but it was a long way for a creature on foot, or a creature sighting the distant lights of others of his kind. Tomorrow was Sunday and he couldn't get on with his dealings with those he must hire or buy from, so after working on the ruins he might walk the borders of the farm and look down the miles from that minor pinnacle.

His lamp made no noise, but called up the strobic hysteria of the moths until he temporarily draped the entrance of the tent with mosquito netting. Some found their way in still, to bash and burn themselves on the hot glass chimney, or to become, briefly, as incandescent as the white mantle.

After he had eaten he went to the old well, by flashlight, and lowered a bucket for the water to do his dishes. The rusted bucket had pinhole leaks in it, but with it he filled a pot with the water that was heavy but nearly invisible in the beam of his flashlight. From the stone-walled darkness of the well came this clear silver weight.

As he did the dishes he thought of twenty years ago, when he had inhabited a body quite similar to this one. He had been singular then, too. He was the editor and part-owner of a magazine that was a filler in the Saturday editions of over a hundred small city and suburban dailies which had no Sunday editions, and for the times and for his age he was comparatively rich. In a year or so he had saved twenty thousand dollars and planned to stay with the magazine, which was called *This Weekend*, for another year at the most. Because of his time in the army he hadn't yet graduated from college, so that summer he went back to the state university to take the two courses he needed in order to graduate. His partners thought it a crazy thing to do, and he hadn't known it then but one of them, a man he thought a friend, was planning to force him out—one reason being that summer school was supposed to have taken so much of his time he abrogated an agreement. Or perhaps he did suspect Ron Sevas, who was older—in his thirties—who in the war had been a major in the air force. Or at least said he had been a major; veterans said a lot of those things in those days, thinking such matters important.

When he finished the dishes he sat at the old table, his chair's legs slowly sinking into the turf. That was the summer he first saw Helen. He lit a cigarette and suddenly, though motionless, he was falling again. Grief was like the void beneath the last lost handhold. He thought how nearly anything could be rationalized, or ameliorated, or made the best of. But all the time he fell too fast to doubt that it was fatal. There was nothing to do but fall and never land. He could shoot himself; that would end the falling. He had never suspected that grief was like anxiety. He had lost what he didn't know how to lose.

He lay on his folding cot, on the thin quilted mattress, the opened sleeping bag over him and a rolled-up shirt for a pillow. The tent smelled of the clean, over-strong canvas fabrics of the army when he was young. He turned off the Aladdin lamp and watched its white light fade into the warmer tones of fire as it died, its last cone in his eyes in the darkness. Moonlight grew like frost on the mosquito netting at the tent's doorway.

So he was alone on the mountain. Surely he was not the first or the most intensely bereaved. He would remember Helen Benton, who had decided, once, firmly and completely, to be his wife—

164

that young woman whose accidental perfections struck him into the acceptance of permanence, literally at first sight, and whose other qualities, luckily and happily, were such that it all held. Pure luck, because in the beginning he would have settled—no, not settled, but gone through it all like a dreaming idiot—for any woman who moved as she did and looked like Helen. Some were lucky in their insanity, when for the first time out of all women in the known world of women the one appeared.

He was twenty-five when he first saw her, in 1957, and she was twenty-two, ages that now seemed immature to the point of incompetence, but then seemed old; he, at least, thought himself more than a little jaded by the abrasions of experience.

He saw Helen for the first time at a New Hampshire beach called Wallis Sands. She was with a fellow whose name he could not now recall, though he believed he remembered everything else about that July afternoon, as though each moment were then set in glass, so that for all the years he could reexamine it at leisure, nothing lost.

He was alone, not lonesome. His current girl was in New York. It seemed to him that in the last few years, after getting out of the army, he had had too many women and had spent too much time having too many women. It had come to be a cloying, even evil game, dishonest because only he could win. At least that was the way it had begun to seem to him then. Those girls, each lovely in her way, each flawed to him, each believing an implication he did not really make; he shuddered, as if he were a criminal being sentenced.

But that day in July, on the beach at Wallis Sands, as if to prove that lust was renewable, that the game was not rigged, he saw Helen walk from the minor surf in a yellow, one-piece bathing suit, pull off her white bathing cap and shake out her dark blond hair. He smelled kelp and the hot salt sand. She was his discovery. She walked to a blanket near his and knelt, the act of kneeling entirely too intimate toward the boy she was with, a mediocre specimen of mankind, a clod just not genetically endowed with the ability to see what was there. Pearls before swine. He thought then, as he watched her, that this woman would have to be a monster in order

165

to disenthrall him, and she never was and never did. No later anger, argument, guilt, pettishness, illogic or stupidity in all the years disenthralled him. Bravery, loyalty, responsibility, care, generosity—these qualities he could not have discerned there on the beach as he lost his judgment and caution. It was his luck.

He watched her. The boy she was with seemed pleasant, soft and bland, made out of inferior materials. Luke had never felt such an imperative; she couldn't get away from him. He had never realized that there were certain dimensions, colors, expressions, sounds that must have been imprinted upon him, or whose necessity to him were as deep as whatever his genetic makeup had come to be through all the generations that had made him. Before he knew her name he wanted to have children with this woman. She was the one. He could hear her voice but couldn't quite hear her sentences. He hadn't known before that a woman had to have certain precise physical characteristics—that she had to be small, but not too small, be narrow but not too narrow in the waist, have comparatively broad shoulders, be slim in her bones yet firm at thighs and upper arms. Strength and delicacy at once. He had never before believed the power of the purely visual; if he'd been asked before he saw her he would have said that such things were superficial, not that important at all. He was wrong; it was all in the way this female animal moved upon her given bones. She seemed so familiar to him he felt that he shouldn't have to introduce himself to her. She was his by the right of her perfection in his eyes. He was aware that the intensity of this reasoning amounted to a kind of dementia, and since he was a practical person, used to the avoidance of failure, he tried to be careful. He thought of following them when they left the beach, of all the ways he might plausibly approach them. She had a book and notebook with her, so he assumed she was a student. It seemed an extraordinary problem; he saw himself disappearing, sinking under too much thought, so he got up, went across the hot sand the few giving, sifting steps to their blanket and simply asked them their names. The boy's name was Chuck something—he remembered the first name now, at least—and hers was Helen Benton. Chuck was not pleased by his company, but was civilized about it. Luke

166

found this civility hard to understand; in all the years he would always be surprised when someone did not covet Helen as he did.

And so they lived happily ever after, except for all the superficial screams and accusations, sulks and the mutually petty interludes of an intense marriage. Of course that was a simplification, but after all the years, and after the particular, instantaneous form of her loss, she and his unfinished children were gone.

His analysis was an avoidance of the unthinkable. Worse things had happened to other survivors. His task of building his cabin, his tomb, was suspect. He detested self-pity.

Or suicide, he thought as he reached for a cigarette. He found the matches and lit a candle so he would be able to see the smoke as it left his lungs, then looked at the white tube of the cigarette. He had begun to smoke late, in the infantry, out of boredom and fear. It was stupid to have a minor pleasure which killed you.

Something moved at the door of the tent. The netting bulged in at the bottom and stretched into pressure lines toward the apex of the triangle. His hand went down beside the cot and came up with the pistol.

A low yet impatient yowl came from out there: *Are you going to let me in? Don't we have an understanding?* No, it was more complicated than that: *I've been waiting here to be let in; why don't you know I'm here, as I know you're there?*

Luke got up, removed the stick that weighted the folded end of the netting to the ground, and let the dog enter. There had been even more said: the dog had implied that he was a dog, man's natural companion, and of course had a right to shelter, no matter how short a time they'd known each other.

"Well, Jake," Luke said. "You're welcome."

Jake looked around the tent, his nose busy in the air, his tail indicating approval. He went to the paper bag that contained the empty tomato and stew cans, nosed it and asked if there were something of the sort for him.

"The question is whether I should feed you, or not," Luke said.

Jake thought he should, though in this area Jake would not be reliable. What a dog knew, he knew totally, and if a man looked and listened, he would understand. But the wants of Lester Wil-

167

son, a dog owner, were another matter. At least Jake was not over-weight. While Jake watched, knowing, Luke went through the canned goods he'd brought from Wellesley and found a can of Prudence beef hash, which he served cold in Shem's old blue-enameled pie plate. Jake found it acceptable, ate it in four or five gobbets and then made himself a nest in the grass beneath Luke's cot. Without further communication he curled up there, sighed and shut his eyes.

"Good night," Luke said.

One white paw moved, a minor adjustment. In the strange way that a dog was company, Jake was company. No small talk, just the primal considerations of food, warmth, proximity, sleep. And in return, if a dog were not stupid or psychically wounded, he con-tributed the skills of his ears and nose. No animal or man could approach undetected this night, which was a small though sur-prising relief. Luke was tired, and now he lay down, that other breathing intelligence his sentinel.

# 13.

He woke in a tent baking in the morning sun, its canvas oils almost suffocating, yet not desperately so because the heavy air, though excessive with the perfume of the fabric, seemed part of an erotic dream he couldn't quite remember. His penis was stiff, electrolytic, acid and base. It seemed an electrode powerful and not understood, precarious to touch. Its ridges and planes were sensitive, almost in pain, yet willing toward a general conception of woman that was hollow, watery, smooth at the center, the woman no one woman. If he thought of one particular woman all the complications, quirks, other needs, demands and schedules would overcome and dissipate the force he held gently between his palms. If he thought of Helen it was of the dead, and all was gone. She passed vaguely, monochromatic as a shadow, over the screen of his vision. Smooth thighs were open, welcoming him past the dark entrance to a needful center that was not darkness but another element in which part of him saw without eyes or light. A strange other entered there and discharged, in a rush of fluid. Too much pleasure and none given: gratitude, but to no one, and the faint aura of sinful excess, the precious slime drowning in the air on the skin of his fingers.

Now why, how, from where, had the need come back to jolt him, when he had never understood the need or its fulfillment? All his life he had experienced it in one form or another, from his earliest memories, such as the smooth young sides of Phyllis Follansbee so long before he knew and could do what made the pleasure culminate in this humid thoughtful limbo.

But it was over now, and he could get on with things. He thought of a shower, shaving, breakfast. Breakfast he could manage. Later, when he walked the borders of the land, he might take a bath at the brook pool. When his cabin was built he would have every small, snug luxury he wanted. He would take a shower while a blizzard buried the woods and howled at his flue.

Jake had left, having found a way around the netting. His round bed of pressed grass and the cleaned pie plate were there on the ground to prove his visit. If he came by again today Luke would have to believe he was lost and take him home.

After breakfast he worked on the house, proceding from the kitchen to places that had fallen in earlier, where the level of rot was more advanced. By noon he decided that he would lever up no more rotten walls, that whatever remained in the house would go down in its grave. When he hired someone to fix the road, the same loader could move all the rotten wood of house, sheds and barn into the cellar hole, then pile dirt on top. He would sow grass over it all and let it work—bluegrass, clover and rye among the plantain, hawkweed and dandelions that would seed themselves.

For lunch he had a can of cold beans and a Spam sandwich, left his dishes for later and began his tour of the vaguely remembered borders of the land. He found ghost pastures, vistas dimmed by leaves, stone walls going through dense woods, barbed wire grown deep into the trunks of trees. In the eighteen hundreds and into the nineteen hundreds all the hills below the mountain were clear pasture or cropland, all open to wind and airy long views, a different world. But there had been migrations, economic changes, wars and years of frost, and the trees that had waited on the ridges and in the swamps moved forward.

He found the northwest corner of the land, where a right angled turn of barbed wire ran through a great beech tree below the dark scars of blazes. On the trunk of the gray tree were the old dashed clawmarks of a bear.

He descended through hemlock and yellow birch, whose golden bark shone against the dark green of the hemlock. Down and to his left, if he could remember, was a place he had found as a child, a dark, wet, rocky place of several acres, where tall swamp maples grew seemingly out of stones and in the wet seasons water dark as rust. It had been a quiet, twilit other world, useless to the farm, where the maples were forced to grow tall without deep roots, so that when a gust caught one at the right angle it would lean, all of its height moved over to rest against its neighbor, its wide pedestal of roots tipped up so that he could see beneath, in that round place as wide as a room, space that had been in darkness as long as the tree was old. It had been still and foreign among the tall columns because no one ever went there. The wood was not worth the trouble of the boulders and water, so the trees grew, sometimes tilted by the wind, and died in their own time.

He found the place again. It seemed exactly the same as it had when he was half his height, so the trees had grown. He stepped over water, from rock to boulder to rock, as he entered its twilight. There a tree that must be seventy feet tall had recently been blown against another. Its roots still held damp earth in the grasp of the new filaments. Probably, if it were blown back, or tilted back upright, those rootlets would again grow down and outward to anchor the tree to the ground. A man with a block and tackle or a chainfall could pull it back upright. He wondered how many years would then pass before a freak gust might again tilt it over, or if it would die sometime hence and lose its sails, so the stump would never move again. A good place to hide something. A body, for instance, if one had to get rid of a body. Who would look beneath a living, fifty-year-old maple? That dense wood was ancient, permanent, slow-grown, its gnarled roots a mesh of inanimate muscle that would block such a thought before it ever occurred. That place would be as invisible as, unthought of as a parallel universe.

171

The roots would grow and proliferate in the absolute dark, surround and rend that nutriment, calcium and all.

Gruesome thoughts to have in this dark place, but why should he mind his thoughts? The land was his world to know in all of its bright and dismal, drained and undrained, fertile and barren places, and if the land jarred his thoughts in strange ways, let it.

The pistol, heavy on his hip, was a dark power worth having there.

He went back to the line, bushwacking among the living and dying trees that were always growing and falling, birth and death everywhere, always reminding. He crossed the brook a quarter of a mile above the pool and bridge, where the line took a jag to the right, following the brook west and up. Then he was lucky to notice old blazes on a hemlock that told him to turn southeast, though from here on his memory was doubtful at best. He climbed to the southeast, hoping that he was not following a false slope. He should have a compass, should have thought to take Johnny's, because the sun always turned confusingly. Here old apple trees, dead for years, had strangled reaching for light. As he climbed he entered spruce, some very old, and finally came to the bald knob of monzonite flecked with lozenges of white felspar. Down across valleys to the southeast was part of the blue lake, a thin crescent from here, and beyond the lake more hills, hills upon hills into the haze of distance. The town of Cascom was invisible in its summer leaves; from this hill on the side of Cascom Mountain, except for the long thin cut of a powerline miles away, the land might have been empty of all but trees.

He sat on a roll of the dry rock, its history of violent fire and glacial wear so ancient it was peaceful here where patches of gray-green lichens slowly worked. Below him was a hardwood forest and behind him the spruce advanced. He lit a cigarette and let his vision move out over the forest as if all of him were levitated on some sort of glider that moved dangerously away from its starting point and was supported only by the air, all that space between earth's trees and a low strata of gray cloud coming in from over the mountain to the west.

From behind him, on his trail, he heard a patter and breathing,

172

but this time knew at once that it was the dog. Before it saw him it came by its nose, casting for the effluvium, invisible and undetectable to a man, that was a dog's best evidence of all. When Jake came within a yard of him he stopped, almost as if surprised, and changed his senses over to vision, then touch as he placed his face against Luke's hands and knees, wagging his tail and expressing something near joy.

"Hello there, dog," Luke said. "You following me?"

Jake suddenly turned, flopped down on his side and delicately bit with his white teeth an itch high on his hind leg. That done, he got up and thrust his head beneath Luke's hand. Luke scratched behind his ears and relieved his collar of bunched hair. Jake was black, tan and mostly white beneath, by Luke's estimation four or five years old. There was a brightness in his eyes one didn't always find in a beagle; even in pleasure the eyes did not go simple, but still watched, expressing something more complicated than ecstasy.

Soon Jake signified that he had been touched enough, and went off to cast around for the scent of a rabbit, hunting with this man he had found in the woods, who should now recognize a dog's clearly superior talent in this matter.

But Luke was not here for that. He felt a need to tell Jake not to expend his energy on the hunt, then was amused by this. There were broad areas of understanding between a man and a dog, instantaneous ones, but to try to go beyond them was stupid. Jake would hunt, and he would continue to follow the borders of the land. Jake would come back if he wanted to, or go home if he wanted to and knew the way.

Luke followed old wire from the knob down and toward the east, then to the northeast, and finally came to the mountain road, the eastern border of the farm. He followed the dirt road for a half mile without a car passing, then turned west away from the road to follow the brook upstream, jumping from stone to stone where the alders were too thick along its banks. He left the brook where wire crossed it, and eventually came to the beech tree on the northwest corner, where he had started. By now it was late afternoon, so he headed back toward the brook pool across woodlot

173

and brushy pasture, past the site he had decided for his cabin, a vision of substantiality there and then not there.

The pool swirled invisibly over its amber floor. It would be cold, but at this moment, in the sweaty exuberance of his exercise, it invited him to enter. He thought of going back to his tent to get soap, towel and fresh clothes, but in his heated physicality decided to wash first and then go naked, except for boots on his tender feet, back up the hill. He took off his clothes and half dove into the shocking water, which after its cruel welcome was numbingly warm. He could take the cold. The sun was behind the low clouds that had slid in across the mountain and now covered what sky he could see through the trees, a gray unstriated ceiling over the land.

He scrubbed himself brittlely, squeaking his half-numb hands over his body in a way that seemed young, pleased by his hard abdomen and pectorals, buttocks, triceps—the terms of youth's pride in its parts. He seemed for this brisk moment recovered from the conception of himself as a bereft, middle-aged being who was only a widower, landowner, taxpayer—a merely civil entity, as vague physically as a statistic. Different, too, from the way he'd felt in New York, with all its constant frantic surges. He did not feel tender here. Here it would be the likes of Robin Flash who wouldn't quite understand, who would mistrust and misread the signs.

He came out of the water and stood where the young woman had stood naked, in that space, a space full of her ghost, and Helen's ghost. He shook himself and wiped the water from his hard flesh with his hands. He hadn't entered a woman for six months, and wondered if he ever would again. It had been in the morning, before he drove them in to Logan Airport. He woke with Helen's hand on him, both of them feeling him grow until he was so rigid he thought of the ball of a trailer hitch. She had to know and feel him grow hard for her, she said, because if she could cause all that involuntary engorgement, that steely purpose in him, it made her forget age and time. He didn't know the why of it; it had always happened. While he grew hard, she grew soft and slippery. That was the way it happened.

174

As he walked back up the hill, his clothes and pistol in a bundle under his arm, a mosquito or blackfly enjoying his shoulderblade, he thought of the words of his trade of words, that there were words he would never use no matter how close they came to the desired meanings. They might flicker through his mind, these summations, but they meant not quite what was real. Now that he was not writing anymore he might, without the small fearful flutter of care, or the fear of breaking his own euphonic or alliterative rules, make a list having no principle of organization whatsoever: anal, oral, nexus, ontology, gnosis, epistemology, phylogeny, positivism, relativism, existentialism, structuralism, methodology, phenomenology, protean, antinomy, quotidian, acculturation, hermeticism, telos, heuristic, aporias, voluntaristic, irredentist, Manichaean, Oedipal—God, what a pile of baggage he'd brought here to this wild land where he walked naked except for his boots.

Before he came into the open he saw that a pickup truck was parked next to his car, so he stopped to put on his dungarees, which was a pain because he had to take his boots off his sticky bare feet before he could put the dungarees on, then force his feet back into the boots. The effort, done for old reasons of tact, irritated him and seemed a waste of the time he had to live.

George and Phyllis Bateman sat in the truck. "Thought you'd be needing the tools in your chest pretty soon," George said. "My son Bill was by yesterday so he helped me load it on the truck. Strong as a damn ox."

Phyllis opened her door but didn't try to get out of the truck. "So the house is gone altogether," she said.

"Was a good house, once," George said. He came around to the back of the truck and he and Luke eased the chest off and onto the ground. "Get some three mil poly to cover it till you get your house done."

"I remember this place so well," Phyllis said. "I can just see the fields and the barn and the cows."

"The woods come back, " George said.

Luke thanked him for bringing the chest and they discussed who he should hire to fix the road and smooth over the ruins.

"Eph Buzzell, if you can get him started," George said.

175

"Eph Buzzell, Junior?"

"No, there ain't any Junior. I mean the original Eph Buzzell. He's only eighty now, still likes to play with his mechanical toys!" George shook his head in admiration for a man Luke remembered, a friend and contemporary of Shem's. "I bet he'd come up here just to see the place again. He's doing some work for the town but I think he's about done with that. Come down this evening and call him up on the telephone. He'll tell you right off if he'll do it. The old bastard's sharp as a tack. Talk your arm and leg off."

"I'll do that. Also I want to buy a pickup."

"New one? What kind?"

"I'm not sure. Chevy, Ford, Dodge, International—I don't know."

"I've had pretty good luck with Fords, but I suppose it's six of one and half a dozen of the other. Depend on what you want it for. Four-wheel drive? Half-ton, three-quarter?"

They discussed it. George was curious and excited by a man just up and buying a new truck, and Luke caught the excitement. A brand new truck, a shiny, powerful new truck. "Maybe I'll do it up brown, George," he said. "Get the deluxe of the deluxe, everything on it you can think of except air conditioning."

"God!" George said. "Power takeoffs, winch, CB, step bumper, trailer hitch and harness, Warn hubs, oil cooler, heavy duty electrical system and suspension—good Lord, Luke, cost you a mint!"

"And those monster oversize tires—they worth it?"

"Well, you got eight to ten thousand dollars to play with?"

"Sure, if I get my money's worth."

"God *damn,* I got to see this!"

"Come with me tomorrow, if you've got the time, and we'll hit every dealer in Leah and Northlee."

"Done!"

"Now, Luke," Phyllis said. "Don't get him too excited. He never did get over playing with trucks."

"I ain't going to have no heart attack, if that's what's worrying you," George said.

"'Course it worries me," she said, and George looked up at her,

176

both of them smiling until a shade passed over both of their faces like a wing of the Angel of Death, and then their clear regard of each other lasted a second more.

George and Phyllis left soon, Phyllis having asked Luke if he wanted to come for supper. He said he needed to do some more work, but that he'd come down later to call Eph Buzzell. And he would come Saturday at seven o'clock sharp; he hadn't forgotten or anything. As he said this he felt foolish—that he was doing Phyllis a favor to come to her house for supper and meet the people she wanted him to meet. Phyllis's instincts, archaic as they might be, were to get him involved with people, specifically with a woman. No man should live alone; we must conjugate, for the hills were cold and empty of cheery hearths and the happy ring of children's laughter, and so on. What a lovely world she had in mind, more than a century out of date.

This made him sad, the sadness coming over him with unexpected force. Blackflies, in the gray light, were eating him, so he put on fresh clothes and put all his dirty clothes in the car to take to the laundromat. He had no more work he wanted to do this evening. It was six o'clock, and it wouldn't be dark until eight or nine, but he was through for the day that had turned an iron gray beneath the single cloud mass that covered the whole sky. The mountain rose like a somber fist.

He washed the coffee cups and his breakfast dishes, then dragged Shem's chest into the tent. He wished for a door to lock when he had to go down the mountain. He was not hungry; the dull sky and motionless trees, the temperature which was neither warm nor cold, made the world comatose, memories of desire weak or false. Only the blackflies seemed desperate for continuance.

Then he heard the dog on a rabbit, far away, the sharp yelps homing in over the valley like pinpricks from that distant chase. The rabbit would be easing along, always knowing where the frantic dog cast for his scent, hopping ahead, loping, waiting, doubling back, making long circles to cross his own scent and try to confuse the dog, whose nearly hysterical enthusiasm he must understand as the desire for his flesh. That, animals must know.

177

But without a man in ambush with a gun, the dog could never mouth the rabbit. A snowshoe rabbit, or varying hare, never went to ground, just moved on. and sooner or later the dog would have to give it up.

The sharp sounds, made faint by distance, dimmed and grew as the circles changed. Luke poured himself a drink of bourbon, lit a cigarette and sat in a kitchen chair by the tent's doorway listening to the new dimension the far excitement gave to the rises and depressions of the land.

In this season he couldn't help the dog, though he felt responsible, his race having bred such instincts sharp through a thousand generations. Hares could take care of themselves.

The sound of the dog hunting was not a sad one. It was just that there was so much of our progress to forget, or ignore, in order to get back to what the body knew. And maybe it wasn't all bad that it was the bourbon, that ancient potion, that helped him out of his despair. It was Jake's voice, though, that turned the valley good again, saying motion, dimension, purpose that couldn't be faulted. Nothing against the hare, who was sacred. We carnivores don't hate our food, our prey, our true mentors. Jake's tail would be wagging, his face eager, no irritation or hatred in him as he crawled through blowdown, jumped, cast about, climbed and ran through brush and thorns.

After a long time the yelps ceased, and with them went the true knowledge that dog and hare had run. At seven-thirty Jake came trotting across the broken pasture toward the tent. He stopped when he saw the man there, to look and think, then came on more slowly until he was certain that they had met before. He came up to Luke and signified friendship, then slipped into the tent to check out the blue-enameled pie plate. It was empty, so he came back, no hard feelings, and lay down at Luke's feet, tongue out and dripping.

"Well, Jake, I guess I'd better take you home," Luke said. "Not that I mind your company." In acknowledgment of the voice, Jake's tail thumped the ground twice; he would rest now.

Luke tied the tent flaps shut and went to the car. With a quizzical attitude toward himself, he put the pistol beneath the floormat under the seat. "Come on, Jake," he said in an ordinary voice, and Jake immediately came over and jumped up into the car. "Move over," Luke said, and Jake did. As they drove out of the farm and down the mountain road, Jake laid his head and lolling tongue on the passenger side windowsill, sifting and utilizing the passing air.

Luke stopped at the Batemans' and asked where Lester Wilson lived, saying he'd be back as soon as he delivered the dog.

"On the River Road to Leah," George said. "There's a whole goddam village of Wilsons out there. Go about a mile past the old mill and when you see four or five trailers and seventeen junk cars, you're there. Lester's trailer's the pink and blue one with the falling down sheds and lean-tos along the backside of it."

Luke had told Jake to stay in the car, and he did. George came out to take a look at him. "Good-looking beagle hound, I must say, 'spite of the shit-for-brains owns him," George said.

"You know, George," Luke said. "I wouldn't want to have you mad at me."

George looked at him, then smiled. "Well, I try not to be too hard on a fella."

Luke remembered when the River Road was the main road to Leah, before the higher road had been graded and widened so that in places it looked like a superhighway. He drove along the winding dark asphalt beneath elms, most of them dead or dying. It was not quite dark when he came to the trailers and the junked, wide and long old cars and station wagons that looked as though they had been deposited over the landscape by a flood. Some were on their sides, chrome and streamlining askew, some were propped up, front or back or both, on cement blocks. He turned in at the pink and blue trailer and stopped between a V-8 engine on the oily dirt and a yellow Dodge with huge tires on its rear wheels that made it look a little hunchbacked. Jake looked around, recognized the place, but displayed no enthusiasm. When Luke got out he remained in the car.

Luke picked a place to knock beneath the louvered window on the narrow metal door. The sounds of television seemed to leak here and there from the body of the trailer. A roof on wooden studs had been set up over the whole trailer, he noticed now, the

179

bare studs driven into the ground so that they would rot out in a year or two. He knocked harder, and after a few moments the door opened partway upon the face of a young woman who was afraid of him.

"Is Lester Wilson here?" he asked. "I've got his dog."

Her red hair was piled up above her pale face in metallic curls, but the rest of her looked undone, unwashed. Her blue blouse was torn or worn out at the shoulder, and her short black skirt was wet across the belly at sink level. Her eyes moved to her right, to the main part of the trailer, then back to look vaguely at him again, a vagueness that made him think of a schoolchild who was too frightened to listen to a question.

"Is this Lester Wilson's place?" he asked.

A large young man appeared beside her, pushed her out of the way and came out the door, forcing Luke to take two steps backward. He stared at Luke without expression or with the intent to have no expression. It was the desire to intimidate, or the need to, and Luke recognized it with a sense of weariness. The man wanted to project, force, possess a presence. His eyes, however, flicked to the Massachusetts license plate on Luke's car—an error, since they should have seen that earlier, seen everything, known everything. Jake was not visible. This poor fellow was not equipped to be the man he wanted to be, and Luke knew that his own calmness in this silent confrontation meant danger, or at least bother; why make an enemy? But his attitude could not be disguised.

"I've brought your dog. Thought he might have been lost up on the mountain," Luke said.

After a calculated silence, Lester Wilson said flatly, "You brought my dog." This meant that Luke's statement was ridiculous, that he had "brought" a dog was a pretentious, meaningless and even embarrassed thing to say, a statement that could only have been made by someone who was frightened and thus dishonest, who needed his comeuppance.

But a front tooth was missing; Lester Wilson was in the country process of losing his teeth early, which meant at least that his dentures would fit better. He did have a pretty good ominous hunch

180

to his upper body, and the skin of his scalp shone between rows of short black bristles even here in the dying light.

"What you got to do with my dog," Lester said. It didn't sound like a question.

"He's been at my place on the mountain for a couple of days. I thought he might be lost," Luke said, trying to hide the weary patience in his voice. "He's in my car."

"Around here you don't mess with another man's dog," Lester said. "Get your ass in a sling."

Another of Lester's mistakes was that he didn't know who Luke was, though Luke had been in town long enough so that he should have known. When he found out he would be startled, and he would probably never forgive that.

"I thought I was doing you a favor," Luke said. "Pardon me." He went to the car, opened the door and told Jake to get out. "Come on, Jake," he said. Jake was pretending to be asleep on the front seat; this dog was indeed out of the ordinary. Jake half-opened his eyes, squirmed toward a more comfortable position, sighed and closed his eyes again. "Come on, Jake. Get out," Luke said. Reluctantly, almost with some truculence, Jake got out of the car. Lester grabbed him by the collar and without a word half threw him into a shed and shut the door, Jake giving one high yelp of surprise and pain.

"You don't have to tell me if he was lost, I guess," Luke said, getting into his car.

"Listen, Buster," Lester said. "What I do with my dog's none of your business, and I mean *none* a your business. You got that?"

In a way, Luke was amused by his own anger. He was tempted to say something unforgivable, something stupid, but he didn't need the trouble. To hell with it. He backed out of Lester Wilson's yard, careful not to hit an engineless pink 1967 Oldsmobile, and drove back to the Batemans'.

"You give him his dog?" George said, keeping a straight face.

"I don't know what he thought I was doing."

"Come on pretty strong, did he?"

"I guess he did."

181

"If we had a need for a chief of police around here, he wouldn't be it," George said. "His dad, now, Raymond—he was a good man, but that whole family went bad. House and barn burned in the '58 fires, Raymond died the following year, and everything went to hell over there. Pigs in shit."

"Well, I'm afraid I made an enemy," Luke said.

"Puh!" George said.

"I must say I didn't like the way he treated the dog."

"Dog's lucky he ain't his wife or his kids."

"But why make him a policeman at all?"

"He wanted it, is why. Took a course with the state police and barely qualified. I still think he used a little M-1 pencil on his scores, but that's neither here nor there."

"Has he shot anybody yet?"

George smiled grimly and shook his head. "Lester, he kind of thinks he's a real old Yankee type. You know, don't take shit from nobody. Trouble is, he don't know shit from Shinola in the first place."

"Well," Phyllis said, "old Eph Buzzell won't give you that kind of reception. You just call him up and tell him what you want done. He'll be through with his milking by now."

Phyllis found him Eph Buzzell's telephone number and then brought him a cup of coffee. She limped, and her stiff fingers curled in a dishlike fashion around the base of the coffee mug, but she didn't seem to be in pain, or at least didn't show it. "You're better now?" Luke said.

She seemed pleased by his asking, almost flattered. "Much better! Why, after riding up the mountain today—all that jouncing—I got right down out of that truck and walked right up the back steps like I used to!"

"You used to run up them steps," George said. "Never saw you walk up no steps." He turned to Luke. "She used to sort of get a jiggle to her and *trot* right up any steps she came to."

Phyllis laughed. "I hardly ever used to just plain walk, that's true."

Luke said, "I remember when I was a little kid you could run like a deer."

182

Phyllis was delighted. "They said I could run faster than a boy!"

"She could run faster'n me, but then I got short legs," George said.

"I could out-run you, George, that's true."

"Ayuh," George said with a grim look. "A few times you had to."

She put her hand on his arm. "Oh, I don't mean those times. We don't think about those times. So long ago."

"Amen," George said.

Between them a sad look passed; whatever it had been, it had never been resolved.

To change the subject they told him about Eph Buzzell, whom he remembered as a friend of Shem's who visited the farm sometimes to help with the haying, sap collecting or some other large task, but never as someone to be paid for that help. He'd been a talkative man Shem liked with a sort of wonder at all that language. Luke remembered wondering himself why Shem never put Eph down as a prattler, but just listened and chuckled with uncharacteristic tolerance.

The money to buy the heavy equipment Eph liked to play with, they told him, came from the Buzzell farm having been along the lake, where cottage lots were so expensive it was hard to believe. So whenever Eph wanted some money he just sold an acre or part of one, which didn't even have to have lake frontage these days, just so it had beach rights. Of course he'd done a lot of lumbering in the area, too, buying when land was cheap, stripping off the timber, then selling the land when it went up in price. He kept up the farm mainly out of habit, because he probably didn't break even with the livestock.

"That's the general opinion, anyways," Phyllis said, "but with an old fox like Eph you never know. He might be a millionaire and he might be broke. He'll talk about anything but money."

"Sometimes he don't seem to care about money at all," George said. "Hard to tell about Eph."

Luke called and a woman answered. "Just a minute," she said. "He's just coming in this moment. He's been out to the barn, has to take off his rubber boots."

Luke heard some clumping in the background. "It's the telephone," the woman said. "Who? Why, I never thought to ask."

"H'lo," Eph Buzzell said. "Standing here in my stocking feet, so speak up." The voice was high, smooth, and didn't have the gratings, seams, cracks and breaths of an old voice.

Luke told him who he was.

"Well, my," Eph said. "You was that little tad nephew Shem had. Running around under everybody's feet. Asking questions. What can I do for you?"

Luke told him.

"Well, now. There's gravel enough down across the brook. Probably all growed up in trees, though. How's the bridge?"

"It's gone altogether," Luke said.

"Well, Luke, you cut me four maple stringers, about eight inches to a foot through, and if they're anywhere near the road where I can grab onto 'em with the cherry picker, we'll put you in a bridge. I got some elm planks we can use on top of the stringers, then we can do the road and what all. You know where the old gravel pit was? As I recall, on the right sidehill beyond the lower pasture. You cut any trees might keep me out of there with the loader. Now, remember—cut them stringers—ash is all right too—on this side of the brook. That might appear pretty obvious, but maybe you ain't as smart as you used to be, having lived in Massachusetts so long. Let's see, now. Today's Sunday. I'm doing some grading and hauling for the town. Be done in a day or two. How about Friday?"

"That's great. Fine," Luke said. He still didn't believe it could be this easy.

"Friday. Unless something breaks, I'll be there. Most likely bring the loader up Thursday evening and leave it. All right, sir, now I can put on my slippers. Good-bye."

"Good-bye, and thanks," Luke said.

"Ain't done nothing yet. Good-bye."

Luke was thinking of the tall maples along the road, trying to remember which ones would do. Later he would replace the maple stringers with steel I beams when the wood grew doubtful as it aged.

184

"He says he'll do it Friday," he said to Phyllis and George.

"Unless something breaks down," George said, "you can count on it."

"That's what he said. 'Unless something breaks.'"

"You think of a man eighty years old," Phyllis said. "You think he's going to be the one to break, not his machinery."

"He's a spry old son of a bitch," George said. "Must have a back made out of spring steel. Sits on his D-5 Cat or his John Deere loader all day long. Funny thing, though; Eph don't like to drive a car or a truck on the road. Tillie does most of the road driving."

"Tillie?"

"She's the one answered the phone. Eph's housekeeper."

"And chauffeur," Phyllis said.

"And about everything else, too," George said. "I once asked him why he never married her—they been together now forty years—and he claimed she don't want to get married. Says he offered to marry her ten, eleven times."

"How old is she?"

"Tillie?" Phyllis said, thinking. "She must be in her sixties. I think she was about twenty when she went to live with Eph. There was a lot of scandal about it at the time."

George interrupted. "She come from Leah. Ran away from home. Her father and brothers come to take her back and Eph damn near killed the lot of 'em. Eph had a reputation as a kind of a sissy, 'cause he talked so much, so you can imagine their surprise!"

"There were three brothers," Phyllis said. "Cole was their name. I wonder what ever happened to that family."

"Died off or moved away," George said. "Been a long time."

"Eph never cared what anybody thought," Phyllis said.

"Never was much for listening anyway," George said. "You get him going and he'll tell you stories, you could write a book."

They were both proud of Eph, as though he were one of Cascom's natural resources.

Luke said he was serious about looking at trucks tomorrow, and he'd pick George up about nine if he still wanted to help him make a choice.

"You come for breakfast then," Phyllis said. "I suspect you could use a good breakfast."

Luke drove in to Leah on the high road. He'd forgotten to think about supper and decided to skip it, so he went to the Laundromat and did his laundry while he looked at a copy of *Gentleman,* which seemed a strange document to find in Leah in a Laundromat. The cover was a collage of the heads of people who were famous though they possessed no talent, each photographed head on a cartoon body—the implication being that they were all, except for the fact of publicity, created out of nothing. Here was *Gentleman* again living off what it pretended to despise. But he did feel a little guilty about his unwritten article, and remembered, as if it had been long ago, Mike Rizzo, Jimmo McLeod, Robin Flash, Marjorie Rutherford, Annie Gelb and Martin Troup, those fragile people threading their lives through the dangerous cliffs and cables, gasses and voltages of New York City.

On the way out of Leah he stopped at a small store and bought a six-pack of beer. He drank one as his headlights probed yellowly, the lines on the road gleaming past, trees thicker and more overhanging as he went through the village of Cascom and climbed the mountain. When the asphalt ended and the gravel made its loose tones he felt as if he were coming home, yet at the same time it would be dark there, totally dark except for any light he made himself. There were no stars or moon tonight. The trees stood motionless in the darkness, only seeming to bend as his headlights passed beneath them. A raccoon crossed the road ahead, giving a masked gleam of a look from the brush before it was gone.

He began to think he might see a human figure somewhere in the woods beside the road, if he looked carefully enough, knowing that if he did look carefully some stump or blowdown would suggest such a presence to him, but not clearly enough to make him stop to make sure, just enough to make him wonder, and that would not be good in the night.

The pistol, its clip loaded, was there beneath his feet.

He turned off down through the tunnel of spruce and came to the farm, where his tent waited in the dark.

That night he dreamed that he deliberately cut off his right

186

hand with a hacksaw, some important idea motivating him. When the hand was completely severed, above the wrist, he found himself holding it by some sort of hand on the same arm, which was impossible, so he chided himself, saying that was wrong and he'd have to change that, not do that anymore, because if he had only one hand left—his left hand—he couldn't hold his severed right hand in anything but that one. But there he was, holding it, now in his left hand, and cutting off pieces of its fleshier parts with a knife that must be held somehow by something or other on his right arm. The white bones stuck out of the wrist, the finger pads and palm meat brownish, as though cooked, and he sliced off the fleshy pieces and ate them. It was Shem's knife he used, and it was sharp. There wasn't much but skin and tendons on the back of the hand, but he sliced off a wide flake of it and ate it.

Then he wasn't really the person who had willfully cut off his own hand—the left hand, this time—because he was standing to the side and a doctor was telling that person in a disgusted voice that the bones in his forearm would have to be cut back and a pad of flesh made to cover the stump. Now the idea of having cut the hand off seemed a little shameful, its importance gone. The white bones, ringed with pale and in places dark red blood, protruded an inch or two from the withdrawn flesh of the forearm. The bones were cut squarely so that the marrow in radius and ulna formed clear red circles. He, however, was the one who had sliced off pieces of palm, finger pads and skin and eaten them.

Awake in the blackness of the night, he pondered his lack of distaste for that flesh. The dream should be more horrible to him than it was, and the sick feeling of loss and broken taboo was not so much from the dream as from his lack of concern or terror. Maybe there was nothing he wouldn't do now. Maybe he was a man who had only thought he was governed by instincts that were civilized, moral, rational, basically kind. Maybe that had all been delusion, but it was sad to feel a whole life's values, whether they had been honored or not, blink out.

So he had quarantined himself up here on the mountain. He would live alone because he was dangerous, and knew it; why else had he the cruelty to survive?

He lay awake until light came slowly to the doorway of his

187

tent—cool, damp light, his eyes' sustenance. Little by little through grayness it came until his tent pole was a hard structural line against it. It came into the tent and all around him, all over the fields, brush, trees, hills, the mountain, its lucid changes washing the dream away until there was only the white bone and pale blood, and it all seemed to have happened to someone else. The brown flesh that had entered his mouth to be ground by his teeth was more like rabbit, or venison, really, or just the meat others slaughter for us.

# 14.

He and George spent most of the day looking at trucks and at glossy brochures, that most thoughtfully seductive form of literature. Here were dashing, triumphant, shining trucks, their handsome drivers given a power that made them not mad but euphoric, alert and potent. No dirt and grease, short circuits, dents, sprung metal, rust, forgotten bolts or welds, bent chassis, misalignments, cracks, punctures—after a while he began to look more closely at the secondhand trucks around the peripheries of the lots, those veterans of truckdom wounded in clashes and campaigns one could only imagine. He didn't trust cosmetic perfection and disliked ornament, yet those trying to sell him thought he must be enamored and wanted to charge him for his folly.

The basic full-sized American half-ton pickup truck, he began to discern through the options and glitter, was one or two hundred dollars less than four thousand dollars—like one that stayed in his mind, a pearlish gray Dodge with a six-cylinder engine and the narrower but lighter and more symmetrical bed that went between rear fenders rather than a bed that contained the wheel wells.

"George," he said while they were between dealers, having coffee at the Welcum Diner, "if you could order your perfect, ideal bloody truck, what would it be?"

"If I was me, or if I was you?"

"Start with you."

"Well, first off, to be honest, I don't need no four-wheel drive. It might come in handy once, twice in the course of a year, but it ain't worth it to lug around an extra thousand pounds the other three hundred sixty-three days. Gas mileage, what it costs in the first place, which is over a thousand bucks extra, not to mention it gets you *in* places you need a helicopter to get back out of—no, you can have your four-wheel drive, far as I'm concerned. It's handy for plowing if you plow, but I got my doubts about plowing with a pickup—won't take the strain. Even a three-quarter ton. You want to get in and out of your camp in the snow, I'd pay the town (course if you lived there permanent they'd have to do it free on account of it's still a town road)—I'd pay the town to do it with the deuce-and-a-half or the grader, and I'd get me a tractor and snowblower to clean up or for emergencies when the town equipment broke down."

"You don't think I need four-wheel drive then?"

"For me, I get *irritated* when I think I paid too much for something I don't need. Gets me down. I get mean, start to hate my own property. Now, that ain't no good. I had a fancy lemon once. Shortened my goddam life. Not worth it."

"Maybe I'll just get a plain truck. What about a limited slip differential?"

"Had that once. Positraction, they called it. Throws you in the ditch. Any crown in the road, you're in the ditch. Forget it. Get yourself a good set of lugged tire chains."

"George, I have a feeling you're going to save me a lot of money."

"You can't hold that against a man," George said, pleased but trying not to show it too much. "That limited-slip rear end—what happens is, both wheels turn at the same time, so if you're on a slant in anything greazy, or on ice, you break free and commence to slide over sideways. It's fine if you're on a flat incline—it' ll take

190

you right out, but there ain't much that's level around here. Roads all crowned, plenty of waterbars."

George's lore, Luke suspected, was real. There were those who wanted to impress with their knowledge, and those who merely imparted it.

"My ideal truck," George said, "is one they don't make. A pretty *fair* truck is the one I got. I like it all right and I can live with it. If it don't blow up I'll keep it probably ten years, or till the salt eats it, whichever comes first."

"You remember that gray Dodge half-ton we looked at this morning?"

"Ayuh. Slant-six engine. Heard good things about that engine."

"I'm thinking about that one."

"Pretty stripped down, ain't it?"

"What do you think it needs?"

"Trailer hitch and wiring harness, set of tire chains, radio, broom to sweep out the bed and you're in business. It ain't the pussy wagon you was talking about yesterday, but if it ain't a lemon, knock on wood, it ought to do you."

Better, better, Luke thought: a plain truck, as plain as one could be these days, to carry real things like hardware, nails and lumber. They stopped back at Leah Dodge, where the smoothing process of mutual desire overcame all technicalities. They gave him an acceptable trade-in price for his car, and said they would get right on the trailer hitch, harness and radio. He could pick up the truck tomorrow afternoon and register it in Cascom, where Phyllis, as town clerk, would assess him his taxes and create him a resident.

Luke picked up his mail at the Post Office, jammed it in the dash compartment without looking at it, and drove them back to Cascom, where he let George off, thanking him again, and went back up the mountain thinking he had done much, though he hadn't really. The glints and flashes of light off chrome, the strange instant relationships one had with salesmen, the fatigue of many short journeys—all these convinced him that he could not get out his chainsaw and begin a new career this day.

He would own a truck he hadn't even bothered to try out; that was sad. Maybe there were no toys for him.

The clouds had thinned, then turned into small white fragments that looked as though they were buttered as they hit and missed the sun. He took his mail from the car, a thick rolled handful of it, and sat in front of the tent to look at it. As he shuffled out the catalogues and junk he came upon a familiar typeface on a stamped envelope, then without thinking went to the car, got the pistol, pulled back the slide to arm it, put on the thumb safety and fastened the webbed belt and holster to his waist. As part of the same reaction he went to the cooler and got himself a bottle of beer, though this did make him wonder, because alcohol would not enhance the alertness necessary for survival, or at least not the kind of survival suggested by the pistol.

He had known people who didn't drink because they felt the world constantly dangerous and needed all their wit and wariness about them. Ron Sevas, his old partner, was one of those. Or in Ron's case sobriety had been more an edge he used against other people who did let down their guard, whether through trust, affection, or booze.

He decided to open the other mail first; perhaps the other messages would be sane. That elite typeface on the unbidden white squareness of the envelope was an intrusion into his life that enraged him. If he were guilty because all of his people had died that was his own guilt, his own miserable property. For a moment he thought of shooting great holes in the envelope, muzzle blast shredding it into the ground. Of course he would have to open it before the other mail.

> Luke Carr:
> Soon we will meet you will die but not before you suffer what you did to here you scumbag. Do you want to know what I look like. Ha Ha! ! ! ?
>
> Mr. Death

"Here" was probably a typo for "her," but "scumbag" was the operative word. He hadn't heard it for many years, but it referred to a condom, and then to a woman. A bag for scum, or gism. "That old scumbag"—from the ancient "baggage." He could tell

192

certain things about the writer, he supposed, providing the writer's brain was not so chaotic that nothing signified. An old word—an older writer. But the word misused. The Avenger, Mr. Death, was either too stupid or too smart for such analysis. Probably too stupid. The letters were all too depressingly illiterate to have been faked, unless faked by someone who knew how not to overdo it. But maybe not. This was the fourth one. It was like an itch he couldn't scratch. He found himself humming, or growling, a low monotone that seemed out of control, so he put the note in his briefcase with the other three, finished the beer and shook himself before opening the the other mail.

Ham Jones sent a document for him to sign—they'd overlooked a water bill, a matter of thirty dollars, which Ham said he'd pay out of his commission. "Where the hell are you?" Ham asked.

Martin Troup wrote to ask the same question, but again reassured him that there would be no hard feelings if he didn't write the piece.

Robin Flash wrote that *Gentleman* had been bought by R.I.C., a conglomerate that owned companies that made everything from resistors to salt water taffy, and the rumor was that Martin Troup was soon to go. Robin's note was written with a wide black italic pen on heavily textured buff stationery. Amy and he were in bad shape, marriagewise, he said, and he was going to be in Boston to shoot a commercial, so if Luke would tell him where he was he'd buy him a cherry soda.

Luke wrote short answers to each of these, wondering what made him so casually reveal his hiding place. It was the compulsion to answer a question, he supposed. Helen, who had taught English at Moorham Community College for the last few years, had told him that he suffered from this even more than she did.

The Avenger might be one of her students. He hadn't thought of that. Some continuing-education student, older, half-literate, infatuated by his, or her, professor. He still wasn't sure if the Avenger was a man or a woman; it was the quality of mind he thought he knew too well, and that could reside in any body. Helen's marking books, some unreturned themes and other papers were in a cardboard box in storage at Joe the Mover's. It would be against probability to find the same typeface on one of those themes, but he might. What he really wanted was that the letters stop, just stop.

He would recognize the typewriter, though. The lower case *e* was slightly bent. The right hand serif of the capital *T* was shorter than the left one. He'd noticed that right away, in the first note, and in the others. One couldn't help noticing, cataloguing, solving the most stupid puzzles.

The first two of the Avenger's letters had been mailed in New York City, the last two in Wellesley. Strange.

Then he looked up to see something that was also strange. Coming along the road from the direction of the mountain was a short fat man in green lederhosen and vest, thick hiking boots, a green porkpie hat with a long red brush in the band, pushing a small bicycle wheel ahead of him. The wheel was connected to a shaft he held in his hand as he walked, his thick red knees rubbing together with each step. When he came even with Luke he stopped, carefully put the wheel on its side and said in a high, delighted voice, "Tickle your ass with a feather!"

Luke's expression was evidently confused, so the little fat man said in the same bright, clipped voice, "Particularly sweaty weather!" Then he took out a large red bandanna and wiped his face and the folds of his neck. "Freddie Hurlburt from the C.M.C.!" he said. "How do you do!"

Luke got up from his chair and said, "Luke Carr."

"Carr! Carr!" Freddie Hurlburt said, sounding like a startled crow. "Oh, yes, the Carr farm! This is the Carr farm! On the geodetic map, of course. Are you the Carr that goes with the farm?"

"Yes," Luke said. "A descendant, anyway."

"How interesting! I'm chairman of the Trails Committee this year, you know. Freddie Hurlburt—that's H–u–r–l–b–u–r–t. Tend to talk too fast sometimes."

"Hurlburt," Luke said. He looked carefully at Freddie Hurlburt's face, seeing no irony. What was strange about it was that in the face crowded by flesh were two large blue eyes, smooth, clear and expressionless. They seemed very young, the skin around them unwrinkled and unpressured, as though they were decora-

194

tive objects meant to be looked at rather than instruments to be used.

"I am now," Freddie said, bending with difficulty toward a little gauge on his wheel shaft, "seven miles from the lodge, having taken the Beaver Dam Cutoff, the George R. Phelan and finally, from Grand Forks Junction, this, which we call the Carr Trail, which hasn't been brushed out or much used for ten years and probably won't be for another ten. Your Trail Committee chairmen, or chairpersons, as they are supposedly called these days, haven't done their jobs, the result of syphilis in the ass of a pig."

"The result of what?" Luke said.

" 'Simply not wishing to get on the stick,' as my father used to say. This sort of corpulence runs in the family, you know, but it never stopped a Hurlburt! Some discussion of that at the last meeting at Beacon Street. Told them they knew my father and some of them my grandfather. 'Fat as toads, never stopped *them*,' I said. 'You want the trails walked and measured, you call on a Hurlburt!' " From a canvas map case he had slung over his shoulder he took a sheaf of maps, a sighting compass and a can of Johnson's Baby Powder. First he uncapped the powder and shook it liberally down into the front of his lederhosen, did a little shimmy to distribute it, then spread a map out on the ground. "Seven point one miles to the Carr House. House not in the best of repair."

"You'd better make it 'cellar hole,' " Luke said. "I'm filling it in."

"Commendable!" Freddie said, marking his map with a felt pen. He folded his map, took a sighting along the road with his compass and put his gear away. "You must come for dinner at the lodge. Is it Luke? I'm Freddie. You must be our guest. Simple fare, family style. Any Friday, Saturday or Sunday from now through October. Plenty of food, no need to call in advance, just drop in. Dinner at seven, come early and have a drink. New cook, I'm afraid, rather too fond of illicit ass to stir his hots, no end of shaping up necessary, but learning."

"Too fond of what?"

"Pasta, great steaming pots of it. Very heavy on the semolina. I don't mind, myself, but some complaints have been voiced. Actually not bad sauce. Well, now, sir, good day! I've another mile to go, I believe, to where we left the Jeep this morning. I wonder what happened to Louise, that tiresome woman."

"Louise?"

"Oh she'll be along, limping exaggeratedly, no doubt."

Freddie righted his bicycle wheel and went on, a fine snow of Johnson's Baby Powder sifting onto his black Peter Limmer boots. Luke watched him go. A strange little man, even from a club noted for its eccentrics, and disquieting with his little slips into doubletalk. The voice was certainly not that of the Permolator-Purfulator telephone call, and the device was different. Or was his own head scrambling syllables, hearing the taboo phrases when they hadn't actually been said? Never, even in what you consider your most lucid moments, he thought, trust any system. Things can be misunderstood, avoided, hysterically exaggerated. He hadn't been too sane since January, and he had failed, or was in the process of failing, to do an assignment he had agreed to do, which was out of character, or at least out of the ordinary.

Then, from the direction of the mountain, a woman appeared, trudging along slowly, her shoulders moving as though she waded through deep water. She didn't see Luke or the tent until she was a few yards away, and then she stopped, startled. Her black hair was wet, her dungarees patched with sweat, her yellow halter top wet through. She was in her thirties, he thought, and though she was terribly disgruntled and unhappy at the moment, which might obscure her general character, he saw in her a kind of rangy neurotic humor that had some appeal.

"Hello," he said. "Hot day."

"Hot!" she said. 'My God, I'm being broiled in Off! Have you seen a repulsive, fat little man pass by here?"

"That's a hard question to answer," Luke said.

"A fat little man, then,"

"Yes, a few minutes ago. You must be Louise."

"Did he say how far it was to the Jeep? "

"A mile."

"Oh, my God! A mile!" She slumped to the ground and sat Indian fashion, her head drooping toward her lap. "Have you got a cigarette?"

196

He brought her one and held a match for her. "Thank God," she said. "Nobody has any cigarettes anymore and if you smoke they look at you as if you're some kind of monster. Mine fell in a stupid brook back there somewhere." Then her eyes, which were an odd olive color, widened in fright. He was startled, and stepped back.

"A *gun!*" she said. "You're wearing a *gun!* My God, you've got a *gun!*"

"Well, yes," he said. "It seems I do have a gun. Don't let it frighten you." He'd been wearing it when Freddie Hurlburt was there, too. Maybe Freddie hadn't chosen to mention it, or hadn't noticed it hanging there beneath the tail of his shirt.

"Oh, my God, that's all I need!" she said. "A *gun!*"

He resisted asking her if she hadn't yet heard about the escaped grizzly bear that had eaten the hikers.

She got to her feet, her eyes on the big holster with the black handle sticking out of it. She was now not so much afraid as judgmental. "Why do you carry a gun?" she said in a voice that meant the verdict was in.

"Are you interested in why?" he asked.

"Obviously you want to shoot someone, kill, see the blood gush out."

"Why did you ask if the answer is so obvious?"

"You're not some redneck. By your vocabulary you're an educated man, so you must be sick."

"Maybe you're right," he said, feeling an improbable change in his attitude toward her. She stood with her hands on her hips, the cigarette rather bravely dangling from her lip, he thought. Her face had a gaunt, almost ravaged look. No, not ravaged, really, but hardened by experience, exercised by gravity. She must be in her late thirties, a tough, slim woman. Perhaps her sanctimony wasn't terminal. She was one of those people who seem to be the same color all over, the same tone—in her case a dark tan slightly lighter than the olive of her irises. Her hair was as glossy black as an Oriental's.

"So you're camping here," she said, "waiting for a poor little deer to come by so you can blast it dead with your big fat gun. Is that it?"

197

"No, it's not deer season," he said.

"That's right. The state tells you when you can murder them, doesn't it."

"Generally in November," he said.

"Sick, sick," she said, shaking her head in a way that was not a signal to him, but to some higher authority she was in communication with.

"I imagine my feeling about guns is more complicated than yours," he said, hearing his voice turn fakely calm and gentle. People who began arguments with strangers, unless severely provoked, always amazed him. What a pain in the ass, he thought; how often someone who looked interesting displayed a flaw of personality as lurid as an open wound.

"Guns are to *kill* with! What else are they for? If you carry one you want to kill something. What's so complicated about that?" she said rather shrilly. "So I suppose you're going to tell me that you only shoot at targets. Well, that's just practice for shooting animals and people and you know it!"

As she spoke he looked at her teeth, which were slightly colored by tobacco, at her pink gums and the lines at the corners of her mouth. He wondered about all the arguments of her life, and the anger her face must have expressed over so many issues. A history in the form of disagreement. He wondered if she ever cried, and what that emotion must have done to the skin around her eyes and mouth. Thank God she would soon be on her way.

She took a step, and winced. Her sneakers were old, and must have thin soles.

"Would you like me to give you a ride to your Jeep?" he asked, motioning toward his car.

"Oh!"

He watched the conflict between her exhaustion and the protection of her righteousness. She was tired and sore and didn't want to walk another mile.

"Who are you, anyway?" she asked, resenting her position.

"Luke Carr, at your service. This is my farm, such as it is." He waved his arm toward the wrecks of barn, sheds and house.

"I'm sorry," she said.

198

"About the farm?"

"No, it's just that I can't think of a reason for carrying a gun. I can't think of a situation, *any* situation, in which it would be better to have a gun."

"You know that doesn't make much sense to my atavistic mind."

"Have you ever shot anyone?" She shivered, and her voice, which had been a little jarring in its clangorous certainty, turned lower.

"Yes," he said.

"Oh, my God, I think you really have. In a war?"

"Yes."

"Ugh! How horrible! And yet you still want to carry that obscene thing? Did you *like* killing people?"

"No, I was scared to death. What I really wanted was to be somewhere else."

"So why do you wear it?"

"Maybe I'm still scared to death, Anyway, this gun belonged to my uncle, who died in that house last winter."

"I don't understand. I really don't understand. But why don't you get sarcastic and defensive, like all the rest?"

"The rest?"

"All you gun people."

"It's a temptation. Sanctimony doesn't bring out the best in anyone. I almost told you there was a grizzly bear loose around here."

"Sanctimony!"

"The word came to my mind."

She was about to say something, but shivered again, goose-flesh spreading evenly over her shoulders and arms as if a thousand pins were trying to push up through her dark skin. Her sweat was cooling her off too quickly now that the sun was in its late afternoon fall toward the mountain. In her damp black hair were a few silver strands. He went into the tent, stashing the pistol under his sleeping bag, and brought her out a large bathtowel. As he put it over her shoulders she seemed to turn smaller, her chill and the silence of her opinions shrinking her until he felt there was a place between his chest and right arm where her shoulders might fit, her salt sweat against his skin.

"I'll give you a ride. Come on," he said, and she followed him to the car.

"No gun, I see," she said as they drove out through the deep spruce. She took off the elastic that held her hair together at the back, and fluffed her hair with part of the white towel, the black glossy and thick now, softening her face and making her seem smaller still.

When they reached the road he said, "Which way?"

"I really don't know. We left the Jeep *some*where this morning and Adrienne drove us back to the lodge. Maybe Freddie left a sign."

They looked, and Freddie had. An arrow had been scratched in the dirt, pointing down the mountain.

"Is Freddie your husband?"

"God, no! Really. My husband was a case all right, but not quite as freaky as Freddie. Actually, Freddie is my cousin."

They came to a yellow Jeep with a white cab, where Freddie pondered his maps, which were spread out over the hood, Freddie standing on the front bumper so he could see them and make his notations.

"Ah, Louise!" he said. "Chivalry, chivalry! Maiden in distress and all that! Did you stalk him into bedding your poor little heat?"

Luke looked at her, but she didn't seem to have heard what he had heard. Maybe she didn't listen to Feddie, who was now folding his maps.

"He wouldn't drive back and pick me up," she said, "because it wouldn't cross Freddie's fat little mind." Freddie didn't listen to her, either. His maps back in his map case, he climbed up into the Jeep, seeming to need three or four more foot and handholds than anyone else would.

She turned and put the towel over Luke's shoulder before she climbed up into the Jeep. He rather liked the smell of the clean towel and the slight sweat together. "What's your last name?" he asked her.

"Sturgis," she said. "And thanks for the ride."

Freddie backed and turned until he got the Jeep facing the right way. Luke wondered why he hadn't driven into the farm

200

road if he were so well supplied with maps of the area. This place was the nearest wide spot on the main road, though. The Jeep bounced at Freddie's inexpert clutching and left a haze of dust which slowly slid off through the leaves to one side of the road.

Back at his tent, Luke put his face against the white towel. There had been that moment, unaffected by memory or loss, in which he'd felt the woman as woman, that faint but immediate proprietary urge. She was a nut, of course, and the name, Sturgis, bothered some wispy, possibly recent memory. Her husband, the "case," was in the past tense, whatever that meant. Divorce, probably; she had that life-peened look about her, and he could sympathize with the husband. In any case, she was gone.

As the sun was about to touch the side of the mountain a cool wave climbed up from the valley to surge invisibly over him. He put on a jacket and made himself a drink, then sat on a kitchen chair in front of the tent to watch the light diminish. Tomorrow he would get up soon after light and do all the cutting of trees and brush Eph Buzzell wanted done, which shouldn't take more than the morning. In the afternoon he would turn in the station wagon and take possession of a new and sweet-smelling truck, mail his letters, possibly get others. He didn't want letters.

A small tingle went down his legs from his crotch, a small charge of static electricity, as though his nerves were slightly overloaded. He had no woman. Several times, in dreams, he'd spoken with Helen, though in the dreams they both knew that she was dead—that strange slippage of logic that always happened in dreams. He couldn't now remember what they'd said to each other, but there she'd been, looking at him and saying things, though she was dead.

It seemed to him now, not dreaming, that it was all right for men to die, but women should not—illogic without dream. Words, words. He had come here to do, not to think of words.

He was hungry, but that urge seemed gross to him; what he really wanted was a chance to make everything all right with Helen, to have his children safe, in safe harbor, Helen's face like the sun.

He drank too much bourbon, his excuse the long waning of the light after the sun had gone. He wore the pistol. The two did not seem compatible. What he ought to do was shoot the next fucking son-of-a-bitch, male, female, human or animal, that came along this road. Or at least shoot in the air a few times and scare the piss out of them, warn them off.

Except for certain violent episodes in his life he had been too passive, it seemed to him now. Passively he'd interviewed and studied the wild or famous, the sorrowing or exulting members of his race, they living, he observing; they outrageous or pompous or whatever they wanted to be, he taking notes. Or as an editor, more passive still, dealing with writers, photographers, designers, printers and the ones who bought in order to profit more, all of them doing, making, risking, considering themselves more vital than he, and probably right. Passively he'd let people take advantage of him, let Ron Sevas take over the magazine long ago. Passively he'd let his family die, and taken himself to bed with his booze and not a peep out of him. He could write the article about the deaths we find so mildly thrilling but the whole thing seemed so obvious it bored him. Of course this and of course that. The assholes always wanted to read what they already thought they knew. By assholes, read the whole asshole race. And one more thing; we are not fit to have too much time to think. Our ambitions should always be simple. The best of these is to starve and want food, or to freeze and want heat.

Craving nothing, he despaired, drank bourbon and pointed his pistol at the shadows.

Somehow he must have gotten into his cot and gone to sleep, or whatever unconscious state it was. Morning light, or moonlight, found him awake. Moonlight; it was one in the morning by his watch. At the flashlight's beam and spot crossing the tent wall, Jake got up from his bed of grass, his night-green eyes searchlights themselves, and came to the head of the cot to lick with his warm dog's tongue the face and hands of his chosen. Decisions were indeed made by others.

# 15.

Eph Buzzell called him "Sonny" until he found that Luke could operate the great Mack dump truck. First, using the cherry picker on the logging truck, they set the maple logs into the dirt at the abutments, axed off a few uneven places and spiked on the elm planks, Eph's two-pound hammer whacking the spikes in with as much authority as Luke's four-pounder. The only thing that seemed to bother Eph at all was his knees when he had to kneel, or when he tried not to kneel; he didn't know which was worse, he said. He didn't talk much while they were working.

When the crude bridge was finished they took the logging truck back up to the farmyard and Luke had to ride on top of the cab of the dump truck with his chain saw, cutting off high limbs that might break the windshield or the running lights and bend the outside mirrors. The big red dump truck was new and unbattered and had cost around thirty thousand dollars, so Eph was a little more careful with it. Luke thought it an honor when Eph ran the rubber-tired loader at the gravel pit and let him drive the dump truck up and down the road, letting the gravel sift as he raised and lowered the dump bed. "Sonny" became "Sir " and then, finally, when the road was in good shape and they were figuring out where to dig the cabin's cellar hole, "Luke." George Bateman turned up about that time, too, so they all conferred.

Eph was a tall old man with a belly that hung out only in front, his belt and suspenders set high above his belly. From front or back, in profile, he looked like an inverted pyramid; only from the side did his hanging sack of guts show his age. He was bald to the top of his head, one saw when he shifted his white cotton painter's cap, and wispy white hair fell from there back down to his collar. His eyes were crinkles of cracked gray ice, bright and at first very cold.

George, as if in respect, became more silent and gruff around Eph. Tillie, who had waited in the cab of whatever truck hadn't been in use, came down to the lower pasture for the discussion about the cabin's cellar hole, though she said nothing. She was a tall, craggy woman in her sixties who wore a blue work shirt and bib overalls—a mark, Luke supposed, of her independence, or strangeness.

The loader's diesel engine idled patiently. With its loader bucket on one end and its backhoe curled like the ovipositor of a giant insect on the other, it seemed a huge yellow live thing, but calm and obedient enough. Eph could run its clutches and hydraulics while looking elsewhere, his large mottled hands moving surely from knob to knob across spaces he didn't bother to see.

"Luke," Eph said in his high, youthful voice, "where do you see this camp of yours?"

"Right about there," Luke said.

"Ayuh," Eph said. "That little rise there. Ayuh."

George looked stern and said nothing.

"What do you think, George?" Luke said.

"Colder down in the valley. Kind of a cold pocket down here, you know."

"I don't care about that. With your advice I'm going to build this place snug and dry."

"Kind of far from the road, though, ain't it?" George said.

"Well, I want that, too."

"Looks like the boy's made up his mind, George," Eph said,

laughing. Hearing the smooth laughter, Luke thought how close to death Eph must be. In their wrinkled green uniforms both he and George looked like veterans of some long-disbanded army, one that had a code of conduct he wasn't quite sure of. He wondered if either of them believed he had the knowledge, the skills and the industry to build what he said he wanted to build.

Tillie had brought cups and a large thermos of lemonade down with her so while the loader idled they drank and discussed drainage, cellar walls, footings, waterproofing, the necessity for a cellar in the first place, bulkheads, windows, vents, the insulating value of earth—sand, clay, loam, gravel, hardpan; here, where the brook had worked across the narrow valley since the last ice age, the subsoil would be largely gravel, with plenty of rocks and boulders.

Should he build forms and pour the foundation walls, use cement block, or stone?

"Not stone," George, the stonemason, said. "For your footings you want concrete or cement block." *Foot-ins*, George pronounced the word.

The lemonade was the taste of Luke's childhood. He wondered if he had ever liked it, or if it were a potion that had simply been there, like iodine, or calamine lotion. Now it was mixed with nostalgia, whether he wanted to remember or not. These people were of older generations in which his relatives had lived and died. Eph had referred to him as a "boy," and now he was an apprentice to their years. It was good, only good. It had been so long since he was a student. He would build well, partly to please them. They might not approve of some of his dimensions, or even materials, but he would work hard to make them approve of his joinings.

They cut saplings to sight upon, white blazes in the dark bark of pin cherries, and measured the hole Eph then dug with both ends of the loader. Large boulders, three or more feet in diameter, Eph pushed in among the spruce on the north side, where the years would gray them into the shadows.

This cabin would work. It wouldn't leak, cellar or roof or chimney. His house in Wellesley, planned by an architect and built by professionals, leaked chronically in all three places. An east wind, with rain, even a small buildup of ice at the chimney cricket, or a soaking rain of any kind, and the house wept in its joints and invisible channels, around the edges of flashing—maybe by osmosis, God knew. Both Ham Jones and the buyer, Clifford Ruppert, knew of it, but the leaks were small and seemed normal enough to them. They never had to him. A house should not leak. Wood and water did not mix and for once in his life he was not going to accept a compromise.

But how much were the complications of the material and technical, when it came to actually building, changing his desire for a wooden cabin and a warm fire? Plastic, asphalt, steel, mastic, silicone, copper, fiberglass (for the toilet, a system called a Clivus Multrum), triple-glazed glass, circuit breakers, pumps, resistance coils, solar collectors and emergency generators; were these part of his romantic vision of a solitary man in "a crag of a wind-grieved Apennine"? Yes. He knew how cold it could get, how the frost crept in and broke pipes and bottles, froze ink, turned oil to cement, canned goods into mush, split flashings and let in the rot. What we knew, we used. If he built an outer wall of stone, he would build it of two faces with four inches of styrene insulation in the middle, the faces held together at intervals by hidden steel bolts. If he wanted for some reason to leave the cabin for more than a week or so in the middle of the winter, he would turn a few valves, empty two or three traps, store his perishables in a specially insulated basement room that utilized from below the unfreezing constant heat of the earth itself. This cabin was where he would live, and maybe, if this joy continued, where he might even work. He wanted right now to be sweating, smelling clean wood as he shaped the skeleton of his house, wired into it its arteries. The winter sun would enter a great southern window to heat an internal wall of stone that would also contain chimney flues, so the wall would be heated from within and from without, forming a reservoir of warmth. At night, or when the sun was not visible, insulated internal shutters would close the window off.

Eph let the loader idle and climbed down. "That ought to do it," he said. "Looks like a hell of a mess, but you can't make gravel stand on end." The cellar hole looked a bit like a bomb crater, but

206

it was deep enough and wide enough. A drilling rig could drive right in on the south side and make his well.

"You get Marple to come in, set the forms and pour you your footings," George said. "No sense trying to do it by hand, less you want to."

"You think the bridge is strong enough for a cement truck?" Luke asked.

"Shuh!" Eph said. "If it worries him you can cut an upright for the middle of it, set it in the brook. After two or three years, I'd begin to wonder myself, but right now, hell, we had five yards of gravel on the Mack and it didn't hardly budge, did it?"

Eph drove the loader back up the hill, its engine roaring and its appendages nodding violently on the uneven fresh gravel. Tillie and Luke rode with George. The gravel was loose, but it would settle down and harden as it found itself. George suggested that he'd need some waterbars here and there to keep the freshets from washing straight down the road and taking the gravel with it.

At the farm, Eph had already begun to push the fallen house into the cellar hole, making a slanted pile like cards fallen over. Finally he stopped, moved the loader away from the pile and turned the engine off, saying he'd had enough for the day and he'd come back in the morning. In the meantime he suggested that Luke throw a few old tires underneath the pile and burn up what was there, so there'd be more room for what was left, including the sheds and junk and parts of the collapsed barn. "You won't need no permit. The lookout's left the mountain, gone down to his cabin to make his supper. Besides, it's going to rain. Light her up. Throw some kerosene on some of them old tires and let burn what'll burn. If it worries you, I'll call up the Fire Warden and tell him what you're up to. Fred Wilson, you know him? He'll bitch about a permit but it won't do him much good."

Luke offered them something to drink. Tillie had a small juice glass of straight Canadian whiskey, and Eph and George each took a beer. They watched him roll four ancient tires from the sheds and shove them into the interstices of the pile. It would burn, and it would frighten him a little, that niggling bit about the permit, and the name, Wilson—a relative of Lester?—and the general old fear of forest fires everyone had been brainwashed into by Smokey the Bear. But the hell with it, he decided nervously, let her burn. He tucked some old, fairly dry newspapers into the tires, poured kerosene on them and lit an edge of the paper. Thick orange flame grew smoothly.

They watched as the flame grew silently at first; then, as the tires heated and curled, it screeched like kittens below the black smoke that raced straight up. It was soon a roar and a heat that made them back up toward the tent. The fire seemed to have no limits to its energy, an accelerating explosion that fed itself and might start the whole town to burning—a terror. Luke thought of the small paper match that had been the seed of this violence, and how he had lit that match. Black smoke and twisting orange flame shot up a hundred feet, then turned to roll to the east in whorls of dense black. It was as if he were responsible, suddenly and disastrously, for this holocaust everyone in the state of New Hampshire must be seeing with horror and disapproval.

He got himself a beer, his hands actually trembling with an apprehension he knew was unnecessary, because after a time the fire would reach its highest intensity and then it could do no more. And soon it did, though it still screamed and billowed and made the air violent and soiled. But he could see that it no longer grew, and would not destroy the world after all.

Eph and George sat on kitchen chairs, sipping their beer and watching. Tillie stood next to Luke, tall and bony, her shoulder bones apparent through the clean blue of her workshirt.

"Now it's lost its anger," she said, "and it will grumble."

It will grumble, he thought. She said it that way: it will grumble.

Tillie said, "Is that your dog? That hound?"

He looked back where she was looking, but his eyes were somehow seared by the fire and for a while he couldn't seem to focus on brush, grass or shadow. "There," she said.

The dog was near the road, unmoving, wondering at these people and the fire, trying to decide whether he should come forward and be recognized, or disappear. When Jake saw that Luke was looking straight at him, the white tip of his tail moved in a small circle, once; in the eyes, in the set of the long ears, in the position of the leading foreleg—the one that would take the first step forward if forward was the way to go—in the set of the body and in the angle of the body to the direction of inquiry, Luke could not help reading the dog's thoughts exactly. "Jake," he said above the fire's grumbling and cracking, and Jake came up to him and nosed his leg, though still a little worried about the others, Luke read in the angle of Jake's tail to his spine. "It's okay, Jake," Luke said. "Though, man, I don't need the complications."

"That Lester Wilson's beagle hound?" George said.

"I'm afraid so."

"I guess he took a shine to you," Tillie said. "They do that."

"He come around often?" George said.

"He came back the night before last."

"You feeding him?"

"Well," Luke said, "I figure that's between me and Jake."

"And Lester Wilson," George said. "That shithead. Pardon me, Tillie."

Tillie smiled and said to Luke, "Why don't you buy him from Lester?"

"Easier said than done," George said.

Eph didn't seem to be listening to all this. "We'll take the Mack, leave everything else here tonight. You ready, Tillie? Got to help Mickey with the milking." He looked at the sky over the mountain. "Rain soon. If it's raining tomorrow we won't be back. If it's done raining, we'll be back to finish up."

When they'd gone Luke gave Jake a can of Alpo in the old blue-enameled pie plate. Lester Wilson could do what he wanted; it was up to him this time. There seemed to be some kind of flaw in this logic, but he didn't want to think about it. He had studying to do. He got out *Architectural Graphic Standards*, a quarto volume that contained all sorts of technical information about building.

For supper he had ham and eggs and a fried tomato, did his dishes and lit the Aladdin lamp when dark clouds came over the mountain ahead of the rain. That evening, with the rain tapping and tightening the canvas of the tent, Jake curled and breathing at his feet, he studied what his heart desired.

209

Next morning the rain had stopped. The cellar hole still smouldered and the house had sifted down into it. The old wood-oil range stood shoulder high in gray ash. He'd thought briefly of salvaging it, but it wasn't the stove he wanted in his cabin and life was too short to start a salvage operation. Bury it all.

Eph and Tillie arrived at nine o'clock in an old Buick that must have scraped a lot on the road in. Before Eph could start the gasoline starter motor on the loader it began to rain again, so Luke made a pot of coffee and they sat in the tent around the old kitchen table, waiting to see if it would stop. About nine-thirty Jake, who had been gone since daylight, came in sopping wet and asked Luke to do something about it. Luke gave him the same towel he'd given to Louise Sturgis and Jake spread it out, more or less, on the ground and rolled himself fairly dry on it.

"You knowed that dog long?" Eph asked.

"For a week or so. He just turns up here," Luke said.

"I was wondering. I'll tell you a story about your uncle, Shem Carr, and me when we was about your age. Of course Tillie's heard it before, and she most likely knows it better'n I do myself. She'll correct me if I disremember, exaggerate or tell a lie; the next bar I go before, being as I'm an old atheist, as Tillie can tell you, though she disapproves, is what I conceive as The Court of Worms, so maybe it don't matter if I do lie. But while we're waiting for the rain to stop, and drinking your good coffee, I'll tell you some ancient history.

"This was the year nineteen thirty-six, the year before you come to live with me, Tillie, bringing the precious gift of yourself to my life, for I was a worthless, brawling, drunken whoremaster, though I worked hard, you got to grant that.

"Now, Luke, you want to be careful what you say about the dead, so I'll stick to the truth. Your uncle, Shem Carr, was one heller when he got in a mood. They used to say that was how he killed all them Huns in the war—he just got in a mood. And when he got that black look to him you never knew what was making him go. I suspect it was a kind of terrible honor and justice the rest of us only think about sometimes, maybe in our dreams, and forget in our regular lives 'cause it's easier to trim and hedge and give a cynical shrug, so to speak, or scream and roar and hit your fist on a wall and get rid of your poor rage that way. Men, in their wisdom, make laws for all men to follow, and the law is like a weight on most men, but not on all men. 'A law unto himself'— you heard the words—was Shem Carr when something got to him deep enough.

"Now, if Shem Carr had anything like a best friend, I was that friend. As a child I was mortally afflicted with a tongue that never would be still, so I learned to fight early on in my life, but I'd always rather talk than fight, so I never meant to hurt, just make them quiet so they could listen, cause for me that was the proper way of things—me talking and the others listening to what my fancy spun out on the end of my cursed and blabbing tongue. I'd feel these dark and wonderful shapes coming to me in my head, and they was the shapes of words and stories that was sweeter to me than meat and drink, peace and dignity.

"Shem kind of liked to hear me talk, and he had no need, like some of the others, to prove me an ass. He never said much himself, or if he did it was straight to the point, leaving out all the sounds and shapes that was more interesting to my ears than how many nails in a keg.

"As I say, the year was nineteen hundred and thirty-six. Shem was born in eighteen ninety-four, so that'd make him a young man of forty-two or so. I was three years younger, hadn't been to the war like Shem."

Eph poured himself some coffee and spooned in some of the white powder that did Luke for cream, giving the bottle a wry look as he screwed on the cap. Tillie sat straight and quiet in her chair, as though she didn't want Eph to know how carefully she was listening. Eph paused to sip his coffee, and Luke thought: 1936. The first thing you did with a year in your own lifetime was to set yourself in it. He was alive then, four years old. He may have had memories of that year, but he couldn't be sure. Shem and Carrie were running the farm. Samuel was fifteen. His own father was twenty-seven, his mother twenty-five. It was the Depression, the source of myth and admonition that had instructed his childhood, though he could never remember it as they'd told him it was.

"That was during the Great Depression," Eph said, "though we

211

never noticed it much around here. We had plenty to eat 'cause we grew and fed up our critters, we had our gardens like always, we slaughtered and pickled and preserved, and there wa'n't no mortgages like out West, or few of them, and we never did have much cash money laying around. Drank hard cider, burned wood, sweetened our gruel with maple or birch syrup. Hell, we hardly knew there was a depression on. You had to go to the city to find out what all the commotion was about—though I believe the state went for Roosevelt that year. I was always a Democrat and a Freethinker myself. Wait till the next depression, though. All the farms are gone and you can't eat wood. I won't be around to see it, maybe, so it's no skin off the back of my neck, so to speak, but it surely is a pity folks these days is so Allmighty dumb.

"Anyway, the dog there minds me of a beagle hound Shem once owned, name of Heidi, smartest little bitch you ever saw— for a beagle, that is. Nose on her you could hardly believe, she never run a back trail, never stopped to dig—and we had all kinds of coney rabbits in them days, they'd go to ground, or in a stone wall, and most of your beagles'd just dig and wail. Not Heidi, she'd pick herself out a jackrabbit and stay on it till you got it. Only dog Shem ever had he'd let in the house. He thought a lot of that dog. Pretty little thing, too, all satin black along her back, like that one there, then a tan like buckskin and pure white on her chest and belly. She had a kind of high, yippity voice, was the only fault she had, that never carried around corners too well, it seemed like.

"One time Heidi, she was about ten years old, a little past her prime but smart—a professional, Shem called her more than once—so smart you kind of forgot she was a dog and considered her another person you was hunting with, well, me and Shem was hunting way over to Switches Corners and Heidi got on this old ridge runner of a jack he'd go clean over a mountain, hours before you'd hear that little yippity-yip way off on the ledges someplace and then it was gone again. All day long we was slogging up and down and across and over and we never could figure out where that goddam straight-line jackrabbit was going to come out. He'd go a mile straight before he'd turn, I swear to God. Finally it got dark and no Heidi, so we come back to Shem's pickup truck—a '34 flathead V-8, went like hell, by the way, which is what got Shem in trouble in the first place with Wallace Ellis, but I'll get to that.

"Shem says, and I can remember it to this day, 'First time I ever got skunked with Heidi, but it ain't her fault,' he says. 'Fact is, she don't have no faults to speak of.' Shem was staring up at Blue Peak where we last heard Heidi more'n an hour before. He took off his coat and laid it down beside the road so's Heidi, when she got done chasing that rabbit, would know where to wait till morning, snuggled up in her master's hunting coat. I could see Shem was worried, afraid at her age she might have a heart attack after all that running.

"Anyway, Shem went back in the morning, got there at first light to find Heidi laying on his coat all right, but she wa'n't in too good shape—half her head was blowed off and she was dead.

"Shem come by my place on the way home, I was up milking, and helps me finish up, not saying anything. Then he takes me out to his truck, pulls off some old burlap bags and there's his canvas hunting coat all brains and blood and the little dog all wrapped up in it. 'Who do you think done it?' he says. 'I don't know,' I says, but inside my head I'm thinking Wallace Ellis. One thing, he lived on that same road. I'm trying to look kind of blank, but Shem he just looks at me and says, 'So do I.'

"That gave me a chill, I'll tell you, so I says, trying to head him off, 'Well, you'll never know for sure, now, will you?' Shem just looks at me for a while. 'Maybe not,' he says, but he takes a spent shotgun shell out of his pocket. 'You drop any spent shells near the truck?' he asks. 'Not that I know of,' I says, 'though I might.' 'Twelve gauge Peters, never been reloaded,' Shem says. In them days shotgun shells, 'cept for the brass at the base, was made of paper, so you could tell that easy enough. Shem looks at me. 'Don't tell nobody about this, Eph,' he says. 'You know and I know, and the lonesome son-of-a-bitch that shot Heidi, and that's enough.'

"You'll be wondering what it was Wallace Ellis had against Shem Carr, that he shot his dog, and that's a story in itself."

213

Eph's big hand, clasped all the way around the white coffee mug, was shiny and rugged, the hairless skin glazed with liver spots. Motionless except for the slight tremor of age, the hand itself might have been ceramic, fired and cooled into its semitranslucent tan and rose. He'd taken off his visored cotton painter's cap when he came into the tent, and put it on his knee when he sat down; his bald dome was so much whiter than his face it looked like brown-grained marble above his faded gray eyes in their red lids. He still had his own yellow teeth, some of them, though they pushed out at awkward angles to his lips. Tillie Cole, twenty years younger than Eph, was at sixty neat, bony, softly immaculate of skin, and her eyes still seemed to recognize an irony and response that Eph in his age had outgrown.

Eph paused to listen to the rain on the tent. "Still coming down pretty good," he said. "Might as well give up and come back Monday forenoon."

"Eph," Tillie said. "Tell us what happened to Wallace Ellis."

"Man was worthless anyway," Eph said. "And I never said nothing happened to him."

"The Ford V-8," Tillie said.

"That was some little truck," Eph said. "Eighty-five horsepower, go nearly ninety on the flats, which was where Shem and Wallace Ellis first got started. The old High Road to Leah, 'fore they widened it and took the thank-you-ma'ams out of it, had this mile-long straightaway where all the young bucks used to see how fast their jalopies would go. Wallace Ellis was a sheriff's deputy, part time, had a Indian Chief motorcycle, and he fancied himself a motorcycle cop. That Indian was quite a machine, too—four cylinders set two-by-two upright in a block about as big as half a orange crate. Heavy machine, but once it got wound up it would go. Chain drive, air-cooled, had a little bitty windshield to keep the june bugs out of Wallace Ellis's eyes. Anyway, one time Shem was coming back from Leah and Wallace Ellis followed him on into Cascom, stopped him by the Grange Hall and accused him of speeding, told him next time he caught him going straight out like that he'd issue him a summons. I guess Shem responded with something you might call fairly inappropriate, and that was the beginning of the bad blood between the two of them.

214

"I guess it was far enough from the war, and what with the state of the country and all, Shem having been a hero had ceased to cut much ice. Seemed like ancient history to most. Shem had long been used to having people treat him with a little more respect, though he never asked for no special treatment. I guess he'd just got used to it.

"Well, knowing Shem you got to realize it was Wallace Ellis's manners offended him most, also the looks of the man. Wallace Ellis was bigger than Shem, for one thing, and he was one of your natural bullies. Most big men, and I speak from experience in the matter, don't have to go through life pushing people aside, humiliating, proving something all the time. Lord knows, people was cautious enough about Wallace Ellis. Nobody went out of their way to get his attention. Don't know what it was about the man made him so ill-mannered. I won't go into details, but one thing led to another and Wallace Ellis pulled his gun and there was all manner of bad feelings and Shem had to go to court in Northlee, it was haying season and he lost a good drying day too, and pay a fine of seven dollars and fifty cents, which was a small fortune in them days. Shem was angry, as you might well expect, so he got the idea to challenge Wallace Ellis to put on the gloves with him. Put a note up in the Town Hall—that was the old frame building that burnt down in the '58 fires. The Legion Hall, which at that time was in the former Christian Science Church, had a boxing ring in the basement. At the time I says to Shem, 'Lord, Wallace Ellis weighs forty pounds more than you and he's ten years younger'n you. What do you expect to prove?' 'I ain't going to *prove* nothing,' Shem says. 'I'm going to take seven dollars and fifty cents out of his God damn hide.'

"Now, the only boxing gloves they had at the Legion, they must have been left over from the Dempsey-Willard fight. They was so small and light you could have done your milking with them gloves on. You could have picked up a ten-cent piece off the cement sidewalk in them gloves.

"As you know, Shem was a fairly big man himself, around one-eighty, and spite of the weight difference there wa'n't much of a reach difference amongst the two of them. Shem had the advantage of having boxed some in the army, but the betting purely had

215

to be on Wallace Ellis, and that's the way the betting went around Cascom and Leah. What I heard, there was more than a hundred dollars altogether, bet on that fight.

"To make a long story short, the evening of the fight the Legion Hall basement was packed so full of men the ring ropes was holding the crowd out, rather than the fighters in. And as for the fight itself, it started out terrible bad for Wallace Ellis and done nothing but get worse. When the bell rung for the first round Shem kind of tippy-toed out to Wallace Ellis—looked like a man about to tangle with a bear. I swear I almost shut my eyes and missed the first punch, which was Shem's left fist splitting Wallace Ellis's lip. Right off you could tell Wallace Ellis never had the first idea there was more to boxing than drawing your right arm back as far as it would go and letting fly, like trying to win a cigar at one of them Fourth of July carnival mallet dingers where you try to ring a bell. His arm wa'n't halfway back 'fore he got stung bad. His eyes opened up so's you could see the whites all around and the poor fellow knew he was in for it. Shem got nicked a few times, and butted, and one of them big arms now and then like somebody dropped a log on his shoulder, but it was Wallace Ellis took the licking.

"After seven rounds young Doc Churchill near had a fit and made them stop the fight, took Wallace Ellis off to Northlee Hospital, he looked like a accident involving raspberry preserves and barn paint. Shem never knocked him down, said afterwards he never meant to knock him down. Said he could if he wanted, and I believe it. Wallace Ellis fell down once in the fifth round, slipped in his own blood it looked like, but Shem wa'n't about to let him off the hook. Said afterwards he only got about four dollars and twenty-five cents worth of satisfaction, so Wallace Ellis still owed him three and a quarter. That remark was widely quoted around Cascom and Leah and never did serve to make Wallace Ellis any happier.

"A year or so later, toward the beginning of rabbit season, was when Shem found Heidi with half her head blowed off, found that Peters twelve gauge shell by the road, which happened to be the road Wallace Ellis took to work."

216

Eph paused and shook his head. "I got to believe this rain has set in for a while." He took a sip of his coffee, which must have been cold by now, and Luke caught a quick, sly look across the rim of the cup. "Ayuh," Eph said with a sigh, "I figure we ought to give up for the day, Luke. Come back Monday forenoon and finish her up."

"Now, Eph," Tillie said.

"Well," Eph said, "I just figured Luke might want to hear that story about his Uncle Shem, is all."

"Now you tell us what happened to Wallace Ellis," Tillie said.

"Wallace Ellis? Wallace Ellis. Where was I? Wallace Ellis. So. We got to go back to that day in October, nineteen hundred and thirty-six, Shem and me was standing there next to his '34 Ford flathead V-8 pickup truck, next to my barn door. Shem put the burlap bags back over poor Heidi and I can see we're headed for trouble. 'Shem,' I says, 'I got an idea how upset you must be, but to my way of thinking what you got in mind ain't worth it. And besides, you ain't that certain who done it.' 'I ain't going off half-cocked, Eph,' Shem says. 'I want you to get me a shell fired from Wallace Ellis's shotgun. I know it's a Winchester 97, hammer-pump, same as mine, cause I seen him at the Fish and Game picnic trying to hit clay pigeons.'

"Well, that wa'n't hard to manage at all, as Shem was damn well aware, cause Wallace Ellis lost his cow that fall to TB, had to be destroyed, and I was delivering him one of my milkers since he had no truck at that time, just his Indian Chief motorcycle and a beat up '29 Chevrolet sedan the roof needed tarring in the worst way. He wa'n't a farmer, had somebody else do his haying, worked in Leah at the woolen mill as a bobbin racker. 'I don't know as I ought to *get* you a shell from Wallace Ellis's shotgun,' I says to Shem. But I did. It wa'n't hard—spent shells was laying all over his front stoop from him shooting at the pigeons lived in his barn across the way.

"Well, it took me a week to deliver that cow and pick up that shell, though I could've done it that same day. I figured a dog is just a dog, not a blood relative, and if Shem had time to cool off some he wouldn't do nothing drastic. Besides, that was the same time they found out Shem and Carrie's son, Samuel, had the epileptic fits, so I figured he had other things on his mind. Figured he'd simmer down after a time.

"Then toward the end of the month Wallace Ellis had the terrible accident on his Indian Chief motorcycle and killed himself—smashed his face off and broke his neck. He always did run that thing too fast.

"Well, I always did wonder about that accident, but then after the first excitement I kind of never brought it up again. Then, just last fall, I come up here to the farm to take a few things to Shem. He looked so poor he'd likely never last the winter, and of course the house was falling in. I asked him for the umpteenth time to come live with me and Tillie, we got six extra rooms, but he wouldn't have none of that. So we sat in what was left of the kitchen reminiscing about old times—his head was still clear—things like his boxing match with Wallace Ellis, the good times we had hunting, and Shem come right out with it. 'It was Wallace Ellis shot Heidi,' he says. 'It was his spent shell I found beside Heidi that morning. There must have been a little kind of dimple on the head of the firing pin of his shotgun you never seen on mine nor any other I looked at, and I went clear to Concord looking at Winchester 97 hammer-pumps, examining firing pins with some care. Ayuh, it was his gun that fired that shell, cause the mark on the primer was the same as on the shell you got me from Wallace Ellis's front stoop.'

" 'Well,' I says, 'he soon got his reward.' 'Ayuh,' Shem says. Then something got into me, I don't know what, and I says right out, 'Shem, did you have anything to do with that motorcycle accident?' He just looked at me. 'Hell,' he says, 'you had that suspicion in the back of your head all these years?' I guess I looked kind of funny, 'cause Shem says, 'Now, you know they give me a hunting license in the war, Eph, and I guess I got my limit on Huns, but just when the hell did they rescind that license? I don't remember nothing like that.' He's pulling my leg, of course. 'No,' he says. 'The unkindest thing to do with a poor son-of-a-bitch like Wallace Ellis is let him live.'

"So you see, for forty years I kind of had the notion my best friend was a murderer. There ain't no limit to what a fellow can hold in his mind!" Eph laughed and slapped his hands down on the table to show that his story was over.

"Why don't you tell the truth?" Tillie said.

Eph didn't seem to hear her at first; his story was over. He didn't want to hear what she'd said. He was rigid, Luke could see now, not physically but with the carefulness of age, a brittleness that needed no surprises at all.

"Maybe he don't want to hear the truth," Eph said, a quavery anger in his voice.

"It was so long ago," Tillie said.

"The truth then ain't necessary the truth now," Eph said. "And what in hell do you know about it, anyways?"

"I slept in your bed forty years, listening to your babble asleep and awake. Tell about how when the REA first come in under the New Deal, there was wire left over here and there. Copper-coated steel. You used to sing that in your sleep sometimes: 'copper-coated steel.'"

"I don't see how you can 'strapolate nothing from some goddam dream I had once. What are you after, anyway, Tillie Cole?"

"I just thought you was going to tell the truth for once, after all the years."

Eph wiped his hands over his pate, shaking his head. "You sure don't humor a man, to speak of, do you?"

"Well, I never married you, Eph Buzzell, if that's what you mean."

Eph's exasperation seemed out of place in such an old man, and Luke recognized in himself one of those wrong, romantic assumptions of youth, that the old have long ago signed their contracts with life, all the paragraphs, subheadings and codicils in order for the calm, resigned autumnal retreat.

"Women, women!" Eph said. "They ain't never satisfied. All right, maybe we made a mistake. Maybe Shem made a mistake. The idea was to give him a wing-ding he'd remember when he was pulling all that gravel out of his skin. I took a couple of turns around a pole, Shem around a maple tree. It was supposed to catch him just above his wheel, on the fork by the stem of his han-

219

dlebars, below that little windshield, but one way or another it caught him just above his teeth, peeled his face off up to his hair and broke his neck. Him and his motorcycle went off in the woods, leaving his face laying there on the gravel. Shem found it with his flashlight, picked it up like you would a used hanky, you know, somebody else's snot in it, scuffed the gravel around to hide the blood, what little there was of it. We found Wallace Ellis amongst the saplings and Shem kind of stuck his face back on. Deader'n a mackerel, of course. Then we took our wire and went on home. There!" he said, looking closely at Tillie. "You satisfied now?"

"You think I never guessed that part?" she said. "Tell us what Shem said to you last fall, then."

Eph looked at Luke, thinking hard. "He said that about the license they give him in the war."

"I believe that part," Tillie said.

"All right! He says when he heard that Indian Chief coming along so proud, he says to himself maybe the son-of-a-bitch has a way to feel gratified by what he done to Heidi. He says he remembered all in a flash how she run her heart out for him time and time again, and how she used to greet him when he come home. Then he says, 'Eph, I just took a higher turn around that white maple.'"

Tillie said, "Eph, it don't matter that much to Luke, that he knows the truth about what his uncle Shem done so long ago. Luke was in a war himself."

"Well, I never was in no war," Eph said. He was silent for a while, and Luke felt that in Eph's old brain, clogged here and there as it must be after eighty years, he was slowly and carefully rearranging the units of his story, his truths and devices.

Finally Eph said, "Well, I says to Shem—this was last November, just before the first big snow—I says, 'Shem, that was forty years ago, when we was both full of piss and vinigar.' I'm looking at him, thinking he won't last the winter out, he looked so poor. He seemed to read my mind. He's setting there in his Morris chair. Lord, the old house was falling in, not a wall was straight, and water had leaked all over his stove, it was all rusty where the splattering grease couldn't reach. He looks at me and says, 'I know you're an atheist, Eph, but I don't know what I am. I got a feeling one of us is wrong and the other's confused, but I ain't certain. I don't know what's going to fall down first, this old house or the old bag of guts you're looking at, but it ain't going to be long, so maybe I'll get some answers. I killed a man for killing a dog, and if you can say it in so many words, and it don't turn your stomach, well, shit on it.'

"That was the last time I seen Shem alive. Ayuh. Well, looks like this rain don't want to let up after all, Luke. We'll see you Monday forenoon, do the rest of the cleaning up around here. Won't take long, once we get to it."

They left in the old Buick, Tillie driving.

The cellar hole still smoked and hissed, live coals beneath. Drops of rain touched the gray ash with little plucking sounds. Jake had come out of the tent with him, and when Luke just stood there looking down into the cellar hole, where rot and fire had taken down Shem's house, Jake curled up in the wet grass and the rain, and waited, his brown hound's eyes alert.

# 16.

At the Batemans' house that evening there had been a great shifting of books so that Phyllis's office could work as a living room. George had piled them around the walls, behind the sofa, to the ceiling of the small closet off the hall. "You don't know how dirty books are until you get your hands on 'em," George said.

"Dirty books? Oh, my," Louise Sturgis said, which disgusted George, though he looked down at his feet to try to hide the expression. He wore a necktie and a dark blue suit that was too narrow and too long for him—his funeral and wedding suit, he told Luke when no one else was listening.

Phyllis had introduced Luke to "Louise and Coleman Sturgis," and for a while Luke thought Coleman Sturgis must be Louise's husband, or ex-husband, but it turned out he was her brother. A young-looking, lanky man in his forties, he had the slightly rumpled, translucent face of a drunk who seemed, for the evening, to be watching his intake. His eyes were blue, watery and ingratiating, and he didn't resemble his darker sister at all.

"Actually we've met," he said, "though you'd have no reason to remember me. It was at a party after a rather bizarre poetry reading at Moorham. I teach in the English Department and knew your wife. I'm terribly sorry about what happened. We were all absolutely devastated when we heard."

Luke could think of nothing to say about Helen, so he made a rather desperate jump in memory, to a time when he'd gone with Helen to a poetry reading. "Was that the reading where the fellow took his clothes off?" he said.

"Yes, and blew his nose in his underwear and everyone had to be so polite, since no one could decide how to react, and we were supposed to admire the man's poetry. In a way, a fairly tense scene. What did you make of it?"

"I was glad I wasn't connected to the college," Luke said.

"And then when his boyfriend demanded a tape recorder and we couldn't find one at that hour. Lord! We were all so embarrassed for the Lectures Committee. But of course that wasn't the end of it, beause *then* we found that the boyfriend was really the poet, and it had been the boyfriend, the actual boyfriend, who had given the reading and it was the poet who had demanded the tape recorder. It's always so damnably embarrassing to be the butt of a poor joke. Don't you think so?"

"I agree," Luke said.

"It's one of the more untenable positions. But why would this poet have done it? Here we were, a rather poor little community college, all of us underpaid, no tenure, trying to do our job with the materials available, and we scrape up three hundred dollars to have the man come and read, and we turn out to be 'The Establishment' or something, deserving nothing but an arrogant switch of his boyfriend's hairy ass. Imagine the hatred and resentment underneath the japing! Or was it just the arrogance of the artist? Can a poet be such a shit? You're a literary man—that is, you're a writer . . . journalist? What do you call yourself?"

"I've never known exactly what to call myself," Luke said.

"Oh."

"I'm not putting you on," Luke said hastily. The blue eyes seemed confused and hurt. "I've done a lot of things for a living, and most of them were literary. None were very dishonest."

"That's as much as anyone can say, I suppose," Coleman Sturgis

223

said. "I've taught for sixteen years, and even teaching's not the purest of occupations. No."

"Once I edited a house journal for a corporation that made, among some useful things, a particularly horrible chemical weapon," Luke said.

"Napalm?"

"No, but something along that line. It ate feet."

"Ugh! But you quit that job?"

"I could afford to at the time," Luke said, wondering why he'd had the urge to do a little confessing to Coleman Sturgis. It had been a shock that the man had taught with Helen, and that he'd had a right to mention her and the accident. At first he'd thought Coleman's washed, faded youthfulness was the result of alcohol, but it could have been any sort of disease, suffering and possible cure. He couldn't decide without more evidence, and didn't want to ask. His own pseudo-confession had been warped by Coleman's need for reassurance, unless Luke himself was slightly insane this evening. His attitudes about corporate responsibility were much more complicated than they had sounded. Also his attitudes toward war; when one compared, say, a .45 slug in a lower intestine full of partly digested C-ration or rice and fish to a compound that had an affinity for epidermal cells, one's judgments became desperate, soiled by the desire to purify. If the former seemed less mysterious and horrible than the latter, that was the result of ignorance.

Louise Sturgis had been talking to Phyllis and glancing over at Luke and her brother. George kept moving, making drinks, handing out hors d'oeuvres he wouldn't pronounce and couldn't help signalling his disapproval of. Luke wanted to talk to George, if to anyone. He felt that out of loyalty to Phyllis he was being forced into dishonesty. On the way here he'd gone twenty miles out of the way, down the other side of the mountain on dirt roads that threatened to end anytime, just to play with his new truck and to think of what good and useful things he would carry in it. The metallic hollowness of the truck, the rugged controls that worked, its new solidity and smell pleased him in simple ways.

Freddie Hurlburt arrived, dressed in gaudy, reddish plaid

224

trousers and a red sport jacket, seeming wider than tall. Luke thought of Shem's wooden rule, and how he might unfold it and measure Freddie to see if he were really wider than tall, a Tweedledee without his Tweedledum. He seemed about to burst out of his skin, though he was not that fat, really; it was the broadness of his pelvis, a large woman's breadth of body on the short man. While he spoke to Phyllis, his words coming across the room as little snaps and pops, Phyllis seeming pleased and slightly hard of hearing, which she was not, Louise came over to Luke and Coleman.

"First, are you wearing a gun?" she said to Luke. She wore a filmy short dress of light brown material, which Helen would have called beige and known the name of, tied at her waist with white cord. The outfit looked expensive, and she herself, her dark skin, thin muscles and black hair, seemed to have been turned, by the kind of preparation women did to themselves before they went out for an evening, into a visual object that, strangely, could talk. There had been a darkening of eyelash, some kind of smoothing, the sheen of colorless lipstick. He looked at the texture of her upper lip and the skin over her cheekbone, her coarse yet smoothly shining black hair, her nipple indenting the expensive fabric, and a small rise of lust and almost detached curiosity came over him. He saw her in his mind with light blue eyes, like her brother's, but she would be too intense and perverse then. Her olive eyes were more consistent with the whole configuration she made, as an animal's eyes would be, and although he felt some perversity in his attraction to her, because he didn't like her that much, he was attracted and would be open to whatever possibilities there were. The whiskey he was drinking had something to do with it, and also the interesting feeling of playing hooky. Then came the emptier realization that he had no need to play hooky.

Since she wanted to be cryptic about the gun, Luke explained to Coleman how they'd met at his uncle's place on the mountain and how he happened to be wearing his uncle's pistol when she and Freddie came by.

Presumably these were people whose accents, vocabularies, ironies and values were also his, so he found it necessary to lie, as he

225

would not have had to lie to Phyllis or George. He could assume, with discouraging accuracy, Coleman's at least public attitudes, and so frivolously explained away the gun.

Coleman then told him about the old house their parents had bought in the fifties—the old Bean house, about a mile up the road—and how he and Louise had inherited it and were fixing it up. Their parents had been members of the Cascom Mountain Club since the thirties and that was how they'd come to know the area. Louise, since her divorce, had taken up ceramics and had fixed up a studio in the barn, a gas-fired kiln in the cement base where the silo had been. He went on to tell how it had been impossible to keep antiques in the house until Louise had lived there the last two winters, because they were always ripped off. They'd lost all kinds of good things their parents had collected. "They simply come with a truck, break in and take what they want," Coleman said. "If a house doesn't look lived in, they'll clean it out." According to the State Police these weren't local people, necessarily, but professionals who sold the stuff out of state.

"Anything old is valuable," Louise said, "and it doesn't have to be very old any more, either."

"Was your husband's name Sturgis too?" Luke asked.

"No, I took my family name back."

"She kept the alimony, though," Coleman said.

"I'm not *that* liberated," Louise said. "At least not yet."

She was beginning to make some money with pots and cups and dishes at the craft fairs, and even had some retail places that bought her things. "You'll have to see my studio," she said. "Tonight, come back and have a nightcap with us and I'll show you my wares. It's on your way back up the mountain."

He thought he would like to see her wares. Danger seemed an abstraction to him. Freddie came over and said hello, again invited him to come to the lodge for potluck, and managed this time to be somewhat unintelligible about trails and distances without suggesting to Luke's ear any stranger meanings. This left Phyllis alone in her chair, so he went over and sat on the arm of the sofa next to her.

"Aren't they interesting people?" Phyllis said.

"Yes," Luke said. "Very interesting people."

"She's very attractive, I thought."

Luke smiled at her and Phyllis looked sly. "Or else George is making these drinks too strong," he said.

"Now, Luke!" She touched his arm with her bent hand, then said, "That little Freddie's an odd one, though. Can you understand what he's saying? We've known him for years, of course, but I never do catch half of what he says, he talks so fast."

George had brought a large young man into the room and was introducing him with obvious pleasure to Louise and Coleman. Freddie evidently knew him already. The young man wore steel-rimmed glasses, green chinos and a windbreaker. He was gaunt, blond, and red-faced from social unease or weather. George brought him over and introduced him to Luke. "John Pillsbury, the new game warden," George said. "It was him and me found Shem that morning, you know. John here used to check on him now and then, and they got on fine."

"Shem Carr was quite a man," John Pillsbury said. "I used to like talking to him. He knew more about that mountain!"

"Shem kind of took a shine to John," George said. "'Course he'd give up hunting illegal by the time John come along."

They both laughed. John Pillsbury said, "He told me he used to need three limits of them little Zach Brook trout just for breakfast!"

Luke then noticed John Pillsbury's wife, whom Louise and Coleman were trying to be nice to and were terrifying. She was a handsome young woman who was so ill at ease she could not be whatever her self was, just smiled tight non-smiles at whatever they were saying to her. Phyllis saw this and went over to her, walking without a cane, and brought her back. Her name was Mary. Luke evidently terrified her too, so Phyllis took her off to the kitchen to be her assistant in serving dinner, at which suggestion Mary looked relieved.

At the table Phyllis had Luke sit next to Louise, with Coleman opposite. Mary Pillsbury, postponing the time she would have to sit down between Freddie and Coleman, fussed over the table after the casserole, salad, hot rolls and utensils were all arranged.

227

Phyllis finally made her sit down. George served the casserole, the recipe for which Phyllis said she had gotten from *Woman's Day*. It contained, among other things, ham, tunafish, green peppers and raisins. Luke said it was excellent, especially after his own haphazard meals on the mountain.

"Single men don't eat what they ought," Phyllis said. "Statistics prove it. They die sooner than married men."

"What about single women?" Louise said.

"Women know better," Phyllis said. "A woman takes time to make things. Men just swill whatever's easy or handy."

George talked with John Pillsbury. Freddie ate. Coleman ate a little and pushed his food around, but concentrated mainly on a strong whiskey and water he'd made himself just before they sat down. When Freddie had eaten enough he began to talk in tongues to Mary Pillsbury, who didn't understand a word, though she tried to smile when Freddie laughed.

While Coleman and Phyllis talked about property taxes, Louise said to Luke, "She's trying to *mate* the two of us. Isn't that sweet?"

"It's what benevolent old ladies do," Luke said, feeling disloyal.

"Well, how old are you and what are your bloodlines?"

"I'm a chap in his forties, of ancient lineage," he said, which she seemed to find impressive and even funny.

"When he looked at me my father used to say there was a touch of the tarbrush in my mother's family," she said.

"You do look a little Oriental."

"Is that good or bad?"

"It's okay," he said, thinking about that—about his saying okay and the sexual rise and tremor in him as he said it.

"What are you thinking about?" she said. "George says you have a brand-new truck. I've been thinking about that because I've never, ever in my life, ridden in a truck. Will you give me a ride in your truck someday?"

"Sure. Tonight. I'll give you a ride home in it."

"Now what are you thinking?"

"I was thinking I always tend to monitor myself for the truth," he said, "though I do tend to lie."

"So it's *not* okay I look like a Slant?"

228

"A Gook," he said. "That's the word my enlightened generation used. Anyway, I'm probably too old for you. How old are you?"

"Twenty-nine. No, thirty-six. I was married at twenty-six, so there was seven years there, then three divorced. That's thirty-six."

"Children?"

"My husband had a vasectomy during his first marriage and neglected to tell me about it. He was like that. He'd already made three kids. So. Anyway, my nipples are still pink."

He looked down at the little points in the material of her dress, she watching him look. She smiled a crooked little smile, a rather aggressive, bitter look.

Later she went after George about guns, having overheard part of his and John Pillsbury's conversation. George manfully restrained himself, though, when Phyllis gave him a hard look.

At ten the Pillsburys left, John a little drunk on George's home brew, so the dinner party was over. Freddie tried to arrange a date when they would all come to the lodge for supper, George being quite skillfully slippery about the matter. As he said good night, Luke told Phyllis he was giving Louise a ride home in his truck, and Phyllis smiled and pushed him in the chest.

"Is Coleman married?" he asked Louise as they drove to her house.

"You mean is he queer? No, Coleman specializes in doomed love affairs. Impossibly young students, other people's wives, broads that don't like him enough—like that. God, this truck is *big*. There doesn't seem to be enough road for it. You could lie down on this seat."

"You could," he said. "My feet would stick out the window."

She laughed, and he felt like a schoolboy. He remembered, because he felt it right now, the nervousness that was the bane of the callow. Would she, or wouldn't she? Could he, or couldn't he? That was a new question to complicate things, one that had never occurred to him before. Then came the warning: they want to involve you. They are after you and will make you care too much.

Coleman came along behind them in his Toyota and the three of them entered the old house together. The front hall was cluttered with lumber, lath and sawhorses, the unplaned sub-flooring exposed. The long room they then entered had been parlor and dining room before the wall between was removed. The room was a familiar combination of objects such as wicker peacock chairs, a modern sofa, cobblers' benches and large, colorful paintings of crosses, circles and other geometric slashes on vast whitish backgrounds. There were many books in pine board bookcases, and a Swedish stove set into one of the high-throated fireplaces. The decor was, with minor differences in the styles of the paintings, one his class tended to superimpose upon the rooms of old New England houses.

They spoke of the paintings, done by friends, and of course the Swedish stove, green-enameled, its heating chamber above the firebox arched and embellished with cast-in designs of leaves and reindeer. Coleman made them drinks, his own pretty heavy on the bourbon, and they went through a big kitchen, across dewy grass to the small barn, where banks of fluorescent lights came on in a room still dusty with ancient hay and cobwebs in its upper reaches and along its square beams. Here were Louise's wheels, racks, glazes, crocks of clay covered with polyethylene, and the cellary damp odor of fresh clay, the floor grayish with clay. On the racks were unfired rows of monochromatic cups, saucers, dishes and pots.

Beyond the barn was the kiln room built within the round cement foundation of the long disappeared silo. Heat from the gas-fired kiln, that was a cave-like stack of firebricks almost as light as balsa wood, could in winter be vented back into the barn-studio, which Louise was in the process of insulating.

Some glazed, finished pots and platters were on shelves in the barn. One glaze she seemed to like was milky, and seemed to drip over the sides of pots with a viscous stopped movement, like photographs of semen. When he examined one of these pots closely Louise said that it began as a mistake, but then she'd rather liked the effect. She'd had a difficult time repeating it, though. "It's hard to reproduce a mistake," she said, "because the data's unreliable."

"We seldom *want* to reproduce our mistakes," Coleman said, "but we do, we do, don't we?"

230

"Speak for yourself, brother," Louise said with a hardness, or bitterness, or a sort of expert sarcasm that gave Luke pause. It seemed unhealthy, suddenly exposed, a disdain that was too heavy.

Back in the long living room, Coleman made himself another tea-brown bourbon, drank it quickly and said good night. Luke sat on the modern sofa, deep into brown velour, while Louise straddled a cobbler's bench, put down her drink and pushed her black hair back with both hands, arching her chest and neck as if she were posing for him, showing him how her spine articulated. Her neat haunches were planted on the dark old bench, her stockinged legs exposed. When she got up to get an ashtray she knew his eyes followed her. She came back and sat next to him on the sofa, bent forward to reach for her cigarettes on the coffee table, moving constantly, puffing on her cigarette, tapping it on the ashtray, sipping her drink.

"I love Phyllis," she said. "Don't you? Isn't she real?"

"Yes," he said. Her nervousness, or whatever it was, somehow calmed his own. He put his hand on her shoulder, thinking that she had, after all, sat down right next to him. He was certain of nothing. She let him pull her back, looking at him quickly with her head bent forward, her olive eyes wide open.

"That doesn't mean we have to do what she wants us to, though," she said.

"No," he said.

"Do you really mean that?"

"I'll mean anything you want me to," he said.

"Are you a *friend*, for Christ's sake?"

"Sure."

"I never know what a man's really like until after he's come, and then he's usually a shit."

"Not me, I don't think."

"Are you still monitoring yourself for the truth?"

"Yes. I don't know what I can do or not do. I've been carrying this weight around. . . ."

"Your family. I know."

His erection faded, and the room came sharply into focus, foreign and somehow casual, as if its items were on display in a store

231

window he passed with only a glance. She was a collection of ten-dons, bones, glands and unpleasant opinions. Except that now she was sympathetic, and put her hand, which was angular and short—he hadn't noticed before—on his leg.

"Let's go to my room and see what happens, anyway," she said.

Her room was across the unfinished hallway, the bed high and white, brass columns and flutings like pipe organs at head and foot. There was the going to the bathroom, he using hers, she finding another somewhere in the old house. The strangeness and familiarity of preparation, the acknowledgment of function, the overcoming desire. She came back still dressed and sat on the high bed, her feet not touching the hardwood floor that was cool to his bare feet. He helped her off with her clothes, and put the suddenly tiny, unsubstantial beige dress over the back of a ladder-back chair, then the silky rope of pantyhose. For a moment they examined each other in the lamplight. She was usual, beautiful to his lust, strange in coloration. Her nipples were not pink, but a light tan, her olive skin not of the blank clarity of youth, but their naked bodies were of a kind, each almost unnaturally preserved and firm. This seemed a bond between them, even at this anticipa-tory moment, and they both said so. He picked her up, weighing her, and put her down easily on the bed.

"You're examining me," she said. He nodded and looked close-ly at her, following his hands with his eyes. Her hand on his erec-tion was like needles. He almost laughed, it was so uncomplicated. Her hollows and creases, the night-black neatness of her small tri-angle there. He took a long pleasure in knowing her body—lips, textures, planes, articulations, tastes—until she insisted that he enter her.

They awoke off and on in the night, neither used to the other. Sometime before dawn they lay awake, her head in the hollow of his arm, her hand gently and idly playing with him.

"You do love women, don't you," she said.

"Yes, I think so," he said.

"Oh, you do. Most men don't. I don't resent you sticking your prick in me. I mean I don't resent it even afterwards, when we get through."

"I feel grateful you let me," he said.

"You don't think the little bitch *needs* a big prick in her?"

"You're pretty bitter."

"You should have known my husband, not to mention the other emotional cripples that came after."

"Why did you finally get divorced?"

"I don't think I want to talk about it. Maybe sometime, if you ever want to come back."

"I'll come back. We're neighbors."

She gave a twisting yawn and stretch, took him briefly in her mouth and then kissed his belly. "God, I hope so. I'm so full, I'm just sloshing with your gism. See, I'm crazy and truthful at the same time, and I never wait for anything, so I scare people half to death. Aren't you scared of me? Don't say anything. Sooner or later you'll think I'm a crazy neurotic grubby-colored bitch who's too ambivalent about sex, life or anything else. I know."

She did have a talent, whether self-destructive or self-protective, for modulating tenderness, or for suddenly changing its environment. He held her, and she pleased him beyond the thoughts she kept pushing at him. But don't ignore the thoughts, he told himself, sad that they couldn't have the same thoughts.

When he entered her again she was like silk.

They got up at dawn and made breakfast, talking about her studio and her work. She had been an art major at Smith, but not in ceramics; should she use fiberglass or foam insulation on the barn ceiling? She liked to work hard, that was one thing she could do. She could turn out the finished commercial stuff in bulk, then fool with experiments, glazes and designs. Their talk was businesslike, and he didn't know if she really wanted it that way or not. Should he, when the time came, say so long, see you, and leave? When the time came, shortly after they heard Coleman groaning awake upstairs, he put his hands underneath her bathrobe on her buttocks and pulled her against him. "Will you come back?" she asked. "When?"

"Tonight, if you want," he said.

"You don't want to, do you? That's too soon—isn't it?"

"No."

"Yes. You want to do your solitary thing up there on the mountain. Listen. You know you've never said my name to me and I've never said yours to you? That's right."

"If I come tonight will you be here?"

"I'll be here and in heat, but don't come tonight. I don't want you to come tonight. I really mean it!" Her strange eyes were a little mad. He kissed her on the lips and left.

He drove his pleasing truck up the mountain, alone, feeling beautifully light, empty of all the fluids and pressures she had relieved him of, and guilty that it had been so natural to take her, the strange woman not his wife. With the guilt, the unreasonable and unlegal guilt, he wondered if she had used some sort of contraceptive. Maybe the pill—he didn't know and hadn't thought to mention the subject. The subject was connection and responsibility, and the ghost was a small, demeaning fear.

# 17.

By the middle of July the mosquitoes were rare, the blackflies had lost their aggressiveness, and only now and then a deerfly, slow and easy to kill against his head when it landed, came to irritate him at his work.

The old farmhouse, sheds and barn were gone, the cellar hole and barn foundations now set like prehistoric stones in smooth new grass that waved at their bases in the wind. Four new poles took the power line down the hill to the valley and his cabin site. Marple & Son had set forms and poured his footings, all plumbing and waterproofing were done, and with his new farm tractor, called a Kubota, Luke had pushed back the soil so that the cabin, as it grew, would sit more pleasingly upon the land, its back to the north and the heavy spruce. The mountain rose to the west, seeming one long slope until, in certain kinds of weather, mist defined the many ridges and depressions that cut between the valley and the bald granite peak.

His tent was now set up near the cabin. Under electric light in the evenings he drew his plans, changed them, improving the not yet existent spaces of his cabin, trying to feel those spaces through the two-dimensional of paper, pencil and rule. It was something he had been good at in his life—to see shapes where blankness or bland solidity hid them, or in the dark to find a wall, drawer or doorway.

Or the parts of women. He had seen Louise Sturgis several times, until a week ago when she had discovered, or treated it as a discovery, that he had arranged somehow to see her exactly twice a week. He didn't think it was that precise, and hadn't thought it deliberate on his part, but she accused him of using her, as she said men had always used her, to relieve an urge that was to them as self-centered as evacuation. He didn't think that was true, either, and he didn't think she thought it true. He wanted to be fond of her; she said that she loved him and then, perhaps with the cold insight of the mad, wounded his ability to love her. They could never think in harmony; her surprises were always jarring. He thought it her fear of trusting him. Last week, before ordering him to put on his clothes and go, she had been near orgasm, he easing her and in his mind a smooth clarity in which she was perfect; he loved her joy and the nearly painful little pullings and cracklings of nerves he felt in her, in her nearness to release. Then she went limp, dead still, and then cried long sobs mixed with hiccups. "Why are you crying?" he asked. "You prick, you're trying to make me love you, aren't you?" she said. "So get the hell out of here! Now! Go!"

And so he left, but not until he was certain that she meant it and it wasn't just a test. But he left with a phrase in his head, which he said aloud out by his truck. "That is a crazy lady, Luke Carr. Watch out, old buddy." The phrases were sane, true, and sad. Gone was some transcendent mood or other, something high and pure that now seemed ridiculous. So she had gone to California, Coleman told him, for a couple of weeks at least, to visit an old girlfriend.

He mixed his mortar in a small, rented electric cement mixer, sifted his sand, added the gray, floury cement, then some masonry cement and then the precise amount of water so that the muck would be plastic enough to hold on the vertical. His trowel became a skillful extension of his hand, and little by little the interior wall grew, a very few square feet of facing each day. He spent much of the time staring at and into stones, turning them over and over in his hands, heavy stones, some of them, that weighed nearly a hundred pounds. His arms and shoulders grew bulky and taut, and hard muscles appeared in his abdomen, symmetrical rises and depressions he hadn't seen since his school athletic days. His gloves kept wearing out at the fingertips, then his skin, so that heat and rough textures were painful. But the wall grew toward the floor level, where it would be visible in his living spaces.

He picked up his mail whenever he found that he needed materials and had to drive to the lumberyard or to Follansbees' in Leah. There had been no new letter from the Avenger. Martin Troup wanted him to come to New York at *Gentleman*'s expense and talk about the article on death and building, or at least call and talk about it, and why in hell didn't he have a telephone?

Jake was gone for three days, then came back limping badly, a tooth broken, a bare abrasion on his head and a round lump on his ribs, the size of an orange, Luke first thought a herniated intestine. Jake had come slowly up to him where he was sifting sand into his wheelbarrow, Jake's tail down and curled under his belly, standing awkwardly, hangdog and as if ashamed. Luke soon found the bruises and then read in Jake's eyes that he should help him, that it was up to him to do something. Jake yelped in pain as he lifted him up into the cab of the truck. He took him to a veterinary hospital in Leah, where the vet diagnosed the lump as a bad bruise full of fluid that would be reabsorbed. It wasn't a dog fight, the vet said, because there were no canine tooth punctures or cuts. Either the dog had been hit and his stretched skin run over by a car, or someone had beaten him with something like a baseball bat.

The vet at first thought Luke must be Lester Wilson, from the tag on Jake's collar. He was a young man just recently come to the area. "Heartworm is here now," he said. "Has he been tested for it? A few years ago they never saw a case up here, but it's coming north." So Luke had the vet take some of Jake's blood and test him for heartworm, and when the test was negative bought seven dollars worth of preventive pills. Jake weighed thirty-five pounds, so he'd have to take half a pill each day with his food. "It's really serious here now," the vet said. "We've had four dogs with it this summer. Two died. After they get it the heart's so full of worms if you kill the worms too quickly you kill the dog." The disease, he said, was transmitted by mosquitoes.

Luke looked at Jake who, though sick with his aches and bruises, trembled with well-mannered nervousness about being at the veterinary hospital among too many distant yips, mews, growls and strong odors. His coat had turned waxy, and stank about twice as strongly of dog as it did on the mountain. Jake belonged to Lester Wilson; it said so right on his collar. Was it Lester Wilson who had beaten him up? No way of knowing. And now Luke would be giving him medication along with the food he probably shouldn't be giving him, so he would have to confront Lester Wilson again, one way or another.

He paid the vet's secretary and went back to the mountain, Jake a little sedative-logy and content to curl up on the seat. Whatever choices had been given to Jake in his dog's world had evidently been made. Unfortunately Luke hadn't been given much of a choice. He'd never thought of having a dog now. They'd had a springer for seven years as the kids grew up, a dull good dog who was killed by a car. He didn't want a dog. With this thought came guilt because he really had enjoyed having Jake around with his ears and nose, his specialized and undemanding intelligence.

So he put the question off and went back to work. Let Lester Wilson come up here and complain. Of course, maybe Lester had already come up and collared Jake; maybe that accounted for the three-day disappearance. Maybe Lester had taken him back to that rickety shed next to his trailer and beaten him with a baseball bat. For how long? How many blows?

In this life one could rarely be sure of things like that. Maybe Jake had been bothering a bitch in heat, and the owner had run him off with a baseball bat, or he had been partly run over; a beagle could practically turn around inside his own skin, and a car tire could have pinched out that orange-sized lump, the bumper, muffler, tie rod or rear-end housing having shaved and battered his head.

238

Jake lay in the grass nearby, still too sick to go off on his rounds, moving a little as the sun's turning rearranged his shade. Luke built his wall. The valley whispered in a light wind and the brook spoke and hissed faintly from down across the field by the eastern hill. In the dry, even warmth of the July day it seemed the most peaceful, meaningful and benevolent place in the world. Luke found a stone that was a near perfect cornerstone, a gift. It was gray, like frozen flannel, with opaque white felspar squares set in it. It seemed to weigh little in his hands, though it weighed nearly thirty pounds. His arms were a smooth reddish brown flecked with dried splashes of gray mortar. Holding the stone easily in one hand he made a soft bed of mortar for it, knew just the pebble that would tilt it correctly, set it into its place and placed mortar around it. Each stone was important not just for itself but for the as yet unfound stones it would support. He had to think ahead and upward, into nothing but the clear vertical spaces he would slowly build through.

At five-thirty in the afternoon, more tired than he'd thought, he dropped a stone on his foot, the pain so sudden and commanding he could not move for a while. His whole left leg was so weak he had to stand and let the pain pass at its own speed—a feeling so momentous it was like a close call with death. He was tired, just physically tired, but he'd built a section three by four by two, a cubic rectangle of sturdy (when it took its first set), respectable adamantine bloody wall. His foot was not broken, or even badly bruised. He was so familiar with his using body now he knew that kind of thing at once. Tomorrow he would hardly notice the residual soreness.

He took a towel and soap and crossed the brushy pasture to the brook pool. He'd cut down alders and pincherries so the afternoon sun could come into the pool and its banks, making the rushing water and the boulders a warm golden room in the green, columned hall of leaves the brook followed. Taking off his boots, socks and dungarees seemed, out of doors, in this active and sighing place, like sexual preparation. His feet, on the unstable organic earth—lichens, hemlock needles, roots, parts of insects left in molt, the paths of salamanders, white mushrooms being eaten by

239

orange, shell-less snails—were a tender part of all the miniature violence and life they touched. Tender in feeling yet strong from labor, his newly tightened body gave him a small narcissistic thrill that eased him into the cold water. He arched his chest against the thudding pushes of the water beneath the chute and felt the openness of his skin to this astounding new element, his anus licked by cold fingers at his ribs and scrotum. He grew a numbed, looping, partial erection. Long ago he and Helen had made love just here in the buffeting water, one warm summer night. Maybe it had been here, underwater, that Johnny had been conceived; he'd always swum like a fish.

A motion at the bank—animal. It was Jake, who, having had to follow, gingerly looked for a place to be. He settled down in a mossy depression between roots, curled and tried to lick himself, but gave it up as too painful. After a few tentative moves, he found a way to prop his head on a root, his large eyes on Luke.

At first even Jake didn't hear, over the rushing of the water, the approach of someone else. Luke was soaping himself and his eyes were closed. He heard Jake's hoarse, short bark of warning, bent down to rinse the soap from his face and came up to see, fuzzily, a woman he didn't recognize immediately because he didn't expect to see her here. His first reaction to her being a woman was to wade toward the stone where his towel was. He wiped his face just as she spoke, and knew who she was.

"I've seen you naked before, Luke Carr, so you don't have to put on your sarong!" It was Jane Jones, in white tennis costume, her tanned skin dark as an underexposure against the white of her tennis dress and shoes. She took a long-legged step and a jump to a nearer boulder and sat on it with one knee up. "Go on with your bath," she said. "I'll wait."

He had been startled, and being startled was not, here and now, exactly pleasant; there was a trail of disappearing fear. Jake made some other threatening sounds and subsided to watch Jane carefully. Luke said hello cheerfully enough, he thought, then went under to rinse himself and wash away the bitter memory of fear, thinking as he pushed through the cold water that Jane Jones was

240

about the last person he had expected to see, and what did she want with him?

He surfaced and stood waist deep, wondering if it was modesty or some other sort of fear to have the water cover him, though she could see through the refracting water and did look there, with an amused look. He resented this somewhat, and said, "Come on in. The water's fine."

Involuntarily she glanced at Jake, as if he were a third party to this immodest proposal, and then she saw that she had lost the advantage, and frowned, again involuntarily, just long enough to realize that she had given herself away. So she had missed that part of a second in which she might have maintained her cool. Luke climbed out, wrapped the towel around his waist and invited her to his camp. Jake followed them slowly across the field and waited patiently, standing while Luke made drinks, entering the painful process of lying down only when Luke sat down.

Jane explained that she had been in a doubles tournament in North Conway, that she and her partner had lost, and she had decided to stop by on her way home. The directions Luke had sent to Ham were bare but adequate, and so she had found him skinny-dipping in the brook. She had the TR-7, which didn't have much clearance, so she'd left it out at the main road and walked in, following the electric wire.

"You're beginning to look like one of those weight lifters," she said. "A stunning body you've got, Luke Carr."

"Yours is pretty stunning, too, Jane."

"I know. I don't look a day over twenty-nine."

"Nineteen, then."

"Too late, Buster," she said, and blushed, he was certain, beneath her careful tan. Some idea or possibility had come to her and made her cautious, or embarrassed, as though she questioned the propriety of coming to see him all by herself. "Ham says we're going to drive up here one of these days and see how you're getting along, so I thought I'd scout on ahead, find out just where you were," she said. "I've got to get on home."

Her embarrassment excited him. Without her knowing looks

241

and sarcasm, or whatever it was she coated all her remarks with, she became the stunning blond golden girl he had desired, at least once in his life, before Helen had imprinted her own characteristics upon him. He look Jane's glass, which was not empty, chipped more ice from the twenty-five pound block and made her another drink.

"God! Easy!" she said. "I've got a long drive ahead. It's six o'clock already!"

"You're welcome to stay over," he said, watching her, feeling a little reckless and even cruel. She became very nervous, her long metallic fingernails clicking on her glass, which she held in one hand and played upon with the other. She was trying to find something to say, and finally looked at him resentfully, then away.

"Ham had a thing for Helen. Did you know that?" she said. "But of course nothing ever came of it except he used to tell me about it all the time."

"He told you about it?"

"Sure. Maybe it's our California ways or something. We confess a lot."

"I don't," he said. "We didn't."

"I know. I used to envy your uptight whatever-it-was. Christ, Ham treats me sometimes like I'm his kindergarten teacher. Every little kinkydink in his psyche and Big Jane knows all about it. But then I'm just as bad, I guess. There's just no goddam dignity. I mean I like to look good and feel good, so I go on the wagon and watch the calories, but then I ask myself what do I want to look good *for?* Because there's no dignity and I just want men to drool over me a little? Why should I ask you this, anyway? I never thought of anything like that before your . . . before the . . . tragedy. I don't want to remind you of it. I'm sorry. What I mean is, I didn't come up here to jump in bed with you. I'm on my way back from a lousy doubles tournament. I can't stand my partner— for one thing, she never comes to the net—so we drive in separate cars; we always do. So I came up here to see you as a person. I did see your whole person, more or less, in the brook. Joke. I'm serious, though, or I want to be, and you're serious. I mean you really *are* serious, maybe because you have to be now, after what hap-

242

pened. No, you always were serious. Maybe all I mean is that you were in love with your wife. Anybody could see it, and it was amazing, fabulous! Like you read in those women's books, so I just naturally respected you and that's why we had all the arguments, not because you never asked to make love to me. Anyway, I never asked you, right?"

"Right," he said.

"When you said to take a swim over there I didn't, right?"

"Right."

"Are you laughing at me, you shit?"

"No, Jane."

"There's no dignity," she said, crying, her lids suddenly red and overflowing. "Christ, I feel like a fool in front of that goddam dog! Why does he keep looking at me? And it wasn't my fault I was for Nixon, either. He came from my mother's hometown!"

She put her glass, clasped in both hands, in front of her face. She was sitting on a kitchen chair, her athletic bottom filling the hard seat, her cute, too pretty, lace-decorated tennis dress unequal to her emotion. The top seam of her ball pocket was tinted red from clay dust, where she had stuffed the yellow extra ball when she had served. Her tears and ragged breaths seemed important because out of character, or out of whatever character he'd thought she had. He went to her, removed her spilling glass from her hands and put it on the ground, knelt beside her chair and put his arms around her. Sympathy threatened to undo him, as though one soft thought might release from him groans and wails that would frighten them both.

She hiccuped, and said, "I stink. I couldn't stand hanging around long enough after the match to take a shower and change."

She did stink, of a prodigious, an Olympic sweat. He thought of her hairy ancestors—Celtic, Saxon, Mycenaean—fierce warrior-women of interminable sieges, survivals, battles and massacres. It rose like heat from her as she sobbed over some vague civilized unhappiness she probably couldn't define. Now he would not dissolve into mush, at least; but he wondered as she leaned into him, needing his arms, to whom his real thoughts might be expressed,

243

and if they were not in violation of the tenderness and sympathy he really felt toward her. As a comforter he had always felt not so much a fraud as an inadequate vessel.

"You stink good," he said. "It's honest sweat. You should have smelled me before I dove in the brook."

"I didn't shower because I didn't want you to think there was any hanky panky," she said. Her arms went around his waist and his towel fell off. "I didn't mean to do that!" she said, nearly in a panic. "God damn it!"

"I know," he said, but the appendage he had never found an adequate word for, at least in any complicated situation, had a willful mind of its own and rose white, pink, veined, a rather shockingly utilitarian instrument. He didn't know if she would take the recalcitrant organ's behavior for a betrayal or a compliment. As he leaned back to retrieve the towel, Jane stared at the thing that pointed at her, then at his eyes. He couldn't read her expression at all.

"I'm not exactly responsible," he said, covering it. "There are certain areas in which our best intentions are subverted, at least in part, by Beelzebub. When I feel tender toward a pretty woman that son-of-a-bitch goes on automatically, but I reserve the final decision, as it were."

"If you screwed me, wouldn't you feel you'd betrayed your friend?"

"You're a friend. You mean Ham. In that case you're talking about two friends. But do you blame me for this growth, or not? I don't know."

"You couldn't have *calculated* to say anything more seductive. All you want is a piece of ass."

He felt his noble ambivalence betrayed by this simplification. How easy and wonderful was marriage, in which action was not necessarily the opposite of care.

He could say to her that, after all, she had come here, where he had been peacefully, ascetically, eremitically performing his innocent ablutions.

Ah, no. She was unhappy and she was not evil. She would never know, this stunning golden girl, whether anyone, except maybe

244

her kindergarten pupil, loved her for herself or her bod—to use a word of her generation. But how much of herself was the great bod she exerted and starved for beauty? This new and near-hysterical flippancy of thought was tawdry, trashy, unworthy, self-protective. He didn't want to have to weep over her unhappiness or his own. If his erection was now licked by flame, now by ice, maybe that was the fire and ice of hell. Maybe she had cheated on Ham a hundred times, but that wasn't his information, and didn't matter anyway.

"I do care for you, Jane," he said with surprising emotion and difficulty, as though the words proved the truth of it. "I'll listen and treat you as a person, okay?" He handed her her drink and went into the tent to put on some clothes. When he came out, a minute later, her tennis costume was draped over the chairback, her tennis shoes and ankleless socks with their little white pom-poms were neatly lined up, and his towel and soap were gone.

The sun was approaching the mountain when she came back across the field, the towel wrapped tightly around her. She walked carefully over stubble and grass, and her hair was a dark rope, now, over one shoulder. Cool air had moved down from the hills, and he had made a fire in his rocked fireplace in front of the tent. Dead limbs, mostly applewood, burned yellow and orange, the small new fire at least visually the warm center of the pasture and surrounding trees and hills.

"Cold!" she said as she came up to the fire. "That brook is beyond cold. It's super-cold. You can't even *feel* it, it's so cold." She knelt next to the fire and spread the heavy, damp strands of her hair over her hands. "God, this is a beautiful place," she said, holding her hair over her head. "It's so green. It's almost too green."

He got her another towel and offered her dry clothes. She accepted the towel and tossed her hair in it as if her hair were wheat and the moisture were chaff that must be gently shaken away, never rubbed. Women were always doing expert things like that, things that rarely made much sense to him, but were part of their common mystery, such as why men caused in them so much tension and emotion all the time. Jane had come here out of some-

245

thing like love, something utterly impractical and compelling. She knelt by the fire, tossing her hair, naked except for the towel that compressed her breasts and covered her to her strong thighs. She was forty, but he had trouble imagining her as a younger woman, as if any smoothing out or firming of the live body that was now almost a cliché of the proper proportions could only make a manikin—thinner, hard, with an airbrushed surface. From certain angles, when she was dressed up and fixed up, she did look like a manikin sometimes, her face simplified and a soft sheen across cheek or forehead that was inhumanly geometrical. Then from this model, as visual an entity as a statue, would come all sorts of ragged, sometimes destructive emotion.

If he made love to her she would, sooner or later, confess to Ham or bludgeon Ham with it, depending upon the needs of that future moment, he knew. Then a connection would be made to all that complicated love and hatred and he would have a line on him like a leash, one that could be jerked taut at any unexpected time. If only he knew exactly what she wanted from him, something she probably didn't know either, he could veto the decision of his inflamed member.

Also he wanted to be alone; that was not an immediate priority because it was now overridden by the persistent itch of lust, each small hair on his body containing a charge, seeming to wave like cilia toward the woman who had come here because of him. But the need for singleness and isolation waited patiently, he knew, and would return with force.

She moved her long arms and basked in the fire as the air cooled and darkened. He felt the alcohol's dangerous evasions of the future. Because she didn't speak he knew what she wanted him to do. He went to her and for the first time since he had known her touched her with that intention. She knew before he had taken his second step, of course, and was so immediately willing and calmly naked she seemed to have lost all of her quirks and hard edges and become a smooth part of him. The mutual expediting, the unity of intent, function, opinion—like the slow tropisms of the green life all around them, nothing could ever be so remorseless and easy. There was the urgent recess for the spreading of the blanket and the removal of his clothes. Warning only came back to him just as he entered her, a moment he would remember later, when her eyes in the firelight widened fiercely, or as if with great surprise.

He awoke from a dream sometime in the night, not having recent memories except for the dream, which was invaded, or surrounded, by actual times and events, so that dream and memory were mixed. Helen had just returned to teaching. No, she had taught for six months or so and had changed in little ways he'd thought not necessarily strange, since one would naturally change with a change of occupation. The children were old enough, now, so that they didn't need constant transporting or supervision, and she went to Moorham only two days each week for her two freshman English sections and student conferences. Was that history, or part of the dream? She grew more outwardly affectionate; she touched him more, with a kind of bawdy, hail-fellow, ribald jokishness that was unlike her usually passionate solemnity about sex. One time she came home with a package (dream?) which she opened late at night on their bed. He watched her take from its box a strange set of black leather belts and buckles, a truss-like contraption the like of which he'd never seen. "I just wanted to show you this weird thing they actually use," she said. It seemed reasonable, even when she took off her robe and was nakedly, patiently, trying on the straps, belting them across her familiar thighs and belly, her brown pubic hair a warm, friendly muff he knew so well. Finally she'd figured out how the thick straps went, and then there was the plastic or horn part that belted over her mons and was a dildo, a huge rigid prick and balls, oversized, molded in precise male detail and yet the color of old ivory, antique as scrimshaw. That had to be dream. Then the dream's memory faded into vague alternatives, one of which was that she told him to get on his hands and knees, which he did, since in their loving there were no limits or inhibitions whatsoever, and she placed her warm, loved hands on his back just before that alternative faded. Another, so quickly fading from the dream now it might have been his own waking imagination, was Helen's round, heart-shaped, beautiful woman's ass, straps cutting waist

247

and thigh, humping and thrusting down between a woman's long tanned legs.

Jane Jones's legs? "Oh, God," he said out loud, remembering more recent events. The dream's details didn't bother him at all, but seemed wonderfully legitimate and interesting, the gift of having seen and touched Helen the dispensation of benevolent gods. But the real events of this night had happened; this was real life with all of its uncontrollable ensuing disasters.

At eight-thirty Jane had begun to worry about Ham, who was in Hartford at some sort of insurance meeting and would be home around midnight. She was more worried than she tried to show, her hands trembling as she put on her soiled, dew-damp panties and tennis clothes. Luke suggested that she have something to eat first, but she had to leave right now. The mountain night was cool, so he put a heavy cotton shirt over her shoulders, and drove her up the hill in his truck, past the somnolent farm foundations, through the deep black of the spruce to the road and her car, his hand at the hip of this woman he had known. That was the feeling, not sexual, not yet anxious because it had all seemed so familiar and normal, but anatomical, or proprietary, because within the moving center his hand lightly rode were vagina and cervix, uterus, ovaries and womb and he had been there, his semen still diving in the moist interior, and that could not be divorced from care.

The TR-7 seemed too low and flat to take her all those miles, but she sat deep in the seat and inserted her long legs toward the engine, then remembered to give him back his shirt.

"Are you unhappy?" he asked. "Is it all right?"

"I don't know what I am," she said. "I'll let you know." It seemed almost a threat.

Then the engine rapped and zoomed, the lights came on and in the form of the red taillights her presence narrowed and disappeared.

On the way back to his camp the truck's headlights swathed the road and the trees, leaving black hollows and distances that shifted, corridors into the night. Halfway down the hill toward the brook he met Jake, who had limped slowly after him and whose

248

eyes, flashing green in the lights, were bothered by this traipsing off in the dark. Luke got out and helped him up into the truck, then down again at the camp, Jake giving only one short, surprised yelp of pain.

And now Luke lay on his cot in the filmy nostalgia of the dream. Jane, in whatever mood this evening might have caused, would be home by now, in bed with her husband and her secrets. Helen and his children were in their graves. Jake sighed from his chosen bed beneath his master's bed.

# 18.

A few days later he stopped in on his way to Leah to see George, but George wasn't there. Phyllis had him come in, made some instant coffee and they sat in her office, which still showed signs of the book stacking George had done for the party, though new glaciers had begun.

"I read so much," she said, "and I sometimes think I remember so little of what I read that it's just like some habit, like biting your fingernails. What's to remember about that? What happens to you, that's what you remember. Yet I have odd memories that come up out of nowhere and I know they never happened to me at all."

"Like dreams," Luke said.

"Ayuh, like dreams. I got them, too. I hear Louise went off to California."

"That's what her brother told me," Luke said.

"You and her get along pretty well?"

"I don't know, Phyllis. We went out together, you might say."

"Huh! Stayed in together, too, I imagine. You don't have to use no euphemisms with me, Luke Carr."

250

"I don't know how much specific information you want. We slept together, but I suppose that's another euphemism."

"You young people, you think you're the first ones to break the rules. I could tell you. Maybe I will. Anyway, I've come to the conclusion Louise is a little tetched," Phyllis said, proclaiming her loyalty to Luke.

She sat straight and thick-bodied, the white flesh of her arms sagging from the bones, her shiny arthritic knuckles around her coffee mug as if to absorb the warmth of the porcelain, though it was a warm day in July. Her swivel chair was well greased in its joints and made no squeaks or creaks when she moved. George would have seen to that lubrication, something he could handle.

"Not badly tetched," Phyllis said. "I don't mean that. She's smart and she's talented, too, but I guess men, and a worthless husband, give her a hard time. She's come and talked to me, you know."

"She said she admired you. She said you were 'real' or something like that. I agreed."

"That's nice. God knows, I feel real enough." She slowly shifted herself on her swivel chair, with the blank look of familiar pain. "You young people think the old are all set in their ways, all the old sorrows and mistakes forgiven or forgotten. It don't work that way. You got to live with them new every day. Nothing ever gets forgiven or forgotten."

He remembered the story, not really a story but just an old piece of information, that one of George's and Phyllis's sons had committed suicide when he was young. And there were things he had heard about George's having been a hard man and a violent one, though the information was so old and vague it might not have been George Bateman at all. Something about throwing all the furniture out on the lawn, with darker implications. He could remember nothing more than that.

"We had our bad times too," Phyllis said. "Some of it was my fault. I made my mistakes. Lord, I once made a terrible mistake."

Her dark eyes, like dots in her round white face, were as black as her hair had once been. They had seemed larger, once, but as her face had grown soft and round with age they remained the

251

same, like mineral beads that would outlast their settings. The little eyes peered off over his shoulder. "I don't know why I should bring that up," she said. "I can't believe it's much of a lesson, if a lesson's anything I'd have a right to give you in the first place." She made a sound half sigh, half judgmental exclamation: "Humph. It was during the war, and you got to know what the times was like. I mean not the way they might have been to you, down in Massachusetts, a young boy. But to a girl from Cascom, her new husband gone off to war, no children to take care of, who liked dancing and going out. Oh, my, I guess it's an old story happened to many a girl. It seems kind of frivolous and even a little cheap, now—the places we went, with sawdust on the floor, and the songs—'Don't Get Around Much Anymore,' or was that 'Lonesome Saturday Night'? 'Rum and Coca-Cola,' 'Moonlight Cocktail,' 'If I Loved You'—unless you knew what it was like then it might appear kind of shoddy, the whole business, the music and the Cuba Librés and the beer. Gas rationing. My father was a Follansbee but he never worked in the store, he run the old farm on the River Road, so we always had T-stamps left over. Such big things was going on in the world it seemed nothing would ever last, everything would change, and we all come to care less about Cascom and Leah and what might happen after. The movies was the same—nothing mattered but the war. Everybody in the world was fighting and going places, sometimes dying. Everybody seemed to be saying hello or good-bye and who knew if the war would ever be over. It just got sort of normal for it to be war and the men gone or going. The places we went, they seemed part of all the excitement. The Rosebud Ballroom in Northlee, or the dances in the town halls of all the little towns, or the Casino Ballroom on the lake, or if I could get a T-stamp or two from my father maybe even over in Vermont or down to Claremont on the Connecticut River. I'd go with a girlfriend, we'd just dance or sometimes just look but then I met this boy he was in the navy, in the Officer Candidate School they had at Northlee College. George was in North Africa, or Sicily, or Anzio, with his Engineers. My girlfriend, her mother was a schoolteacher, so we had a car we could use, a DeSoto, it was. Howard—that was the name of

252

my Officer Candidate, Howard Gould—he'd always find a date for Loris. To tell you the truth, Luke, it don't sound like me, not now. It seems like history, like it happened to some other young girl married and without her husband—like something I read in a book a long time ago and can't recall the name of the book.

"Meantime, I had this sweet boy in his handsome uniform, and one thing followed another and I was pregnant. Shortly after I knew, Howard flunked out of the Officer Candidates and was sent off to sea someplace. I heard the Seventh Fleet, in the Pacific. I never knew the name of his ship or whatever happened to him. Maybe one of them kamikazes got him, or he's living back in Philadelphia, where he come from, or he's dead of natural causes. Men don't live as long as women and he'd be sixty years of age. It don't seem that long ago, just that it happened to somebody else.

"Later events seem like they happened to me. I went off to Manchester and worked as long as I could in a defense plant, making canvas duffel bags. The allowance from George's pay kept coming, too. Then when I got too big I just waited and had the baby, a boy I called John. There was no natural way he could have been George's child, no way in the world. I considered putting the baby up for adoption, but for one thing I couldn't do it and for another I figured I could never keep a secret like that anyway. When the war was over and George was in a camp in France I wrote and told him everything, saying it was up to him to do what he thought right, and I'd go along with whatever he thought best.

"Which he did. Which he thought he did. Instead of divorcing me he come home and took John as his own but John wasn't his own. George tried, but something in him denied what he thought he could do. He never could forgive me, and whenever he laid eyes on John it was like he was looking at a spider or some little beast that was ten times more dangerous than its size. It drove George crazy, and that's the truth of it. He never forgive me, though you never seen a man try so hard.

"Bill was born in 1947—George's real son.

"George's mother died insane, you know, down to Concord, and George always had the terrible suspicion the same thing would happen to him. It was bad. Bad years. George worked, but

253

at night he drank and whenever he was on the hard stuff he broke up the house and wrecked his cars. They was terrible years for all of us, but it was worst for John. God knows I tried my best to give him what he needed, but at the age of fifteen, that was in 1959, January 15, John hung himself from a crossbeam, out in the shed.

"So who's to forgive what all there is to forgive, Luke? Maybe it fades a little, but that's the best we can ask. You live in and around and about whatever happened, but it's always with you and you you just live every day, starting over each time."

Phyllis moved too suddenly, then gave a blank stare of pain for a moment as she lifted herself, using the arms of her chair. She let herself settle back again, her spine as straight as she could make it. "I've got to go to the little biffy George made for me," she said, lifting herself to her feet this time. "It's the coffee. I drink too much of it." Using her cane, she walked slowly across the room.

He thought of the shed, where he and George had talked and smoked, the crossbeams and the body of the fifteen-year-old in the January freeze.

When Phyllis came back she sat down slowly, giving Luke an icy twinge of sympathy pain in the vicinity of his prostate. She said, "You're not building a camp up there, you're building a house to live in."

"Who knows?" he said, startled into the inane question.

"George described it to me, so I guess I know. You going to live by yourself, like a hermit?"

"Maybe."

"Hmm."

It was as if she looked straight at him for the first time. Her small eyes, black shiny things in the soft white folds of her lids, might almost have been evil, or else he was suddenly too much on the defensive. Not so much on the defensive as on the very edge of any knowledge of his plans or desires, where he had no sure footing at all.

But her eyes were not evil, only old and curious; she meant no harm, she just wanted to have a hand in things. Here was this rarity, an unencumbered man, a widower, a curiosity indeed. That and their old fondness for each other when he'd been a child and

254

she a young woman. He wondered if she had any recollection, and if she had, whether she thought it strange or important in any way, that she had let that child climb upon her smooth, naked body, the child in a kind of night-warm paradise.

He didn't know how to ask that, but she looked at him with a tolerant, fond, knowing expression as they said good-bye.

He went on into Leah on the High Road and bought groceries at Follansbees' and a ten-cubic-foot refrigerator from the Electric Coop Store. Two men helped him slide it off the loading platform into the truck and he roped it, still in its crate, in a front corner of the truck bed. He would decide how to get it off the truck later, probably with a couple of two-by-eight planks. Lumber for joists, roof, sills and beams had been delivered by the lumber yard and was stacked by the cabin site, shrouded in black polyethylene that whispered and flapped.

He forgot to stop at the Post Office for his mail and was on the road back to Cascom when he thought of it, decided to get it another day, then turned around and went back for it. He didn't want any mail, yet, in order to avoid closer confrontations, needed to know who exactly did want to communicate with him. This seemed a trap, unfair; but then he had foolishly told people where he was. In time, maybe, if he slowly and carefully retreated, no one would think to write to the Hermit of Cascom Mountain. So far he hadn't been doing too well.

He picked up his mail, paid forwarding charges and went back to the truck to read it, the hot, fumy breezes of the town square blowing through the windows.

The August issue of *Gentleman*; he wondered if he would actually read any of it. A letter from the Avenger, postmarked Wellesley, MA. He held the envelope in his hands. It was as if he were blind, trying to get hold of someone in a room in which the other could see. It was addressed to Luke Carr, General Delivery, Leah, N.H. One step closer. There was a letter from Jane Jones, and another from Martin Troup on Martin's own stationery. The rest was junk he could throw away without opening.

First the Avenger. As he opened the envelope he felt almost sick. This asshole, this shit-for-brains, was soiling his freedom.

255

Then he tried to imagine someone who would actually be flattered by such attention. Maybe he could imagine that person; maybe even himself, once, when he wasn't known and wanted to be known.

Luke Carr:
You will die slow with you're dirty, nasty gonads and prick cut off. How would you like to eat it???

Mr. Death

So the Avenger now seemed more interested in method than in justification. If Luke had any insight into the matter at all, he had to find this note somewhat reassuring, since literary creation of this sort was rewarding in itself—a nice thrill to write nasty like that. Maybe the Avenger's kick was just creative writing.

The pistol was stashed under the dash, however, where he could reach it quickly. He'd spent some time arranging a hidden but accessible place there for the holster.

He opened Jane's letter, which was written on flowered blue stationery, her name and address embossed at the top and on the envelope by one of those pliers-like gadgets.

Mrs. Hamilton Jones
206 Winthrop St.
Wellesley, MA.

Dear Luke,
I arrived a few minutes ahead of Ham—about 11:45—so he didn't have to worry about me, thank the Good Lord and I-93! I keep thinking of everything that happened in your Mountain Greenery. I was a fool to barge in on you like that, but that's the way I am. It was so lovely. We mustn't do it again but I shall always remember those wonderful moments.

I'm sorry I was so anxious to get back. I was nearly out of my mind when we said good-bye. Forgive me.

If you ever get down this way again, please come and see us.

Love,
Jane

\*   \*   \*

Hmm. It didn't sound like Jane, and because it didn't sound like her, what could it tell him? Perhaps Jane was one of those people who spoke one way and wrote another. But which was the truth? He wanted out of it, and she seemed to be allowing him to be out of it. Her handwriting was nervous and angular, the tails of letters stabbing straight down into sharp points before they shot upward again. Lord, he thought, this wasn't over. She'd get the itch for some more adultery and turn up again. Maybe he was being small and mean. He felt shame. Hadn't he loved her at all? Whatever power of desire she'd caused was gone, and now all he wanted was cool freedom.

He was sweating in the hot wind from the pavement and the passing traffic, a bad sweat. The two notes mixed in his head, reinforcing each other. He put them in the dash compartment and opened Martin Troup's.

Dear Luke,

As you can see, I'm not using Gentleman's letterhead this time and I'm typing this myself. We've been friends, I fondly think, for a long time and I've got some questions I'd like to ask that I don't want anybody at Gentleman to know about. Anybody. Mainly, what have you heard about Gentleman and specifically me, lately? I'd like to stop right here without telling you any more and see what you'd have to say, but, ' ¹ Buddy, I'm about to blow my top, there's about nobody else I half-way trust, Charlene and I have parted but that was no surprise (I know why you shied off coming to supper and don't blame you), I've got five kids by three goddam horrible marriages, one in an expensive college, two in expensive prep schools and two in an expensive grade school where they wear leotards a lot.

Don't know why I got onto that, but stay with me, boy, you're hearing a lonesome roar of pain from a trapped bear. I can see the white of my own leg bone in the steel, and there's a couple of poisoned arrows in my back.

Maybe you and me weren't meant for this fucking political-ego-power-performance shit, where a man's word's nothing but a fart in a whirlwind or a piss hole in the snow. If you trust a man, like I trusted Merlin Richards, or for Christ's sake even Jimmy Barnes—

can you believe that? Jimmy? Why, son, you're just a fool. I even find myself wondering about Annie Gelb, for Christ's sake.

Anyway, to spare your sensitive hide from too many details, what happened was when the new owners came around, Merlin, a man I brought in here and treated like a son—he's talented enough—and trusted, along with Jimmy Barnes, who I once thought was my friend, or at least a fairly honorable man, began stabbing me in the back, making up, and I mean made up out of nothing but their wily imaginations, all kinds of things I was supposed to have done, said, not done, etc. How do I know about it? For one thing, finally, when I began to get ominous little signals from upstairs, I asked Merlin if he knew what was coming down and with the straightest face you ever saw he told me how he heard with his own ears and saw with his own eyes these fictions. He said that I said things to him that I do not remember saying and that, in fact, are not even in my psychic language. He evidently made them up, and now—what chutzpah, Luke!—he tells me what I am supposed to have done and said that hurt morale, sowed dissention, convinced my colleagues I was a sadist, a drunk or a nut.

You've met the fellow. I suddenly know more about him now, and it makes a bad list. Plausibility is his talent, omniscience is his delusion, and power is his game. I was so sick when he told me all this shit I thought I might do him a favor and end his miserable existence on the spot. I guess I looked kind of funny, because he asked me if I was "getting any help." From a shrink, I guess he meant. That night I went home and fucking blubbered. The death of friendship, the death of trust, Luke. That's a wound that never heals.

I know you're up there in the clean woods someplace, where you won't hear much, up there in that strange state of New Hampshire that's more of a culture lag than Mississippi these days, communing with the deer or something. But I've got to try to fight this thing, make a stand somehow, keep my pride in my work, which you might think frivolous sometimes but, dammit, has always been receptive to your kind of thing, too. So if you know anything, have heard anything, or can think of anything, buy a pencil and a piece of paper and let me know. Or if they've got a telephone over to the village you might even try one of them infernal instruments. Just ask the operator for Martin Troup, in New York City, where a man's as good as his word.

Martin

Luke read the letter again, feeling empty, like loss, and distant; Martin had never claimed anything from him in the past but decent work. He must be truly hurt, not just because of his job, because there were other jobs and it was musical chairs in the profession—but who knew? Martin had been there for a long time, and had been part of *Gentleman's* transition from slick, girly sophistication to whatever lively mixture it was now. The feeling was like hearing of the destruction of something old, dependable and more meritorious than not, or even like hearing of a death. As for the truth of Martin's accusations, one incident came immediately to mind. Several years ago, when he'd met Merlin Richards, Merlin had addressed Martin as "Sir," no irony or humor implied. Luke had been a little startled, and had looked at Merlin's bland face to see. He felt then that Martin liked Merlin enough, for some reason, to overlook small indicators, but hadn't thought much more of it.

This outburst, however, was all wrong; this last roar was fatal by definition. How could he help? If things had gone as far as Martin said, with ominous signals coming down, he should be out of there already. No one was ever considered, except in his own delusions, unexpendable. And gratitude was not a chip to be cashed.

He had to call Martin and didn't know what to say to him. Of course he couldn't remember *Gentleman's* telephone number and his address book was in the tent, so he would have to call information; the complications of that, on top of all the other complications, made him want to run back up the mountain. He always did what other people wanted him to do. He never did anything he wanted to do, just responded, responded, all of his life. He got some change in Trask's Pharmacy, went to the telephone booth and with weary, nearly panicked clumsiness deciphered the instructions in the telephone book, got the number and called collect. He finally got Annie Gelb, who said she would accept the call. Martin was in conference.

"Mr. Carr . . . Luke," Annie said.

"Martin asked me to call," he said.

"I know," she said, meaning that she knew everything.

"Tell him I don't know anything except what Robin Flash told me about the new owners. What's going on?"

"It's awful. Everybody's looking for other jobs."

"Is Martin okay?"

"No, I wouldn't say so. He's upset. He says nobody will give him any answers." She was silent after that, and then, just as he decided that he would have to say something, she said quickly, "Your name was on a list of people they wanted information about. Your name keeps coming up and Martin worries about that, too."

"I don't know anything about that, Annie. In any case, I'm not for hire. Tell him that. Tell him my word's still good and I'm a hermit, now, terminal case. Tell him to keep his pecker up, okay?"

"All right."

"Good luck to you both, huh?"

"I'll tell him. I wish you luck, too, Mr. Carr."

So he'd got out of it without having to promise to call back. Feeling a little dishonorable, he went back to his personal, singular, paid-for, registered, inspected and insured, functional truck. He sat behind the wheel and lit a cigarette, which he soon put out. In this truck, or while working on the cabin, and lately on his equipment shed, he found that he rarely smoked. It was as though he had forbidden himself any of those small, addictive rewards until some major part of the construction was finished. Then he would sit down and have a slow, solitary, contemplative little celebration. He yearned for walls and ceilings now, protective spaces.

He drove around the square and back to Cascom, through the green hills and the warm summer air. What happened to anything as ephemeral as a magazine was hardly cause for thought. He wondered why even Martin Troup cared, really, aside from salary and benefits. It was all words, words, glossy photographs, drawings, jokes, stuff blabbed out over and over again, opinions that were standardly fashionable and amusing or pseudo-shocking. It was hard to remember his own interest in reading *Gentleman*, or any other magazine, but then he'd read it, usually, while sitting on the hopper, a captive position that precluded deep seriousness.

What suddenly did seem important was that a canary yellow Dodge was following him. The car was so elevated in the rear by its springs and oversized rear tires it looked like a tracking animal,

260

nose down, snuffling after him. It had closely tailgated the truck for the last mile into Cascom, where it could easily have passed, and now followed him up the mountain road. It was Lester Wilson, of course, his thick shoulders and wide head visible when the light changed on curves and the shadows and reflections of branches or sky wiped across the car's windshield. Luke first thought *cop*; was he guilty? Then of the power Lester would assume, then of the ragged, almost pitiable man who acted out his fantasies of authority. There was no one certain way to treat the man if it came to a confrontation. He might be properly civil and even meek toward this fantasist, or cite the law, or use his class-given authority composed of literacy, property and influence; but from beneath these practicalities he heard a more primitive voice asking, *Are you following me? Are you following me, you son of a bitch?*

He had begun, he realized, to consider the upper part of the mountain road, where there were no more year-round houses, his private road, as if it were his own driveway, and the farm turnoff itself as private as the doorway to his house. The long days of solitary work, no sounds but his, Jake's phlegmy sleeping breaths nearby, the cries of birds and the sighing of the brook, were reality now, and anything else an excursion or an interruption.

The yellow Dodge followed him past the asphalt, onto the dirt road. A morning shower had damped down the dust, unfortunately, or Lester Wilson would be eating it. In the narrow places between banks and trees Luke could hear the half-muffled roar.

The bastard was pushing him, trying to intimidate, changing him toward rage, the fool. When he came to the farm road he would stop right there, and if Lester wanted anything he would have to stop with his own car still in the middle of the main road. Or if Lester wasn't alert enough maybe the Dodge's grille would kiss the truck's step-bumper and trailer hitch. Luke would have it out on the edge of his property.

When they came to the farm road he waited to put on his turn signal until the last moment, a chilly compromise between his anger and legal foresight, turned in and stopped instantly. The Dodge swerved, drifted on the dirt, straightened and went on up

261

the road, its engine cutting back in with a long, blapping rise and the clack of gravel in the wheel wells.

Luke waited, lighting a cigarette this time, and after a minute or so, having found a place to turn around, the yellow car came back, accelerating past him down the narrow road with such noise and recklessness Luke thought Lester might lose control on the next curve. He backed out on the road to see, but Lester had made it, at least that curve, and was out of sight.

He drove on in, down the hill, across the log and plank bridge and across the field, stopping within the framework of his equipment shed. He trembled in the aftermath of this violation, this invasion. Jake appeared from within the tent, where he had no doubt been sneaking his rest on Luke's forbidden pillow. Out of sight, out of shame. Though he felt weak at first, Luke's strength came back as he walked the crated refrigerator down planks to the concrete, removed the skeletal crating and plugged the shiny white box into a heavy-duty extension cord. It rumbled, clicked its relays and the hum of its pump began, so he wiped the dust from it, inside and out, and transferred to it his perishables, those that hadn't already perished in the ice chest, then rigged a tarp over it to protect it from the rain until he possessed a roof.

Jake followed him into the tent, looking fairly innocent in his joy at Luke's return. "Jake," Luke said, "you know and I know you've been sleeping on my pillow." This meant nothing to Jake except that it was nice to hear a voice. He scratched Jake's back just forward of his tail, an area unreachable by Jake and the stimulation of which, for some personal reason, made Jake grin, wag his tail and raise a brushlike line of hair from his tail to his collar.

Jake belonged, legally, paralegally, conventionally or whatever, to Lester Wilson. So why, he asked himself again, didn't he either take the dog back, or, if he wanted the dog around, offer to buy him from Lester? Why keep putting off a possible solution? It had, he thought, aside from his not wanting to talk to or even look at Lester Wilson, to do with Jake's freedom of choice in the matter. Jake was, after all, a unit, a sentient being with his own desires; how could he be owned? One could own a machine, a house, a knife. One could not own another person. Did one own one's wife, for instance? Did Ham Jones own Jane Jones? Should he have felt like a thief? It had been Jane's choice, right or wrong; if he had not done what she wanted him to do because he didn't think she should cheat on Ham, wouldn't that have been cruel? Was this clear? It would have meant to her that she was not a person but a possession. Had he made love with a singular, independent, self-contained, free animal, or to another man's wife?

And then, the accident. Should he have been paid all that money because someone's negligence or bad luck had killed his family? Had someone, then, destroyed his property? The possessive we so casually used; the vet had referred to Jake as "your dog," and that had made him think, No, not *my* dog, just a dog. I own no one.

# 19.

He had just hosed down and turned off his rented cement mixer when he heard a car, or some machine, coming down the hill toward his bridge, engine and gears whining. Jake heard it and rose painfully to his feet, giving a single warning howl, his hair up along his back. Luke didn't think it was Lester Wilson's supercar, or George's truck. Because of brush he could just see part of the bridge, where whatever it was would have to pass. His hand went to his hip: cops and robbers, small chills and a suspicion of melodrama. He went quickly to the truck, got the holstered pistol from its hanger up under the dash, took it to the tent and hung it on a nail on the center pole. He didn't want to be unprepared for attack, to show his resentment of this intruder, or to look silly, like some idiot imitating Wyatt Earp, though that last hesitation had no doubt killed many of the overly civilized. Clear ultimatums were seldom issued.

There would still be several hours of daylight. He wanted to continue to work on his cabin, toward that vision of blowing snow and warm windowlight. The car came to the bridge and stopped, still hidden, then moved across the bridge. It was dark blue, new-looking, an American car of some kind. It came slowly toward him on his driveway across the pasture, the wide grille dipping. A Massachusetts license plate. Because he had no idea who it was, and couldn't make out the driver, he looked for clues in the car itself, in its posture and expression, in the width of its eyes, as if in the mass-produced design there had to be small defects that might show its intentions.

He stood in the entrance to the tent, waiting. A step backward and he could reach the pistol. Shem's other guns were in the wooden chest. An ax imbedded in a small stump three feet away tilted its handle toward his hand.

The car stopped. The wide door opened on the driver's side and it was Robin Flash, his kinky blond beard and hair vaguely fuzzy until the bright blue eyes stabilized his face as he recognized Luke. He wore a plaid leisure suit with lots of red in it.

"Hey, man!" he said. "I wasn't sure it was you and I've been lost for ten miles. Didn't want to get my balls shot off for trespassing. You look like a goddam pioneer or something! I mean, Jesus! What are you *doing* out here?" He reached into the car for a camera and put its carrying strap over his sharp shoulder as he came closer. "It is you, isn't it? Or am I a goner?"

"It's me," Luke said. "How are you, Robin?"

Robin looked around the valley, at the mountain rising toward bald rock, into the nearer spruce with their corridors that led into twilight. "Gives me the creeps," he said. "I don't go for all this green. There wasn't another car on the road for miles back there, and I thought what if this Avis iron breaks down? Photographer lost, dies of exposure, bitten by snakes, shot by hunters, eaten by bears."

"Well, it's not hunting season. You've got enough red on you to keep from being shot, anyway."

"Yeah, but is it wise-ass New York Jew season? I'm just a city boy and don't know the local customs. I have this vision, see? I keep going down this one-way road, unpaved, and I come to this rundown farm, there's this retarded kid playing the banjo and these fat, inbred weirdos with guns, kind of giggling softly to each other and they tell me to get down on my hands and knees."

"You're safe now. Relax. You want a beer? Coffee?" Luke brought out a chair for him.

"Coffee and a Valium. No, hold the Valium. My nerves are coming back. Maybe I'll have a beer. Yeah."

"I thought you didn't drink."

"Maybe I'll take it up. Things not so good in the big city, Luke." He took a beer and held it in his hand without trying it. "Amy split with the kid. This time I think she really means it."

Jake nosed Robin's shoes, limped slowly over to piss on one of the car's tires, then lay down by Luke's chair. Robin paid no attention to him.

"She's done it before?" Luke asked.

"Once after Marjorie blew the whistle, twice so far in July."

"Twice?"

"Yeah. She's totally irrational. Flipped out. I love her and I love the kid, you got to believe it. I told her, you know, I said none of this other shit means anything, it's just the way I am. She says, 'What about the shit with me?' and 'How'd you like it if some big stud was laying me?' I said, 'Amy, I'd have to try to understand.' That's when the shit really hit the fan. You figure it out."

"It's not too hard, I guess. Have you thought about it much?"

"Yeah. It sounded pretty reasonable at the time, but reasonable doesn't apply. Like why I keep going back to Marjorie, for instance."

"You do?"

"Yeah. I can't help it. There's something about that big smooth long-legged innocent broad I can't fucking resist. She's with me now, at the motel down on the lake."

"With her kids?"

"They're back in the Bronx with Sheila Ryan. Remember that cold-turkey Harp bitch? Does she hate my guts? But I've got Marjorie to jump up and down on for a few days. The world's crazy, *n'est-ce pas?* So I was born a sex fiend, how can you fight it? Marjorie's mad at me too, sort of in a sultry semi-sulk, just because I was looking cross-eyed at this cute little yokel waitress this morning. Cute but freaky. You ever noticed how many of the chicks up here have tops that don't go with their bottoms? Freaky, freaky gash.

266

You know what I mean? Long skinny legs with short torsos and big boobs? Or teeny-weeny petite tops and tits and great solid asses and legs like elephants? What is it, inbreeding? Long cold winters? Too many porks and beans? Oh, God, Luke, all I know is I want to bang 'em all!"

After this outburst Robin was thoughtful, and stared across the field, seeing, Luke supposed, amorphous green with no nameable parts to it but light and shade, texture and composition.

About Marjorie Luke felt, if he had any right to have feelings about her, sad that she had been so uprooted, startled and changed.

"Didn't she want to come up here with you?" he asked.

"You think *I'm* scared of all these man-eating trees, you should see Marjorie. It's like I suggested we paddle up the Amazon. Anyway, she's embarrassed she lets me hump her; in some freaky Waspy way you're her conscience. But she'd like to see you. Figure that one out."

"Well, I'm fifteen or sixteen years older than she is."

"Yeah, yeah. Lots of things. Like . . . death, you know. You've been where she's been." Robin looked at him, worried, and they spoke of other things. Luke showed him around the construction. The shed was now roofed, and sided with board and batten; the cabin's joists and sub-flooring were in, and the interior stone wall, or heat well, had grown several feet above floor level. Luke explained how the low winter sun would hit the wall, which would also be heated internally by the stove gases. Robin seemed impressed by all this, not as if Luke were a mere mortal like himself who had learned to build a house, but as if Luke were one of them, those others who did such things and sometimes deigned to hint at their mysteries.

"Far out," Robin kept saying. He seemed to look as often through the viewfinder of his reflex camera as he did with his naked eyes. "But Luke, you going to *live* out here? Man, that's sick!"

"Maybe it is," Luke said, "but I'll only have to cope with my own illness. When winter socks in here it lasts from November till April mud season. Six months or more."

267

"But what'll you do all that time?"

"Stoke my fire."

"You can't haul your own ashes, unless you've got an awfully sexy mitt."

"I'm going to try it, anyway."

"Creepy."

Robin told him the latest he'd heard about *Gentleman*, that they were going to try a new format, making it more topical, thinner and bringing it out every two weeks, or else they were going to make it thicker, glossier, sexier and have it appear every other month, or else it was folding, or else it was going to print nothing but high-class intellectual stuff and old-fashioned line drawings, monochromatic from stem to stern, or else it was simply going to be a house organ-tax loss deal for R.I.C. Corporation, and so on. Luke didn't tell him about Martin Troup's letter.

At five-thirty Robin looked worried again and asked him if he'd come down to the motel and have dinner with them; Marjorie had made him promise to ask.

"And I want to get back down to what is laughingly called civilization before it gets dark and the Sasquatch come out," Robin said. "I'm not kidding, either. All this nothing around here is sucking out my juices. I need carbon monoxide and neon signs that go on and off, man. Maybe it's irrational, but as nameless dreads go, it's not bad. Marjorie's got it worse than me. I mean, there ain't a berserk taxi driver or a Spade mugger within a hundred miles of this godforsaken wilderness."

"If she feels so funny about you two, why does she want to talk to me? I don't get it either," Luke said.

"It woman bidniss," Robin said in a deep, mysterious black accent. "Yo cain unnerstan it cause yo ain got no pussy."

Luke didn't see how he could not go, if they had come all the way from Boston, where Robin's assignment had been, just to see him. He must, just this one last time; they would both have to go back to New York and their wrenched lives. He shook Jake's pill bottle and Jake, resigned and sad over the inevitable, came slowly over to him and sat down. He broke a pill in half, opened Jake's wet, toothy mouth and stuck the pill down into Jake's throat as far

268

as his finger would reach, shut the mouth and rubbed Jake's throat to force him to swallow. Jake didn't object to all this, but could be clever in holding the pill in clew or gum somewhere and later spitting it out. Luke opened a can of dog food and put it in Jake's blue pie plate, formerly Shem's. Jake was mildly pleased by this, though he preferred human food.

"A watchdog to keep the wolves at a distance, huh?" Robin said.

"Oh, he's small but fierce," Luke said.

He washed up at the hose, which had warmed in the sun, rinsed in the cold water that came after and put a kettle on his Coleman stove to heat for shaving. Robin looked into the tent and saw the pistol hanging there. "Is that for real? Jesus!" he said. Luke took out the clip, unloaded the chamber and handed it to him. Robin quickly handed it back. "What do you shoot with it?"

"Nothing yet, but you never can tell."

"That thing scares me more than the Sasquatch," Robin said. "I mean, do you really need it around here?"

"To me it's just a friend."

"Weirder and weirder," Robin said. "Let's hurry up and get the hell out of here." He was even more puzzled when, before they left, Luke reloaded the pistol and put it back in the truck.

He followed Robin down the mountain, through the village and out along the lakeshore road to the Lake Cascom Motel and Dining Room, an old wooden inn that had grown outward into long, one-story motel units, nearly every one, now, in the summer season, with a car nosing its parent cubicle. Across the broad blue lake the hills rose up toward Cascom Mountain, which did look impressively steep and rocky from here.

Marjorie had just come back from the beach across the road. She wore a filmy light blue dressing gown open upon a bright orchid bathing suit, a two-piece semi-bikini that revealed smooth reaches of white skin now tinted pink, a near sunburn, on those curves that by their amplitude had been offered directly to the sun.

"Hi, Marge," Luke said. She was shy, yet prepared, as though she had thought a lot about this meeting and was as ready as anyone could be. She smiled and said hello, but was terribly embar-

269

rassed. She seemed bound by it, kept back a certain distance from them toward the far wall of the room. She was larger than he remembered her to be, a tender giant in the clashing feminine colors. She looked directly at him once, as if to say, "Look what's happened to me, of all people," with some of the wry humor of the fallen. They talked about the lake, the clear cold water, the greenness of the hills, her first time way up here in New Hampshire, the difference from the city. Robin made gin and tonics for them, plain tonic for himself.

Marjorie was grave, impressed by the ceremony of all of this. It was as if her body were the immensely important but somehow shameful offering that had caused it all. She was excited, prepared to be shamed or praised, knew she was in a foreign land in a compromising room with two men who were strange, attractive, rich, glamorous and judgmental, and who had nothing to do with her real life. Yet she was here, and they all knew she had lain naked with one of them. At least that was the way Luke had to read her high emotion. She, Marjorie Burns Rutherford, her life, soul, worth, morals, her freaky licentious behavior, her cheapened but still sinfully magnetic sexual attractiveness, was at the center of this moment.

Luke suddenly thought that if Robin had any meanness in him now was the time he would show it.

And then, another thought that frightened him: by requesting his presence she had given away her right to treat her liaison with Robin as a lark, a whimsical thing she had decided to do, and given him a license to ask her any question at all. In fact demanded those questions, and he didn't want the responsibility. No. But if he were imperviously polite and casual, and went away having dealt with nothing of high seriousness, then she would be abandoned and truly hurt. He didn't want to be anyone's confessor, not even his own, and they were after him as they were always after him.

Maybe he would have to get drunk in order to take her confession and dispense his paternal indulgences, as he had been at the Joneses' when their repetitive marital cataclysm demanded his goddam mediation.

270

And now Marjorie, this twenty-nine-year-old woman, so awed by the strange turns her life had taken; big Marjorie, Marjorie in all her voluptuous warm flesh chilled by the cold lake and warmed again by the afternoon sun, now indoors with men, drinking gin, still in the diaphanous blue of her gown, her sinful places struck by scant and violent orchid. They must be so important to her, these next hours, but did he need them? Demeaning thought. Poor Marjorie.

"I ought to change out of my bathing suit," she said, but sat in one of the shiny motel easy chairs, next to the door that led to the inner hallway. Sunlight striped her. With one hand she pushed and carded her hair that was damp at the ends. "And wash off all the Coppertone, though I got burned a little anyway. I burn so easy I guess I ought to stay in the shade and look like a white worm."

"Some worm," Robin said.

"Now, Robin," she said with a touch of sternness, or dismay, then changed the subject. "How are you doing now, Luke?"

"I'm building myself a cabin in the woods," he said.

"He's going to be a hermit," Robin said.

"A hermit?"

"I just want to live alone for a while," Luke said.

"But it's awful living alone. Why do you want to live alone?"

"I don't know," Luke said, though the unformulated answer loomed in his mind, anxiety around that gray shape like a nimbus. "What are you going to do, Marge?" he said.

"Be a receptionist-secretary at the clinic again. The girl they got now's leaving the first of September, her husband's going to college in Indiana."

"So you've got a vacation till then."

"I got to go back and take care of Mickey and Marcia, so this part's nearly over. Sheila's mad at me, anyway. I said we only live once and I'm a widow now, so why not? Do you disapprove, Luke?"

"Why should I disapprove?"

"It's like, well, I mean, I never did anything like this before."

Robin said, "I'm going to take a shower, so you two Wasps can

271

discuss the finer points of sin." He went off cheerfully to the bathroom, and the shower started.

"You do disapprove. You disapproved on the phone when I called you," Marjorie said.

"Well, I got the impression that you kind of disapproved of the whole thing yourself."

"I did at first, but I liked it too much. You only live once. That's what I told Sheila. She's Catholic, you know."

"It's just a matter of what's good for you, that's all," Luke said, sinking, doing his duty.

"Robin's so good in bed. I need a man in bed," she said, a little breathless at this confession.

"Just so you know how temporary it is."

"I don't know about that," she said.

"He's married and has a kid. Do you think he'll leave them?"

"She left him!"

"I doubt it. She'll be back when he gets home."

"He loves me!"

"Not to marry you, Marge, for Christ's sake. I was hoping you knew what you were doing. Treat it as an outing or something. You only live once. Robin's a nice enough fellow, it's just that he's a little sick in certain areas. He wants to go to bed with every woman in the world. I'm sorry, and I shouldn't get exasperated, but if you think anything's permanent, you're a fool."

"Why did Mickey have to die?" she said, crying. Fluids came to her nose and eyes, and she reached for the Kleenex. When she'd wiped and blown, her eyes glossy, she said, "I wish I could live with you, Luke. Not to sleep with. No, that too. I don't care how old you are. Maybe you don't even do it anymore, how should I know? I've just been so alone!"

"You're an attractive young woman who likes men and you won't be alone for long, believe me. Go back to work in your clinic. I wish my prognosis was as good. Meanwhile, have fun on your vacation."

Though the shower still ran, she looked conspiratorily toward the bathroom. "He's so good, you know, in bed. He goes on and on. We do awful things, too, that I never did before. I mean, I

272

heard the words for the things we do, but I never knew people ever really did them. Now I'm embarrassed, telling you that." She pulled her gown over her long pink and white legs. "I just need a man's arms around me at night. I thought there for a while I was a mother, so I'd be a mother and that was it, the rest was all over. But the rest wasn't over. I'm still too young, I guess, and too hot-blooded. I'm on the pill now, even. I mean, I'm a good mother, too, but I get wild for a man. I'm unnatural that way. I just got to have a man."

"You'll get a man, Marge. Don't worry."

Robin came out of the bathroom in flowered blue shorts, toweling his hair. "Next," he said. Marjorie glanced once at his hairy, gleaming body and the bulge caused by his randy little apparatus, blushed and looked away as she rose to take her bath.

Robin retrieved his leisure suit from the bathroom and Marjorie went in. Then he, too, looked conspiratorily at the bathroom's closed door. "Pardon my crudeness, or whatever you'd call it, but if you want to try her, old buddy, I'll take a walk."

"For Christ's sake, Robin."

At dinner Marjorie looked purged, absolved. She was gay and laughing, Robin going on about the dangerous animals he'd come across on the way to Luke's mountain home. They ate in the dining room of the old hotel, Marjorie a little worried about silverware and how one should hold a wine glass. Occasionally she gave Luke quick, serious glances he thought grateful, this somewhat formal dinner and his older presence making it all more legitimate. Just having another person know must institutionalize it somewhat, make it a social rather than an aberrant act. Well, he knew, and having known would say good-bye to them soon.

Robin asked about the article. "*Gentleman* doesn't pay that well—notorious tightwads—but I wouldn't mind the credits, if you ever do the thing."

"I wouldn't know how to tell the truth about it," Luke said.

"I called Mike Rizzo, you know," Robin said. "He told me once I could come and photograph his apartment, but on the phone he was scared or embarrassed or something. He's a big talker. He said he was afraid some nut would come and get him and his fami-

273

ly. 'They get your address, Robin, you follow me? They find out where you live, you follow me? Some nut's going to come and kill you.' Our brave paratrooper."

"What about Jimmo McLeod, the crane guy?"

"Jimmo's gone to Alaska, his family and all," Marjorie said. "Maura, his wife, called me up to say good-bye. She said they were going to get rich in Alaska."

"A crane operator makes good money," Robin said, "but a crane operator does not get rich."

"Or a photographer," Luke said.

"But films, films," Robin said. "Who knows?"

When Marjorie went to the ladies' room, her fawn colored slacks drawing glances as she walked between the white-clothed tables, Robin said, "You could take her, you know. Don't get mad, now, but she's ripe. The two of us turn her on, I can tell. She's hot as a pistol, if you're up for that sort of thing."

"Robin."

"Don't go all fucking moral on me. I'm thinking what she'd like. I'm not being a shit. She'd like to get gang-shagged, is what she'd really like."

"I'm not a member of the gang."

"You mean you couldn't get it up for poor Marge? Listen, she likes you so much that when you act sort of dignified and moral and like that she acts that way too, but I'll bet anything—I'll bet you a hundred bucks, right now, we can take her back to the room and have her clothes off in five minutes."

"Maybe you're right, but I don't want it to happen. I deeply don't want it to happen, Robin. I want to say good-bye to Marge without making her unhappy now or in the future. I want out with a good conscience, if that's possible."

"Back to your hermitage, huh?"

"Right. No guilt, no more tears, no orgasmic convulsions, no voyeuristic amusements whatsoever."

"Oh, well. It would have been funsies for all. Whatever else she is, Marjorie is one fucknutty cunt. I was just trying to do my old buddy a favor, but forget it, forget it. Maybe I'm a pimp at heart. What do you think?"

"Maybe."

"And I guess you're never going to do the article, huh?"

"Too much new data keeps creeping in. I want to creep out."

"Maybe you're a creep at heart."

"Maybe. Just don't turn over my stone and I'll be satisfied."

Marjorie came back across the room, her eyes glittering with interest and shyness as she looked at Luke and Robin.

With their coffee, Robin ordered brandy for Luke and Marjorie. "Live it up," he said, "for tomorrow we head back to Logan and the shuttle to the real world."

"You can have it," Marjorie said.

"Would you like to stay up here with all the trees and creepies and crawlies?" Robin asked her.

"I don't know," she said sadly. "I guess I got to do what I got to do, the same as everybody."

They walked Luke back around to his truck to say good-bye. Marjorie suddenly stepped up to him, put her arms around him and kissed him on the mouth. He'd never touched her before, and hadn't realized that she was just his height, which seemed strange—strange that he hadn't known it. His arms went around her broad ribcage, her large breasts squashed alarmingly against his chest. "It helped so much talking with you, Luke," she said. "You make me feel I'm worth something, you know that? I'm so grateful." She squeezed him hard, forcing some breath out of him. She seemed a continent, and he thought of her oversized sexual parts, female parts, which in his mind were muscular and tough, meant for hard and constant use, yet her mind and emotions were so delicate and fragile they might break. He was probably, hopefully, wrong.

She held him until he wanted very much for her to let him go, and finally she did. Good-bye, good-bye, they called to each other as she and Robin went back to their cubicle.

He got up into the cab, feeling free, and had the key in the ignition when a small woman in a white dress came running across the dimly lit parking lot toward him. At first it might have been a child, but then it was Louise Sturgis.

"Can I get in?" she asked in her husky voice. He opened the

275

passenger door and she climbed up. "Well, what did you do for that statuesque broad?" she said.

"Not much," he said. "I thought you were in California."

"I changed my mind. Will you give me a ride home? I'm with a jerk I don't want to be with, savvy? One of the cripples I told you about. Not that all of you bastards aren't cripples in one way or another."

"Okay," he said.

She didn't speak until they stopped in her driveway. "I'm too old for this dating crap," she said. "Second-hand goods. The bastards are always peeking at the book, like second-hand car dealers. Come in and have a drink."

In spite of everything that had happened to him, that might happen to him, his pulse rose at her offer and he wanted to be inside her, to slip into her darkness. It seemed an absurd activity, all that soft wrestling, the changing of positions, the goatish jerking and plunging. He would have thought he had outgrown it. He didn't want a woman with all of her sudden resentments, who didn't want what she wanted, or hated what she wanted. A crazy lady, he had said to himself once in another, safer mood.

He thought briefly, as if the time had been years instead of weeks ago, of the young woman and child he had seen bathing at the brook pool. Now that young woman had Helen's face, but it had been so long ago the memory had turned grainy and bluish, like an old color photograph exposed to too much light. There had been sweetness in that scene, now changed to loss.

Louise led him into the house, past the unfinished carpentry of the front hall. Coleman was out, she said, on some no doubt doomed venture of the heart, some lost cause, some romantic expedition into the devouring jungle. Poor Coleman.

"You did go away, though," he said as she made the drinks.

"My ex-husband, the con man, is in the money again and I wanted some back alimony. Sordid story. I went to Fire Island with him for a week. He's really a pitiful slob. But now he has some nefarious relationship with a conglomerate called R.I.C. I know it's nefarious or he wouldn't be involved."

276

The *Gentleman* conglomerate, he thought, also into comic books, heavy metals, tennis court surfaces, razor blades, imported booze and oil. All this, presumably, for money, power, the world. Right now they could have it, because he wanted another kind of oil and slippage, the power of touch, nerves connecting to this woman through more than the epithelium, liveness to unsheathed liveness—all the nerves that now wove themselves into his leash.

She sat down next to him on the couch, her thin shoulder beneath the silky white, her hair a black wash. The pale flat paintings glowed around the dark walls. He had asked himself before how it might be possible to make a woman happy, if it were at all possible. He wanted her because he wanted to love her.

When they were naked in her bed he tried to prove to her how sweet and valuable she was. How could she not turn, all of her, not just her flesh, open and equal? She seemed enraptured by what he gently did to her. It was all smooth and mutual, but if to her each new wave of rapture was a theft of power, then he was helpless, no matter how she warbled and turned liquid under him and over him. If he could only reach the center that screamed thief, usurper, alarms and excursions.

When she did convulse, skim and then glide down to come, he did, grateful to her loved center where he'd left himself. She held him and said nothing. Time had passed in sleep, he knew, when he woke. The night felt deep, climbing toward morning. She had turned on her bedside lamp, propped herself on an elbow and now smoothed him with her squarish hand. When he was wide awake she said, "Luke Carr fucked me. You want to know who fucked me? It was Luke Carr that fucked me." She seemed tender, angerless. "He's got a gun, though. Do you have a gun?"

"A real question?" he asked.

"Yes. Have you got your gun?"

"It's in the truck," he said.

"I'd like to see it. Go get it."

"We don't need a gun, Louise."

"I mean it. Go get it. I want to see it," she said. He looked at her closely, for signs. Her olive eyes seemed just curious, as when

277

she'd asked him to do different things to her—to see if he would do them, or to see what they would be like if he did, he was never certain.

"To hell with the gun," he said.

"I'll go get it. Tell me where it is," she said, then quickly came over him and took him in her mouth so deeply she gagged and momentarily recoiled. He felt her breath and the naked little points of her teeth, then her tongue.

"Let's fuck," he said. "Hell with the gun."

She brought her face over his, her black hair falling around him. "I'm in heat, don't you know? I'm dripping for you. But go get the gun."

He entered her, but she wrenched away. "I just want to see it," she said.

He went out through the hallway, wondering, not certain how curious or apprehensive he was, barefoot and naked in the chill darkness. The grass, the trees and the house were drenched and silent, the road empty. Coleman's Toyota was parked next to his truck. He took the pistol from its holster and carried it back through the silent house to the lamplight, where she sat cross-legged on the white sheets, the heavy black weapon wrong near her tender nakedness. He took out the loaded clip and put it on her bureau, then pulled back the slide to make sure the chamber was empty, the hard clicks of internal stops and cams loud in the room.

"God, what a sound," she said. "Is it empty? Let me hold it." Her voice was low, as if in dread. She took the black gun in both hands. "It's cold. It's too heavy. God, it's black and cold! It smells of oil." She put the cold gun flat against her belly and winced at the shock.

"It's cocked," he said. "Now let me uncock it and put it away."

"But it's empty? It's empty?" She pressed the gun against her with both hands.

"It's empty. The hammer would just click against the firing pin," he said, "but it might pinch your finger. Anyway, come on, let's put it away now." He reached for it.

"Wait! I want to feel it. It's warming now." She turned it around

278

so that the barrel end was against her navel, fitting into that soft depression. "God," she said. "It's death, isn't it? That's all it was made for." She squeezed the gun, her forefingers depressing the grip safety, her thumbs on the trigger, and the hammer fell with a dull, high *pink*, unreverberant yet powerful as a sledge on an anvil.

He took the gun away from her so quickly he twisted and hurt one of her fingers. She looked at him, holding her finger in her other hand. "That hurt," she said.

He shuddered out of the horror of whatever absolute taboo she'd broken. "I'm sorry I hurt you," he said. "I shouldn't have brought this thing in here."

"What's the harm if it's empty?" she said.

"It's the idea."

"The whole ugly, cold thing is an idea," she said. "You're the one who carries it around with you all the time."

"I don't point it at myself and pull the trigger."

"You're too squeamish. You know what I'd like you to do?" Her eyes were bright with an idea, her teeth showing. "I'd like you to cock it, and I'll get on my hands and knees, like this." She got on her hands and knees, her behind toward him, her dark round anus in its condensed, pigmented skin, her vagina wet amber wrinkles in the black silk. "Now," she said. "Now. Put the end of it up my ass. Put it in deep and pull the trigger. I want to feel it."

He wanted and did not want to do what she asked. He could not do it. It was clear to him he could not do it, not with the ghost shell and projectile, his too close knowledge of that murderous process.

"You can't do it," she said.

"You're right. You've got me," he said.

She turned over, her legs apart, thighs leading down to her silky places. "And you thought you could do anything the kinky bitch wanted."

"I can't even pretend to kill the kinky bitch," he said.

"You don't mind putting your other thing in there."

"It's not a gun."

"Why don't you take your fucking arsenal and go home?"

"I don't want you to be a kinky bitch."

"But I am, right?"

Unanswerable woman logic.

"And who the hell are you?" she said. "What right have you to want me to be anything you want me to be?" She was shrill, and he thought of being overheard.

"I want you to make me feel good when I make you feel good," he said, thinking that it was possible she faked it all, all the moans of pleasure. It was possible. He could be near tears, or he could redefine everything. What he thought sounded stupid—that she should find his intensity fulfilling, defining. Helen had—or had she? Marjorie would—or would she? Jane? Certainly Jane had wanted and found pleasure in his maleness, or in something about her clandestine visit to his mountain. And then he thought, Leave this. Leave it. Somewhere there is a cool uncomplicatedness that can be tested by time.

# 20.

In the next week and a half he didn't leave the mountain at all. He finished his stonework, except for the upper part of the chimney, and went on. The cabin took on shape, now, as though it hadn't been quite seriously a house before. The first log, bolted to the footings, seemed rough, bent and uneven compared to the straight lines of the cement and sawn joists; in this part of the construction he would have to use his eye, and match one log's characteristics with another's, trimming and shaping with adz, ax and chain saw. Splines of thin pine furring would fit in grooves down the length of each log, to tighten as the logs shrank down upon themselves. The logs were fresh and clean, and though heavy were of a density and texture that pleased him and felt good to his hands. He ran out of milk for his coffee, bread and vegetables, but put off going down the mountain. He ate whatever he found in cans. Jake had to eat dry chow with water, which he ate but not without reproachful looks. In the middle of the second week the cabin walls were up and ready for windows, doors and the sills that would carry his rafters. He was out of cigarettes, so could not smoke with his celebrational drink.

At night he slept as he had as a child. He lay down on his cot, slept, dreamed, and woke at first light, the night having passed as if in an instant.

One morning he woke to the heavy tatting of rain on the tent, so he decided to go down for supplies. And the mail, which he didn't want. He wanted nothing to happen out there, but of course the bashings and dismemberments, plots and betrayals would go on. The hurt, the neglected; the last week and a half—it was August now, he calculated—had been pure, with a pure purpose cleanly fulfilled, no crazy unhappy vengeful creatures sighting in on him. He put a canvas tarp in the truck to cover his supplies and went down the mountain, planning to eat breakfast at the Welkum Diner in Leah.

When he passed Louise's and Coleman's house he had to look at it. Coleman's Toyota was there. Then he was past it—an old house like many others. George's truck was gone from his driveway. Then the high road to Leah.

He would get his mail last. At Follansbees' he shopped for food and whatever else caught his eye, taking interesting things from shelves, vegetable and meat counters with a pleasant lack of accountability. Everything was just for him, except for the canned dog food, so he could take anything into his cart. Everything fit into the wide cab of the truck, so he didn't need the tarp. He had deliberately shopped while hungry, and now went to the Welkum Diner and ordered coffee, orange juice, scrambled eggs, ham, home fried potatoes and English muffins with blueberry jelly. He could eat anything. He wanted to read nothing, write nothing, not talk; he wanted to put a roof on his cabin, to make doors and glaze windows to look out of beneath the sturdy roof. At night the deer came to the brushy pasture; he would, when the cabin was complete and furnished, prune and fertilize the apple trees around the field, free up hawthorn, maybe in season plant concord grapes, autumn olive and other food and shelter shrubs for the wild mammals and birds. He would leave aspen for the partridge, near the spruce that was their shelter. He would make a pool near the brook, and let the brook trout grow into giants. It would be a temperate paradise. Ducks would breed there—black ducks and wood ducks. Bear would come to glut themselves on the apples

282

and shit great piles of sweet smelling seeds and cores. Bless the wild, the independent, those who minded their own business.

At the Post Office the teller told him his mail was due to be returned to the senders but they'd kept it a few more days just in case he came in for it, so there it was. He paid the postage due and took it out to his truck to look at it, the rain tapping the hood and cab. First he lit a cigarette; poison as antidote. His hands were wet from the rain and the truck's door handle, moisture seeping into the pile of mail. There were five letters from Jane Jones, a letter from the Avenger, a letter from Ham Jones, a letter from Martin Troup, a windowed letter for Helen from the American Association of University Professors, material from Common Cause, the American Civil Liberties Union, Senator Brooke, Orvis, Gokeys and Brookstone. Bills from Mobil and Mastercharge. What he wouldn't bother to open he threw on the floor next to his groceries. Bills went into the dash compartment. He was left with the real letters, the envelopes seeming heavy with portent, threat, adhesiveness. Why this barrage from Jane Jones? All he did was what the lady wanted. Lonely widower humps horny housewife. Lord, Lord, these ragged wounded splintery women! He read the letters according to the postmarked dates. The first four were friendly and chatty. What she did Monday, how Ham had made love to her in the morning while she thought of her indiscretion. She really wanted to talk to him. Her period (she was off the pill because of the bad things she'd heard) came Tuesday, sort of. Her innards were a little out of whack. So were her emotions. She wanted to see him, to talk to him. Where? When? Discretion advised: no return address on notes to her, though she always got to the mail first, no sweat. Love, Jane. Then: "Dear Luke, I told Ham, I had to. I never heard from you. I didn't know he would take it the way he did. He says he's never been unfaithful to me, 'really,' whatever that means. . . ."

Ham's note:

What are your intentions now that you loused up our marriage? Jane, my wife, is sick. Don't ever come around here again. You are not welcome.

*　*　*

The Avenger's note:

Luke Carr:
    You murder what you touch, but I will touch you last.

                                                            Mr. Death


Martin Troup's note:

Luke, I've just got to come to the conclusion that you are fucking
with me. I brought you to New York because I thought it would be
good for you, get you out of your doldrums. I knew about the accident. Hell, who didn't? But this character, Sevas, he says he "used"
to know you. Are you after my job, Old Buddy? I'd just like to
know. When an old friend turns out to be a slimy scheming shit,
well, you may not want to know it but you got to know it or you
might step in it and track it all over the rug. I also happened to gather the information that you are jabbing his ex-wife. Too fucking
neat, Old Buddy, too fucking *neat*.

                                                                  M.


To try to explain anything to any of them was simply, clearly,
plainly beyond his powers. He could not say the first word. And
why should he try? He was the one continually struck by astounding information. They would all find out sooner or later, or they
wouldn't find out sooner or later. He refused to be in their world
anymore. He had to get his perishables back up the mountain and
put away. He had been happy there for more than a week.

The Avenger's note was literate; the ear that had tested that
sentence was too good, and that was ominous, as though for the
first time real intention and the fixing of a time of revelation were
at hand. He reached under the dash, above a wire harness, where
the holster hung, removed the pistol and jacked a cartridge into
the chamber, then replaced it, cocked, with only the thumb safety
on.

Ron Sevas, it seemed indicated, was Louise's ex-husband. A con
man all right; the man had always shown a strange joy at being
caught doing something sly or dishonest. It seemed to energize
him and raise him up onto a plane of intense life. Luke had heard

of him on and off over the years, notably as one of the proprietors of the quick death of a famous magazine, ten years ago. It would appeal to Ron, after all the years, to be in a position to enter into some conning, manipulating, perhaps even guilt-absolving strategy by using Luke's name. There was a kind of glistening, boyish yet mingy survivorship about him that was irresistible to some. To Louise, he supposed, and to R.I.C. in their new, probably reprehensible venture. It was just the place for Ron to surface.

But let them all assume what they wanted. He would write no instructive notes, make no calls. No more explaining. The world of manipulation was out there, not where he was going.

He drove around Leah square and back toward Cascom on the high road. Somewhere on the flats the yellow supercar, the hunchbacked Dodge, nose down, appeared behind him in the swirls of mist from his wheels, then seemed to leap as it passed him at almost twice his speed and disappeared in its own streaming turbulence.

There was a quick thrill of apprehension at the sight of Lester's car, but it went away. The rain streamed against his windshield, then was thrust away by each beat of the wipers. In the cab he was warm and dry, and he was going home, the engine's familiar song of good, harnessed power all around him. He went through Cascom and up the mountain road, the trees softened in the rain and mist. Soon he would have a roof on the cabin and rain would be welcome, part of the weather for which he planned and built.

He turned in the farm road and drove down through the spruce, his wheels in rivulets, then out into the more open land by the old farm foundations. Cascom Mountain was gone behind gray. On the way down the hill toward the bridge he looked for tire marks in the gravel that was still soft in places, but the tracks he saw were probably his own. The bridge rumbled as he crossed the brook. He still looked for the yellow car, but it was not there. Jake was, and greeted him with a few howls of anger and affection.

"Hello, Jake," he said. Jake looked at him, suddenly quiet, as if some large thought had overcome him. "What are you thinking about, friend?" Luke asked, thinking himself of that strange line

285

across which simple need and gratitude changed toward more complicated emotion. He thought of wolves and jackals, their tribal relationships, loyalties, orders of importance and dignity. Then man and man, dog and man, the latter combination hardly fair to the dog. A dog could run, and a dog had a nose. Jake was nearly over his bruises. The lump on his ribs was now the size of a walnut, growing smaller and harder. For a moment longer Luke squatted in the rain and ran his hands over the dog's body, Jake still, unwagging, submitting to medical examination, which was not petting or scratching and elicited a different response. Then a pat on a flank said the examination was over, and Jake could wag his tail again, turn away and get out of the rain.

Luke put away groceries and supplies, then took off his slicker and dried his hands before getting out Shem's single-shot shotgun and the old Marlin .22 rifle. He cleaned them both and lightly re-oiled them, Jake bright-eyed at the looks and the metallic sounds, maybe even the odors, of the guns. The old ammunition Luke would get rid of somehow, not by taking it to the town dump with his other trash, however. He didn't want to try to shoot it because of the mercuric primers and subsequent cleaning problems, and wanted to give no one a dangerous fireworks display at the dump when the fires that always licked through that maze of rat tunnels reached the old cartridges.

It was early afternoon, the rain beginning to lessen, when he looked out of the tent to see fragments of the mountain appear, long writhing shawls of clouds moving eastward over his head.

Jake, at his feet, sensed a foreign presence across the field, growled and moved forward with his hair up along his back.

Luke stepped back into the tent and fastened the webbed belt and holster around his waist, then put on his olive drab slicker over it, having a sharp memory that there was a cartridge in the chamber, the pistol cocked and the thumb safety on. He stepped evenly across the pressed-down grass in front of the tent and stood among young pasture pines, searching the field toward the trail, where Jake pointed. If someone were over there and meant him harm, the weapon he carried was not the right one for that distance. A rifle, any rifle, even the .22, would be more effective.

He didn't really believe someone was over there, but he had to take it into consideration—a small fear and a dullness. Jake moved slowly forward, growling, his tail down between his legs. Whatever it was, Jake thought it larger than a beagle. If it were a bear, it would have heard Jake and departed. Jake would not be afraid of a deer, but then he must have merely heard something, or the scent had come to his nose in a confusing eddy of wind, because the main push of the wind came upon him laterally, from the west, and Jake pointed south toward the trail.

Following Jake, Luke moved from the pines to a group of young aspen a little higher than his head. He would be visible, but not a clear target, and a moving one. Jake glanced back at him for courage and went ahead. When they came to the trail the evidence had vanished and Jake relaxed. Maybe a tree had twisted and cracked in the wind, or a branch, heavy with water, had fallen and made a sound only Jake had heard.

No one had been there, Jake said. He took a few casual casts back and forth and then said by his expression that they ought to go hunting—a bright new look.

"No, come on," Luke said, and went back to the tent. There was a hollow place in him, now gradually filling because of the usual, normal expectations and probabilities. But he had felt excitement and a kind of angry fear.

It was unfair. He went through a smooth convulsion of self-pity and anger, aware of the names of the emotions he felt. Had what he had done in this life justified the treatment he had received and was receiving? Did he kill what he touched? Was this justice? Infantile residues; the breast had been removed long ago, and he had been of the world too long to believe in justice. That lack of belief was not merely theoretical; it had been gained from experience. He was not a hurtful man, he believed, and yet his presence seemed to hurt people. He did what they asked, and then they were hurt, but he didn't mean to hurt. All he meant to do was to survive. There were, he hoped, enough miracles for him in his woods, or looming over his bald mountain. Or he was owned by the woods and the mountain.

His children had been mysteries to him, their power over him

287

having something to do with their perfection in spite of the roughness and vulnerability of their characters. They needed him and tolerated him. Helen was the only woman he wanted to make children with. She died at forty-two, Gracie at twelve, Johnny at fifteen. No scenes from those lives; it was forbidden, except in dreams, where he had no authority.

It was as if he wrote the notes from the Avenger and mailed them to himself.

You fool, what will you do when your cabin is finished and you have to walk in the door?

The dog lay on the towel it had appropriated for its bed, breathing with a slight snore, now trembling and paddling its feet in a dream. A happy dream, the tail said, the feet now stilled. Love for this good dog, the recognition of it, opened in him frighteningly. He had to solve that problem, then. He had a hundred-dollar bill in his wallet—more, probably four times more, than Jake was worth, a calculation from another world. The money was probably worth four times more to Lester Wilson than it was to him. Equations, problems, the brutal, coarse weight of Lester Wilson. Such a man could always surprise.

He administered Jake's half-pill and gave him a can of dog food. When Jake saw him leave in the truck he didn't try to follow; any half-intelligent beagle knew you couldn't outrun a truck. He drove down the mountain road steeled, he hoped, for this task. When he came to the Sturgis house he was startl d to see Lester's yellow Dodge parked next to Coleman's Toyota. It was more than disconcerting, because these people should all be where they ought to be, revolving in their own courses. But he had come down to see Lester and he would.

Coleman came to the door in a bathrobe and bare feet, his pale, wrinkled face and moist blue eyes showing some kind of strain and apology. "I was about to take a shower," Coleman said. He began to move aside, as if to invite Luke in, then stopped that movement just too late for Luke not to understand.

"Is Lester Wilson here?" Luke said.

"No. Claire does some housecleaning for us. Lester, presumably, is at his trailer babysitting and getting sloshed on beer. You'll probably find him there."

"Thanks," Luke said. He began to turn away, then asked, "How's Louise?"

"Much better. They're letting her come home tomorrow."

"They?"

"Northlee Hospital, in its collective wisdom. Louise ingested too many pills with her booze, something she does occasionally, and accomplished what is called, for lack of the exact truth, 'an accidental overdose.'"

"My God! I didn't know that!"

"Well, she's all right this time. I've got to rush, now, Luke. Why not stop back around five? I'll give you a drink and fill you in on the Perils of Louise."

It was three-thirty. "All right. Thanks," Luke said.

Louise was a little crazy, but no matter how clear and simple the indications had been, he would have nothing to do with a more precise diagnosis. He didn't want to. He drove on toward Lester's trailer on the River Road. In what measure couldn't he understand suicide? She was a healthy, attractive animal, possessing all of her senses, and the world was green and fascinating, its lights, temperatures, shades, odors and winds changing and forever new. She had her clay to make into the nearly eternal, as he had his wood and mortar. She had, with the lovely shapes and textures of her body, helped him so easily. But she must see it all through different filters and lenses. To make a statement that one might like to die. Of course he had no one to make that statement to, not anymore. With a feeling of superiority that shamed him he thought that if he were to make that statement it would be once, and final; if he ended himself it would not be an act of communication at all, but the shutting of a door, no one on the other side but the light of day. But a young, healthy woman in her thirties, with the equipment, the instruments—no words for the miracles of perception. He would love her if she would let him (shame: take your small coin and spend it elsewhere). There were places he could not go. He couldn't dive that deep. But maybe he could help her. Then a voice said clearly, the same small voice that in other circumstances told him not to have another drink, that he should stay away.

There was another dangerous thing going on at the Sturgis

289

house. He could smell it, divine it with the most primitive sense, the one that was never wrong when it nosed the primitive. Maybe Coleman was more than a little suicidal himself. He remembered the metal sheen of Lester's wife's red hair, her soiled clothes and her pale skin, but mainly the fear of Lester that had made her appear stupid.

There among the dying elms were the dead and wounded cars, the detritus of a battle or a flood, and the pink and blue trailer beneath its stilted second roof, like the wreck of the Burlington Zephyr, or some once glittering streamlined wonder, windows fashioned into parallelograms signifying speed. The V-8 engine still sat in its oil on the ground.

When he turned off his engine he heard the murmur of television and a child's high, gasping whine, a lament that sounded practiced and tired. He wished he had gone to George and Phyllis first, and discussed with them his coming here, but that would have been a weakling's attempt to gain courage. He wasn't a child, but he didn't want to knock on the metal door. His pistol, that tool of the simpleminded, was in its place under the dash. It all depended upon what world within a world he was about to enter.

He went up to the door. There was a doorbell but its square, cream colored button was stuck flat into its orifice as if by the thumb-grease of generations. He knocked on the tinny door, the sour stench of poverty flowing from its brown, tinted jalousies.

The frame of the trailer shook as steps came to the door, and as the door opened upon not much but the big body of Lester Wilson, in green chinos, Lester's voice blared back into the trailer a word, or words, that Luke thought at first foreign, or inner trailer language: "*Shunnerap!*" Harsh, strangled language Luke figured out, he thought, to mean, "Shut her up." Then the big head turned down toward Luke, almost the deadly, sclerotic, smooth-bristled, stupid bully of a child's nightmares. The lips were wet where the teeth were missing or rotten, and there were shoals of black dots of stubble, but not many yet, for the fellow was only in his twenties. "What do you want?" he said, with some emphasis on the "you." He stood there to intimidate what was on his doorstep, his eyes too bleary for his age, his green belly soiled.

290

"I want to buy your dog from you," Luke said. Again, because there might be a real reason to fear this man, Luke could not keep a countering disdain out of his voice.

"You want to what?"—to make Luke repeat himself.

"I want to buy your dog. He seems to want to stay at my place, and. . . ."

"He 'seems to want'? What fucking dog you talking about? I suggest you twirl your ass around and get along home."

"I'll be glad to do that, but I want to get this business straight first. You know what I'm talking about."

"You giving me some lip, mister?"

"Jesus," Luke could not keep himself from saying. "Do you live like this all the time?"

"What's that you said?"

It had been so many years since these youthful wells of adrenalin had been tapped. What a dance it was, the tarantella of violence! He could say, then Lester would say, then he could say, and soon they would cleanly transcend the compromises of civilization. Lester was not wearing his revolver, but for authority he would be the police, and his property was in question. Luke would have the possible beating of that property, the dog, who had certain vaguely specified rights, too, but mainly Luke would have middle class, landowner, old family status; the prior discussion would have to be violent enough to cause amnesia on both sides before the action became primordial, but that could happen, if Luke wanted it to happen. He didn't want it to happen, and so he controlled himself in order to be in control.

He said, "Just to get it all straightened out, the dog's name is Jake, and I'm offering you a hundred dollars for him. I brought him back to you once, but he didn't choose to stay. I have witnesses to say I brought him back to you." If the man could, or would, listen, Luke could choose his own weapons, which would be words fashioned into plausible lies. He went on, "As you may know, the animal's volition in this matter is a small but valid point of law, and in any case it remains a civil matter. The dog, however, was later beaten, a fact documented in the records of the Leah Veterinary Hospital, and this matter is not civil, but a case in tort,

291

or criminal law, animals having certain rights generally espoused by the ASPCA and written into the codes having to do with humane treatment. Of course you may not have actually beaten the dog, but a beating did take place, and given your general reputation, as I understand it, a *prima facie* inference would certainly exist. However, I'm willing to ignore all that, not press charges, and in fact buy the dog from you."

"You going to stay around here after I told you to git?" Lester said, but he had been gravely touched.

Luke saw it so clearly, and had seen it so many times, how the essentially powerless feared the word. Lester was a bully and a brute, but he had only a minor clientele, in a small circle of hell. It would be so much more honorable to hit Lester with a fist. It was disgusting, boring; how could he have ever considered Lester Wilson a real danger, or have been so angry at the beating of a dog?

"Who says I beat up a dog?"

"No one; the fact remains that the dog was so badly beaten he had to be taken to a veterinary hospital for treatment. That is a fact; the rest, as the law would imply, is a presumptive inference." What a fluent liar he was. He could see that Lester suspected that he was being had, but didn't quite dare to call.

"None of your goddam business what happens to my dog. Now you move your ass out of here and take your money with you. I'll get my dog back when and how I feel like it!"

How poor, that "when and how," and how stupid of Lester to try to fight with words.

Ten minutes later they sat in the trailer's kitchen, at the chrome-legged Formica table, the kitchen grimly polished where hands and feet had travelled it, a jade plant strangling on the counter beside the sink, diapers fuming in a corner. Through an archway could be seen a torn red sofa bed, a figured carpet, the pink-green-blue cyanotic faces of television and a pale child; a baby cried somewhere down there.

Lester had no doubt decided out of caution, which was a sort of fear, to trim and deal. He may have suspected that to Luke the money was shit, a small purse tossed to a peasant. Tense joviality did not become him, and even he would be afraid that he might give the impression of groveling before his better. They discussed the size and number of trout in Zach Brook. Luke made out a bill of sale for the dog and Lester pretended to gloat inwardly over the high price by saying too many times what a good rabbit dog Luke had there. He had a beer opened already, and he opened one for Luke.

"Lots of deer up there, too, though the dog ain't one to run deer. Building yourself a camp, I hear. You got yourself a good deer rifle? I got one I bought at the State auction, Marlin .35 Rem. Sell it to you cheap. Fish and Game took it off some deer jacker last year."

Luke thought about this offer; if Lester could think he got the best of it in a matter unrelated to the dog, one in which he hadn't any reason to suspect he'd been manipulated, it might be helpful when the resentment flared again, as it would.

Lester got the rifle from a corner, where it and several other guns leaned, wiped the kitchen dust from it with his hand, and handed it to Luke. It was fairly new, with only a little superficial rust from sweaty hands. It was lever action, with iron sights and a leather sling. Luke opened it, put his finger in the breech and looked down the barrel at the light reflected from his finger. The rifling seemed good.

"Ninety dollars," Lester said, "and I'll throw in a box of shells, five missing from the box of twenty."

The last time Luke had to research commercial rifles was several years ago, but even then this rifle, with the extra sights, sling and sling hardware, would have cost more than that. So if he bought it he would have a bargain anyway, especially with the fifteen shells, each worth about a quarter.

"Sold," he said. He made Lester a check on the Leah Trust Company, and wrote, "Rifle, Marlin Mod. 336" on the bottom of the check.

Lester said, "You got a good buy. Got the new Microgroove rifling, you know. You're going to like the way she shoots." He folded the check and put it in his breast pocket. Now there would be, hopefully, some genuine triumph in it for him.

As Luke was leaving with his rifle and box of shells, the yellow

Dodge rumbled up outside. At the door he met the young red-haired woman whom Coleman Sturgis had called Claire. She was astounded to see him, and flustered. Her white face seemed grimy with a kind of general abuse, ghost bludgeonings. She lowered her head without speaking and went into the trailer. Lester, standing large in the kitchen, looked steadily at her, saying nothing as she went past him.

# 21.

Luke sat in the Sturgises' long living room with a too-dark bourbon and water in his hand. Coleman was both drinking and smoking. Luke had taken a couple of drags from the fat yellow joint Coleman had made, then said he didn't need any more. As Coleman spoke he held the joint in sterling silver roach tweezers.

"To tell you the truth, Luke, though it might not sound too brotherly, Louise has begun to bore me with her drills, so to speak. I love her dearly and all that, but the constant repetition of sheer panic somewhat dulls one's edge." He took a long drag on the joint, held it with eyes and cheeks bulging, then seemed to hold it for a second long breath, or non-breath, before he let out a diminished gray wisp. "By the way," he said, "what business had you with the loathsome Lester?"

Luke explained about the dog, and said he'd finally bought him. "I gave Lester some pseudo-legal doubletalk, accused him of beating the dog beyond what the law allows, and finally he let me buy him for about four times what he's worth."

"And did he beat the dog?"

"Oh, yes. With a baseball bat or a two-by-four. Lucky he didn't kill him. But dogs are pretty tough critters."

"A violent man," Coleman said, and his eyes flicked to Luke's.

Maybe Coleman needed a confidant. He remembered when he'd felt the same. Once he'd always had, it seemed, a good friend to whom he could confide things, nearly anything. He'd had Helen, too, depending upon the nature of the thing to be confided. But now he had no one. Everyone he knew seemed flawed, dangerous, too interested or needful, and so he kept things to himself, like a plotter. Whatever had happened to his equals, his friends, except that they were gone to far places and age? That was enough, that was enough.

Coleman was about his age, but aware.

"I gather, as they say," Coleman said, "that you smelled a rat this afternoon. I shouldn't say, 'a rat,' though. What should I say? That I was, indeed, alone here with Miss Claire—Mrs. Wilson— and so on. You may read it that I like to live dangerously."

"I suspected something like that," Luke said. Coleman was wearing dark slacks, loafers, a white shirt open at the collar, and he seemed quite dapper and jaunty in the face of his danger. Luke wondered how he had so easily left the subject of Louise, whose situation, repetitious or not, didn't seem all that casual. But this was Coleman's drama, not Louise's and Coleman had from the first struck him, with that winsome, watery look that peered around as if for credit, if not for praise, as a little boy.

"You might well ask how I dared to get involved with the young wife of such a violent man, and I'd have to answer that I think it's utterly insane, dangerous and doomed. But Claire, strange Claire, is more than she seems."

"Most people are," Luke said.

"Not necessarily. Perhaps if you'd been a teacher for sixteen years, as I've been, you'd come to realize how repetitive the gene pool actually is, in everything from hair color and handwriting to the distribution of adipose tissue and analogical thought patterns.

"But Claire—how interesting it was when I first saw that though she was terrified of me by definition, because I was a man, she did have submerged needs that hadn't been destroyed by her experiences. At twelve, and thereafter, she was raped by a brother. Her father beat her mother bloody with whatever came to hand, including split stove wood. There was no romance, tenderness or even seduction involved in her marriage to Lester. She can barely read or do simple arithmetic. She knows little about the household arts, such as hygiene, medicine, nutrition, anatomy or sex. We had to teach her many of the simple chores she comes here once a week to do. Television itself is quite often a mystery to her, its jokes and simple ironies over her head. What she sees on the screen are moving images, seeming alive and energetic but essentially motiveless.

"Physically she was given that garish hair that makes her look, in some lights, almost artificial, and with it eyes as clear, green and simple as emeralds. Many so-called red heads have unfortunate skin—freckles, coarseness, bristles—but hers is that rare, pure white that comes as close as any Occidental skin to deserve that adjective. Because of a lack of the proper exercise and horrendous nutrition she has a protuberant belly that hasn't and won't recover from the trauma of two pregnancies, but it, too, accented by her gaudy orange pubic hair, is white. One thinks of snow, of percale—no, more of a satin, or even velvet, there being on that skin an infinitesimal velour. The bluish to green bruises caused by Lester are the only flaws in this admirable dermis, and they of course come and go."

Coleman placed the extinguished roach in a small tin box and added bourbon to his drink.

"More and more dangerous," Luke said.

Pleased by Luke's attention, Coleman went on, "But since I'm not enjoined, not in any way, to evaluate Claire's intelligence, to give her an *F*, so to speak, I've been journeying with her to countries other than those of the mind. As for the initial seduction, that was nothing. After she'd got used to my presence, and I hadn't hit her with a piece of stove wood, or a belt, which I don't wear in the first place, and had smiled at her, even touched her lightly several times, I came into my bedroom where she was changing sheets and pillowcases and gently, firmly but somehow *neutrally*, told her that we would lie down together there, right there, you see, Claire, for a minute, to see how it is. Strange customs have these rich summer people. No, I doubt if such a complicated shadow of thought crossed her obedient mind.

"But where did we journey? We began, I suspect, in what was to her Cascom, New Hampshire, but to me seemed like some dense archipelago in, though I may slander the place, New Guinea, where the men wear their sexual parts strung up to their belly buttons on strings and the women are humped quickly, grossly, publicly and upon male whim. And when they are not 'presentable,' as it were, the females are considered filth—of course by themselves, too—and a cause of disease and other abominations. I may be confused in my geography, but not terribly much in my anthropology, and I apologize to the Cargo Cult or whatever if I have my archipelagoes mixed. But do you understand what a *tabula rasa* I'd found? Can you realize that the girl had never been allowed the time, or given the slightest motivation, to find that the vagina lubricates itself and that male penetration is not as painful as shoving a splintery stick up between the legs? Ah, how slowly and carefully, how tenderly, did we our pleasures prove. Ah," Coleman said and took a drink. "Ah, our tender loving levers and orifices, her sweet clitoris on my tongue unbrutalized. Luke, it was a whole history of the evolution of love, like having lived since the Eocene."

"Just so you don't find a certain troglodyte sniffing after you through all those misty ages," Luke said.

"Amen! Amen, but it was worth it."

"What about Claire now that she's found that it can be fun?"

"God, I don't know. More bruises, I suppose. And she seems to be making small hominid noises about leaving him, but where could she go?"

"With two kids, one a baby?"

"Yes, yes! Lord Cupid, what have I done?"

What a fine moment Coleman thought this was. Luke believed very little of the story, though Coleman might believe most of it. The basic, most dangerous part of it Luke did believe.

"But Louise," Coleman said after several sighs, a pacing across the room and back, and a drink. "Louise. You'll be curious, I imagine. I don't know much about the . . . intensity . . . of your affair, which seems rather off and on, but there *is* an intensity, I do feel that. Of course I don't know how candid you want to be, or if you want to say anything at all, but I'm sure you have questions, such as your earlier one, 'How's Louise?'—which is rather complicated and I couldn't go into it very deeply then because Claire was at the moment warm and dewy from her bath."

"Would she want me to come and see her tomorrow?"

"That's the sort of question it's always hard to answer with Louise."

"Why did she divorce her husband?"

"Maybe *all* questions are hard ones when it comes to Louise," Coleman said. "It seems to me I remember a Louise who was a fairly happy young woman, who met this older man, a publisher who was in the process of divorcing his wife, or who *said* he was— you just don't assume things with that character. Anyway, Louise did marry him, and that was the beginning of the nightmare."

"Who was the guy?" Luke asked, surprised that he'd asked the question so easily. He'd had a little time now to cope with his sick feelings about Louise and suicide, with Martin Troup's and Ham Jones's accusations and denunciations, with Lester Wilson's brutishness, and he was thinking of the Avenger, and all sorts of little evidential coincidences. He usually tended to trust anyone he was dealing with, thinking that the truth was more or less normal— except in a poker game, and there deception was honorable, mutually agreed upon. But he watched Coleman with care.

"His name is Ron Sevas—perhaps you've heard of him, since he's more or less in the same business you've been in," Coleman said. He was watching Luke, trying to seem casual himself, unless Luke imagined all this caution.

"Yeah, I've met him," Luke said.

"Louise told me you had. I guess she found that out from Ron."

"Why did she go see him?"

"To get him going again on the alimony. He's not the most conscientious of men, to put it mildly."

"So I've heard," Luke said.

"He's a strange man, and he did strange things to Louise in

299

those seven years—and since, for that matter," Coleman said. "He's a natural crook, I believe. What I mean by that is that he doesn't just cheat for profit, he enjoys the *process* of cheating. Anyone, for instance, might steal something he wants, because he wants it badly enough, but Ron steals, cheats and cons because he simply likes to do it. There's a sort of wild bravado or looney bravery in him. Also the practical jokes, the constant practical jokes. Anyway, Louise was married to him for seven years or so, and you can't blame her if her mind is slightly boggled. Some of the things he pulled on her are quite simply beyond the pale."

"Like what?"

"For instance, the constant money business. It was as if he demanded that she connive and con and try to cheat *him* in order to get any money from him. His idea of a great joke was to have the electric company shut off the current because of delinquent bills. He owed everyone, all the time. He borrowed when he didn't need the money, just to do it. If Louise took a car to be repaired and tried to use a credit card, the garage would call an eight hundred number and find that the card had been voided for non-payment. She rarely dared to write a check. He made her jump through hoops to get any money at all. That was just a level sort of thing, a constant, but she's told me about other things that happened soon or late in that marriage. Not pretty things, such as the time she woke up in the night being fucked by one of his friends. Nice. Right out of the blue, that was, before her real education had commenced. Later there were all the faddish things, the drug of the week, the kicky kink of the month, and he talked her into all sorts of episodes—like the blue home movies such as *The Gang Bang,* starring Louise. I'm not really exaggerating, and I don't think Louise was when she told me.

"But in spite of everything, and there was much, much more, she couldn't get loose from the guy. I'd hesitate to call it love because I'm an incurable romantic and to me love is a pretty private and idyllic sort of episode. But she did love this crook, I guess. Maybe she still does. The suicide stuff began when the divorce was final. And of course there were shrinks, shrinks and more shrinks, anal shrinks, oral shrinks, primal shrinks and vaginal shrinks, and

Louise always trying to get money out of dear old Ron, who countered just for the fun of it with lies, jokes, threats and this and that, like using the home movies, and so on. He's married again—at least I think he is—but he can't stop teasing her. She's sort of a hostage or something to this monster. She could do without the alimony. Maybe she can't do without Ron, and he can't do without her brain to fuck with, I don't know. So you ask, 'How's Louise?' Come and see her tomorrow and ask her."

Coleman had been drinking a lot of bourbon as he talked and paced back and forth. As first he'd had ice in his glass, but then he'd just sloshed in more whiskey from the half-gallon bottle.

Luke had finished the one very strong drink that Coleman had made him, but couldn't feel that it had done anything to his head at all. Too much raw data, true or false, had been fed to him this day. He felt danger all around him, danger more shadowy and pervasive, as if it stooped over him, than all the unhappiness and cross purposes he'd seen today could warrant. He felt as if this moment, right now, in the long room that had been so self-consciously and tastefully decorated with the abstract paintings and interestingly mixed furniture and Scandinavian stoves and miniature metal sculpture and books and pots and platters and hooked rugs and polished pine flooring—at this moment, or the next, or a second after that, something would happen that would change everything for good and blow all this away.

"What I want to say—don't know why, don't know how," Coleman said, humming the words. "Don't know where, don't know when, but I know we'll meet again some sunny day." Thoughts went in and out of Coleman's mind, his loose, now drunken face reflecting them, wriggling in and out of humor, or irony, or confrontation. A mood change was taking place in him, toward some drink-inspired drama. Luke didn't know him well enough to predict what mood was coming, but he suspected aggression. The affected locutions had been trying to become more parenthetic, more self-consciously superior in tone, until the gradual disruptions of the booze, and maybe the marijuana, had made their transitions less crisp and less satisfying. So now an aggressive, mind-clarifying attitude was perhaps necessary.

301

"I was in love with your wife," Coleman said. "Did you know that?" Said with a dramatic pose, arms akimbo, drink sloshing at hip.

"No, I didn't know that," Luke said. "But I was, too, so we have something in common."

"Common? Common?"

"More like 'communal,'" Luke said. "Not to signify the ordinary, the prosaic, the *infra*, Professor. Different connotation."

"You cold, *cruel* shit!"

"That's nice."

Then they heard the deep explosive rumble of a car out in front of the house, the scraping slide of dirt and gravel, a car door slamming and heavy steps at the front entrance.

Luke thought at first of the common, the ordinary—everyone had heard such sounds throughout a life that had been mostly invaded by the ordinary. Then he thought, not at all in panic, that it had to be Lester Wilson. He himself had not had anything to do with the man's wife, though he was here with the criminal, and Lester might think him somehow in cahoots. And minor as it might seem, there had also been the defection of the man's dog. Lester's anger would encompass him too, and he'd better jump out a window and head for the trees; then came the idea that he ought, as a more or less responsible citizen, to try to prevent Coleman's murder as well as his own.

But there was nothing but a sedate rap-rap-rap on the front door, Coleman displaying no worry at all, and it was Freddie Hurlburt strutting fatly in after his merely protocol knock.

But it seemed only very precariously Freddie, as though time could plausibly back up ten seconds and the first heavy steps on the stoop had been followed by the breaking of a door, sawhorses kicked out of the way against the walls of the unfinished hallway and it was Lester Wilson, half-drunk, in soiled green chino, fuming with sweat and rage, his .38 Smith & Wesson in his red hand.

"Well, here we are!" Freddie said. "Here we are, two turds with one bone, so I can ask you both to come and dine with us at the Club!" He wore his green lederhosen, his fat knees peering out above his ribbed stockings like two chubby faces similar to his ac-

302

tual face, but slightly smaller, and without his enormous blue eyes. "Cousin's rather sloshed, at first glance. Despondent about Louise, I imagine, though I saw her today and she seems well on the way to recovery, so let's pop in our vehicles and off to the Club, Coleman obviously not driving, wouldn't you say? Cheer us all up!"

Coleman had just achieved the moist, bright, glaring stage of his drunkenness and wanted to argue with Luke. He ignored Freddie, poured himself more straight bourbon and said, "Of course the possess—the possessor—is unaware of the value, which is not to be had, you see. Owned, so. . . . " His incoherence infuriated him so much his face turned even paler than usual. "Hell with it! Mere slick cliché journalist anyway. Beneath contempt. Fink."

Freddie shook his head, his shoulders moving too. "Poor fellow's drunk, mouth like a Christian sewer, I believe. All snotted up in the groins. He does get a little combative sometimes, Mr. Carr—Luke. It never lasts long because he's not a bad sort, tons of apologies coming, but in the meantime an excellent lasagna, one thing the new fellow really knows how to make . . . "

"You're a fink!" Coleman shouted at Luke. "I don't care what . . . "

"Oh, shut-shut-shut-shut up, now Coleman," Freddie said, "and take your jacket. That night air, you know, fools and kills."

"There he sits, you see," Coleman said in a new tone, this one a try at sarcasm, "with the look of a martyr cursed by the gods, a famous living grave legend to us all. You can tell by his unctuous fucking pseudo-dignity."

"Shut up, now, I said! That man doesn't look like that to me—he looks like a man about to give you a knuckle sandwich, so shut your mouth and take a breath. Here!" Freddie walked over, took Coleman's drink from him and put it down on a table. Coleman, thinking hard, didn't seem to notice. Freddie took him by the arm and led him, Coleman's feet clumping down as if he were in the dark, to the hall closet, selected a tweed jacket and put it on him. "Chilly-chilly," he said as if talking to a child.

"Would you turn out all but one of the lights? Watts, volts, amps

303

and such considerations, right?" Freddie said. "We don't want poor Coleman to spend the night alone. Get some food into the poor fellow and see if he can hold it, bed him down at the Club for the night and let him sleep it off. Then he can compose his apologies, as usual. I'll make him in the Jeep—knocked my muffler up today, did you hear it? Outrageous noise. You follow in your truck, or if you want to spend the night at the Club—plenty of room—you can come with us and I'll spring your crack in the morning."

"Fink," Coleman said. "Keep his pecker in his pants."

"Oh, shut up, Coleman," Freddie said patiently. "Awfully distraught about Louise. Forgive the poor fellow."

"Pay-no-tention-poor-fellow," Coleman said, trying to imitate Freddie. "Yeah, yeah, yeah. Usual garbage. Bullshit. Get me a beer. Won't go less I get a beer."

Luke went to the kitchen and got two bottles of beer from the refrigerator, put one in his own pocket, turned all the lights out except the one in the downstairs bathroom, and followed them out to Freddie's Jeep, where Freddie folded Coleman's long thin legs, one at a time, into the cab.

"Give him his little bottle to suck," Freddie said, "and we'll be on our merry way."

"Bullshit," Coleman said, accepting the bottle.

"Maybe I'd better be getting back to my place," Luke said, but Freddie said, "Oh, come on and have a drink, anyway. It's early." It was just about to get dark.

He didn't know why he didn't go back to his camp. It was Jake's usual feeding time, but Jake could wait. Maybe he wanted to hear some more of Coleman's anger, but he had to doubt that. He was still thinking about the Avenger, but was he really looking for him? If Coleman were the Avenger, what would he do then? Or do with Coleman? He thought of the tilted swamp maple in the dank slough of woods and in a blink of vision the ground water black among the trunks and boulders, silver in small streaks where it reflected what seemed a very distant, unrelated sky.

He followed the Jeep around the town square. The road to the Cascom Mountain Club left the high road to Leah and went up

304

the southern slopes of the mountain, so it was several miles before they turned right and began to climb. His new rifle began to rattle against a seat strut so he bent down to change its position and nearly swerved off the gravel road, a small fright. The Jeep's lights went on and he put on his own. He thought of opening the beer, but then put it in the dash compartment to drink on the way home—one for the road. He didn't know why he'd agreed to follow Freddie, but maybe there had been an urgency in Freddie's voice and in his expression, as if Freddie were really saying, "I can't explain now, but it's important." If so, what should he make of that? So he followed, prepared to be bored at the Club and eager to leave. He must be up at first light to start roofing in his cabin.

Everyone he knew, it occurred to him, the Jeep's tail lights winding in and out of sight ahead, was old, mad or some kind of obvious freak. Except Jake. But they were not; they were what they were, for bad or good, measurelessly complicated, not definable. Maybe he was the simple one, his sense of reality destroyed with his family.

But essentially, not to let this word restrict all, what he was doing was a form of suicide, because he was building his mausoleum, in which he would retire for good, forever. No, he must depend only upon what he had learned from experience, that reality before words. He would kill anything that threatened him there. He would have to, if it came to that, because any animal had to protect the place where its short mortal blink of perception was, of the trees, the night odors of the woods, the leaves that bowed and were suddenly green in his headlights along the summer road.

After several more miles, then a quarter mile of rocky, washboarded road, a section not kept up very well by the town because the Cascom Mountain Club was non-profit and paid only token taxes on its thousand acres, they came to the lodge and parked next to several other cars in the graveled parking lot. A lanterned light on a post illuminated the walk to the wide porch, behind which yellow lights shone through the low, diamond-paned windows of the old log building.

He had come here as a child with Shem, to pick up swill for

Shem's pigs. It had been one of several stops for them. They would back around, up a driveway that must be over there to the right, hand off an empty fifty-five-gallon drum, then slide a full or partly full drum up a garbage-greased plank to the bed of Shem's pickup, where it would be roped in place, the cover clinched on firmly to prevent the slopping of the sweet, bitter-sour stuff. Later, when he helped Shem bucket the swill to the wooden troughs in the pens, he would sometimes find a cheap bright knife, fork or spoon, which would be added to the kitchen cutlery of the farm— each a prize, wonderful to the child, like finding a pearl.

The trees were not so thick, then, and hadn't leaned in so fully over the lodge and across the way. He had been proud of his high leather boots and farm-tanned arms, helping with great and even nervous attention his uncle who thought so much of him and was so fierce and expert about every task.

He followed Coleman and Freddie into the lodge, where the walls were decorated with sunbursts of antique skis, snowshoes, crampons, and ice axes. In a large stone fireplace a small summer fire was like a bonfire seen at a distance in a field at night. Down the long, gabled room with its log beams was the dining area, with many long tables, and beyond that, through open double doors, the brighter lights of a kitchen. Iron bridge lamps stood around the room among cushioned easy chairs made of ash with the bark left on, and bookcases that had once been light pine but were now cured by smoke and age into the color of old leather, all of them seemingly full of books with red covers faded into pink and rose.

There were other people in the room, the older ones regulars, members of the club and Freddie's old acquaintances. A few transients who were camping out nearby stayed by themselves in another light island in one corner. Freddie introduced him to the nearer people, who were tanned, city-outdoors types, pleasant enough, whose names he would never recall. Coleman went to the kitchen, came back with another bottle of beer and sat with these people, morosely acknowledging what they said to him.

Then Freddie turned Luke around to the younger ones, saying they were neighbors. Two men looked to be in their late twenties or early thirties. They wore their hair to their shoulders, one in a ponytail. One had a beard so pervasively black and curly very little of his face showed, though what showed seemed friendly. This one, whose name was Bob, introduced his wife, a plump girl in Mother Hubbard and hiking boots, as Marcia. The other man, whose name Luke hadn't caught, said that his wife was back in the yurt babysitting for all. The other person was a slim, rather short blonde girl who seemed familiar, so familiar it was bothersome, more than merely puzzling, but then a small child came running in, boy with black hair, two fireflies in a bottle to show his mother, and she was the young woman who had bathed with the child in the brook pool while he'd watched like a thief.

"I got *two!* I got *two!*" the child shouted. His mother knelt down to stare with him into the bottle at the pulsing cold lights. She was seriously interested in the fireflies he had caught, and looked at them closely, gravely, her lack of false excitement understood by the child, who now also looked carefully into the bottle. When she stood up again Freddie introduced her as Adrienne, and she put out her warm dry hand for Luke to shake, looking straight at him with the same grave, friendly interest she had given her child and his fireflies.

She wore jeans and a faded blue work shirt. The cloth of her shirt crisply defined her arms and shoulders, the open collar a subdued flare against her throat and a rise of collarbone. He was struck by a presence, before he'd heard a word from her, and it was from his past. She was Helen, at least in this dimension, without sound. Surely she would immediately show by voice or action, or even by an aggravating habit of speech, that she was herself, not Helen, not only not his but not at all caring to be.

"Freddie's told me about you," she said. Her voice was not at first Helen's, but then it was. No, it was her own. It was higher, though not harsh or nasal; he couldn't find the flaw there, at least not yet. This was painful and dangerous. He didn't need this, of all things. She must do something to offend him and give him back the balance, or even sanity, he felt going from him. He was breathless, his pulse high. It was nothing he showed, but there must be a way to stop or at least slow what was happening to him. You could go through a whole life and not have this sort of moment, and now he was having it again as he'd had it on the beach at Wallis Sands so long ago. But this time he was old, in the worst way helpless and constrained. He would be the fool.

"He has?" he said, then had to take a breath. He was for the first time that day conscious of his sweaty work shirt and his dungarees that were stained with pitch and ripped where they had worn at the right knee. He was the fool already to consider such things.

"I'm never sure I understand Freddie that well," she said, "but you're the one building a cabin on the Carr Trail, right?"

"Yes." He had the absurd, disastrous urge to tell her about having seen her and the boy at the brook—to describe her to herself—but didn't do it. Or even confess to her that she was his wife come back from the dead, made of the synthesis of memory, safe now, uncrushed, untorn, unburned. And the young boy was his to nurture and protect, though their family was not yet complete because there was a daughter, too, as yet uncreated by them. Oh, the value, the perfection—a moan of joy he heard at an interior distance, thinking he was insane, his outer self unmoving. He would be polite and attentive to this stranger who tormented him, knowing that she would not suspect what she was.

"What's your last name?" he asked. No one seemed to be around them except the boy, who had placed the bottle on a chair and knelt on the floor, chin in hands, to observe the strange green light.

"Gilbert," she said. "This is my son, Harwich, the proto-entomologist—at least for this summer." At the sound of his name Harwich looked up, saw that his mother perhaps patronized him because of his youth, and looked back at his fireflies. Who took love to be a constant didn't need that fond smile.

"It's not easy to catch fireflies, " Luke said, "when your hands are small, without squashing them."

"I squashed one," Harwich admitted. "The light gooed on my fingers and then it went out. It didn't burn."

"Cold light," Adrienne said.

"It wasn't cold," Harwich said.

"I meant that it wasn't hot," she said, and Harwich resumed his study of the fireflies.

"Do you live in a yurt?" Luke asked.

"No." She smiled, glancing over toward where the yurt people must be. "We've just been coming up to the lodge on and off this summer."

He couldn't look away from her. Surely she must see that he was unstable, that it was unlike him to stare at her so.

"From the city?"

"Yes, from Boston. My mother and father were members of the Club from way back, and I've been a member since I was Harwich's age."

"They're not alive?" he said.

"They were killed. An accident several years ago, on the Cape."

"An accident," he said, not having meant to say the word.

"Yes. A car accident." She looked down at her hands and he measured the shape of her head, the bones that had miraculously fused, the clear strands of dull gold covering her head. She looked up, and then said, "Freddie's signalling from his portable bar. What would you like?"

"Nothing, nothing," he said.

"He'll feel hurt if we don't let him play bartender."

"Whatever you're having," he said.

They walked together across the room, where Freddie had set up what looked like a large plywood suitcase on a table.

"White potions, magic effluvia," Freddie intoned. "The grape, the grain, the poison that liberates, the water of life!" His wide round eyes were like windows through which nothing could be seen but blue. He selected a small brass key from his key ring and with a flourish of his pudgy hand unlocked a panel that came down to reveal bottles, stainless shakers, long stirring rods, forks, strainers, openers, corkscrews, lemon peelers and all the gleaming professional gear of a bar. Two young men came from the kitchen, one bearing a wine cooler, the other a large silver bowl full of cracked ice. A young woman brought a basket of limes, lemons and oranges.

"Alcohol without ceremony is anathema to the gods," Freddie half sang. "The curse of the solitary, devil's sweat, the piss of Beelzebub, death, corruption, madness, murder and beyond."

"Stick your ceremonies up your ass!" Coleman called across the room. "Pour the booze and shut up, you fat little fuck!"

"Here, " Freddie said, "we have a living cautionary tale, a souse, his eyes bleary, his arse a pinhole, his jewels paste and his leather a feather."

To Luke all of this seemed beside the point. He looked at Adrienne, having to see what she made of it. She turned toward him, shrugging her shoulders, not at all upset. Who should be upset by Coleman Sturgis? She said something to Freddie that Luke didn't catch, Freddie nodded, got to work at his magic effluvia and soon turned around to them with a small dewy glass in each of his round pink hands. They took the glasses and moved off somewhere. No one else seemed to be near them. She led him out to the porch, Harwich a dark shape small as a dog moving in and out of the bright green around the lantern light, chasing fireflies with silent intensity.

He wanted to tell her that it was all right now, that whatever terrors and dangers she had been through were over. He would be here to build for them all. She sat on the porch railing, her slim center leaning there against a vertical.

"Try it," she said, holding her glass out toward his, as if for a toast. "I don't know what's in it. Freddie won't tell me."

He placed the cool glass against his lips, as she did with hers, and sipped the strange, evaporative liquid.

"What is it?" she said. "What's in it?"

"Ethanol, no doubt," he said. "What else, I don't know. Anise? Bitters? Vanilla?" The fluid seemed to pass straight into his lips and tongue, nothing left to swallow.

"Are you going to stay and eat with us?"

"Yes, but I'm not too hungry for lasagna."

"What are you hungry for?"

He could not answer that, so he shrugged and said, thinking this also dangerous, "You know, I saw you at the brook, at the pool on my land, you and your son."

"Zach Brook!" she said. "What a beautiful place."

"It was beautiful that day. I heard the boy crying and didn't know what the sound was. I thought it might have been the blat of

310

a wounded fawn, so I moved down through the hemlocks very quietly and there you were."

"And you watched."

"I felt like a thief, but I watched."

"I don't mind," she said.

He had never, in spite of his profession, been very curious about what people did for a living, how many brothers and sisters they had, where they lived, where they went to school, even their names. For one, they revealed all soon enough. Just a presence revealed more than he could assimilate anyway, or try to make accurate with words. She showed no shock, coyness or cute modesty, though he had painfully expected something of the sort, and now he was more anxious because his possible loss would be the greater. How few times would one ever encounter a voice that leapt a generation and was still unshoddy and precise.

At the dinner table he sat across from her and they talked, Adrienne mostly. He was in love; he had that secret that should be demonstrated but never told. What did the young talk about? Nothing much, endlessly and excitedly. The old always wanted to choose a topic, form a committee, categorize and only then endlessly repeat, though they had heard it all before, each surprise more a compulsion than a surprise, like hearing an unfunny joke or, more likely, given the dust and worn bearings of age, being tone deaf at a concert. But watching her he heard again the immeasurable in the ordinary. Nothing could ever end or be definable. It didn't matter what they said. Harwich sat next to his mother, liking the lasagna, Freddie next to Harwich, both talking with mouths full, evidently understanding each other. Adrienne spoke to him as if there had been months to make up, so many things having had to wait to be said. He heard his own answers and questions without remembering the effort of formulation; so this was how easy it had been.

Freddie looked across at him, his bland blue eyes undecipherable, and just then there was a noise at the main doorway, at his back, across the long room, not that it mattered, but the eyes of those across from him glanced over there, including her eyes, which grew in intensity from even the lively regard she had

311

shared with him. "Daddy! Daddy! Daddy!" Harwich yelled, jumping back over the bench he sat on, his paper napkin tucked in his collar. She followed Harwich down the long table and around, both running toward a young man in city clothes who put down a suitcase so that he could hold both of his arms out to them, a man who might have been himself disguised by a dark wig and the taut, smooth posture of youth.

# 22.

He guided his truck down the southern slope of the mountain on the narrow gravel road, branches reaching out at eye level in his headlights, then sweeping skyward as he passed beneath them, as though his truck were a submarine forcing its way through a green sea. At his camp all would be dark, wet with dew, the new wood clammy and slippery, the tent silver and cold. But out of the dark Jake would be there to greet him, an intelligence mostly affection and need. "Hello, Jake," he said aloud in the cab of his moving truck, alone, with the bottle of beer in his crotch. After the first hysterical flurry of greeting and accusation, when the light went on Jake would look up at him, thinking as hard as he could about joy and guilt, having slept in the fragrant, forbidden hollow between Luke's pillow and blanket. Joy and worry all at once. Jake couldn't help it; it was a terrible dilemma of love and obedience.

As for his own found and lost love, he cursed himself for a fool and an idiot; his head might well be as flat above his sad brown eyes as Jake's. There had been a time in his life when he was the one to triumphantly return. He might say to that young man, Beware. Do you know what you are getting into? You can't keep it, and you can't have it over.

The memory of Helen, or of Adrienne, hurt him so badly now that he moaned. Over the engine and road noises he heard his foolish moans.

He was a few miles past Cascom square and up the mountain road toward his camp when headlights cruised in behind him, swirls of mist dimming them, then blowing aside in the night wind so that they turned too bright again in his mirrors.

"What the hell is this?" he said. He couldn't make out the car or truck behind the headlights. They were there, glaring, a presence following him. They didn't turn off onto the last side road, they didn't stop at the two hunting camps, they kept their light on him, on his truck. It shouldn't be Lester Wilson because he had paid quits to Lester, hadn't he? George? Coleman or Freddie in the Jeep? No, the headlights were too far apart for a Jeep. He got out the pistol and put it on the seat beside him. Oh, God damn it, he thought, I'm the wrong one to mess with right now, you son-of-a-bitch, whoever you are. The old rage at being followed grew in him until the skin on the backs of his hands burned. He turned off into the farm road and the headlights followed him in. He let them follow until they reached the darkest growth of spruce and then, with a precision that was past rage, stopped the truck, put it in reverse so the backup lights were on, took the pistol and fell out the door to the ground. In control, he felt like a cat as he sprinted the few yards to the other car. It was yellow; it was Lester's. It tried to reverse but ground gears and stalled as he pulled open the door and reached in with his right hand for the driver. His hand grabbed an arm or a neck and hauled that person out onto the ground. He was shouting or he would have heard sooner the counterpoint of immature and female screams that came from the car and from his feet. What he had grabbed was too soft and filmy, and had been too easily bent and jerked from the car.

"You following me? You following me?" He had stopped shouting the words but they were still somewhere between echo and memory. Before him all was hysteria—a baby strangling on its own rage, a young child's terror as pure sound, no quarter expected, and the woman bawling and shrieking at his feet.

Though he felt a primal urge to join them, to add a contrapuntal tenor to the despairing choir, he put his pistol in his pocket and lifted Claire to her feet.

"I'm sorry," he said. "I'm sorry. I'm sorry."

She bawled at him as if she were talking to him, pure connotation. How these animals communicated their suffering; again he wanted to join the pack and howl.

"Come on, now. It's all right. I'm not going to hurt you," he kept saying, or crooning, to their fear, no denotation really meant, and after a while there did seem to be a subsidence. She raised her hands from her sides and placed them on her face, at least, to show that a lesser state of disorganization had been reached. Inside the car the baby still screamed for what it wanted, but the older child had quieted.

"All right, stop crying now," he said. "What do you want? Why were you following me? Claire? That's your name, isn't it?"

She wiped tears and mucus from her white face; he knew that she cried for more reasons than his sudden attack upon them. Her voice was constricted and hoarse. "Waiting at Sturgis's," she said. "Nobody home and I seen you come on by."

"Well, what's the matter?"

The child in the front seat looked to be a boy, with the pale bony face and bluish eye hollows of the malnourished or maltreated. His hair was straight and black, and his small round ears stuck out from his head. The boy watched with the concentration of one who is totally and unselfconsciously in danger.

"You give him all that money and he bought the hard stuff!"

Her hair in the reflected lights of the cars was a varnished, wiry red that seemed to have drawn all the color from her face. White as paper, he thought. Translucent, dangerous; he couldn't have her and her children here.

He found out, finally, in phrases, words, parts of sentences and odd references he was evidently supposed to understand, that Lester had bought whiskey—bad, bad news with him—and broken up the furniture, beat up the boy, her, threatened the baby, and when he passed out she tried to find the rest of the money but couldn't find it. She wanted to take the children to her sister's in Providence, Rhode Island, but she didn't have any money for gas,

315

so she'd gone to Coleman Sturgis but he wasn't home. Then she recognized Luke's truck and he must have lots of money because he gave Lester so much. But she really had nowhere to go, she cried; she wouldn't be welcome barging in on her sister with a kid and a crying baby. Her sister had her own family, her own problems, her own life. In the island of light in the overhanging spruce, mist rising along the ground and flowing underneath the cars, Luke stood and listened to this young woman whose disasters seemed older than she could possibly be. The baby's mewling seemed exhausted, beyond need. The yellow car's interior smelled of old beer, bundled feces and tobacco smoke. Claire seemed too immature to have been laden with breasts tumescent with the milk that came through her clothes to stain her red blouse in splotches. The boy in the front seat stared at his mother and the stranger, his levels of fear and expectation in a region of helplessness Luke could no longer bear to think about.

He took out his wallet and found thirty-five dollars, thank God, and put it into her hand. "For gas. That ought to be plenty for gas. Can you back out of here?" he said in a panicky haste he though unseemly. "Let me back it out to the road." Before she could say anything he pushed her back into the car and carefully, carefully revving the huge zooming engine, using the brake lights, a touch at a time, for orientation, backed out until he reached the gray opening at the road. He turned the car so that it pointed down, away, out toward the wide world to the south.

He got out and she thanked him with emotion and gratitude for the little he had given, saying that she would pay him back when she could. "Coleman never had five bucks in his pocket anyway," she said, and he came out of his controlled panic long enough to look at her. The green eyes Coleman had called simple were now illuminated by the lighted face of a large tachometer mounted on the steering column, and Luke saw that Coleman's story was nearly all fabrication, a creative effort. Louise had once mentioned that he wrote fiction.

Then the straight-through mufflers rumbled and the car went down the road. Let them be safe elsewhere, let the car not run off the road, let them pass out of his ken forever. He walked back toward his truck through the dark vault of spruce until he could see his own backup lights, the empty truck making its silent light in the woods.

Jake was there in front of the tent, joyous and anxious as he always was when Luke came home after dark. After the greetings, when Luke brought the rifle into the tent and worked its action a few times before putting it away, Jake found that weapon fascinating.

"Well, old friend," Luke said, "we are now officially each other's property." It had cost him a hundred for Juke, ninety for the rifle, and thirty-five to get rid of the family. Strange to be customer and broker for Lester Wilson, to separate the man from his possessions.

Suppose he had comforted the young woman, the boy and the baby, taken the three waifs down to his camp, fed and gentled them, vowing his strength and protection, which in fact he had to give. He thought of Shem, up there all those years alone, where even the ghosts of the buried farm slowly faded from memory. Shem had lost everyone—Carrie, Samuel, his dogs one by one, no matter how sharp and skillful he'd been all through his life.

In the morning he began his rafters and the framing for his main solar window. As the beams rose the cabin became even more real, though not as real as it would become when the roof panels began to block out the sky. The inner dimensions seemed larger as the long reaches of the outdoors were excluded and kept from scale.

He didn't go down the mountain for two weeks, and by then the long lights of triple-glazed glass were set in the framing of the big window, caulked and anchored. The plywood roofing panels were on and squared, the sky no longer his ceiling.

He took a day to cull hardwood—maple, beech, ash, cherry, yellow birch, white birch—to thin out a grove and let the trees lie so their dying leaves would suck moisture from the wood. Then, in late fall, he would buck them up and split them for his winter supply.

He made a list of what he needed in the way of materials, gro-

317

ceries and other supplies. When he went to the truck, Jake came
along and suggested that he go, too, which would have been all
right, now, but this time the cab and the body of the truck would
probably be full.

"You stay, Jake," he said, and Jake sat down, sad but still eager
for a change in that decision. He lifted one white forepaw and
then the other, shifting his weight back and forth, his question as
simple and wholehearted as a question could be. Luke continued
to look at him, at the dog full of the one emotion. He remembered
what some theologian or other had written in a chiding way about
the essential frivolousness of the human race, that upon their entrance to heaven, "There are those who would not sit down with
angels, 'till they had recovered their dog."

Jake kept asking, saying that of course it was all right, really, if
he had to stay here, but how much nicer it would be if Luke would
change his mind. Luke had a shiver of the fear of losing this
friend, and said, "Okay," opened the door and Jake was there immediately, ground to floor to passenger seat, where he sat up,
sniffed and looked out as though they were already passing
through the interesting air.

Luke drove down the mountain and on into Leah, where he
made his stops, managing to put everything in the truck bed, and
paying by check. Jake howled if Luke went out of his sight, but
never tried to jump out of the open window, which seemed to be
relatively sophisticated behavior, or at least somewhat complicated behavior; from what Luke knew of beagles, their immediate
desires usually voided all commandments. In the matter of howling when unhappy, however, Jake was normal for the breed.

Luke went to the Leah Trust Company to find if the mortgage
payments from the Rupperts were coming in, which they were;
then, with the usual misgivings, he stopped at the Post Office.

Again they had kept his mail past the return deadline for general delivery. He paid a dollar and thirty-eight cents and took the
bundle to his truck. With relief, and yet at the same time a surprising feeling of abandonment, he found not one first-class letter.
Not one. No person, for good or ill, had sat down to write to him.
That intensity was not out there, so maybe he was free, untarget-
ed.

Coleman was at the truck window, the man's usually loose, pale face looking like a clenched fist. He seemed to have been running, or he was in the midst of some frantic emotional progression Luke couldn't understand.

"Why didn't you come and see her?" Coleman said.

"Why? I don't know," Luke said. "I wasn't sure she wanted. . . ."

"You could have taken time from your goddam fucking hobby horse."

"My what?"

"Well, she made it this time."

"Made it?"

"Yeah, she made it, Buffalo Bill. She wasn't fucking around this time."

"Tell me what you mean, Coleman," Luke said, though he knew. He thought he knew.

"You just used her when you wanted it, right? Little poontang, right? Get your ashes hauled, huh, buddy? Fuck 'em and forget 'em, right?"

Luke thought of Jane Jones. Out of the instantaneous guilt came Ham's letter, and the sentence, "Jane, my wife, is sick." But was there a reason for that guilt? And how sick? What sick?

"Coleman, hey," Luke said. He got out of the truck and put his arms around the man, who had almost fallen down. Luke held him up. "Hey, hey," he said, chiding, trying to comfort. "Come on, get in." He pushed Coleman up into the truck, Jake moving over, and got in himself. "Now, tell me what happened."

Coleman sniffled and sobbed.

"Come on, tell me what happened."

"You got a drink?"

"A case of beer in the back. You want some?"

"Yeah."

Luke got a six-pack from the back and brought it into the cab. Jake was nosing Coleman in a friendly fashion, trying to get some affection out of him but not succeeding.

"I never thought she'd do it," Coleman said. He sobbed and hiccupped, then nursed his beer, or the beer nursed him, Luke thought, thinking how the thought was avoidance. If Louise was

319

dead, she was dead. That was the first and last impression; one tried to avoid the others in between. When people were dead, the most obvious effect was that they were never around again, and had so little effect on the world. It was hard to believe how little effect the dead had. He thought of Patrice Lumumba and Tom Mboya—but why had he gone to Africa for the absent ones? And they had been murdered.

"We went to Wellesley to get her car. She got her license back—there was the D.W.I., I guess you didn't know about that. Six months' revocation and all that shit. I had something to do, so I . . . . " Coleman was quiet.

"So you?"

"So I wasn't with her, see? So she went and had all her prescriptions refilled. She was good at that. I mean, getting doctors to give her all kinds of renewables. Plausible. I never thought she meant to go all the way. Maybe she didn't mean to."

"When did it happen?"

"I was out last night. She thought I was coming back, but I got drunk and drove to Wellesley and stayed there last night. When I got back today and found her and got her to Northlee she didn't have any brain waves left. She died a couple of hours ago. I've got to go make some telephone calls. Aunts and uncles. Her stepmother." Coleman made motions, and Luke let him out. His Toyota was parked a few cars down the street. He held his beer in his palm, the neck of the bottle up his sleeve. He walked rigidly to his car, the guilty drinking driver.

Was there going to be a funeral? Luke might have asked that question but he hadn't, because no matter where it was or when it was, he would not attend. He had perishables in his truck. He drove back to the mountain, Jake scanning the wind with his lively instruments. Visions of Louise were fragmentary—a curved plane of dark skin, a swatch of silky fur. Sounds of smoothness. The face was as obscure as its expressions had been unexpected. Warmth, motion, liquid, now still as a photograph. Some of us survive.

By dark, both planes of his gable roof were felted, the edging on all around and the chinmey flashed to the tiles. Tomorrow, in the sun that would make it flexible, he would nail, tar and apply his double-coverage roofing.

Jake didn't like it when Luke was on the roof; he wanted to be up there too, but couldn't manage the ladder. He tried, but could only brave standing with his front feet on the third rung, one hind foot nervously on the first rung. Dogs, he cried, must go where you go, but can't climb trees.

Two more days and the chimney was done, curing under a dampened bandage of mortar bags so the sun wouldn't dry out the narrow beadings before they set. It was a good square chimney, expertly vertical. He was proud of his work; he walked around the cabin, seeing how it set into the land and the trees. It was new and the logs were still shiny, but when they weathered the cabin would grow into the valley and seem inevitable, part of this wild place, defining by its snug interior the breadth of the wilderness outside.

One clear day in September he struck the tent, folded it and took it back to George. He was on his way into Leah to pick up his wood stove and the wiring, fuse boxes, relays and circuit breakers George was going to help him install.

"You must be coming right along," George said. "We ain't seen you in near a month. Thought you might have throwed it all up and gone back to the city, 'cept Phyllis seen your truck going past now and again."

George went into Leah with him to make certain he got the right electrical gear. Jake was happy to share the front seat with them. "Hi, there, feller," George said to Jake. "Good-looking hound. You heard Claire Wilson run off, I guess, left Lester and nobody can blame her. And that about Louise Sturgis, that was a shocker. Coleman still shows up weekends sometimes, though he's back teaching at his college. Life goes on, don't it."

In Leah they loaded on the crated stove, which weighed over five hundred pounds, though Luke would be able to disassemble it somewhat when he moved it into the cabin. After they'd been to the electrical supply house on Northlee Street, Luke thought of the Post Office, but finally drove on by and back to the mountain.

321

George was really impressed by the cabin, impressed beyond politeness. "Crackerjack!" he exclaimed over and over as he examined joinings and stonework with a professional eye. "Crackerjack!" Then a look at Luke that said all sorts of assumptions about his cityness had been wrong. There was admiration there. "But this ain't no hunting camp, Luke Carr," he said slyly. "This is what they call a whole goddam way of life." There was friendly suspicion there, and a narrowing of the eyes. "You going to *live* up here?"

Phyllis had guessed that earlier, and Luke wondered if she'd ever discussed it with George. If she hadn't, that was a strange reticence. But there were many reticences in Cascom; he had quite a few himself.

"I'm going to stay here this winter, anyway," he said.

"Ah, yes," George said. "You're still in mourning, kind of, ain't you."

They worked all afternoon with the speed of George's real professionalism, and by five o'clock all of the wiring was in, 220 and 110. George insisted that they install the stove before Luke took him back down to the village, so they did, George strong and proud of his strength, Luke a little worried about the old man's exertions.

And of course he had to come to dinner with them that night, the meal a strange reverse payment for George's help. Before they left he showed George the Marlin he'd bought from Lester. George admired it, hefted it. "Best lever-action deer rifle still made," George said. "Only one trouble with it. In cold weather, you got heavy gloves on, the damn trigger's hard to find. Ain't that bad a problem though. Seems to me I read an article in *The National Rifleman* a year or so back, how that Microgroove rifling, it don't distort the bullet so much as lands and grooves, you know, so the accuracy is damned good, for a lever action."

"I'll zero it in tomorrow," Luke said, "since I'm waiting on a few things."

Phyllis had made dinner for them. She was getting around pretty well these days, she said. And how was Luke eating, up there all alone? He looked skinny to her. Men didn't know how to feed themselves. She'd prepared sweet corn, peas and small potatoes in milk, meat loaf, pickles and steamed chard, tapioca pudding for dessert. "You've been working hard. You ought to eat right," she said.

"I eat good things," Luke said. "They just don't taste as good as this. I eat to live, I guess."

"You going to live up there all winter, huh?" George said. "Long about February you're going to get a bad case of cabin fever, I wouldn't be surprised. Start thinking about Boston and all them city lights."

"Ugh! Boston!" Phyllis said. "You get restless you come down and see us. Enough going on right here in Cascom to keep your mind occupied. Interesting people moving in to town these days." Then, thinking of Louise, she made a strange face and the three of them had to smile, not without pity or dismay.

At ten-thirty he came back through the spruce onto his land, that darkness surrounded by miles and hills of night-black woods. Jake greeted him and they went into the bare cabin. In there it was cool, fresh-smelling of paint and cut, planed and sanded wood. He made a small fire in the stove, open now in its fireplace mode, and Jake, who knew what hounds and fires were for, lay down in front of it to warm his white belly. One bulb on a drop-cord lit up the beamed ceiling with faint but glaring light, the large solar windowpanes dark mirrors to the room.

He set up his cot near the fire and lay down to sleep, but after a while he rose up, saying, "Oh, God!" out of a great and desperate unhappiness he couldn't understand. Then he said to Luke Carr, "You shit, what have you ever done to prevent or to help?" But the dead were not there. They were, in the plainest way, not there, and meant nothing.

# 23.

Luke awoke at dawn with no memory of dreams, the cool light printed on the big window, Jake scratching at the door to get out. He made breakfast, getting coffee water from the hose outside.

It would be a good day to go to Wellesley to Joe the Mover's, rent a large U-Haul trailer and bring up those things he had stored. He could go through them later and discard or keep. The bookshelves were ready for the books he had saved—books of plausible history and presumed fact, reference books and also the fiction of the few odd voices he trusted. He would have no book here that he didn't trust. Maybe some winter night he would start reading again.

Before he left he was bothered by a phrase, or a vaguer memory, something he'd said. It was yesterday, and to George. The rifle—that he would zero it in, or at least see where it shot. That didn't sound like a promise, or anything binding or important, but he took out the rifle, cleaned it with Shem's equipment, carefully dried the oil from the barrel with several patches and loaded its magazine with six shells. A rifle shot differently with its tubular magazine loaded than it did when one shell at a time was fed into its chamber, and the first shot was always the most important, so he would target it from the loaded magazine.

With a felt marking pen he made a three-inch black dot on a piece of typewriter paper, paced off fifty yards and tacked the paper to an expendable aspen. He put a rolled-up blanket on the hood of his truck, laid the rifle over it, then breathed correctly, held it, squeezed and the rifle pushed back against his shoulder. The sound washed off into space and wind. From here he could see no mark at all on the paper, but when he walked up he saw that the back of the tree had been blown out into white splinters and in the bullseye was a crisp hole. Either it had been a fluke shot or whoever had zeroed in the rifle had happened to have taken the same sight picture he did. He put two more shots into the bull and one touching it; he wouldn't have to fool with the sights at all. Jake showed up then, all excited by the shots, but was disappointed when Luke put the rifle away.

He couldn't take Jake with him for the whole day, or didn't want to have to deal with Jake's needs, so left him with meaningless reassurances and drove on down into Leah. Here he remembered that the pistol was still under his dash, and that in Massachusetts there was a mandatory, supposedly non-avoidable one-year prison sentence for having an unlicensed gun in your possession. Signs on the highways leading into the state made this clear enough, and he certainly didn't need the worry of breaking that law. Then, as if it were a breakthrough of the mind comparable, say, to the formulation of the theory of relativity, he realized that Joe the Mover could easily put the pallets containing his household goods on a truck and bring them to Cascom and to his cabin door. He wouldn't have to go to Wellesley at all. He made a telephone call and it was arranged. Maybe his brain was growing weak from the solitude, the altitude or the company, mainly, of a beagle.

He went to the bank and got some cash, then stopped at the Post Office. He really expected to get nothing but bills and junk, as he had last time; no one should want to write to him, none of the living, not if they had any sense. He wrote to no one. Nothing could make him write a letter. When he'd got out the piece of pa-

325

per for a target he'd noticed a light frost of mildew on the black leatherette of his typewriter case.

He went through his mail and found nothing personal, no letter even from the Avenger. It was not there, the elite typeface on the stamped envelope. It had been so long since he'd seen one of those envelopes, and he had done so many things, the memory of them had actually begun to fade, as dreams faded.

He wanted to be back at his cabin, on his land, as if that place were a sanctuary, Jake an incorruptible sentry, the woods his outer fortifications.

He drove back toward Cascom with too much urgency, as though his trip to Wellesley would have been a disaster and he had, by a quirk of insight or luck, barely avoided it, or almost avoided it. He couldn't be certain until he returned to his safe, good place. He drove faster than usual, with an anxiety that seemed to restrict his peripheral vision, he was so intent on getting there. He was going over sixty on the high road, thinking only of where he must go, when strange signals came to him as a distraction, not at first concentrated upon at all. Flashing headlights or reflections, then a siren; then he looked more deliberately into his rearview mirrors and a green car was behind him, strobic blue lights coming not from the top as they would have from the bubblegums of a police car, but from behind the grille. But strobic blue meant police, and he pulled over to the shoulder, cursing, saying out loud, "You asshole! You idiot!" What a stupid time to get caught speeding, by whatever sort of police had caught him. He hated being caught this way, for any reason, which was why he was always alert for police. Even in his hurry he couldn't understand how he'd failed to notice the green car behind him.

He opened the cab door to get out, and the passenger in the other car got out too, a short, thick man in green work clothes, wearing pale yellow shooting glasses, a big leather holster on his belt. It was George Bateman. "Luke!" George called, and motioned him to come over. As he went to the green car he recognized the driver as young Jim Pillsbury, the game warden. George tried to keep a stern, professional face, but there was a marvelous excitement in him. He opened the rear door of the car and got in

326

the back seat, motioning Luke into the front. A radio hissed and barked fragments of words and numbers, as if doors were constantly shutting in the middle of sentences, cutting off, along with breath, the necessary pauses for understanding and acknowledgment.

"Lester Wilson," George said. "He went crazy and killed his family, shot his wife and the two kids, shot his brother-in-law in the stomach, though he's still alive. Shot himself, too, or tried to, but he botched it up."

"What?" Luke said. He heard all this but he was still getting over the fact that they were not after him.

"Shot his ear off or something. Rhode Island police got that from the sister-in-law. Anyways, he come back here before they could catch him, State Police seen his car—that yellow hopped up Dodge—on a I-89 off ramp down around Baker. 'Course he's got the radio, too, so's he could hear everything, took the back roads, most likely. Armed and dangerous. Fugitive warrant. They figure he's somewheres in Cascom, is where he's come to hole up, where he knows the woods. He don't know much else, that's for certain."

"He *shot* them?"

"Ayuh," Jim Pillsbury said. "It ain't that rare. Kind of out of my line of work, though."

"Husband shoots estranged wife and children, kills self," George said. "Only that dumb shit Lester, you got to figure he couldn't finish himself off. Anyways, you'll find a State Police roadblock up ahead. We're going around the Leah side of the mountain—old logging roads, camps and all, some ain't even on the geodetic map."

"They can't find his car?"

"Not yet," Jim Pillsbury said. "When they do they'll bring on the bloodhounds and it'll be over shortly. They'll be a helicopter looking too—I just heard that on the radio."

"Luke, if I was you," George said, "I'd keep me a gun handy till they flush Lester out. Never know where he'll show up. Just wanted to warn you, is all." George's thick, compressed head shone with sweat, his gray bristles shining. "Killed his wife, his boy and the baby. Shot 'em!" His excitement made him tremble beneath the stolid flesh. His hand crossed his lap below Luke's vision, probably to touch his holstered pistol. The thin metal clips of a gun rack came over the top of the front bench seat, and Luke's hand, over the back of the seat, felt the steel of a racked gun.

Luke got out and they made a U-turn, tires whining.

At the roadblock, a State Police car and some red rubber dunce caps, he was questioned and warned by a large trooper, then allowed to go on. He turned on his AM radio to country music. He wasn't sure where the local station was on the band, thought he had it once when a bulletin stated that a "massive manhunt" was on in New Hampshire, but the station turned out to be in Wentworth Junction, Vermont. The rest of the information was about the same as George's.

The yellow Dodge was around Cascom somewhere, no doubt. He believed the information. Where else would Lester go? He was not about to run to Rio, or hijack a plane to Algeria. He'd tried to shoot himself; Luke believed that, too. On the way up the mountain he passed a pickup, men with guns in the back. They waved, and he waved. He looked for the yellow Dodge too, but had no idea what he'd do if he saw it. He wouldn't turn around now, he didn't think, even to report it—or maybe he would, he didn't know. Lester must have got the car back from Claire, maybe the day he'd shot her and the children. Christ, did all that really happen? It happened every day; why did he have to think it strange, even for a few transitional minutes, before it became fact hard as rock.

But there was no sign of Lester. When he reached his valley, his cabin, shed and equipment were untouched, waiting for him, though Jake was gone. He wished Jake were there, but Jake had his daily travels to attend to, his favorite rabbits to exercise.

Now that he had a real, an official, reason to wear the pistol belt, he didn't want to, and left it in the truck. He did load the .35 caliber Marlin, however. The day was mild clear September, the leaves darker and a little dry now toward the end of summer, crisp against the blue. A small breeze twirled the round aspen leaves on their stems, as though it touched only them. He thought to listen for Jake's distant voice, but heard only birds—bluejays complaining back of the spruce, a robin's long melody and the five clear notes of a white-throated sparrow, that wistful plaint that was really a warning.

He had some work to do outside, some shoveling around his basement bulkhead, work too close for the tractor, so he did that until noon, then wheeled some humus over, spread it and seeded the dark stuff with bluegrass and rye before dampening it with the hose. In a few days it would all be pale green needles.

The man hid somewhere in the woods, in an unused camp or even in his car, where he could listen on the police and CB bands to the coded words of pursuit he must understand very well. They were after him and would find him. Maybe at this moment he put his revolver against his head and tried again to keep it there as he pulled the trigger, the crisp metal of the sear sliding its fraction of an inch, the hammer spring's energy waiting, the mass of the hammer about to begin its fall toward the silver primer. Then the real energy. If he'd tried to do it once and blasted his ear, he must be mostly deaf on that side, burned black because he wasn't ready for darkness at the last tic of intent. Then he must have been called to his home, thinking that if he could get back to the woods and mountains of his childhood he could find his way out of the present, back to a time when he wasn't yet what he was.

The day was changing, the blue over the mountain sifting into white, as though the blue were the overcast and the white of the high mist the base color of the sky. Weather always came over the mountain, masked by dark spruce and rock until it was nearly overhead. The breeze had died, and he thought he heard, far up the mountain, Jake's excited yelp. He waited, listening, but it didn't come again. Then, as he turned to wash his hands at the hose, he thought he heard it again. *Ki-yi, ki-yi.* Silence, then just as he'd stopped trying to listen, *Roup, elp,* so far off it seemed lonely. He wished Jake were here, as though the small dog were a missing possession he needed to have safe here with him. There might be intruders in the wilderness up there inclined to hurt an animal so intent on his pursuit he saw nothing but a haze of brush and branches leading him through the tunnel of scent. Luke would go up the trail and see if he could hear Jake's voice more clearly and

329

perhaps intercept him somewhere on the rabbit's long circle. He might even shoot the rabbit for Jake, though the season didn't begin until another two weeks. He was not a breaker of most laws, though, so he wouldn't take the shotgun. Bear season was on, but he doubted if he would shoot a bear, not now, even if a miracle of chance and timing happened and a bear let himself be seen. The woods were full of their bounty of meat, but the meat was not prisoner and had its ways of avoiding death.

Because it weighed less than the other guns he took the pistol, fixing the webbed belt around his waist with its brass connector, the holster and gun a familiar weight at his hip, and climbed the Carr trail, up from the hiss and splash of the brook. Several times he thought he heard Jake's voice, but the sounds, filtered by the trees, would not grow closer. First they seemed to come from the mountain, which he could no longer see through the trees along the leaf-drowned stone walls; then from the brook valley below and to his left. The distant cries were never quite clear enough to be sufficient evidence to leave the trail and bushwhack into a climb or a descent.

It seemed more and more possible that Jake could be in danger. Maybe it was just the anxiety of the days, and of this day, but life was too fragile, Luke knew. The young boy with the straight black hair and ears like cup handles, his white look at a life that ended soon, shot by his father. Shot by his father. And the baby, who never knew what hit it. An estranged wife—what sort of monstrosity was an "estranged" wife?

Was that Jake, over there on a ledge, the little dog frantically casting and calling? He left the trail and pushed through blackberries and juniper. Just to be nearby, in the vicinity of the dog, might be protective enough. He heard a yelp that was certain, though it might have been a yelp of pain or fear. Maybe Jake had hit a strand of old barbed wire strung taut by the growth of the trees that held it, or a sharp broken branch had stuck into his soft lips or his eye. When Jake was on a rabbit, the cool, dignified rabbit loafing, turning, easily keeping far ahead of the noisy pursuit, he had no time to be careful. He was the one driven, locked by genes into his single mission. Why couldn't Jake be more careful, though? No one was careful; only he was careful. He climbed up the side of a gulley, not hearing as the sticks and brush crunched under his boots. A wand of hemlock brushed lightly over his face, but in it was a sharp dead stick that stung his cheek and made his right eye water. He was sweating, hot along his back where his shirt stuck to him like tape, needing still more altitude up through the thick saplings and hemlocks so he could stop and try to listen. The trees here stifled his hearing. He could stop his crashing now and listen, but he wasn't high enough. A dead branch held him back with the insistence of a turnstile, and when he broke it off he thought he'd simultaneously heard a shot—his luck to break the branch at the precise time of the shot. He wasn't certain about its direction.

What he saw in his mind as he climbed were some local, self-appointed posse-vigilantes going through the woods, spread out, shotguns and rifles held at the ready, eager to shoot. A strange dog then appears and the instinct, the eagerness of the excited man is too much so he shoots and the number one buckshot whacks across the woods and one pellet travels through the body of the dog; the man then shouts ecstatically that he got a dog that was running deer. "Ran this little spikehorn right by me, near as me to you!" The dog writhes in the hemlock needles, gut-shot and screaming, so the fellow points his gun at the head and finishes it off, just as Luke appears.

Maybe he didn't hear a shot. Though why not Jake, too? Was Jake being saved just because he was a dog and didn't matter that much? "I cared very much for that hound," he says to the vigilante. "In fact, I loved that hound dearly." The pistol is at the small of the man's back. "Why do you people do such dangerous things?" Luke asks reasonably. "Don't you know the consequences? Why do you take such risks?" He lowers the muzzle of the pistol and fires downwards into the man's coccyx, the big bullet traversing down through bone, anus, prostate and the penile root. Lots of writhing and screaming now, and lots of satisfaction: you have sacrificed your innocent dog just because you want to punish a man.

Luke came out into tall beeches on a minor ridge, breathing

331

heavily, wet and shaking. Silence. The sky was darkening quickly now, so that it was almost twilight among the gray, skinlike trunks of the beeches. He almost called for Jake, feeling the name, Jake, in his throat and lips. But that would be stupid, a sign of panic. He rested, listening.

The other man must be listening too, at least with his one good ear. There must be some place he wanted to find, where he could rest and be safe. There would be no reason now for defense, for rage or the desire to hate or kill his pursuers. His guilt had taken all of that out of him and left him empty, just an organism abhorring simple death. No matter what he had done. He couldn't kill himself and that was that, so he moved away, as well as he could, from nonexistence. No matter that he didn't have a chance, that he wasn't a bear but only a man covered in thin green chino, with bad teeth. Lester wouldn't think of his teeth.

When a helicopter came toward you it went fluff, fluff, fluff, fluff, and when it left it sounded more like a light plane. It went on over, looking for Lester.

Luke listened for Jake. The dog couldn't help it; he was not responsible for giving him this pain, yet he felt anger toward him along with the impossible feeling of the infinite value of the being that caused the anger.

"God damn it, Jake," he said. "Where are you?" The timing was all off; Jake shouldn't be out in the woods now, but Jake couldn't know because he hadn't the equipment to know. Luke knew that; his irritation was anxious and foolish. How easy a drama it was to sentimentalize a dog.

Rain was coming. The sky, visible only in leaf-enclosed patches, was now darker than the saw-edged beech leaves and their smooth gray branches. Maybe the coming rain would convince Jake to let up, or if it was heavy enough erase the rabbit's scent.

He was a little lost, disoriented because he couldn't place the sun in the sky. A cool invasion of wind from the storm felt its way through the trees, and his sweat was quickly not warm, just damp. Which side of this knoll had he come from? Memory said there, from what he thought was north. The storm came from the west, but in the woods the wind could sweep and counter-sweep. The

332

dark sky, though it must be moving, was a solid tone of false night. Thunder began, a shake and a thud, valleys echoing without giving him a bearing. He moved with his memory down through the trees that were here wild, unlike those around houses, and couldn't be remembered from the side he hadn't seen in coming. Too many burls and forked branches imitated each other. And the levels of the woods moved their declinations around slopes so that the world turned but not in his mind. He went down where he really knew he hadn't climbed, the false compass of his mind more powerful than logic. He could move and cover ground, so he moved, wanting this to be the way home. He heard the gray noise of the rain before the trees let it come through to him, and when it came, gathered into dollops by the leaves, it was cold. This September storm must be high, from a reservoir of ice.

Then he was at a steep embankment, almost a cliff, but he didn't stop or try to find a way around. Cherry and basswood branches were slippery in his hands as he eased and slid his way down, stepping occasionally on shiny embedded stones. Green swamp grass in hummocks let him cross water frothed by the rain. On the other side he climbed a steep soft bank among hemlocks, using their rough trunks as handholds. The rain was solid and visible now and there was no dryness anywhere. All this place was roofed, dark, a submarine cavern in which it seemed strange that he could breathe. The water came into his boots with a naked feeling, his socks liquid, the soaked leather of his boots flexible as skin.

He couldn't stop going, though he should wait and try to think. It was as though he would, if he kept moving, come through something like a doorway out of the cold swamp into the clear day he had left, his cabin there and Jake to greet him. Or he might just pass out of all of it, back to anything predictable. He should be back at his cabin now, right now, or in some looming way it would be too late. George and Pillsbury might stop by on their way around the mountain, and even that little thing increased his worry. He couldn't stand to wonder what they would think if they found his truck there but not him. It was ridiculous, but still he crashed on, too careless of his footing, between trees and boulders, the wind moving everything but rock, the thunder so directly overhead he felt he was about to be hammered flat on an anvil. He didn't know where he was or which way he was going; the geodetic map, green, brown and white, flickered there in his mind, no doubt oriented wrong. There were too many small hills and valleys in the woods. Sooner or later he would have to come out somewhere. He thought he might be near an old logging road that came out by the two hunting cabins, but he might be a mile in another direction.

He nearly fell over a ridge of tilted ledge, but caught himself on sharp wet rock that numbed his hands. Below him was a brook, but it couldn't be Zach Brook because he had crossed too many ridges. It must be Carr Brook. It became Carr Brook, the white water and rain-speckled pools not Zach Brook. Every stone and flow of the dark water and the white rushes of it were unfamiliar, elsewhere, in another valley, where he now was. It flowed, according to the flickering map, more or less to the east, where it met Zach Brook at a bridge. He could follow it down until it met Zach Brook, then go up Zach Brook to his cabin, or take the longer way by the road and come to the entrance to the farm. He stood there, seeing Carr Brook, these rational processes going on in his mind while the sky fell through the trees in gushes and whirls. He was under water, as wet as if he had been submerged, scratched and buffeted. It was like trying to think in the midst of battle.

Something big moved to his right, soundless in all this sound. A gray shape; two shapes, one darker and larger. Then the larger one leapt upward and outspread a tail like a linen-white flag, as did the smaller one, and the tilting flags flicked from one side to the other as the two deer flowed bounding through the rain and were gone between and behind the trees. They had been so close to him, he half-blind in the storm, that their great hunch and starting of weight had made his pulse jump, with a hesitation between each throb of blood that seemed too long, and made him short of breath. It was that, and the force and purity of the wild lives escaping from him.

He went down the brook, which rose steadily, every gulley in its banks now a tributary. The rain came down his forehead and passed over his open eyes in a blur sharp at its edges. His eyes

334

cleared for a second at a blink, then were blurred again. He tripped over a dead alder and fell to his knees, the cloth sucking as he got up, a bent finger hurting. He asked himself to slow down, even to wait for a lull in the rain, but whatever made him run said hurry, hurry, be there right now, and there was such a long way to go. If he could just break out of here into the clear where he could put one foot after the other and not have to wrestle branches, duck his head, worm under and over and have to stretch his body past where it hurt.

Nothing pursued him except an anxiety not justified by events. He was not hunted with guns, though he too was a lone man without allies. He must get safely home, his possessions around him, and never leave that place. It was Jake who was threatened; if he didn't own that dog, if he hadn't been hung with that responsibility, he would just be a wet man out in the woods finding his way back to his camp, no hurry or panic at all. He should get rid of the dog as he had shed himself of his family. This pain was too strong.

In a clear blink something moved. It was down the brook, on the other bank. The brook was all white now between black rocks, and the only sound was the crashing water. Something bulky and slow moved down there. It was dark, almost black; at first he made a bear out of it, but it had white and red splotches that moved with it against the mist-green and black of the woods in a strangely loose, toppling yet connected way. He couldn't seem to think it a man, or to make himself trace out a whole man there.

He melted back into evergreen boughs and watched the awkward progress of the thing as it came up the brook. It was a man, because it was more upright than not as it climbed and leaned its way through the alders. It was not armed, at least not with a long gun, which was the first warning of its identity. Then it was a big man, young but broken, a man who was followed. Long before the face could make its statement the signs of the hunted were there in the bones.

"Oh, no," Luke said, a soft exclamation he was unable to hear over the rushing water. It was Lester, who had to be somewhere because, after all, he was not yet dead. He had nothing left, but he was not yet dead and didn't want to be dead. Luke said no because

335

in all the miles of hills and swamps around the mountains he had to be here to observe what was real. Lester came up the brook toward him, staggering as if whipped by each alder trunk that was only a stationary bar to his passage, but often looking back. He seemed to be trying to hear, though nothing could be heard over the white water. When he turned his head Luke saw that one side of his neck was grizzled white and pink, his ear enormous and a darker red. His black bristles of hair stood up straight, washed and shiny. His awkwardness said fear, exhaustion, despair, a knee locked half-bent and whatever other disasters could beset a man. He didn't seem to know where he was going, but he looked back, knowing what he tried to escape.

He tripped and fell to his knee, and his mouth opened as wide and round as a child's, his random teeth and red gums showing. It was a cry Luke couldn't hear, repeated after a short breath. Lester was not armed; he didn't even have a belt, and the pockets of his soaked green chinos had been torn off or cut off, showing white, hairy thigh that seemed cold and vulnerable. One of his workshoes was unlaced, the black sock down and his Achilles tendon silver.

Still on his knee, he retched, one hand on an alder, his head down. He seemed to hear something behind him and turned, his face so wrinkled with terror Luke had to look where he looked. Nothing was there, but Lester's mouth squirmed like part of a phantom face seen in the embers of a fire. He still thought he might have seen a man back there, and all men were against him.

Across the brook, Luke felt himself to be lateral to this hunt. He could step across the brook on stones and ledge, draw his pistol and remove the last of Lester's possessions, but that was not the direction in which he was going. Having been given an excuse, in this fellow's case, the men with guns would have him soon enough.

Wet and friendless, Lester got back to his feet and began to move again. Fresh blood washed down the cloth below his damaged knee, where he might have taken a buckshot pellet or a bullet. A wound was like a little leash or hobble, giving the hunters a certain edge.

336

Luke was not without pity for the animal that didn't want to die, but he had nothing to say to the man. What he saw across the brook was an animal about to be destroyed by its own kind, like a brown rat touched with a foreign scent. He would not join the hunt, but responsibility, he knew, would not be so easily denied, whether the man was supposed to deserve it or not. He had touched the man's life. He was not neutral, even if he seemed to have no control over the curse of his touch. He watched Lester go on up the brook, the wide face, when it turned to look back, so beaten and simple he wondered how the man could ever have inspired caution or fear. Lester's fear, however, spoke to Luke and made him cold.

He hurried down the brook, a little faster because the rain had lessened and he could see the traps and hurdles that had grown into his path. After a while he came to a bridge that couldn't be there, made of maple logs and boards. As he recongnized it for what it had to be the world shifted with a giddy lurch, like a slide in a projector, and he had been on Zach Brook all the time and was at his own bridge, on his own land, a hundred yards from home.

He climbed up out of the brook bed and sloshed across the field toward the cabin, his disbelief at where he was fading slowly because it seemed that he had spent hours in another valley, on another brook. When he was halfway across the field, Jake came from the cabin porch, looking as hard as he could, hesitant, suspicious, shy, eager, wanting the upright figure who came toward him to be the one he wanted. When Luke spoke to him he trusted his eyes and came running and howling, prancing sideways out of joy and the torque of his tail. He stopped to shake a mist of water from his coat and came on, safe and happy—this time.

In the cabin the warm dryness was another shift in the way to look at the world and the human condition. To be dry instead of greasy, the penetration of the cold solvent gone. The cabin was still warm from the morning's sun, but before he took off his sopping clothes he took some lumber scraps and made an open fire in the black iron stove, the wood dry and light, the paper rustling. The new clothes were light and soft, and slid furrily over his skin

337

as he warmed. He gave Jake a towel and Jake took it to the hearth to roll in it before he settled himself down to lick and steam before the fire.

Luke took the pistol out of its holster, removed clip and shells, wiped it and left it on the table to dry. His soaked clothes he took to the porch to wring out before they steamed dry on the back of a chair. The long log walls were bulky and tight, gleaming in the light of the fire, and his windows, though they let in a cold gray light, kept out what they let him see.

Another singular man, wounded and cold, tried to escape over there in the dripping swamp of the woods, climbing up along a brook that began in farther and higher wilderness where there was no warm haven like this one, and not even a hound for company. Luke made himself a drink of bourbon, death's little antidote, to try to fool reality somewhat and perhaps to reconcile his own comfort with the agony of another. And of others, the poor wounded and self-wounded that were all he seemed to touch.

He pulled Shem's old Morris chair up to the fire, the new cushions clean and tailored as once the old ones had been new and clean for Shem, and let his tired bones into it. How good to be rewarded for industry and foresight, to be dry and warm in a snug harbor, plenty of food and tobacco and booze. These were the realities after all. He was not out there bleeding and weeping.

# 24.

In October, as the sun waned, the animals grew sleek for winter. After the first hard frost the deer came under the apple trees for the softened fruit already pecked over by grouse, among others. A bear, glutted on apples, left recognizable cores, skins and stems in the loose piles of his spoor. The sun was clear in cool blue, not a force now, just a broad light the hardwoods transformed, each species and then each tree in its own way turning luminous, as if answering the sun's departure with a last bright signal from earth. There seemed to be no air, it was so clear. Warmth during the day was just radiance, from everywhere, and the cool nights seemed to go all the way to the stars, as though the whole universe were a perfect benevolence.

Luke used this harvest time to prepare his place for the winter. All of the machinery and appliances had come and been installed. In his shed, now closed by sliding barn doors, was a small diesel generator, his tractor, storage tanks, room for his truck and several cords of wood, though as much wood was stacked on the cabin porch and in the wood room off the living room, drying quickly under cover. His books, furniture, pictures and miscellaneous

339

items, some handy and others not, had arrived by Joe the Mover. Other furniture he had bought or made, and now the cabin's main room was warm, a little spare in furnishings, but there were a comfortable leather sofa, chairs, Shem's Morris chair, a long old table desk by the main window, drawers, cabinets, lamps, books in shelves, a view of the mountain through triple glass above the kitchen end. The room began to have its patterns of use, to be his, or even him, as if it were an exoskeleton, or a finely, genetically perfected organic shelter made of his own labor and glands, in which he was comforted in all functional and aesthetic ways. Jake had a little self-closing, insulated tunnel next to the eastern door for his use, and the bedroom had a door which kept Jake's hairs and dense musk from Luke's pillow. A small thick rug near the hearth was Jake's, though he had alternate places on sofa and chairs, according to his temperature and other atavistic hound necessities, such as elevation or the mammalian need for a kind touch.

As the sun's route across the southern arc grew lower, its heat entered the southern window, crossed the room and was absorbed by the stone column. At night the column was warmed internally by the long sloping tiles of the stove's flue, the window shuttered and the stove in its closed, controlled mode so that it gave even heat for twelve hours or more. He would see how this worked in the real cold to come; in October he often didn't fuel the stove for a day or two at a time, or used it as a fireplace only, and that mostly for the sight of a fire. He hoped not to have to use his backup heating at all.

In his cellar were shelves for foodstores and that category of former possessions he hadn't decided what to do with. Among these were the boxed contents of Helen's desk at home and another box of papers and books her department chairman had collected from her office at Moorham.

He didn't know what to do with Helen's relics. Maybe they were sacred, each unclaimed theme, annotated schedule, calendar or text. If so, they should be in a monument, or laid to rest with ceremony, and he hadn't any monument or ceremony. A musty cardboard box in a cellar seemed less respectful than incineration. He should go through them, but what news would he find there except loss? Every paper he touched would proclaim that she hadn't planned to die, and if he began he would read every one.

That night he brought the boxes up from the cellar. There had been on this bright day a sense of the near-completion of his cabin. There were more things he wanted to do to it, and to the land, but most of those would wait until spring. He was almost ready for the long sleep of the wilderness. With Shem's knife he cut the paper tape on the boxes. An open fire waited; he was not here to fondle relics and mourn, but to try something else.

The Moorham teaching, committee and personnel material went into the fire, as did marking books and catalogues, the slick paper of the catalogues opening slowly, like black flowers. The letters to a woman who didn't exist, letters concerning recommendations, schedules, salary, the strange half-democratic governance of a college, went into the fire. From that box, the one from her office, he found nothing that wasn't to or of the official person she was.

The other box, in which he had piled the materials from her desk at home, was at first not much different. He had seen most of the letters here, because mail was read in common at their house, and Helen was not a saver of correspondence. Most had been received within the few months before the accident. The household bills had all been paid and dated. She hadn't yet answered, and hadn't noted that she had answered, her mother's last letter, which must have made her unhappy as she flew toward her mother's funeral.

When he came to a typewritten note in elite he read it before he recognized what it was, not expecting or wanting to find, with a sudden loss of breath that was also the loss of mystery, the Avenger's certain identity this close to Helen.

Dear Helen,
    Yes, I'd have to say it's plagiarism, if only because of internal evidence. I can't quite lay my memory on the lines that seem so uncharacteristic of this student's other work (especially the in-class theme), but I know so much about *her!* Examine, for instance, the

341

word "Tho." I'd say lower middle class, a note-passer in high school (in the in-class theme she dotted her i(s) with little circles). Also the multiple exclamation marks and question marks, the possessives that are plurals half the time and vice versa, willy-nilly; a carelessness or grayness of the mind rather than error. I mean that in such a messy cranium the *possibility* of error has not inkled. Contractions, such as "you're," are also used for the possessive, and question marks are left off questions. Oh, Lord, what hope *is* there?

We must talk. Lunch Wednesday?

Coleman

There, without the possibility of doubt, was the short serif on the capital *T* and the bent lower case *e*. How could this not be proof of identity, the puzzle solved? The other question was how long had he really known without wanting to know. Mr. Death; it was all just a little too sick, a disease that couldn't be left untreated. He could not ignore or withstand pathological malice. It had to be dealt with.

With this note was another:

Helen: I can't bear to be near you in the presence of others. I am blinded and struck mute. It is passion; it is an obsession. Can't you arrange to stay the night somehow? The gift you have to give!

C̄.

And another:

Helen: I can't bear to face you, your irridescence—it blinds me. I apologize to you, but not, never, to the swine who possesses you. You are in thrall, sick, infected with the banal, and that is your only flaw. I hate him, not you.

C̄.

Helen had saved these notes, and never shown them to him. She must have been flattered, no matter what else her feelings might have been. She couldn't have known that after her death this madman would play with threatening letters. Luke could not follow the mind that called itself Mr. Death.

342

He was, he thought, cool as he went to his truck. It was Saturday and Coleman might be at the house in the village for the weekend. He would shake Coleman like a rag doll, shake some reason from him. He would not break Coleman's scrawny neck. It was as if he had taken a step off into nothing; he couldn't understand, and Helen was infected by the void that kept opening, now here, now there.

His headlights pushed away the darkness as the truck climbed out of the valley to the mountain road. He was going to initiate an action he didn't think would work. Surely reason wouldn't work, nor would threats or violence. He might dislocate Coleman's ankle, for a start, and maybe, if Coleman found that unpleasant enough, he might see the light. No, he would be dealing with madness, with a man who would punish someone who had just lost his wife, son and daughter. He must remember that. Should he carry the pistol in his hand, in his pocket, in his belt, none of these? He could kill Coleman easily with just his hands. Murder was just a thought, yet it was plausible. Death was not that odd, or that rare, Mr. Death.

The Sturgis house was dark, no cars in the driveway. He left the pistol in the truck and walked up to the house, to the front door. In his strength the house seemed flimsy. The front door was locked so he kicked it in easily, with little noise, as if the frame were made of cardboard. He turned on the hall light. The flooring was still unfinished; nothing had been done since he'd been here last. In Louise's room her bed was unmade, the wrinkled sheets as still as carved marble. If no one had touched them of course they would not have changed. He shut the door again on that room and went on into the living room, his hand remembering light switches. The pale paintings gleamed from the walls, Louise's pots and platters silent on their shelves and tables.

In the kitchen the dishwasher was full of washed dishes and in the refrigerator a quart carton of milk hadn't soured, so Coleman must have been here recently. He went upstairs to Coleman's room, his right to enter this house or any room in this house the incipient rage that made his arms tremble with strength. Coleman's double bed was stripped to the mattress. The room was bare, the patterned wall paper faded and in places water-stained. On an old pine desk were manuscripts, books and an office-sized typewriter, its type not elite. In spite of its clutter the desk did not look worked at, more as if the books and papers had been placed upon it long ago and just left there. The manuscript on top was titled, "Dream Images in Stearns Sloan's *Repetitions*."

He went downstairs to the telephone table, found a Wellesley telephone book and called Coleman's number there. No one answered. He let it ring until he stopped counting rings and began to think that he didn't know what he would say to Coleman if he answered. He didn't want to speak to the man, he wanted him, simply, eliminated, he and his letters nonexistent. He could do nothing about it now, however, and surprised that he had come to that sane conclusion he shut off the lights in the house, jammed the front door shut upon its splintered frame and left.

He drove back up the mountain in the dark. Why had Helen never mentioned a nut she worked with called Coleman Sturgis? Was it possible to be jealous over the dead? His anger now might simply have been caused by the violation of his own freedom; how selfish and cold he was if that were true. If she had told him, would he then have become demeaningly suspicious and angry? He didn't know the logic of love, if it had any, and there were no reliable witnesses to whatever had happened.

In the morning his anger had passed and could not be summoned back; he was not the initiator of confrontations and had no hope for structure or resolution.

The hardwood leaves paled and thinned, and the woods opened up to long columned vistas that revealed the old field lines and the rises of hills that were once pastures. Evergreens were dark islands here and there, hemlock groves far up a hillside revealed themselves and were walls where vision ended, though they were vague, seen through skeins of graying branches. Maple leaves twirled like yellow and orange stars down the brook, and the beech held their fading sienna leaves longer than the rest. Ash, that had turned dark mauve at first, were now altogether bare of the stems and branchlets of their compound leaves, and seemed over-simple, as if drastically pruned.

Jake, as if he knew the season and the opening of the floor of the woods to Luke's surveillance, became more nervous and curious about Luke's entrances and exits, watching him closely, the brown eyes full of one question: now? Is that a gun? (No, it was a brush scythe). Jake didn't mind hunting by himself, because he had to when the scent called and crossed his senses, but that was not the real thing, which was to cast ahead, knowing the man was there, checking back, circling, needing the man as well as the vivid rabbit. So one day Luke took down the single-barreled shotgun and a pocketful of number eight shells and without explanation left the cabin. Jake had seemed asleep but knew perfectly the click of the opening of the shotgun's action, the hollow, musical clunk of the shell entering the chamber, and he flowed through his tunnel and was there with Luke before he could cross between the porch woodpiles. "Which way?" Jake asked with a pause and a look. Luke pointed west, toward the mountain, and Jake began the hunt.

Luke walked slowly through the woods, Jake ranging far out of sight. Jake came back once, on Luke's trail, an approaching gallop of small feet coming on so fast from behind Luke was startled, then saw that it was Jake, who passed him in a rush and went on ahead with no greeting, busy and serious. The day was dry, crisp, the blue above the mesh of trees so constant and pure it seemed opaque. From far to the south Jake found a cold trail and howled sporadically, minutes in between, not with the intensity a fresh scent would have caused in him.

An hour later the voice came back high and sharp, this time from the west, and continued to ask a constant hysterical question as it moved. Luke tried to guess its course, and moved as quietly as he could up the hill, feeling and thinking himself into an arc of an imaginary, uncreated circle that existed only in the intentions of a rabbit. When Jake's voice seemed to turn toward him he stopped and studied the slopes and rises he could see, to find which planes of the forest's surface he could actually see behind folded dry ferns, witch hobble, low spruce seedlings, banks of windrowed leaves and the columns of hardwoods. Jake came on, closer and more piercing of voice, and passed just for a moment within sight,

345

the white tip of his tail whipping back and forth, the dark back in sight and then gone. The rabbit had passed there, probably hadn't seen Luke, and might traverse this general area on his next round. Since Luke could see fairly well here, he stood still as Jake's voice receded in an invisible arc defined only by sound.

In twenty minutes he seemed to have learned by heart each rock, tree, bush and dead fern within his view. Jake's voice kept moving, far away now. Then he heard a light tick and jump, stop, the movement of something, Jake's voice far behind, not in this hollow of vision, and a brown rabbit appeared thirty yards away, disappeared, came up over a hummock between trees, was there, hopping along, a little gray on his belly in the beginning turn toward his winter white, his paws white already. He was about to go out of sight for good, or for another long unpredictable circle when Luke without conscious thought of the mechanics of the gun leaned into it instantaneously and shot, an invisible cone of energy flailing across the air and the rabbit was brushed away, rolling once and then out of sight. Luke ran over, loading another shell as he ran, and the rabbit was still there, bunched soft hair, awkward legs and the brown eye still bright though it was dead.

He waited for Jake to come along the still-live trail of this rabbit, to find what he had earned. In a few minutes Jake came in sight, casting, weaving along the still-bright scent. When he came near Luke the trail was gone, blown away by the shot, and Jake cast desperately though still joyfully in circles until he smelled Luke, a surprised quick look, and Luke said, "Here." Jake finally saw the dead rabbit and came to it all wagging and friendly, curious, mouthed it without biting, smelled it and licked the soft fur. "Okay, Jake," Luke said, feeling good because of Jake's approbation, even triumphant. "Jake, here is the first tangible product of our relationship, right?" He took the rabbit, made a nick in its warm belly with Shem's knife and pulled the belly skin softly apart. He hadn't killed for a long time. Then the knife point slit the hard belly and hot blood warmed his fingers. There was the liver, fortunately clear and healthy, and he pulled it and the kidneys firmly against their tethers out for Jake, who gobbled them delicately from his hand, then licked the blood from his fingers.

Another happy nosing of the rabbit and Jake was ready to hunt again. "Which way?" he asked. Luke pulled the skin from the long muscular body of the rabbit. He would clean it above the diaphragm later, at home. The entrails, on the leaves speckled with blood and their own bloodlike pigmentation, still moved in waves, but they would soon cool and stop.

"Home, now," Luke said, but Jake went on ahead, hunting again. Luke carried their meat back through the woods to the cabin, the firm dark flesh of legs and backstrap speckled even darker by a few shots. He remembered now, from odor, texture, heat and the stoppage of death the prize that was the weight of good meat. He had been allowed to hunt with Shem one fall. His parents were away somewhere and left him at the farm, lonesome and a little apprehensive of the fascinating real world of slaughter and game and of his fierce uncle who knew how to do everything and do it right. But Carrie had made rabbit pie, with a light pastry crust that when crumpled by the serving spoon emitted rich steam. He would see if he could find such a recipe in one of Helen's cookbooks, and this evening he and Jake would divide and eat, the absolving act, the one absolving act, for this small vivid harvest.

One day George came by hunting grouse, stopped in with some diffidence, and said that Phyllis would like to see the cabin sometime. "And Eph and Tillie," Luke said. "I had you and Eph in mind whenever I did something right, and I'm not exactly ashamed of my joinery. Anyway, you'll be tactful enough now it's done."

So the four of them were to come, bringing food. "You know Phyllis," George said. "She's got to pay for the privilege of you inviting her or she won't be happy about it." George was the same way, of course. "Well, don't bring any beer or booze, then," Luke said, a concession he wasn't sure they'd honor.

The day when they were to come was cold, though bright. October was changing toward its end, and the colors were gray, purple at a distance in certain light. The sun was only slightly warm, if the wind didn't get to the body first, the pale light seeming as dimin-

347

ished as a reflection as it lay briefly across the fields. When a small white cloud crossed the sun the valley grayed into winter.

They arrived in Eph's old Buick, driven by Tillie Cole, and from the trunk brought hampers, casseroles, plates, silverware and all the equipment of caterers, Tillie and Phyllis supervising this treasure as Eph and George helped carry it in.

Then was the time for the inspection tour of the cabin. "Looks like it'll make the winter," Eph said, "Rugged enough. You sure do like strong studding!" He laughed, referring to the logs. "Tell you the truth, Luke," he said seriously, "I kind of thought you'd give up on the logs, get somebody to put you up a frame camp and let it go at that." Eph seemed a little shaky, slower and more hesitant when he moved. He'd missed a patch of hair under his chin when he'd shaved that day. He leaned on his arm when he stood, walking slowly toward where he could get an arm down on a railing or on a log in the wall so he could lean on it. His belly sagged from his tall body like a sack beneath the wide chest. His cheeks were splotched with islands of veins, and he glistened with sweat as though he might have a slight fever.

They all thought the cabin good, the kitchen handy, the composting toilet a wild idea because it was actually inside the house. They asked if it smelled. Luke explained the venting system which took care of this. With the eagerness of his comparative youth and its desire for approval he explained this, and his solar window. He demonstrated the internal shutters, and explained, perhaps over-explained or waxed enthusiastic beyond the proper taste. Of the heat absorbing column George said, "That's a lot of stone wall in a room. Don't it make you think you're living in a cave sometimes?"

"It's a warm cave, anyway," Luke said.

"It is comfortable in here, and no fire in the stove," Tillie said.

"It's cozy, sort of," Phyllis said, "though different." She stood with her cane looking at Luke's books. "George, you make me some bookshelves like this, we won't be tripping over books all the time." Then she said to Luke, "George don't like bookshelves—can you figure that out? He just don't like bookshelves in a room. Says it reminds him of a library and he never wanted to live in a library."

348

When it was time to get the food ready, Phyllis and Tillie took over the kitchen end of the room. George, saying he'd done it a hundred times when he was a kid, opened up the old kitchen table and put in the center leaf, and soon the feast was on.

George and Eph would be more at ease sitting at the table than afterward, having to sit on sofa or chairs in the living room with all its clues, such as the books, to show that Luke was indeed a city type who had in a sense recreated his world in this room. Then they would make noises and gestures about leaving. But when the table was finally cleared they did sit a while. Tillie stood at the sink, having insisted upon doing the dishes, the sleeves of her cotton blouse rolled up her long arms above her elbows.

George sat on the front edge of the sofa, Eph beside him, though deeper, with his long legs stretched out. Phyllis was more comfortable in a straight chair, wishing out loud that she were helping Tillie and Luke with the dishes and saying how she hated to be a shirker.

"I read in the *Manchester Union* they found Lester sane, down to Concord," George said. "He'll have to stand trial."

"They got two witnesses seen him do what he done down there in Rhode Island," Eph said. He took out, with some effort, a large blue bandanna and wiped his face and neck.

"You got the sweats, Eph?" Phyllis said, worried. Tillie turned from the sink and looked at Eph, a steady look, then turned back to the dishes. Eph didn't want to respond to Phyllis's question, so ignored it.

Lester Wilson was in Concord, the state capitol that was synonymous with the hospital for the insane. George's mother had died there. Lester had come out of the woods on his own the day after Luke had seen him by the brook. Bloodhounds hadn't been used because of the heavy rain.

"He give himself up," George said. "Was me, I'd of been in the woods till hunters come across my bones, but Lester, puh! They used to be good blood in that family but it all went bad."

"Ayuh," Eph said, shaking his head.

"If I found the son-of-a-bitch in the woods I'd of saved the state time and money," George said. He had begun to tremble with an-

349

ger, his gray eyes small in his head. "I just wished I come across the murdering bastard, I'd of blowed his worthless goddam head off."

"Well, now," Phyllis said carefully, "he did give himself up."

"And now they give him three squares a day and a dry place to sleep. Probably let him go free in a few years. The son-of-a-bitch killed his wife and two innocent kids, one a baby." George hummed with hatred, his voice as restricted and pressured as his eyes. Luke didn't want one of these older people to be irrational or unpredictable. Whatever George's personal reasons were for hating the murderer, they should long ago have been resolved. He wanted to be fairly judged by these people found good.

"I heard from Louise," Phyllis said.

At first Luke thought she was speaking about someone in Lester's family, and the name meant somebody else and didn't mean anything to him.

"That was a shocker," George said, willing, at least for the moment, to let his anger go. This began to mean to Luke that it wasn't Lester's case they were referring to. He was at that moment taking dishes from Tillie, wiping them and stacking them on the drainboard.

Phyllis said, "She said the funeral's going to be in Wellesley. That would be tomorrow, come to think of it."

"Wellesley?" Luke said.

"She wrote me the time and all, but I don't remember. The letter's on my desk at home."

"Whose funeral is that?" Luke said.

"Why, Coleman's. Haven't you heard? Louise had to make all the arrangements, too. And him so young, but he would drink and drive, and now he's dead. You can imagine how it is for Louise, her only brother and all, and she having her own troubles."

"Will you look at that!" Eph said in his high voice, surprised and pleased. Jake had just come through his little tunnel, and stood for a moment cautiously assessing all these people, though he was not antagonistic or afraid. "By the gods!" Eph said. "That hound's got his own private door! Now what do you think of that?"

350